I want to give all the children, whether extraordinary or not, whether typical or not, a beautiful future and a gentle happily ever after.

The things that cannot be done in reality, I still hope to present it to them through the story. At the same time, I also hope that all of you, outside of this story, will be able to gain some warmth from the words written within.

Per aspera ad astra

A special group of people, a special progress of life, and a special love.
My silence, and your affections.
Please, world, treat us a little more warmly.

SILENT HEARTS

JING SHUI BIAN · WORK

Silent Hearts

Author: Jing Shui Bian
Translators: Alex; Katniss
Editor: Michaela M; Seven

978-1-77408-219-5

Published by Via Lactea Ltd
twitter.com/ViaLactea_press

Via Lactea
Publishing Co.

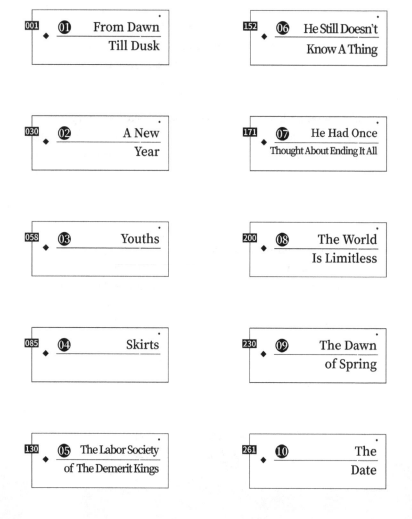

CONTENT

KUNQIAN HIGH SCHOOL
GRADUATION SEASON

SILENT HEARTS

From Dawn **01**
Till Dusk

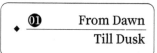

01 From Dawn
Till Dusk

In a cross-legged position, Lin Mu sat in front of the dressing table, dressed in Lin Zhao's sundress. The person behind him was bending over him, adjusting a wig and the hair net attached to it before carefully pulling it over his hair.

Lin Mu signed at the mirror, "It's too warm."

Lin Zhao pursed her lips, her fingers moving swiftly. "You have to wear it even if it's warm, or you'll be easily exposed without it."

Lin Mu rolled his eyes. As he grumbled about how troublesome girls were, he received a knock on the head from Lin Zhao.

Lin Zhao narrowed her eyes. Her fair fingers were like sharp, thin blades fanning out as she signed leisurely, "I can understand what you're saying, Little Liar."

In the city's East Zone, community sessions were held monthly for people with special needs. Lin Zhao had attended them a few times and then refused to participate further. Lin Mu had initially been worried that she'd been getting bullied, but he'd later found out that the girl had privately accepted an invitation to become a Go mentor, and that these two demands on her time clashed.

Because of this, Lin Yanlai and Jiang Wan had called for a family meeting. Lin Zhao had stood there with a dark face and folded arms, having just received a scolding from Lin Mu.

They were fraternal twins, a pigeon pair, but they were miraculously as alike as two peas in a pod. Lin Zhao had greeted the world first, one second earlier than her brother, yet Lin Mu had been the first to cry aloud. A month later, Lin Zhao had been diagnosed with congenital deafness.

After going through the immense pain when the diagnosis was first confirmed, Lin Yanlai and Jiang Wan had begun to search everywhere, hoping for a cure for their daughter. However, the results had only made them even more depressed. Lin Yanlai had quit his job abroad to become a full-time househusband. He'd taught himself sign language while taking care of his daughter, Lin Zhao, and brought up his son at the same time.

At two years old, the first thing Lin Mu had learned to say was to call Lin Zhao, "*Jiejie*."

A year later, Lin Zhao's first words to Lin Mu had been "Little Liar" through sign language. Lin Mu had sneakily eaten all the nougat that Lin Yanlai had made, and then he'd lied to her that their dad hadn't made any.

Under normal circumstances, Lin Zhao should have attended special needs schools since primary school. However, due to Lin Yanlai's unremitting efforts, other than not being able to hear or speak, she had not fallen behind other children in any other matters of her education.

As such, the elder sister had shuffled off to the same school as her younger brother, and both had been in the same class. After four semesters at school, Lin Zhao had started to pick up Go officially.

At first, Lin Mu too had followed along and learned the game. However, half a year later, he'd found that he didn't have enough patience for it, and eventually he'd given up on the lessons. Lin Zhao had been infuriated over this. In the middle of the night, she'd kept kicking his bed, refusing to let him sleep.

Lin Mu had been extremely sleepy. From under his pillow, he'd taken out a little torchlight, shining it at his sister.

This was a habit of many years. Lin Zhao could not speak, so when she wanted to speak to Lin Mu at night, her younger brother would have to use the light of the torch to sign in the dark.

"Why did you quit learning Go?" The bright light from the torch had shone gently upon Lin Zhao's small, delicate face. Her expression had been stern, and she'd looked just like a little grown-up.

With half-closed eyes, Lin Mu had signed quickly, "I can't keep hanging out with you. The other boys are no longer playing with me anymore, and it's embarrassing."

Lin Zhao's lips had tightened. She'd seemed furious. After kicking Lin Mu's bed some more, she'd finally flipped over and ignored him.

After that day, Lin Zhao had no longer gone with Lin Mu to school and back home. She would only attend the morning classes, and Lin Yanlai would then take her to the Go Institute after lunch.

However, Lin Mu also had not ended up making more friends.

He'd still gone to school and left it on his own, occasionally dropping by the Go Institute to deliver Lin Zhao her meals.

"Little Liar," Lin Zhao had signed at her little brother while eating, "you said you wanted to make friends, so where are your friends?"

With his head resting on one hand, Lin Mu had lazily signed back with his other, "You're so annoying, go practice your Go."

Lin Zhao had managed to achieve the amateur fifth dan rank when she'd been in junior high. During Lin Mu's first year of high school, Lin Zhao had defeated her opponents in a professional ranking tournament, becoming a young professional Go player.

However, Lin Yanlai and Jiang Wan had still felt that one should not completely give up on academics. As such, they'd sent their daughter to Kunqian High—the high school where at the time Lin Mu had been studying at, as well as the only high school in the East Zone that accepted special needs students.

A year later, Lin Zhao had been promoted to a higher rank. She'd moved onto a more prominent Go institute to hone her skills, and no one in the family had ever imagined that she would accept a job as a mentor.

"You're not yet eighteen." Despite having a busy work schedule, Lin Zhao was Jiang Wan's greatest concern, and she could not bear to see Lin Zhao go through even the slightest bit of hardship. "Being a Go mentor is a job, and we are not short of money. Why did you accept it? Is there something you'd like to buy? Just tell mama."

Lin Mu had not been able to help but laugh in irritation. He'd signed the words that he'd simultaneously said aloud, "As if she has anything she wants to buy! She just has too much time on her hands!'"

Under the table, Lin Zhao had kicked him, her fingers moving swiftly. "You're so annoying!"

Lin Yanlai too was rather disapproving. He'd removed his glasses, signing gently, "What about the zone's monthly community sessions? You have to attend them."

Lin Zhao had been unhappy; her fingers had moved forcefully in response: "I'm nothing like those people, why do I have to attend? Just because I'm disabled?!"

Lin Mu had frowned, signing at her, "Who are you looking down on?"

Lin Zhao had sneered, rebutting quickly, "You're the ones looking down on me, every single one of you!" She had then stood up and headed upstairs, ignoring the looks of consternation on the faces of Lin Yanlai and Jiang Wan.

Lin Mu had nearly exploded in anger. He'd also stood up, wanting to chase after her, but Lin Yanlai had called him to a halt.

"Don't argue with your sister," Jiang Wan scolded. "Your words shouldn't have been so harsh."

Lin Mu's head had spun with rage. "Who exactly was being harsh? What did she mean by us looking down on her? Which 'we' was she alluding to, huh?!"

Lin Yanlai had given him a look, and Lin Mu had abruptly fell silent. It'd been as though his raging fire of anger had been extinguished, and he'd stood there, alone.

Putting his glasses back on, Lin Yanlai had thought it over and said, "If she really wants to be a Go mentor, then let her be. We'll think of something else with regards to the community sessions."

Only after the twins graduated from primary school had they

then obtained their own rooms. Lin Mu had stood outside Lin Zhao's door for some time, and the moment he'd opened it, his face had been met with a flying pillow.

"Little Liar." Lin Zhao had raised a middle finger at him. "I can't believe you tattled on me."

Lin Mu had thrown the pillow back, his expression serious as he'd signed, "Tell me the truth, are you being bullied at the new Go Institute?"

Lin Zhao had rolled her eyes, responding, "I just don't feel like attending the community sessions."

Lin Mu had asked, "Why?"

Lin Zhao had lifted up her hand, her finger twirling in the air as though she'd been drawing a blossom. With pursed lips, she'd looked somewhat wilful. "There's no reason for it. I just don't want to."

In all honesty, Lin Zhao was really good at makeup. Although Lin Mu was a little taller than his sister, as a high school student, he had no time for exercising to train his muscles, so he was thin. The twins both had extremely fair skin, their limbs slender and long. Apart from Lin Mu's flat chest, Lin Zhao's dress was nearly a perfect fit for him.

"Do I have to wear a bra?" Lin Mu asked.

Lin Zhao took out a NuBra, waving it wickedly. "Put this on."

Lin Mu was speechless.

The thin muscles on his chest were forcibly squeezed together by Lin Zhao as she tried with much difficulty to shape a pair of "breasts." Then, Lin Zhao found her brother a cardigan and finally tied a ribbon around his neck.

"We're done." Lin Zhao gave him an OK sign. Her fingers dancing through the air, she praised her brother, "You're actually quite pretty."

Looking in the mirror, Lin Mu raised his chin slightly. His lips were pursed, feeling a little disdainful of the compliment and a little embarrassed at the same time.

Lin Yanlai and Jiang Wan did not know why their daughter had suddenly changed her mind and was willing to attend the community session. When they received a call informing them of her attendance, they were of course caught off guard.

"She's there..." Jiang Wan was still a little in disbelief. She confirmed again, "Is she really there?"

The voice of the community teacher was so loud that even Lin Yanlai, standing next to Jiang Wan, could hear her clearly. "She's here, she's here. Lin-*tongxue* is very obedient. It's just that she doesn't like to interact with anyone. I'll keep an eye on her."

It was true that she did not like to interact with others. Although Jiang Wan still could not understand what was going on, she could only accept it and left the teacher a few reminders. After she hung up, out of the blue, Lin Yanlai casually asked, "Where's Lin Mu?"

Jiang Wan was still thinking about their daughter, and so she waved him off without much thought. "He's probably hanging out somewhere. Who knows? Just let him be."

Lin Mu was sitting in the last row of the classroom. Turning drowsy from the heat, he had to keep himself from crossing his ankle over his knee. There weren't many people in the room, and everyone seemed to know each other except him. Occasionally, a few deaf-mute members would try to interact with him, but after signing at each other for some time, the conversation soon fell silent after they ran out of things to say. In the end, Lin Mu still remained seated there alone.

By break time, the heat got too much for Lin Mu. He went out by himself, sitting down under the shade of a tree. Finally, he could cross his legs, and he relaxed for a short moment.

However, that moment was over in a flash as another tactless person came over.

Unwillingly, Lin Mu straightened his legs and put them together demurely. Tilting his head, the dappled sunlight fell upon his face as he looked at the newcomer with a squint.

"Hello." The boy was very tall, looking much more muscular than Lin Mu. His skin was very tanned, and he had a very good-looking face. His signing was rather jerky, exposing him as a beginner that had only just learned it. "Are you feeling warm?"

Lin Mu signed shortly, "I'm fine," not caring if the other person could understand. He studied the boy, concluding that he was neither intellectually disabled nor had any obvious physical handicaps. As such, he was uncertain as to why the boy would strike up a conversation.

"I'm Lu Rong." The boy clearly did not know how to sign his own name. Clumsily, he straightened his thumb as well as his index and little fingers while curling down the other two fingers. Raising his hand to his temple, he shook it slightly.

Lin Mu was tickled. He did the same gesture, and then signed, "This gesture is referring to an animal, a 'deer.'"

Lu Rong understood. He seemed somewhat embarrassed, standing there at a loss. A while later, he again repeated the question. "Are you feeling warm?"

Lin Mu looked at him, unable to suppress his smile. He held his hand out, waving his five fingers, and tapped them twice lightly on his forehead.

"Not anymore," he signed.

Honestly, Lu Rong did not look like the type of person that would initiate a chat with others; the conversation went dead again as they ran out of things to say. As Lin Mu's character was currently a pretty, deaf-mute girl, he would definitely freak the boy out if he were to speak out loud. Later on, Lin Mu realized that Lu Rong might have seen him as someone of a similar age to him, and therefore approached him to see if he could spark up a conversation. However, once they started chatting, due to Lin Mu's character as an "aloof and icy beauty," he was unable to maintain the conversation.

The two sat together on the bench for a while. Lin Mu felt that there was no point if they continued sitting there. Just as he stood up, Lu Rong quickly followed.

"I'm going to get an ice cream," Lin Mu signed. "Would you like to come along?"

Lu Rong nodded.

Lin Mu led him to a nearby store. The shopkeeper was sitting next to a freezer, snacking on melon seeds.

"Auntie," Lu Rong called out, "two Wall's ice cream, please."

The shopkeeper took two out from the freezer, handing them over. She asked Lu Rong, "How's your granny?"

"She's attending a class."

"Is it ok if you're not watching her?"

Lu Rong nodded. "It's fine if it's just a short while."

Surprisingly, the shopkeeper knew a little sign language as well. She signed at Lin Mu, "You've grown taller."

Lin Mu had no choice but to wave her words away modestly.

Lin Mu and Lu Rong ate their ice cream while walking back. Thinking about what the shopkeeper had said, he signed at Lu Rong, "You came here with your granny?"

"She's ill." After signing that, Lu Rong thought for a moment, then tore off the ice cream wrapper and took out a pen from his pocket. He wrote on the wrapper, then passed it to Lin Mu.

Alzheimer's Disease.

As though afraid that Lin Mu would not recognize it, Lu Rong added a few more words to the note. "It's a type of dementia."

Lin Mu raised his head, glancing at Lu Rong. The boy was a little shy, and he did not smile often. With incredibly long eyelashes, his eyes did somewhat resemble those of a deer.

"Is it tiring?" Li Mu knocked on the crook of his arm and drew a question mark.

When Lu Rong understood the question, he remained silent for some time and then shook his head. "Not at all."

They could not return to the classroom without finishing the ice cream. As such, they again returned to the bench under the shade of the trees.

With the wrapping paper, conversation became much easier. Lin Mu realized that Lu Rong could understand sign language fairly well; it was just that he was not fluent at signing. If there were any words he could not sign, he would write them out.

"Are you taking care of your granny alone?" Lin Mu slowed down his signing speed so that Lu Rong could understand.

Lu Rong would mumble softly as he wrote, "My parents passed away a long time ago, so I'm the only one taking care of Granny."

Lin Mu asked, "What about school?"

Lu Rong wrote, "She comes with me to school."

He then signed, using simple vocabulary, "I've been accepted into a new high school, and I'm going to be a first-year student."

The situation in East Zone was rather complicated. Many students would choose to attend the high school affiliated to their junior high. In Lu Rong's case, even a fool would understand his reason for doing so. Lu Rong would be accompanied by an Alzheimer's patient, and Kunqian High was the only school in the area that fulfilled his needs.

"Soon, you'll be my junior." Lin Mu smiled as he signed.

Seeing his smile, Lu Rong blushed. Wiping sweat away from his forehead, he wrote slowly on the paper, "I know, I've read about you on the newspaper."

Lin Mu's mouth fell open. Only then did he remember Lin Zhao had been the youngest member in their city when she entered the qualifiers. Due to her unusual identity and her extraordinary accomplishments, she had appeared in newspapers before.

"You're very good at Go," Lu Rong continued writing. "You don't look like a dis—"

He stopped abruptly, a little flustered. Forcefully, he drew a strikethrough across "dis." After some time, he finally glanced at Lin Mu.

Lin Mu could not even put on a smile. He now seemed to finally understand Lin Zhao's reluctance to come. Perhaps when interacting with others, Lin Zhao had never been treated as an ordinary, healthy person, despite her ordinary, healthy appearance.

"You've always ignored everyone else," Lu Rong wrote carefully, "so, I guessed you came here unwillingly."

Lin Mu could only sign, "Well, here I am, no?"

He looked at Lu Rong and continued signing, "Is it convenient for you to have your grandmother following you all the time?"

"It wasn't convenient at first, but I got used to it. There's no other choice; she needs someone to watch over her."

Lin Mu gestured, pretending to hit someone: "Did you get bullied?"

Lu Rong did not speak. He clenched a fist and lightly pounded his chest twice.

Lin Mu laughed.

Lu Rong pointed at him. "How about you? Do you get bullied?"

Lin Mu had not expected that Lu Rong would turn the question back. He was a little dumbfounded, and so he hesitated for a moment, trying to figure out how he should reply.

It was impossible for them not to have been bullied. Things had still been fine in primary school, as the teachers were strict and the students innocent and guileless. They could complain to the teachers if any argument happened. However, things hadn't been so easily settled once they got to junior high.

The twins had appeared gentle and weak, the very model of well-behaved, obedient children. Boys entered puberty later than girls, so in junior high, Lin Mu had been even shorter than Lin Zhao. Most of the time, she had been the one protecting her little brother instead.

The bullying had appeared within Lin Zhao's textbooks. Her textbooks had always had a few extra pages missing from them. By the time Lin Mu had noticed it, his sister's English textbook had been half its original thickness.

Lin Zhao had said nothing of it, only signing that she'd torn it by herself. Lin Mu had not believed her.

"I saw Sun Hai next to your table in the afternoon." Lin Mu's actions had been very agitated as he signed, his face flushing red. "Was he the one who did it?!"

Frowning, Lin Zhao's fingers had moved lightly, "No."

After a moment of silence, Lin Mu had said, his voice cold like ice, "I'll ask him."

Lin Zhao had caught hold of him, refusing to let him go. Her fingers had signed swiftly, "What are you going to ask? If he says yes, what can you even do about it? Fight him?"

Gritting his teeth, Lin Mu had wiped his face with the back of his hand. When he turned back, his eyes had been red, and his voice had been filled with anger. "I'll fight him until the end even if I can't win! Let's see if he dares bully you again!"

Lin Zhao had frozen. Then she'd cracked up over her brother's reaction—he was too adorable! Yet, the slight bitterness in her heart had not abated.

"I'm fine," Lin Zhao had signed at Lin Mu, "just let him be."

The phrase "let him be" had not lasted longer than one day. Junior high students had been required to attend evening classes, and by the time Lin Zhao had returned from the Go institute to pick Lin Mu up, the classroom had already descended into chaos. Her seemingly thin and small brother had been sitting on top of Sun Hai, whacking his head forcefully with an English textbook.

As his back had been facing her, Lin Zhao had not been able to read her brother's lips, and she had been able to only vaguely make out what Sun Hai had been shouting.

From his lips, she had read things like: "Sissy," "I'm going to complain to our teacher," "Stop hitting," "I was wrong," and then, "I won't do it anymore."

Lin Mu's attacks on Sun Hai had become more violent when Sun Hai had called him a sissy, his strength enough to even crumple the pages of the textbook. Some classmates around them had tried to stop him, and it had seemed like they were telling him that his sister was here. Lin Mu had jerked his head back, the fire blazing in his eyes having yet to die down. Injuries had been scattered across his face, and he had cut a sorry figure as he looked at Lin Zhao.

The siblings had looked at each other silently. Lin Mu had been a little tired, and he'd slowly clambered off Sun Hai. The bully underneath him had still been crying, and Lin Zhao's had gaze slid away from her brother. She had walked over to Sun Hai, looking down at him in a queenly manner.

She'd raised her chin slightly, and her fingers had drawn through the air elegantly yet flippantly. "You can bully me, but you can't hit my brother."

Lin Mu had pursed his lips, refusing to say a word. He had then been kicked by Lin Zhao.

"Tell him what I signed!"

Clicking his tongue, he had sneered at Sun Hai. "You can hit me, but you can't bully my sister!"

Lin Zhao's eyebrows had drawn together, very confident that Lin Mu had not passed the message correctly. She had picked up the English textbook off the ground. To no one's surprise, it was hers. She had already finished studying the missing pages from the book, so the issue of them being missing had not really affected her.

Taking the book from her hand, Lin Mu had thrown it onto Sun Hai's face, speaking fiercely, "Fix the missing pages, or I'll beat you up again!"

In the end, the pages had indeed been pasted back. However, Sun Hai had also reported the incident to their teacher. As violence was never the solution, Lin Yanlai and Jiang Wan had been called down to the school. Jiang Wan had a bad temper, and, upon knowing that her daughter had been bullied, she had nearly destroyed the teachers' office in a rage. Instead, it had been Lin Yanlai who calmly said, "We'll definitely scold Lin Mu properly when we're home."

At the same time, he had given the twins standing in a corner a thumbs-up.

Later on, Sun Hai too had been admonished. His "punishment" had been to help, protect, and take care of his classmate, Lin Zhao, for a semester. Since then, Lin Mu had discovered that there was a pest called Sun Hai following Lin Zhao persistently, even fighting with him over tasks like carrying Lin Zhao's schoolbag.

"Your sister is so cool." Sun Hai imitated the movements of Lin Zhao's fingers. His tone was earnest when he asked, "Why do her gestures look so good?"

Resting his head on his palm, Lin Mu burst his bubble: "Don't you know that those gestures are how my sister calls you 'stupid'?"

Sun Hai had been dumbstruck.

"I've seen your brother before," Lu Rong wrote suddenly on the paper, "the two of you look very alike."

Halfway through signing, Lin Mu's gestures stiffened, and he felt a little apprehensive. Thinking it over, he recalled that during the few times Lin Zhao had obediently attended the community sessions, he did come by and pick her up.

As such, he could only blink innocently. With feigned calmness, he signed, "We're twins."

Lu Rong continued writing, "I never thought that he'd be so good at fighting."

Lin Mu did not know how to respond to that.

Lu Rong thought for a moment, and added, "He looks too delicate. With how gorgeous he is, no one could bear to hit him."

Lin Mu narrowed his eyes. His smile was a little fake, and his fingers signed forcefully, "You're wrong, my brother's extremely good at fighting."

Lu Rong looked a little shocked. Perhaps he didn't understand why an elder sister would emphasize how good her little brother was at fighting. After a moment of hesitation, he wrote, "Did that Sun Hai boy ever bully you again?"

Lin Mu sulked a little. He felt that this person was definitely looking down on him. However, he was currently pretending to be Lin Zhao, and so he could not embarrass her. Hence, he started exaggerating about how "her brother" had taught Sun Hai a lesson, embellishing the entire incident. With how animated Lin Mu's gestures were, Lu Rong reacted like he was watching stand-up comedy.

"After that, Sun Hai became my lackey and my brother's buddy," Lin Mu signed excitedly as he concluded the story.

Lu Rong's expression did not change much, but his gaze turned a little cold. He replied with his fingers, "That's nice."

He then wrote on the paper, "You can even become friends with someone who bullied you."

Lin Mu froze as Lu Rong's words slowly sank in. Just as he raised his hands to sign his reply, someone walked out from the classroom some distance away.

It was one of the teachers of the community session, and he called out to Lu Rong, "*Xiao* Lu, your granny wants to go to the washroom."

Lu Rong looked up and acknowledged him, "I'm coming!"

He signed at Lin Mu, "Shall we head back?"

Lin Mu nodded, standing up as well. Lu Rong was walking rather hastily; Lin Mu had to sprint a little to catch up. The members in the classroom were still the same few people, all as

friendly and harmonious as before. Some of the deaf-mute members were standing around Lu Rong's grandmother, and when
they saw him, they all signed at him enthusiastically.

Lu Rong signed his thanks back. Bending down, he softly
coaxed the old lady.

Lin Mu could hear the old lady mumbling, "Meimei doesn't
want to go to the toilet alone, Meimei is scared."

She added, "Meimei wants to hold hands."

As such, Lu Rong held her hand, helping her up.

The old lady saw Lin Mu as she turned her head. Her lips parted abruptly, revealing her broken teeth. She then asked, "Want to
go pee-pee with Meimei?"

Lin Mu did not know how he should react.

Feeling a little embarrassed, Lu Rong spoke quietly, "Meimei,
we'll just go together. We're not going to trouble others, alright?"

His grandmother seemed to understand what he meant. Her
eyes turned downcast, and she pursed her lips unhappily.

Lu Rong heaved a breath of relief and signed at Lin Mu, "Sorry
about that."

Lin Mu bit his lip. Deliberately, he signed, "What did Granny
say?"

For a moment, Lu Rong hesitated. But he still replied honestly, "She wants to go to the washroom with you."

Lin Mu smiled. Suddenly, he stuck out his hand, tucking it
around the other arm of Lu Rong's grandmother and moved his
fingers gently.

"I want to hold hands with Meimei and go pee-pee together."

The grandmother of Lu Rong was called Chen Meihua, and she
liked to refer to herself as "Meimei." She loved bright, colorful
dresses that were not very fashionable, and insisted on painting

her cheeks red every day. Sometimes, she would even dab a red dot between her brows.

Lu Rong combed her hair every day, tying it in all sorts of neat and pretty braids. She liked presenting herself brightly and colorfully all the time, and Lu Rong tried his best to satisfy her.

The school holidays during summer were quite long. Ever since Lin Mu started attending the sessions on behalf of Lin Zhao, he would be able to see Lu Rong and Meimei almost every time.

There were times when Lu Rong would be so busy he did not have time to chat at all. Each time Meimei went to the washroom, she needed someone to watch over her and hold her hand.

However, later, it seemed that Meimei preferred going to the washroom while holding Lin Mu's hand.

At first, Lin Mu felt a little awkward going to the ladies' room. However, after a few experiences, along with him being dressed as a girl, he became resigned and started getting used to it.

Helping the old lady into the cubicle, he then closed the door for her. As he stood on guard outside, he could even hear Meimei singing happily.

Meimei must definitely have had a beautiful voice when she'd been younger. Every word she sang was clear as a bell, even when she was singing in Cantonese.

Her voice drifted out as she sang "*Qian Qian Que Ge*":

"*In the days to come, thousands of songs will drift along my path.*

"*In the days to come, thousands of stars will shine brighter than to-night's moon.*"

Lin Mu could not help smiling as he listened to her sing. However, as soon as he remembered that he was supposed to be a deaf-mute girl, he quickly straightened his face again.

Aside from individuals with mental disabilities such as Lu

Rong's grandmother and people with hearing impairments attending the community sessions, there were also a few others with visual or physical impairments. The people managing the sessions were all volunteers, like the teacher in charge of Lin Mu's class. He had just graduated from university, and he had volunteered at first because of his interest in sign language. After volunteering a few more times, he'd developed an interest in the community, and started fussing over everyone like an old mother hen.

There were a few instances where Lin Mu had been annoyed by him almost to the point of having a breakdown.

The reason for the annoyance was that the teacher felt he was too much of a loner.

"Lin-*tongxue*." Mr. Ma's sign language was even worse than Lu Rong. "You have to come play with the others; you can't always stay by yourself all the time!"

Lin Mu signed back lazily, "I'm playing with Little Deer."

There was a distinct difference between Mr. Ma's and Lin Mu's understanding of the deer. Baffled, his response was stern: "There's no deer here. You have to play with people, understand?"

Lin Mu laughed his head off. Noticing Lu Rong walking over, he cocked an eyebrow as he raised his right hand. Keeping his index and little fingers straight, he placed his thumb next to his temple and waved his hand lightly a couple of times.

From his height, Lu Rong cast his eyes down, looking at Lin Mu.

Lin Min signed gloatingly at Mr. Ma, "See, the little deer is here."

Even as the summer holidays came to an end, the matter of Lin Mu attending the community sessions as Lin Zhao had yet to be revealed to the family. In fact, Lin Zhao suspected that her brother was enjoying it.

"Sun Hai keeps contacting me lately." Lin Zhao waved her phone, signing at her brother, "He wants to know why you're always so busy."

Lin Mu was currently wiping his face with Lin Zhao's make-up remover. He had one eye open and the other closed, and he signed perfunctorily back, "Am I not attending your community sessions on your behalf? I'll see him anyway when school begins. Why is he so anxious?"

Lin Zhao gave Lin Mu a disapproving glance. She had found the handbook that her brother had brought home, which was now full of messages from the other participants. This handbook was like a license declaring your handicap; as long as you attended a session, you would receive one. When Lin Zhao had been the one attending the sessions, she'd only ever had a few messages in it. Now, Lin Mu had most of the pages filled up.

Flipping through it, Lin Zhao was tickled to laughter by some of the messages. When Lin Mu was done drying his face, he saw his sister reading the handbook and joined her.

"Uncle Wang cannot see, so he dictated his message as Mr. Ma wrote it down." Pointing at some of the messages, Lin Mu signed at Lin Zhao, "This one is from Auntie Li; do you remember her? She has a prosthetic right arm, but her handwriting is especially nice."

Lin Zhao glanced at him. "Why are you even more enthusiastic about this than me?"

Lin Mu looked stern. "I'm trying to let you experience the warmth of humanity. Next time, don't skip the sessions anymore. You should attend the sessions yourself."

It was a rare occasion for Lin Zhao not to argue back. She

seemed to have suddenly remembered something, bending over and pulling a shoebox out from under her bed. Acting unbothered, she pushed the box at her brother.

Lin Mu gave her a puzzled look. "What is this?"

Lin Zhao seemed unruffled, but a nervousness could be seen in her eyes, and even her hands were trembling as she signed, "I bought this for you. If you don't like them, I'll return them."

Lin Mu could not be any more delighted. As he exclaimed over how much he liked the present, he opened the shoebox and put the shoes on straight away. Admiring them, he came to a sudden realization and signed agitatedly at Lin Zhao, "Why didn't you tell me when I asked you about it? Did you work as a mentor just to get me a pair of shoes?!"

Lin Zhao would of course never admit this. Raising her chin, she signed back elegantly, "Idiot."

Lin Mu paid no heed to his sister's harsh pride. Basking in joy, he took a photo of his new shoes and sent it to Sun Hai.

Lin Zhao did not understand his actions. "What are you doing?"

Blissfully, Lin Mu replied, "I'm sharing the photo with him so he can drool over it."

Lin Zhao was speechless.

School started again in September. Lin Mu belonged to the rare category of students who did not need to rush through their summer homework before school began again. A week ago, Sun Hai had requested to borrow his workbooks for copying. The two of them arranged to meet at Starbucks, and Lin Mu brought along his laptop, surfing the web as he waited in boredom.

The first thing Sun Hai noticed was his new shoes. With great emotion, he expressed his plain jealousy, and it got onto Lin Mu's nerves. "Aren't you going to copy the homework?!"

Clutching onto the workbook, Sun Hai did not let him snatch it back. "What have you been doing this entire summer break? I asked your sister, but she didn't say anything about it. I tried to ask you out, but you didn't come. Look at the world outside. Isn't it nice to be out there?!"

"It is nice," Lin Mu responded lazily, then rushed him, saying, "hurry up and get your work done."

Sun Hai was unhappy now. "How could you not have any love for your classmate? And why are you in such a hurry? Are you meeting someone else?"

Resting his chin in his hand, Lin Mu smiled. "I'm meeting a little heron too."

"Xu Yilu?" Sun Hai shrieked. "Why are you meeting him? Is he going to fight over your homework with me?!"

Of course, Xu Yilu would not fight with Sun Hai over Lin Mu's homework. His vision impairment was classified as being between Class Two and Three, and he could only see very minimal light in his left eye, whereas his right eye was slightly better, and he could see vague shadows with it. Apart from wearing his special corrective glasses, he had to carry a white cane when he was outside.

Initially, Lin Mu had wanted to pick Xu Yilu up, but Xu Yilu had turned him down. As such, they'd decided to meet at a café located between where they stayed, and Sun Hai was only there out of convenience.

There weren't many customers in the morning. When Xu Yilu arrived, Lin Mu went to the entrance specially to await him.

Folding up his cane, Xu Yilu grasped on to Lin Mu's hand. "Is Sun Hai here already?"

"He's here." Lin Mu smiled, looking at him. "You cut your hair?"

Xu Yilu was slightly shorter, fairer, and thinner than Lin Mu. Smiling elegantly, he said, "Just a little. How does it look?"

Lin Mu was unbothered whether or not Xu Yilu could see the earnest thumbs-up he gave him. "Looking good, little birdy."

Xu Yilu had always completed his holiday homework on his own, and this fact left Sun Hai in admiration. To encourage interaction between special needs and ordinary students, as well as to develop the independence of special needs students, Kunqian High had implemented a collaborative learning system—special needs and ordinary students, including the elite classes, were required to share some classes together.

However, only students with excellent academic grades were eligible to enroll in an elite class. Xu Yilu was the only special needs student whose grades could compete with the elite class's curve wreckers.

Although Sun Hai was now furiously copying Lin Mu's homework, he had a good head for examinations. His grades were quite decent despite him making no attempts to study.

"Has your vision deteriorated recently?" Lin Mu could not help but ask when he saw Xu Yilu's glasses.

Xu Yilu shook his head. "It's fine. My mom sought some opinions from an overseas optometrist, and he recently prescribed me a pair of new glasses. Now, I can vaguely make out things with my left eye."

Lin Mu leaned closer to him. "Can you see me?"

Xu Yilu laughed. "Yes I can, you handsome fellow."

Kunqian High was a highly reputable school, so it was not

surprising that the former alumni had the highest university promotion rates in East Zone. Apart from the governmental support they got, the fact that they accepted special needs students as well as the strong education system they provided to their ordinary students had pushed their profile and prestige to the top. Furthermore, as soon as the school had become famous, more patrons had stepped up to provide aid, and more rich families had begun to send their children there. There were various motives for the enrollment in this school—it could be due to parents who were too busy to look after their children, or the worry that a child would follow the examples of the bad students in other schools, etc etc. However, no matter what the reasons were, as long as the students were enrolled in Kunqian High, a strict, regulated, and disciplined education system would be imposed upon them. In turn, the standard of teachers and the adequacy of school facilities had in effect risen to a high level.

Xu Yilu's parents were quite well-to-do. Just the amount of money they spent annually on his eye care was an astronomical sum to many ordinary families.

Speaking to Xu Yilu, Lin Mu was a little distracted. His mind drifted off to Lu Rong. After a couple of days hanging out with him, he'd gotten an idea of his family's circumstances. He was not living in poverty, but neither did he live much better.

"Have you guys heard anything about the new students this year?" Sun Hai, unable to bear his loneliness, asked them both while copying his homework. "I heard there are a few of them in the special needs class."

Lin Mu said, "The special needs class is just a name, and they will still be studying with the other ordinary students. Can you please stop making them sound like a different species?"

Sun Hai pompously disagreed, "No way, your sister is one of a kind in my eyes. She's the beauty of Kunqian, a silent and exquisite lotus of snow."

Lin Mu felt so disgusted that he felt a pull in the pit of his stomach. His voice turned colder and responded, "Just give up now. You're not going to woo her, not with your face."

Sun Hai was left dumbstruck.

Xu Yilu seemed a little curious about the new students too. "We might be able to see them during the new student military training, right?"

Lin Mu was amused. "So what would you like to see? A pretty female junior?"

Xu Yilu blushed with Lin Mu's teasing. He spoke quietly, "I can't see them anyway..."

"So what if you can't?" Lin Mu grinned. "What you see in your heart is nothing less than us."

For a second Xu Yilu was speechless, falling into silence. He seemed to be a little embarrassed, a flush of red rising to his cheek and spreading to his ears. Unable to stop himself from pinching his earlobes, he changed the topic. "How about your sister? Is she doing well at Go?"

Most people who wern't involved in Go didn't know how the ranking system worked. Even if they asked Lin Mu about it, they would only ask using the most basic terms.

Besides, even if the conversation went deeper, Lin Mu himself didn't understand it either. All he knew was that Lin Zhao rose astonishingly quickly to the top ten rankings of the Association of State and Provincial Go Boards during the first half-year, and she would be competing at the national finals on the next half year.

With such an impressive elder sister, the younger brother appeared rather average in comparison. On top of that, due to Lin Zhao's unique situation, she was the one standing in the center each time the media reported on any matter of Go. As such, whenever the neighbors thought of Lin Yanlai's family during neighborhood gossip, they would hold her up as the role model for the children of the community, and Lin Mu wouldn't be mentioned very much.

The three of them were chatting and updating each other about their recent lives while waiting for Sun Hai to finish copying his homework. Since Xu Yilu's corrective glasses were pretty odd, when there were more people in Starbucks, many unknowing eyes fell upon him from time to time.

It seemed as though Xu Yilu was unaware of them, but Lin Mu was not feeling comfortable about it. Nudging at the diligent Sun Hai, he quietly said, "Let's move to somewhere quieter."

Sun Hai was utterly engrossed in copying. Confused, he raised his head. "Huh? Why are we moving?"

The moment he finished asking, he saw a man sitting across him staring at Xu Yilu. Not only was he staring, he even pointed at the cane in Xu Yilu's hand and gestured to his female companion with a movement that rudely implied blindness. Then, he gave a disdainful and malicious laugh.

Sun Hai's overbearing temper rushed up. Just as he was about to burst out in anger, Lin Mu held him back and lightly shook his head.

Xu Yilu had no idea what had just happened. He had his head bowed and was earnestly sniffing at the beverage Lin Mu bought him. Lin Mu refused to tell him what flavor he had bought, only saying that he would definitely like it. As such, Xu Yilu could only guess the flavor by smelling it.

Perhaps he got too close. The tip of Xu Yilu's nose became

smeared with some cream, and he exclaimed in shock.

"Ooh, there's cream." Xu Yilu had an extremely sweet tooth. Like a child, he asked delightedly, "Did you buy the matcha frappuccino?"

"This is sweeter." Lin Mu packed his laptop away. Holding onto Xu Yilu's arm, he supported him as he stood up. "Let's go to another café; we'll have something even sweeter."

Without any doubt, Xu Yilu extended his white cane happily. The raging fire in Sun Hai was still smoldering, yet he understood that Lin Mu did not want Xu Yilu to find out about the incident just now and become upset. Shooting a fierce glare at the man from earlier, he threw an arm over Xu Yilu's shoulders.

"There's a new dessert shop next door, and their cream puffs are loaded with cream." Sun Hai's voice was deliberately loud as if to show support for Xu Yilu. He generously said, "*Gege*'s treat, I'll buy you ten!"

Xu Yilu frowned, looking somewhat scornful. "Ten cream puffs to be my big brother? Are you trying to take advantage of me?"

In the end, not only did Xu Yilu get ten cream puffs from Sun Hai, but he also got an egg tart from Lin Mu. The little heron's mouth was filled with sugar and he was happily calling the two boys his elder brothers. The three of them only separated after dinner; Sun Hai took Lin Mu's workbook as they sent Xu Yilu home together.

When Lin Mu got home, Lin Zhao was still playing Go in her Go room. Although Jiang Wan was not good at being a housewife, she shone brightly in the business arena. The family of four had moved to a townhouse the year before, and Lin Zhao had an extra room for her Go practice.

In the stillness of the night, their parents had already fallen asleep. When Lin Mu came out from the bathroom after his shower, the light in the Go room was still on. With bare feet, he went up the stairs; it was so quiet that he could only hear the clacking of the Go pieces.

He counted in his mind; his every step was like stepping on the square board. Lin Zhao's back faced the door, and she never knew her brother had been there and left again.

That night, Lin Zhao stayed up until midnight and spent the entire next day in the Go room practicing. Until the night before school started, Lin Mu finally saw Lin Zhao at the dining table.

"Did you lose the game?" Lin Mu signed at her.

Lin Zhao's expression was placid, and her fingers moved, "I lost a game. It was a practice."

She raised her chin and smiled. "But I'll definitely win the next time."

Lin Mu smiled back. He gave her an encouraging gesture and slightly gathered his fingers together as he bent his elbow. Then, as if he were attempting to catch the last remnants of summer, he clenched his fist tightly.

SILENT HEARTS

⑫   A New Year

02   A New
Year

Lunch break at Kunqian High was short. Even though it was just the first day of school, students were asked to distribute books to their classes, and then they had to attend their various club meetings in the afternoon. The first half of the semester for the second-year students was not stressful, but, under the school's strict education system, no class was allowed to fall behind.

With what little freedom that he barely squeezed out of his schedule, Lin Mu sprawled across the balcony railing in the second floor corridor, looking at the sports ground not too far away. With Lin Mu's bright, keen sight, in his words, even if there were a housefly rubbing its feet on the ground, he would be able to see how many times its feet had rubbed together.

After dealing with his books, Sun Hai too stared out at the grounds with him. A while later, Xu Yilu joined them as well.

While watching, Lin Mu broadcasted the proceedings to him. "They're marching now. Damn, this instructor is so fierce, and his voice is so loud. Can you hear him?"

Xu Yilu laughed. "Yeah, I can."

Sun Hai continued, "There's a pretty junior there! She's in the second last row; her legs are so long!"

Lin Mu had noticed her too. His eyes stayed on her for a while time, and noticed that the way she marched was a little different. A moment later, he saw the girl leaning down and rolling her trouser legs up.

Sun Hai was astonished.

As Xu Yilu could not see, he did not understand why his friends had fallen into sudden silence. He could not help but ask, "What's going on?"

Lin Mu's voice was a little light and breezy. "That kid has a prosthetic for her left leg."

Xu Yilu blinked. With a smile, he sighed as he expressed his earnest admiration, "How impressive."

Exactly, Lin Mu said within himself. He stared at the girl for a while. Upon turning his head, he discovered Meimei sitting in the shade of a tree.

Startled, Sun Hai clasped Lin Mu's arm, warning him, "Be careful, don't fall over."

Lin Mu ignored his warning; almost half of his body was leaning out over the railings. After searching around, he finally saw Lu Rong walking towards Meimei with a bottled drink.

It had been a while since they last saw each other. Lin Mu felt that Lu Rong seemed to have grown a little taller, and his skin was not as tanned as the first time they met. His hair seemed to be a bit longer too. Lu Rong opened the bottle cap with a twist, tasting it, and only then did he give it to his grandmother. His grandmother took a mouthful of it, then smiled so very brightly, revealing her teeth.

Sun Hai saw them too. Curiously, he asked, "Did he bring his family to school with him?"

Lin Mu responded casually, "His granny is an Alzheimer's patient, and she needs to be watched the whole time."

"Oh," Sun Hai replied. After a moment of thought, he realized something was not right, and so he asked, "How do you know that? Do you know him?"

Lin Mu answered placidly, "Lin Zhao knows him."

Upon hearing that Lin Zhao knew Lu Rong, Sun Hai was immediately filled with a sense of crisis. He stretched his neck out, desperately searching for him to see how he looked, yet Lin Mu shoved his face away.

"Don't block me," Lin Mu started fussing. Just as he was pushing and rowing with Sun Hai, Lu Rong suddenly turned his head towards them. Lin Mu got a shock, and without thinking, he dragged Sun Hai down, ducking down behind the balcony wall.

Xu Yilu had no idea what was going on, standing there blankly. After looking around for some time, he was dragged down by Lin Mu too.

The three of them huddled in a circle, crouching on the ground without any reason. Sun Hai looked at Xu Yilu, then glanced over to Lin Mu. Much like Xu Yilu, he did not understand what was going on. Like a thief, he lowered his voice and asked, "Why are you hiding?!"

Lin Mu imitated his volume, answering solemnly, "I can't let him see me."

Xu Yilu responded naively like a child, "Why not?"

Lin Mu did not know how to explain his actions, yet he had no choice but to say, "I can't let him see me, at least not for now."

Sun Hai gave him a suspicious stare. "Did you offend him in any way?"

Of course, Lin Mu would not admit it. "No such thing."

He added, "It's nothing like what you think anyway."

Question marks could be seen all over Sun Hai's face. *I wasn't thinking anything anyway*, he thought. When he looked up, he saw that Lin Mu was again sneakily peeping at the boy.

Meimei had already finished drinking, so Lu Rong returned to his position in the marching contingent to continue his training. The girl who had previously caught the attention of Lin Mu and his friends was now taking a break and sitting next to Meimei.

Looking at the girl's rolled-up pants, Sun Hai could not help but marvel, "That metal leg is so cool."

Right now, Lin Mu's attention was focused solely on Lu Rong. Therefore, he was not aware of anything else. He looked at the boy repeatedly practicing his turns under the command of the instructor. Surprisingly, he was not bored at all. Instead, he rested his chin in his hand, watching in great interest.

Xu Yilu could not see a thing; all he could do was listen to both of them chattering about their own topics.

One spoke about Lu Rong while the other talked about the "Metal Leg Girl." In the end, he was a little confused, and the expression on his face looked even more perplexed.

This situation continued until someone called out to Lin Mu.

Lin Mu was still in the midst of chattering away. Frowning unconsciously when he heard the voice, he clicked his tongue and lazily turned his head towards the person standing at the classroom entrance. "What do you want?" he asked in an unpleasant tone.

It was An Jincheng, the Young Master of Kunqian and a pretty boy. In Sun Hai's words, Young Master An was basically overflowing with the genes of nobility—every strand of his hair was carved with the word aloof. If he had to speak with the common folk like them, he would have to wipe his mouth ten times thereafter.

Right now, this nobleman was expressionless. His gaze, when looking at them, was as though he was looking at a bunch of idiots. With a detached voice, he said, "The teacher is calling for you."

Lin Mu pursed his lips. He clapped Sun Hai on the back, then supported Xu Yilu up, and responded to him unwillingly, "We're coming back now."

An Jincheng glanced over the balcony. The first-year students had to go through three days of military training, and he had no idea what was so interesting that had Lin Mu and his friends so entranced.

Lin Mu walked up to him, sounding rather impatient, "Make way."

An Jincheng did not move. He glanced at Xu Yilu. "It's not like there's no space."

They could walk past the door, but Lin Mu would not be able to support Xu Yilu with the tight fit. His brows knitted, and just as he was about to erupt, Xu Yilu let go of his hand.

"You should go first." Xu Yilu seemed a little scared of An Jincheng; he shrank into himself like a quail. Quietly, he mumbled, "Sorry..."

Xu Yilu then leaned towards the other side of the door. As he was not aware of the distance, he accidentally bumped into the doorframe.

Lin Mu's face darkened. Gritting his teeth, he repeated, "I said, back off."

An Jincheng and Lin Mu stared at each other for a few seconds. Then, An Jincheng averted his gaze first and quietly stepped out of the way.

Xu Yilu was dragged into the classroom by Lin Mu. Sun Hai

seemed accustomed to the contentious attitude between them. Although he had a better friendship with Lin Mu, he did not dare provoke the Young Master of Kunqian. As such, he could only smile awkwardly at An Jincheng before returning to his seat.

The form teacher of the elite class was an old, balding man with the surname Yang. He had been their form teacher since their first year, and, despite his short stature, he was extremely ferocious when scolding them. Most teachers of Kunqian had been headhunted from Qidong, and they were truly elite teachers. Once Lin Mu entered the classroom, he was immediately called up to the front.

"Hand out the papers." Teacher Yang adjusted his glasses; his eyes were bright and clear. "How was your summer holiday? There will be a mock test in two days; it's up to you and An Jincheng to decide who comes first and second."

An Jincheng was a child of a wealthy family, and he was also an exceptionally bright student. Of course, even if Lin Mu were to be punched to death or forced to jump off the building, he would never admit this fact.

Periodically, Lin Zhao would browse through the school forum and happen across the posts on her brother and An Jincheng battling things out. She did not really understand how her brother managed to engage in a conflict with character like An Jincheng, and somehow, it had even driven him to strive for excellence in his studies just to rise a step above An Jincheng.

As a matter of course, Lin Mu would never tell Lin Zhao the true reason—his conflicts with An Jincheng had arisen because of her.

"He didn't do it intentionally," Sun Hai quietly said to Lin Mu after the papers were given out. "With your sister's appearance and temperament, no one can tell that she has a disability. She's just like a goddess descending from heaven. Besides, there are so many students in Kunqian High, yet your sister became the school belle upon enrolling. How is she different from others, right?"

Lin Mu pointed at him warningly. "Lin Zhao is no different from others, watch your words."

After a pause, he continued, "She doesn't like us talking about her like that."

Sun Hai sighed, "Your sister is just too sensitive. No one has any ill intentions."

"You're not them, how would you know how they feel?" Lin Mu looked rather stern. "Exaggerated sense of pity and discussing over them are ill intentions to them. You must respect them, get it?"

Sun Hai raised his hands in surrender, his tone helpless. "Alright, alright... I'm respecting your sister from the bottom of my heart, okay?"

Lin Mu shot at him, "You even bullied her before! You were the one who ripped her books."

Seeing that Sun Hai wanted to retort, he immediately added, "Stop telling me that you're bullying her because of love, my sister and I are not going to fall for that. Whoever dares to express his love in that way again, I will beat the crap out of them."

Sun Hai snapped his mouth shut obediently.

Finally feeling a little more pleased, Lin Mu took out his notebook. Looking up to see An Jincheng watching him, he glared back stubbornly.

After a moment of thought, he sent Lin Zhao a text in worry.

"An Jincheng is really ugly." After sending that text, he hummed a song as he started on the paper.

After some time, Lin Zhao replied, "What sort of crazy are you dealing this time?"

"Nothing," Lin Mu replied, typing with his phone with both hands. "I'm just commenting after having not seen him for the entire summer holiday."

Lin Zhao's reply was rather quick this time, and she even attached a link to the school forum.

Lin Mu asked, "What's this?"

"It's the new ranking of the best-looking boys in school."

Lin Mu was puzzled.

Lin Zhao sent an emoji of evil laughter. "*Didi*, you're now number two."

Lin Mu had always known about the school forum. He had gone online and browsed through it a few times, but was not intrigued by it. It mostly consisted of An Jincheng's fans, and he was always scornful about how they paid obeisance to the rich.

Unlike the school belle, the decision of who was the most handsome boy in school was not so decisive. Lin Zhao dominated the position as Kunqian's school belle, and students had even formed a group to share her photos. After Lin Mu taught them a lesson a few times, they no longer dared to do it so brazenly. Therefore, it caught Lin Mu by surprise that his elder sister would actually pay such attention to the boys' ranking.

This time, Lin Mu was number two, yet neither did An Jincheng get the first spot. Looking at the photo for some time, he realized that it was actually Lu Rong—the boy had been captured sitting down in the shade of the tree with Meimei.

He probably did not realize he'd been secretly photographed— a shadow of a tree was cast upon his face, like a cloud concealing a glare, or a wind rustling through the leaves, the atmosphere around him warm and cozy.

Lu Rong was extremely tall—his towering physique gave him a steady, mature look that did not match his age. Even when bending down to speak to Meimei, his back was always straight; it seemed as if he were under some pressure, and there was a strength in him accumulating slowly.

Lin Mu repeatedly opened and closed the forum link, looking at the photo many times over, and then sent another text to his sister.

"There's something I want to tell you," Lin Mu typed.

Lin Zhao sent a "?" in response. After all, as twins, they could read each other quite well. "Did you stir up trouble for me again?"

"I'll tell you after school." He thought for a moment, and with a desire to survive, he added, "I promise I didn't stir up any trouble for you."

Lin Zhao was in Class Three. There were five classes in each grade; Class One was the elite class, whereas the rest were regular classes, including the special education class as well.

Special needs students who excelled in academics like Xu Yilu would attend compulsory subjects' lessons with Class One students, and join the special education class for the last two periods before the school was over, along with the evening self-study sessions. There would be a specially trained teacher there to take care of them and guide them along.

The special education class was not divided by grade. All special needs students from the first year to the third year would gather in special education class before school was over. It could be seen that the school had put great effort into this aspect as they were afraid that new students would feel isolated, helpless, and with no companions.

Lin Zhao, on the other hand, was a little more special from

other special needs students. After lunch, she would head to the Go Institute and only return to school to pick up her brother after his evening self-study sessions.

In Kunqian, with such an intense studying environment, the evening self-study sessions were the rare moments of freedom during which students could ease up a little. To bridge the gap and promote positive social interactions between ordinary and special needs students, each class would arrange a few ordinary students to join the special education class so they could have the self-study sessions together.

Because of Lin Zhao, Lin Mu would often run over to the special education class in the evening; he was familiar with everyone who was friends with Lin Zhao. On the first day of school, when Lin Zhao returned from the Go institute, she saw Lin Mu sitting in front of Xu Yilu, spinning his pen as he chatted with Cao Zhan.

On the IQ test, a score of 100 was considered average whereas scores below 70 would be classified as intellectual deficiency. Cao Zhan was the unlucky one—his IQ score was 69.

Such a slight intellectual disability would not affect his life too much, and Cao Zhan only seemed a little slower than others of his age. In psychological terms, he was classified as mildly impaired.

Lin Mu enjoyed teasing him. "Have you done your homework properly?"

Cao Zhan widened his eyes. He rarely spoke to people with whom he was unfamiliar since he could only respond with one sentence in the same time as the other party saying twenty. However, this was not the case for Lin Mu. They were familiar with each other and often talked a lot.

"What did you learn in Math today?" Lin Mu continued to

ask, not minding Cao Zhan's slowness. "Let me take a look."

Naturally, Cao Zhan would not refuse him.

Perhaps due to his intellectual disability, Cao Zhan looked a lot younger than he was. The baby fat on his face had yet to recede, but he was very tall. Slowly taking his workbook out, he was muttering indistinguishably while flipping through his book vigorously.

"I've done a few questions," Cao Zhan said. He did not control his volume, and thus his voice was a little loud, but soon he realized it. He tried to lower his voice as much as he could, speaking earnestly, "All these... I don't know how to do them at all. What should I do?"

Lin Mu looked on his workbook. "I'll teach you."

He sounded natural, as if nothing could be any more ordinary than this, listing those questions out on some scratch paper. Writing out the steps one by one, he explained them to Cao Zhan.

Cao Zhan's expression of studying the paper was serious, but it seemed likely that he did not understand.

Lin Mu called out to him, "Dopey."

Cao Zhan raised his head blankly.

Lin Mu asked him gently, "Do you understand?"

He shook his head. "No."

Lin Mu could not suppress his smile. "I'll explain it to you again."

And so, Cao Zhan continued to listen attentively.

Lin Mu repeated three or four times, but Cao Zhan was still lost. He felt that he could not let Lin Mu go on like this, so he took the workbook back. "I'll just copy it over and over again."

Lin Mu rested his chin in his hand. "Are you going to memorize it?"

Cao Zhan thought for a moment before he responded, "It's

better for me to memorize it."

Lin Mu did not stop him and handed over the scratch paper to him so he could copy from it. Sitting next to them, Xu Yilu was reading his braille book, not finding them noisy. A moment later, he looked up from the book as if he had sensed something. Groping about and nudging at Lin Mu's arm, he asked, "Is that Lin Zhao?"

Lin Mu turned his head without thinking. With no surprise, Lin Zhao was standing behind him.

"You're back?" Lin Mu signed and said it aloud simultaneously.

Lin Zhao acknowledged him. Her eyes fell onto Cao Zhan, and she signed, "Dopey."

Cao Zhan knew she was calling him. Half a beat later, he nodded.

Logically, a deaf-mute person and a blind person had no way to communicate, but Lin Zhao was obviously not bound by such logic. With no hesitation, she reached out to Xu Yilu, her palm running through his natural curls as though she was tugging at wool.

Xu Yilu could not help but laugh. "Did you win your game today?"

He slowed down his speaking speed so Lin Zhao could read his lips; Lin Zhao was able to do so as long as the speaker did not speak too quickly or complicatedly. She pressed on his curls lightly.

It meant that she won.

Wordless, Lin Mu felt that the tacit understanding in this friendship of rebels was a little too much.

After making a round of greetings, Lin Zhao sat down next to

Lin Mu.

"Tell me now." Lin Zhao's slender finger tapped at her lip. She spread her palm out, her fingers moving, "Is there anything you want to tell me?"

Lin Mu's signing speed had obviously slowed down, and his expression became a little ingratiating. "Remember when I attended the community sessions on your behalf?"

Lin Zhao raised her chin slightly. "Then?"

Lin Mu studied her expression. "I made a friend."

Lin Zhao narrowed her eyes, frowning slightly. A vague sense of doom welled up within her. "What did you do?"

"I didn't do anything, I just simply made a new friend," Lin Mu raised his hand and vowed. Again, he peeked at his sister's expression, then pointed at her phone, speaking cautiously, "He's the most handsome boy in the school."

Lin Zhao was at a loss for words.

Lin Mu smiled sheepishly. He coughed and tried his best to hide any tell-tale signs of wrongdoing. "I have a pretty good eye, don't I? Isn't he handsome?"

Lin Zhao was on the verge of vomiting blood, and her gestures became vehement. "You actually dare seduce someone when you were pretending to be me?!"

Lin Mu shook his head firmly. "I didn't seduce anyone! We're just friends! It's a pure friendship!"

Lin Zhao stuck out her thumb, drawing it across her throat savagely. Expressionless, her fingers danced deftly, "There is no such thing as pure friendship between males and females!"

Lin Mu rebutted unhappily, "I'm a male! What can happen between the two of us?"

"But you were 'me' on those days!" Lin Zhao jabbed his chest fiercely. Her mouth opened in agitation, but she could not make a sound. "I even pushed up your breasts for you! I dare you to swear that he didn't mistake you as a female!"

Lin Mu was speechless.

Paying no mind to Lin Zhao's worry, he said, "He might not even like you in that way..."

Lin Zhao moved to hit him, but Lin Mu dodged. Catching hold of his sister's hand, he swung her arm like a spoiled young child. "Don't be angry with me anymore... I swear there's really nothing between us. Just act normal, don't let the cat out of the bag when you see him next time, and stay friends with him, okay?"

Lin Zhao's face was grim. She tried to pull her hand back a few times as hard as she could, but Lin Mu's grip was too strong, as he grasped at her arm with an expression saying that he would never let go unless she agreed so.

Lin Zhao sighed. Feeling a headache coming, she rubbed her forehead, signing with one hand, "You're lying to him. What are you going to do if he finds out the truth in the future?"

"He's not going to find out so easily." Lin Mu noticed that she was giving in and immediately gave a crafty smile. With great confidence, he said, "We're almost identical, he's not going to find out."

Lu Rong closed the water bottle and looked down at Chen Meihua, who was seated demurely with her knees together.

"Does Meimei want to go to the washroom?" He asked quietly.

His grandmother looked up. Today, her hair was tied into two plaits, with the few loose bits of straggling hair neatly combed and tucked behind her ears, and her lips were painted a cherry-red.

"Meimei wants to go to the washroom with *Jiejie*." Chen Meihua pouted, asking, "Where is *Jiejie*?"

Lu Rong fell silent for a moment, then only he answered, "*Jiejie* is not around. Why don't Meimei go to the washroom with me instead?"

His grandmother was not very happy about it. Lu Rong waited for a while, and his classmate, Mo Xiaoxiao, came over.

"Meimei, how about going to the washroom with me?" Involved in a car accident when she was ten, Mo Xiaoxiao's leg had been severed below her knee, and her father had lost his life. Now, she lived alone with her mother. Surprisingly, she loved laughing, and she had a cheerful and lively character, making her even more lovable.

Apparently, Chen Meihua seemed to like this cute little girl a lot. She stood up obediently and held Mo Xiaoxiao's hand as they left for the washroom together.

Lu Rong and Mo Xiaoxiao were the only special needs students in their class. Consequently, they got closer during the military training.

The new students had all heard about these special needs students, but this was the first time they met them. All children would always be intrigued by something novel to them, and as for whether there was malice or kindness in this intrigue, Lu Rong did not want to think about it.

The three days of military training were tedious and exhausting. Cliques began to form during those three days, and it was not surprising that Lu Rong and Mo Xiaoxiao were ostracized. Lu Rong did not feel much about it, but Mo Xiaoxiao did not feel comfortable.

"I have a close friend from junior high." Even if Mo Xiaoxiao wanted to, she was unable to train along with her classmates for a long period of time. While resting, she removed her prosthetic leg, allowing the muscles of her left leg to relax. "But she didn't manage to get into Kunqian."

She sounded a little gloomy as she chatted with Lu Rong. Students around them were frequently sneaking looks at them, and most of their gazes were drawn to Mo Xiaoxiao's oddly shaped metal leg.

Meimei was singing. Her voice was not loud, yet it could still be heard quite clearly. Distracted by it, Lu Rong listened to her singing for a little while before saying, "Well, that's what most students are like usually. It'll be fine once you get used to it."

Mo Xiaoxiao widened her eyes in surprise, and she chuckled. "You don't like it here?"

Lu Rong paused before speaking, "When I was in junior high, things didn't go well."

Mo Xiaoxiao nodded. She thought for a moment, and advised him earnestly, "Not everyone is bad. Kunqian High is excellent, or else I wouldn't have given my all to enroll here."

Lu Rong was noncommittal. Chen Meihua began to clamor for water again; Lu Rong bent down to pick up the bottle.

That was what dementia was like—the person would behave like a child, their actions spontaneous, and you would not be able to stop them. Despite knowing that drinking too much water would lead to frequent urination, causing trouble for others when she wanted to urinate or she would pee on herself, Lu Rong had no other choice. He had already grown used to this over the years.

He was obviously a healthy individual. If there were no Chen Meihua, he would be going through a bright yet frustrating youth, just like most ordinary students. He was neither missing any limbs nor deaf or blind, but he was still different from every-one else. Mo Xiaoxiao knitted her brows. Momentarily, she could not decide whether she was more pitiful, or if Lu Rong deserved more sympathy. Coming from a mediocre family, her life was kind of tragic, yet she had received so much more love—from her mother, friends, and relatives. During that accident, her father had sacrificed his life for her. Despite losing a leg, she very much cherished this life that she had regained.

Of course, it was not the right time for her to say this to Lu Rong. Putting themselves in each other's shoes and empathizing with each other was not something suitable for them.

There were different kinds of pain and suffering, and no one could decide if one was able to bear with them or not.

Furthermore, silence was always better than any word; if she ended up saying too much, it would only make her sound like she was showing off.

After sitting there for some time, Chen Meihua seemed a little bored. She wanted to walk around, so Lu Rong could only seek out the instructor and ask to be excused so that he could accompany her, leaving Mo Xiaoxiao sitting alone under the tree.

Halfway around the sports ground, they happened to bump into some older students, who had just been dismissed from class. Holding onto Meimei's hand, Lu Rong did not let her obstruct anyone's way, and the moment he looked up, he saw Lin Zhao who was walking in their direction.

Chen Meihua saw her too. She shouted, "*Jiejie!*"

Of course, Lin Zhao could not hear her, but Chen Meihua was so conspicuous in the crowd that she could not help but notice her.

Standing next to Chen Meihua, Lu Rong smiled at her slightly. He raised his hand, gesturing next to his temple—the sign for
"deer."

Lin Zhao did not respond.

She really could not understand why she had to be involved in
this act of Lin Mu. Moreover, did Lu Rong even know what this
gesture meant? Or did Lin Mu mislead him?!

Seeing that she did not have much of a reaction, Lu Rong
was a little startled. He was not an enthusiastic person, but he
thought they had become friends after hanging out together
during the summer holiday. Yet, looking at her expression, it was
evident that he was getting snubbed instead.

Lin Zhao hesitated, then signed, "It's been a while. What are
you and your granny doing?"

The look in Lu Rong's eyes changed subtly, and he signed back,
"We're taking a stroll."

After a pause, he continued moving his fingers, "You've always
called her Meimei."

Lin Zhao was speechless.

Before the evening self-study session ended, Lin Mu made a
deliberate detour to the sports ground. He had received a message from Lin Zhao in the afternoon—an image of someone saying they had nothing to live for.

Lin Mu replied her with a string of question marks, and it
took Lin Zhao a long time to reply. "I saw Lu Rong and his granny today."

Without even thinking, Lin Mu was full of praises. "How was
it? He's a good boy, isn't he?"

"You didn't tell me that you called his granny by a nickname."

Lin Mu was baffled. "Meimei isn't a nickname; it's his granny's childhood name."

Lin Zhao did not even bother to talk to him anymore. Finally, Lin Mu registered that Lin Zhao had met Lu Rong, and he asked her anxiously, "You didn't expose yourself, did you?"

Lin Zhao typed for a long time, but only a sentence appeared. "I think I managed to bluff him."

The moment when Lin Mu saw the word "bluff," he felt a little guilty and could not suppress his urge to go over to the sports ground, despite his self-study session. Lu Rong was training with the contingent, while Chen Meihua was sitting alone under the banyan tree, next to the sports ground.

The evening breeze was a little chilly, and the golden-red rays of the setting sun gently scattered through every crisscrossing leaf it touched. Lin Mu did not hide, standing at a distance that was neither near or far away, and Chen Meihua managed to see him.

Meimei stared at him for a long time, so long that Lin Mu could not stop himself from smiling at her, and she too grinned back at him. She held onto the smile for a while, then suddenly stood up and shouted at Lin Mu, "*Jiejie!*"

Lin Mu got a shock. He held out his index finger and pressed it to his lips, shushing her for very long time.

Meimei did not listen. She ran over as she shouted, "*Jiejie! Jiejie!*"

Lin Mu had no other choice and could only step up and stop her. A short while later, Lu Rong came running over.

He was stunned when he saw Lin Mu's face.

Lin Mu had no choice but to take the initiative to say hello. "I'm Lin Mu. Umm, I guess you know my sister?"

Lu Rong treated him like a stranger, and his expression was distant and cold. Nodding slightly, he answered, "Yes."

Then he added politely, "Hello."

Chen Meihua called out to Lin Mu again. "*Jiejie!*"

Lu Rong lowered his head to see his grandmother. Supporting her, he answered expressionlessly, "He's not *Jiejie*; he is her younger brother."

Chen Meihua seemed unhappy again. Her forehead creased tightly, and stubbornly repeated things like, "He's *Jiejie*" and "Meimei wants to go to the washroom with *Jiejie*."

Lu Rong was a little helpless. He glanced over to Lin Mu, and in a low voice, he said, "Sorry."

"It's fine." Lin Mu looked at Chen Meihua with a bright smile and explained patiently, "I can't go into the girls' washroom, but I can accompany Meimei there. I'll wait for Meimei at the door, is that okay?"

Naturally, Chen Meihua would be fine with anything as long as she could go with him. She held Lin Mu's hand, while Lu Rong remained standing there, motionless.

Lin Mu looked up and realized Lu Rong was staring at him.

"You called her Meimei." Lu Rong's eyes seemed to be dyed with the hues of twilight. He said slowly, "Did Lin Zhao tell you about that?"

The smile on Lin Mu's face stiffened. Scratching his head as a cover, he calmed himself down before meeting Lu Rong's eyes.

"Who else could it be?" Lin Mu's smile was bright and sincere. "Didn't you see her today?"

Lin Mu believed himself to be the type of person who was great at social interactions, and it was all thanks to Lin Zhao. He remembered that one time as a child, Lin Zhao and he had gone out to play together. It gad been rare to for them have no parents around, and they could only go to the places such as the playground near their home and the convenience store.

The twins were very pretty and adorable. Along with their quiet, obedient, and likable personalities, they had always been the center of popularity wherever they went.

At that time, Lin Zhao had been obsessed with the banana flavored Bingrae ice cream sold at the convenience store. She'd been unable to buy it alone; every time, she'd needed to wait for Lin Mu to accompany her. Ten-year-old boys tended to be very playful. No matter how close the twins were, there had been times when Lin Mu had considered her as a burden to him.

There'd been a swing at the playground—the spot that all children desperately fought for. When Lin Mu won the spot, he'd been unwilling to leave, and he'd pretended not to see Lin Zhao signing at him from the side.

In the end, Lin Zhao could only go to the convenience store alone.

Lin Mu had swung by himself for a while, yet his mind had inevitably wandered to Lin Zhao—he'd been worried about her. He'd stretched out his neck, looking across the road while his playmate had chattered alongside him.

"Doesn't your sister know how to speak?" Children had no concept of the deaf-mute. Hence, his playmate had found it strange to see the twins so focused on each other.

At this time, Lin Mu had still been a little self-conscious, afraid that Lin Zhao would embarrass him. As such, he had only mumbled in acknowledgment.

The little playmate had spoken again, "Whenever I speak to her, your sister ignores me."

Lin Mu had been a little unhappy. He'd explained on behalf of Lin Zhao, "She doesn't mean to ignore you, she just can't hear."

The little playmate had understood, and he'd exclaimed loudly, "Is she deaf?"

Lin Mu had glanced at him, an unpleasant feeling of anger rising in him, yet he hadn't known what he was mad at. He'd leapt off the swing and stumbled his way out of the playground.

"Hey!" the little playmate had called out to him. "Aren't you going to play any longer?"

Lin Mu had turned his head, replying loudly, "I'm not playing with you anymore. I'm going to find my sister!"

Standing outside the convenience store, Lin Zhao had been a little hesitant. She'd poked her head inside and discovered a different person at the counter than usual—a young girl she hadn't recognized.

Frankly speaking, Luo Yu had not been happy about having to watch over her family's convenience store, but she hadn't had a choice. Her grandfather had sprained his ankle, so her parents had been preoccupied taking care of him in the hospital. As such, they'd ended up asking Luo Yu, currently in the middle of her first semester break of university, to take over the store temporarily.

How could a university student stand such mundaneness? Even now, Luo Yu's morning grumpiness had yet to dissipate, and she had just painfully rejected her close friend's invitation to karaoke. Forget about greeting customers with a smile; even when collecting money for goods purchased, her face had remained extremely dark.

The convenience store's automatic door had chimed with a welcome when Lin Zhao entered. Luo Yu hadn't even looked up, so it had taken her a while to realize there was a little girl standing in front of her.

The ice cream freezer was kept behind the counter, so customers would need to ask the person at the counter to get the ice cream for them.

Assuming that the little girl wanted some ice cream, Luo Yu had stood up, asking lazily, "What would you like?"

Lin Zhao had stared hard at Luo Yu's lips, and she'd vaguely understood what had been asked, so she'd reached out and pointed at a poster on the counter.

It had been a "Binggrae" advertisement, along with many others.

Luo Yu had frowned.

She hadn't known why the little girl hadn't spoken, and she'd become suspicious that the girl had been playing some sort of prank. So, her face had become sterner, and she'd repeated her question impatiently, "What exactly do you want?"

Lin Zhao's cheeks had blushed rapidly. She'd seemed to feel ashamed but she'd still been unwilling to just give up like that. Mustering up her courage, she'd raised her hand to touch her mouth, and then she'd waved her hand slightly.

Luo Yu had finally realized what was going on. "You can't speak?"

Lin Zhao couldn't hear, so she'd pointed at her ear, waving her hand again.

Luo Yu had been a little shocked. Subconsciously, she'd glanced towards the door, then left the counter and held Lin Zhao's hand. "Where's your family? How could they let you come alone to buy ice cream?" Only then had she realized that the little girl could not hear, so she'd brought her behind the counter and opened the door of the freezer chest.

Lin Zhao had looked up at her.

Luo Yu had smiled in response. "What do you want to eat? Just take it yourself."

Lin Zhao had managed to understand what she was saying. She'd hesitated for a moment, then she'd reached out and picked the banana flavored Binggrae ice cream.

Luo Yu had assisted her in removing the wrapping. Lin Zhao had wanted to pay, but Luo Yu had refused to accept it, saying, "It's on me."

Perhaps she'd thought Lin Zhao was a lost, deaf-mute child, and so she'd been worried about letting her go like this. Thus, she'd situated Lin Zhao in the counter and decided that she would call the police if no one came in to look for her.

Lin Zhao, on the other hand, hadn't realized what was going on. She'd sat obediently behind the counter, slowly eating her ice cream as she swung her legs expressionlessly.

Soon, Lin Mu had come looking for her.

His forehead had been covered with beads of sweat from anxiety, and he'd been called to a halt by Luo Yu. Her expression had been a little stern as she'd reprimanded him, "How could you leave your sister out there alone?"

Lin Mu had been unable to justify himself. Feeling both aggrieved and ashamed, he'd held on to Lin Zhao's hand, saying quietly, "I'm sorry."

Lin Zhao had not heard him, but she'd reached out and patted her brother's head.

After that, Luo Yu had spent her entire summer break watching over the store. Her parents had been clueless regarding what had changed their daughter's mind; she had been so reluctant at first, but now, while watching the store, she'd even brought with her a stack of children's books.

The time Lin Mu spent playing in the playground had become significantly shorter. He would seldom fight for the swing now, and he'd even started playing house with Lin Zhao.

If other girls wanted to speak to his sister, he would be their interpreter.

"You'll be Mama." He'd looked at Lin Zhao's hands and then asked the other girls, "Who will be Baby?"

Nobody had been willing to be the baby. Sighing exasperatedly, Lin Mu had ended up taking the role himself. "Alright, I'll be Baby."

Naturally, among seven- and eight-year-old boys, there were always a few irritating, hateful ones. They'd stood in the playgroud, making fun of Lin Mu for being a sissy. Lin Mu had been furious, but before he could react, the girls who'd been acting as "Papa" and "Mama" had started attacking them instead.

At that age, gender did not matter in children's fights. In fact, some girls developed physically faster, and thus they'd had the advantage in height and strength over boys. Holding the boys down in the playground, they roared sincerely, "Don't bully my baby!"

Around Lin Mu's neck had been a girl's handkerchief—used to represent a bib. At that moment, he could only continue to pretend as if he were a baby, and he'd tried his hardest to cry like one.

"I should've realized this sooner." Lin Zhao sat on the bench outside the convenience store. Sucking on a banana flavored Binggrae ice cream, she signed slowly, "Since we were young, you've always been fantastic at acting."

Lin Mu was speechless.

Luo Yu had inherited the family store after graduation, and she'd expanded the business. From its modest start of a store, the business had grown to include numerous stores spread across the entire East Zone. Even though the twins and their family had later moved away, they still went to her shop out of habit.

"You should work hard, too," Lin Mu advised his sister patiently. "Don't end up spilling the beans; I almost let the cat out of the bag today."

Lin Zhao smiled wickedly. "So, did you really go to the washroom with Meimei?"

Lin Mu signed resignedly, "Of course not. I waited outside, okay?"

Lin Zhao laughed so hard that she had to hug her belly. Luo Yu carried her son outside. The baby had just celebrated his hundred days of age, and she could not help but ask when she saw the two of them, "What are you laughing at? Something happy?"

Lin Mu hurriedly replied, "It's nothing!"

Luo Yu did not believe him. She looked down at Lin Zhao with a questioning look. As his elder sister, she considered her brother's dignity. Shaking her head lightly, she then reached out, wanting to carry the baby.

Luo Yu carefully tucked her son into Lin Zhao's arms. She had picked up sign language too, and signed at Lin Zhao, "Tell me if Lin Mu ever bullies you, I'll beat him up for you."

Carrying the baby, Lin Zhao swayed a little, looking at Lin Mu with meaningful eyes.

Lin Mu felt extremely maligned. With an aggrieved expression, he called out to Luo Yu, "*Jie!* You cannot be so biased!"

No matter what Lu Rong actually thought, Lin Mu optimistically felt that he had fudged through the situation without any issue. He chose to use the term "fudge" with Lin Zhao, instead of "lie" as if it were less dishonest.

There was only one day left to the end of the military training for the first-year students, and the official "military parade" would be conducted in the afternoon. While the third-year students had to focus on their studies, second-year students would participate in the parade as the audience.

When the time came to assemble the contingent, the instructor called Mo Xiaoxiao and Lu Rong to meet him separately.

"Neither of you have to participate," the instructor said. "You can rest in the stands."

It did not surprise Lu Rong. He had no intention of saying anything more, so he stood there quietly.

Yet, Mo Xiaoxiao was upset about it. "Why? We can march too; we're not going to drag the contingent down."

The instructor wrinkled his brows, seeming to think that she was too stubborn. He suppressed his impatience and explained, "Both of you have special circumstances. Look, isn't it good to rest in the stands? Everyone is only looking out for you, don't overthink it."

Mo Xiaoxiao wanted to say something, but Lu Rong stopped her before she could. He raised his chin, his eyes glimmering like black quartz under the brim of his cap.

"We're not overthinking anything." He swept his gaze across his classmates standing before him; some averted their eyes, muttering to each other.

The corners of Lu Rong's mouth quirked up a little, curving into a small, false smile. He looked straight into the instructor's eyes and said, his voice cold, "Those who are overthinking things, they themselves are the most aware of it."

SILENT HEARTS

03 Youths

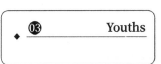

♦   ⓪③   **Youths**

Xu Yilu finished the test alone. After checking the paper one more time, only then did he raise his hand and call for the teacher. Straightening his white cane, he slowly felt around to stand up, making his way outside. When he reached the door, he heard a familiar voice.

"Little Heron." Lin Mu reached out to support him. "How was the test?"

Xu Yilu was a little bashful. "It was ok. How about you?"

Lin Mu's tone was a little pleased. "As long as An Jincheng doesn't get full marks, I'll definitely be at the top of the class."

Xu Yilu did not suppress his laughter. Then, he suddenly remembered the gossip from the school forum that Sun Hai shared with him, about the most handsome boys in school. He asked Lin Mu quietly, "Is the new number one really that handsome?"

"Yup, he is." Lin Mu thought for a moment. "The first year's military parade is about to start; we'll be able to see him then."

This time, Xu Yilu did not say anything like "I can't see," that might spoil the atmosphere. The two of them walked through the corridor and happened to run into An Jincheng.

Young Master An had always remained cold and aloof, disdaining to mingle with the ordinary folk of the school. If they happened to bump into him, it was clearly on purpose. As such, Lin Mu could only stop and ask impatiently, "What's the matter?"

An Jincheng glanced over at Xu Yilu, speaking with an indifferent voice, "The new students are practicing their marching, and their Head Teacher want some second-year students to watch over them. So, he called for us."

Lin Mu asked, "Who else was called?"

An Jincheng did not reply, but Lin Mu understood that it was probably just the two of them.

Lin Mu said, "I'll send Little Heron back. Why don't you go first?"

An Jincheng shook his head. "It's fine. I'll wait for you."

Lin Mu was a little surprised, but if Young Master An was willing to wait, he would just let him be. After sending Xu Yilu back to the classroom, only then did he go to the sports ground with An Jincheng.

All the teachers of the first-year students were present. Lin Mu and An Jincheng were assigned to monitor the rehearsal as the representatives of the second-year students, but it was only for show. With An Jincheng's family background, the teachers dared not offend him, while Lin Mu was as sweet as candy floss, and thus he was very popular among the teachers and students.

There were no issues with the practice at the start. The teachers and the instructors took turns to adjust the contingent, and the flag-holders in charge of giving commands were once again reminded of their duties. Sitting at the podium with his chin in his hand, Lin Mu was a little bored. Looking around him, he found Chen Meihua sitting by the sports ground.

Meimei caught sight of Lin Mu as well. She stood up, waving her arm at him. Today, the old lady was dressed in a bright red dress; her white hair was tied in a ponytail that kept her looking fresh and clean. For a moment, Lin Mu looked at her with a smile, and then suddenly noticed Lu Rong walking towards her from a short distance away.

"He's not practicing...?" Lin Mu mumbled to himself. It was already Class Three's turn to practice, yet Lu Rong had no intention of joining his classmates. Lin Mu's brows slowly knitted together.

Chen Meihua seemed to have said something to Lu Rong. The boy looked up, and his eyes met Lin Mu's directly. Giving him a radiant smile, Lin Mu raised his hand and was about to greet him, but Lu Rong looked away after giving him a quick glance.

"..." With his half-raised arm, Lin Mu awkwardly scratched his head.

Now, he was no longer in the mood to watch the rehearsal. He kept his eyes focused on Meimei and Lu Rong, and after some time, Mo Xiaoxiao joined them as well. Lin Mu had a deep impression of the girl, since Sun Hai had described her as the "girl with the very cool metal leg."

On the sports ground, Class Four's rehearsal was almost over. Seeing that Lu Rong and Mo Xiaoxiao did not look like they were about to rejoin their class, Lin Mu could not remain seated anymore and stood up.

An Jincheng looked at him in puzzlement. "What's wrong?"

Lin Mu did not respond and ran down the podium alone.

The contingent of Class Five was getting ready. When Lin Mu

arrived, both the instructor and the form teacher were present. The teacher's face looked a little unfamiliar to him; she appeared quite young, and it was likely that she had just joined the school this year. Lin Mu greeted them loudly, and both of them turned to look at him.

With a smile on his face, Lin Mu pointed at Lu Rong and Mo Xiaoxiao who were by the sports ground. "*Laoshi*, why are there two students not participating in the parade?"

The form teacher exclaimed, seeming to have just realized it. Sounding uncertain, she asked, "Are they from our class?"

During the military training, most of the time, the students would only interact with the instructor. Subsequently, it was reasonable for the new form teacher not to be able to recognize her own students. Counting, she discovered that there were two missing indeed. With a little surprise, she turned to the instructor. "Did they request to be excused?"

The coach glanced over at Lin Mu, his smile a little stiff. "Yes, they did, as the parade would be a little more tiring for them."

The form teacher frowned slightly; she seemed a little disapproving. Lin Mu spoke up, lazily, "Why don't we just call them over and ask?"

Hence, Lu Rong and Mo Xiaoxiao were called over.

Although they had been informed that they did not need to participate in the parade, they were still obediently wearing their military uniforms handed out by the school. Mo Xiaoxiao looked at Lin Mu curiously, and he gave her a smile.

The form teacher was a sensible person; she took the initiative to ask Lu Rong, "Did you asked to be excused?"

Lu Rong swept a gaze across his classmates who stood still in position, his response indifferent. "I didn't."

The expression of the instructor standing by the side worsened. Suddenly, a boy in the class raised his hand.

"The military parade will be graded." That boy shot a glance at Mo Xiaoxiao's leg; his tone was a little unhappy. "We won't be able to receive a good score if someone is dragging us down."

Lin Mu inhaled sharply; a swell of anger rushing to his head. Just as he was about to scold the boy, he heard a burst of mocking laughter from the last row of girls.

"Are you referring to yourself?" That girl was not tall, and she had a short, neat haircut under her cap. She raised her chin slightly. "Mo Xiaoxiao never missed a beat when marching in the contingent; which of your eyes saw her dragging us down?"

Lin Mu was surprised.

The boy standing in front probably did not expect that someone would contradict him. His face flushed red with anger, and he argued, "Li Zi, what do you mean by that?! Who are you trying to scold?!"

Li Zi looked up from under the brim of her cap. Raising her arm, she flipped the boy off. "Who else but you? What a piece of rubbish, trying to ostracize people in the class."

Obviously, no one seemed to expect Li Zi to have such a sharp tongue, and a ruckus occurred in the contingent. Even though Lin Mu had yet to vent his anger, he now had to help the form teacher and the instructor control the situation.

High school students were young and vigorous—without careful supervision, arguments could quickly turn into war. The form teacher was, after all, still young and inexperienced, but just before she was about to lose control over the situation, someone roared through a loudspeaker from the other side of the sports ground, "Why is Class Five making a fuss?!"

The anxiety in Lin Mu vanished as soon as he heard this voice.

Just as he was feeling a little puzzled as to why Chu Lin would come over so early, he understood as soon as he saw An Jincheng standing beside her.

Chu Lin—the head teacher of special education class, the inspector of the school's board of education, the secretary of the board committee, and Kunqian's number one tigress.

Today, she was wearing a pair of heels, which, when combined with its thick soles, was twelve centimeters high. Halfway through walking towards them, Chu Lin removed her heels and held them in her hand, striding over to Class Five without giving the prickly grass under her feet any concern.

Lin Mu straightened up, looking polite and obedient. "Ms. Chu."

Chu Lin glanced at him, then turned her attention to the young form teacher. "What's going on?"

The form teacher succinctly reported the matter, and near the end, she did not even dare to look at Chu Lin's face. In Kunqian, aside from the principal Zhong He, no one dared to butt heads with Chu Lin—she could be said to be the one who singlehandedly established the special education class and supported it. With the immeasurable glory and honor as well as the vast amounts of donations and aid she gathered for school, not to mention the contributions she had made to society and the government, her accomplishments were sufficient to bring all the teachers and students of Kunqian to line up and kowtow to her.

With a grim expression, Chu Lin listened to her. Anger seemed to manifest gradually on her face, and she spoke coldly, "An Jincheng, recite the school motto."

It was a few seconds of silence before An Jincheng recited every word clearly, "Kindness, Courage, Equality, Love."

Chu Lin studied the faces of the students in front of her and abruptly asked, "Do you know why I wanted all of you to hear the school's motto?"

No one dared to speak a single word; even the boy in front had his head bowed. Lin Mu could not help but look at Lu Rong, and the latter happened to look over as well. Time stood still for a moment, then Lu Rong averted his eyes nonchalantly.

"Lin Mu," Chu Lin suddenly called out to him.

Lin Mu straightened unconsciously. "Here!"

Chu Lin nodded her head.

"Well done," she said, then looked over to An Jincheng. "An Jincheng too."

An Jincheng remained silent. He frowned, looking down at the ground, while Lin Mu pursed his lips silently.

Although Chu Lin knew their estrangement, she had no intention of acting as a go-between for them. Her compliments were as blunt as her scolding, direct and straightforward. "You don't understand the school motto, and you're not learning from example. Why did you want to come to Kunqian?"

None of them had enough courage to provide an answer, and the class was dead silent from the rebuke.

"Since you all have decided to study at Kunqian, you had better engrave the four words of the school motto right into your soul. Whoever thinks they're unable to learn it, you can step forward now." Chu Lin put her heels back on. Standing tall and straight, she looked down at the students and spoke calmly, "I will personally help them with their school withdrawal application."

Lin Zhao heard from Cao Zhan that her brother was once again being a busybody.

Cao Zhan did not know sign language, and so he wrote it down for Lin Zhao to read. His handwriting was messy and sloppy, and his narration was a little unclear, but if one read it a few times, they could still understand what he was trying to say.

"An Jincheng helped too." Cao Zhan wrote down whatever he thought of. "Even Miss Chu came."

Lin Zhao took the pen. "What else?"

Cao Zhan continued writing, "They were both praised by Miss Chu, along with another new student."

Lin Zhao had heard about the new student Li Zi too, as well as Mo Xiaoxiao, the girl with the metal leg.

"That one, Lu Rong," Cao Zhan waved his hand above his head, putting on an expression of envy as he spoke earnestly, "he's really tall!"

Lin Zhao recalled the day they met, then she wrote on the paper. "Is he as tall as Jiang Tianhe?"

The moment Jiang Tianhe's name was mentioned, Cao Zhan became a little unhappy. He wrote down forcefully, "He's even taller!"

Lin Zhao suppressed her smile. "Did Jiang Tianhe bully you again?"

Cao Zhan wrote furiously, erasing and rewriting. The cycle repeated, and he seemed to be really angry. Finally, he pushed the paper away and spoke loudly, "He's so annoying!"

Lin Zhao did not manage to read his lips clearly when he spoke. She wanted to write, but suddenly, a hand inserted between the both of them and snatched the paper away from the desk.

Jiang Tianhe had a hand in his pocket while holding the paper with his other. Looking at it for a while, he laughed, trying to create trouble. "I thought it was something fun, but turns out it's just Foolish and Deaf Girl trying to whisper to each other?"

Cao Zhan was a little fearful of Jiang Tianhe, but he understood what he was implying, and responded, stammering, "I-I'm not foolish, I-I'm dopey!"

"Dopey?" Jiang Tianhe threw the piece of paper at his head, sneering, "Why? Are you Lin Mu's puppy? Lin Mu can call you Dopey, and yet you refuse to accept the nickname that I gave you?"

Lin Zhao could not hear what they were arguing over, but looking at it, Jiang Tianhe probably was not saying anything nice. She stepped forward, shielding Cao Zhan behind her, then succinctly flipped Jiang Tianhe off.

Jiang Tianhe's voice was disdainful as he spat, "Both the sister and the brother are just the same."

Cao Zhan's eyes turned red from anger. He knew that Class Three and the elite class were different—most students here had paid a selection fee to enroll in Kunqian. Some students in this class were studious, but there were also many people like Jiang Tianhe, so much so that different cliques could be formed. Jiang Tianhe did not look like a student—he was very tall and muscular; his hair was shaved in a crew cut; he never wore his uniform properly, and the sleeves of his T-shirt were always rolled up and tucked in. With how loose his collar was, he looked as though he was wearing a sleeveless tee.

He had a group of so-called followers, but he was the only one who always bullied Cao Zhan.

It was not that Jiang Tianhe would beat people up, but his tongue was very wicked—he loved finding ways to agitate people with no rhyme or reason. Although Cao Zhan had a little problem with his intellect, he was an incredibly earnest person. To reason with Jiang Tianhe, he often butted his heads with him, but he had never won an argument. Instead, Jiang Tianhe would scold him even more harshly after each fight.

Jiang Tianhe would even snatch his books, but he never read them. Instead, he would mock Cao Zhan's notes, asking him why he was still studying since he was so stupid.

Cao Zhan was about to burst into tears of anger. Again, he fiercely retorted, "I—I'm only just a li—little stupid! My mama s—said so!"

"Mama, mama," Jiang Tianhe mocked him in a sing-song tone. "Did you pee your pants? Why are you calling out to your mother?"

Cao Zhan's reaction was slow, and he really looked down to check his pants. He stated earnestly, "I-I didn't pee on my pants!"

His words made Jiang Tianhe laugh even more, and for the rest of the day, he called Cao Zhan an idiot.

Lin Zhao passed Cao Zhan a note, it said, "Dopey, just ignore him, he's such a bastard."

Cao Zhan thought for a long time before writing his reply below. "Bastard is a swear, and it's not good. Zhaozhao, don't learn from the bad examples."

Lin Zhao was speechless.

Cao Zhan added another line. "It's not right to put up your middle finger too, don't do it anymore."

His words drove Lin Zhao crazy. Honestly speaking, she really admired the way her brother could interact well with Cao Zhan, and how he was able to hold a good conversation with him. She felt that her brother was like the sun, radiating saint-like rays of golden light upon the world.

Now, the aforementioned sun was sitting on the sports

ground, preparing to watch the first-year students' military parade.

Sweat dripping down his face, Lin Mu looked down and sent Lin Zhao a text. "Can you request to be excused today? Skip the Go institute and watch *Xiao* Lu with me."

Lin Zhao replied, "Why? Is he still ignoring you?"

Lin Mu felt no embarrassment after being exposed. "Well, you're the one who has a better friendship with him after all."

Lin Zhao sent a emoji of mocking laughter, along with another text. "I've already requested to be excused; I'm coming with Dopey."

As though he had received an imperial edict, Lin Mu raised his head, looking around. Sure enough, he saw Lin Zhao and Cao Zhan walking towards the stands. He immediately stood up, crossing over the row before him, cupping his hands around his mouth as he shouted, "Dopey!"

Cao Zhan turned his head on hearing his name and saw Lin Mu waving at him. He then grabbed Lin Zhao along, sprinting to where Lin Mu was standing.

"Is it too hot?" Lin Mu was concerned to see his sister's face turning red in the sun. "Why didn't you apply any sunscreen?"

Lin Zhao looked at him scornfully, signing, "I did."

Lin Mu then covered her head with his school shirt. "Use this to shield yourself from the sun."

Lin Zhao pointed at him. "You're all covered in sweat."

Lin Mu wiped his sweat away, signing unconcernedly, "I've always perspired easily."

Cao Zhan seemed to be very happy to be able to sit with Lin Mu. He held Xu Yilu's hand and called out to him in an uncontrollably loud volume, "Little Heron!"

Xu Yilu acknowledged him in return, then asked, "Did you pay attention in class this morning?"

Cao Zhan snapped his legs together, looking like an obedient student answering a teacher. "Yes, I did. I learned about surface area in math, and memorized an ancient poem in language class."

Young Teacher Xu Yilu asked earnestly, "Which ancient poem did you learn?"

Cao Zhan tried his best to remember, then replied guiltily, "I'm too stupid, I haven't memorized it yet."

Xu Yilu laughed and then groped around to pat Cao Zhan on the head. Discovering that Cao Zhan was a little too tall when sitting down, it took him some time before he was able to give him a pat.

"Dopey is just a little stupid," Xu Yilu said, "sixty-nine is only a point below seventy."

It was rather conspicuous for the four of them to sit together, but it was mainly because of Young Master An sitting in the back row and staring straight at Lin Zhao. Lin Mu turned around, shooting him a warning glare, but An Jincheng only glanced over at him with his expressionless face.

Sun Hai had run off to get some drinks. When he came back, he was only left with a seat beside Xu Yilu, and he was very upset about losing his chance to interact closely with his goddess.

While Lin Mu chatted with Cao Zhan, a frown suddenly creased his forehead. He pointed at Cao Zhan's eyes. "Were you crying just now?"

Cao Zhan blinked, looking confused. "No, I wasn't..."

Lin Mu was able to make some sense of what had happened. "What did that asshole Jiang Tianhe do this time?"

Cao Zhan was silent for a while, and then he spoke, "Asshole is a swear, you can't use it."

"Oh." Lin Mu took his advice. "So, what did that rotten apple do?"

Cao Zhan was speechless.

Lu Rong and Mo Xiaoxiao stood in Class Five's contingent, going through their final preparations. During the break, Mo Xiaoxiao saw Lu Rong staring at the stands a distance away.

"What are you looking at?" Mo Xiaoxiao asked. She followed the boy's line of sight and eventually saw Lin Mu and his friends.

"By the way, what's the name of the upperclassman who helped us out?" Mo Xiaoxiao could not help asking.

Lu Rong looked away from the stands, his response nonchalant, "I don't remember."

Mo Xiaoxiao did not seem to believe him. "I clearly remember seeing you speak to another female upperclassman that look very similar to him."

Lu Rong glanced at her and replied indifferently, "You've already said that it was a female upperclassman, so why would I remember a male one?"

Mo Xiaoxiao had no response.

She was a little skeptical, and she asked dubiously, "Are you angry?"

Lu Rong pulled his cap back on. After a moment of silence, he said, "I'm not."

"Then who were you looking at just now?" Mo Xiaoxiao tiptoed, looking at the stands. "The boy or the girl?"

In the glorious, blazing sunshine, the first-year classes marched past the podium one by one in their contingents. Lu Rong was in the last row of the Class Five's contingent, and occasionally, he would turn to look at the stands closest to him with worry.

Chen Meihua was sitting there obediently with his form teacher accompanying her.

Lin Mu's attention was naturally focused on Lu Rong. As Cao Zhan told him how Jiang Tianhe bullied him, Lin Mu listened with vague attention as he watched the Class Five contingent about to come closer.

"Ready—March!" Class Five's flagbearer waved the flag. The students followed the command, marching towards the stands.

Cao Zhan's voice grew louder, as well. "Jiang Tianhe called me Foolish!"

While looking at Lu Rong's face that was slightly hidden under his cap's brim, Lin Mu responded to Cao Zhan, "What did you say?"

Cao Zhan said earnestly, "I said, I'm Dopey!"

The flagbearer shouted, "Salute!"

Lu Rong raised his arm, his fingers tapping against the brim of his cap. Even as Lin Mu admired the boy's truly handsome appearance, he had to simultaneously contend with Cao Zhan.

"You're not listening." Cao Zhan was a little unhappy, so he huffed, "I'm not going to talk anymore."

Lin Mu opened his mouth, about to respond, but he saw Lu Rong's gaze directed at him before he could utter a word.

Lin Mu was surprised.

Under the intense sun, even the breeze was warm, and it seemed as though the clouds were about to burst into flames. However, in this hot weather, Lu Rong was as cool as a mint leaf. His gaze lingered like a boat cruising by, the water rippling in its wake, swaying through without a sound.

Lin Mu held his breath and gave him an appropriate smile, but the other party turned his head away and did not look at him again.

Cao Zhan leaned into Lin Mu, quietly asking, "Who are you looking at?"

Lin Mu heaved a deep sigh, grumbling, "I was given the cold shoulder."

Cao Zhan was unable to understand what Lin Mu meant, so he could only nod in a vague understanding. Lin Mu gave him a complicated look, then reached out and ruffled his hair. "Is Jiang Tianhe coming for the evening self-study session today?"

Cao Zhan was confused. "Why?"

Lin Mu smiled, baring his teeth and looking a little savage. "I'll help you beat him up."

Cao Zhan did not know how to respond.

The principal gave a speech once the military parade was over. Lu Rong returned to the stands, to the space allocated to his class. Chen Meihua had been very well behaved, giving the teacher no trouble at all.

She seemed to enjoy seeing Lu Rong dressed in the military uniform, but she kept calling out for "Zhengnian" instead.

Lu Rong took off his cap, allowing his grandmother to see his face clearly. He spoke placidly, "Meimei, I'm not Granddad. You've got the wrong person again."

Chen Meihua was a little unhappy. She hit him twice on the shoulder, but after a while, she seemed to have forgotten about it and began to sing as she swung her legs.

Lu Rong inhaled deeply. He waited for a moment before turning to look at where the second-year students were. Suddenly, Chen Meihua shifted closer to him, whispering, "Meimei saw *Jiejie*."

Lu Rong's gaze dimmed slightly, but his expression remained unchanged. "Which *Jiejie* did Meimei see?"

Chen Meihua pointed, speaking in earnest. "The *Jiejie* that accompanied Meimei to the washroom."

Lu Rong stared at Lin Mu for some time, then he bent his neck and shifted his gaze to his grandmother, his emotions unchanging. "He's *Jiejie's* younger brother, he's not *Jiejie*."

Chen Meihua shook her head furiously, sounding just like a little girl. "Meimei knows, that's *Jiejie*."

Lu Rong seemed to smile. As though directing the question at himself, he asked, "How do you know?"

Chen Meihua paused a moment and thought about it, then twisted her plaits proudly as she laughed. "Meimei just knows."

The first-year students were released from school early that day, but the second-year students had to return to their classrooms for their self-study sessions. Since Lin Mu could not think up any new excuse to look for Lu Rong, he had no choice but to go back reluctantly.

After marking attendance, An Jincheng realized that Lin Mu was about to slip away again. Frowning, he called him to stop. "Where are you going?"

Lin Mu's response came as though it could not be any more natural. "Next door."

Young Master An fell silent for a moment. Suddenly, he said, "I'm going, too."

Lin Mu was baffled. "Why are you going?"

"Don't you know that ordinary students have to take turns to go to the special education class every day?"

Lin Mu of course knew the rule, but he also knew it was optional—students could decide whether to go or not; the school did not make it compulsory.

Since Young Master An wanted to come along, Lin Mu could

not stop him from doing so. Furthermore, with his accomplishment of having called Chu Lin over earlier in the day, Lin Mu did not dislike him as much as he used to.

With one walking behind the other, they arrived at the door to the special education classroom. Lin Mu was very familiar with the students and the teacher in the class. After giving a round of greetings, he sat next to Lin Zhao. An Jincheng, on the other hand, stood alone at the door for a while, and only then did he sit at a corner stiffly. There was a strange look in everyone's eyes.

Lin Zhao nudged her brother, signing, "Why is he here?"

Lin Mu signed back swiftly, "Who knows? Maybe he's having a mental episode."

Lin Zhao could sense that the prejudice in Lin Mu's heart was high as a mountain. A little disapproving, she turned to look at An Jincheng and unexpectedly caught his gaze on her.

Perhaps he did not expect her to look over so suddenly, and he flinched.

Unconsciously, Lin Zhao gave him a sweet smile.

In the end, An Jincheng tightened his lips and looked away, frowning.

Wordless, Lin Zhao's smile froze on her face.

Seeing his sister turn her head back in anger, Lin Mu thought she had suffered an indignance. "What's wrong?"

Lin Zhao ran her fingers through her hair agitatedly. Kingly, as though she had a crown on her head, her fingers danced icily, "It's nothing, I just happened to meet a crazy person."

Lin Mu was left questioning.

The self-study sessions of the special education class were different from the other classes—unlike the rows in which students were normally seated, they would cluster in small groups, and they always looked as if they were not studying properly. The deaf-mute students formed the largest group; they would stick together, signing at each other energetically as though they were miming. Lin Zhao and her other friends were discussing trendy television dramas, just like any other ordinary girls.

At a time like this, Xu Yilu would be reading his braille books seriously. The teacher would specially prepare textbooks for him to revise what he had learned in the day.

Lin Mu would often read the questions aloud to him, but halfway through, he would have to tutor Cao Zhan.

Today, before Lin Mu could finish tutoring Cao Zhan, Lin Zhao was suddenly called over by the teacher.

Her friends were even more excited than she was, signing vigorously, "It's Lu Rong!"

Lin Mu froze for a moment. Without thinking, he turned back and immediately saw Lu Rong standing at the door, with Meimei smiling brightly at his side.

Lin Zhao's expression was uncertain too. She glanced over at her brother, then stood up slowly. When she walked to the door, Lu Rong pointed to the side, signaling that he would like to speak to her privately.

Lin Mu could not stop himself from shifting about; his chair screeched loudly. Xu Yilu looked up from his book, groping around and tapping the back of Lin Mu's hand. "What's wrong?"

Lu Rong and Lin Zhao were almost completely concealed behind a wall. From Lin Mu's angle, he could barely make out the edge of the boy's T-shirt. Meimei was still standing at the door, looking at Lin Mu with a silly grin on her face.

Cao Zhan glanced at Lin Mu. Thinking for a while, he finally asked, "Why is Lu Rong looking for your sister?"

Lin Mu could only say, "They both attended the community sessions during the summer holidays... So, they know each other."

"Oh." Cao Zhan did not seem very interested. Looking down, he studied the questions he had just done, then raised his head and looked at him again. "So, why are you so anxious?"

Lin Mu reeled back, nearly falling off his chair. His expression was rather awful, and he forced himself to say, "I'm not anxious at all."

Cao Zhan's expression showed that he did not believe him at all.

Lin Mu's back stiffened. His urge to turn his head towards the door grew stronger, yet he was afraid that Cao Zhan would again ask another embarrassing question. Scratching his head in frustration, he jabbed at the scrap paper, his tone a little fierce, "Do your practice!"

Cao Zhan was aggrieved, and said loudly, "You're bad, you're lying!"

Lin Mu was clearly a little conscience-stricken when he heard the word "lying." Blocking Cao Zhan's view of his face, he looked over to the door. Meimei was waving at him, but Lin Zhao had yet to return.

Lin Mu started getting anxious again, grumbling and complaining, "It's improper for men and women to be interacting so closely with each other... What is there to discuss that is taking so long!"

Lin Zhao actually did not speak too long with Lu Rong. He was not adept in sign language, but he was still able to roughly express what he wanted to say. It seemed like he was asking if she would be attending the community session this weekend.

"Probably," Lin Zhao signed in reply.

Lu Rong thought for a moment, then signed, "Is your brother

coming too?"

Lin Zhao blinked, then moved her fingers deftly, "Maybe."

Lu Rong lowered his gaze. No one was able to tell what he was thinking. As Meimei was standing in the way of the classroom door, blocking the way, Lu Rong finally signed, "Then I'll go off first."

Lin Zhao stopped him.

She asked, "You don't like my brother?"

A wrinkle appeared between Lu Rong's brows. He did not express his thoughts, only shaking his head lightly.

Chen Meihua was still smiling when Lu Rong held her hand. "Let's go home, Meimei."

She nodded. Waving enthusiastically at Lin Mu inside the classroom, she said, "Goodbye, *Jiejie!*"

For a moment, Lin Mu did not know how to react. When Lu Rong glanced at him, he shot him a friendly smile without thinking.

"*Jiejie* smiled at me!" Chen Meihua exclaimed happily. Strangely, she had been very cold towards Lin Zhao instead. As the girl could not hear, it was not easy for them to interact.

Lu Rong's lips tightened. From Lin Mu's angle, he could only see the boy lowering his head and saying something to Meimei. Meimei then pursed her lips, looking rather unhappy. Before they left, she looked over to Lin Mu a few times reluctantly.

Lin Zhao's expression was a little unfathomable when she came back in.

Unable to wait any more, Lin Mu signed, asking her, "What were you two talking about?"

Lin Zhao thought for a moment. She cocked a brow and suddenly signed, "I'm going to the Go institute this weekend."

Lin Mu gave her a look of confusion, not catching her drift. "There's a community session this weekend."

Lin Zhao smiled insincerely at her brother, her eyes narrowing.

Do or do not. Regarding cross-dressing, as long as one had done it before, there was only a difference of never having done it before or doing it a hundred times.

Shivers ran down Lin Mu's spine the moment when he recalled Lin Zhao's smile. His sister even had an excuse prepared, telling him sternly that she had already informed Lu Rong that she would be going.

"Last time, you told me that I shouldn't lie," Lin Mu signed. Today, he wore a black velvet dress with a high collar, and the wig was forced onto his head.

Lin Zhao contoured his face with makeup, making his features stand out even more delicately. She was very surprised by how her brother's facial hair grew so slowly.

"This is why you need to explain and apologize to him," Lin Zhao signed earnestly. She applied blush onto his cheek. "Good luck, little liar."

Lin Mu had no response.

The community session this time was a large-scale bazaar. The East Zone management committee had rented a flea market space so that the handicapped people in the community could set up booths to sell some of their crafts.

Lu Rong and Chen Meihua arrived early in the morning to set up their stall. They were selling some hair ornaments that girls especially liked, and many of them had been made by Meimei personally.

Lin Mu paced outside the bazaar entrance for a long time, until he was caught by Teacher Ma.

Teacher Ma's sign language had finally improved a little. "Why didn't you set up a booth?"

Lin Mu signed perfunctorily back, "What kind of booth should I set up?"

Teacher Ma thought for a moment. "A booth for Go, you could teach them how to play."

Lin Mu kept quiet. He thought that it was fortunate Lin Zhao did not come, otherwise she would have to play Go with random passersby off the street.

Many people who came to the bazaar had no disabilities. East Zone had always publicized an aura of humanistic care to the community, cultivating it. Many came to the bazaar with the kind aim of making "donations," but there were also quite a number of troublemakers taking advantage of the situation and demanding for exorbitant discounts.

It was the fifth time that Lu Rong saw the same drunk man.

"This?" The man gave a drunken belch. Squinting, he picked up a little yellow duckling hairclip Meimei made. "You're selling this for ten yuan?"

Although the management had assigned staff to patrol the bazaar, and Lu Rong only had to step away to call for someone, Chen Meihua would still be left alone, so it was not convenient for him to leave. Hence, he could only restrain his impatience. "If you don't want to buy it, you can have a look elsewhere."

The drunk man shouted, "Who says I'm not buying it?"

He held two fingers out, waving them. "Two yuan, how about that?"

Meimei was about to burst into tears from anxiety. She reached out and tried to snatch the hairclip back. "No! No! Meimei is not selling it to you!"

The drunk man raised his arm to keep her from snatching the hairclip back, and then laughed maliciously, "Well, well, well, look what we've got here? An unreasonable, silly old woman. Don't you know that the customer is always right? ...How dare you scratch me?!"

Before he could finish, his hand was suddenly empty—someone behind him had taken the hairclip away.

Lin Mu was expressionless as he held onto the little yellow duckling hairclip. Next to him, Teacher Ma was glaring fiercely, extremely angry.

"Why are you here again?!" Teacher Ma took out a walkie-talkie, calling for other management staff to come over as he stepped forward alone and tried to catch hold of the drunk man.

The man was still cursing and shouting. He reached out to grab Lin Mu's wrist. Lin Mu dodged, but failed, and his arm still caught.

"Stupid bitch," the drunk man swore, but in the next second, he was sent careening into the air with a kick by Lu Rong from behind.

Lu Rong caught Lin Mu's other arm, dragging him to himself.

Teacher Ma finally managed to hold the man down, thanking Lu Rong at the same time. A few other management staff too rushed over, and they dragged the drunk man out together.

Lin Mu was still in a daze. He looked up to see Lu Rong's chin. Lu Rong released him, watching him calmly.

Lin Mu was silent for a moment, feeling a little guilty from his stare. "Thank you," he signed.

Lu Rong watched him a little while more before he pulled his gaze away, his eyes falling onto the little yellow duckling hairclip in Lin Mu's hand.

Lin Mu held it out, wanting to return it to him.

But Lu Rong shook his head.

He moved his fingers, "It's for you."

He smiled. "Meimei personally made this for you."

Lin Mu did not know what he could do here, and hence, he accompanied Lu Rong and Chen Meihua at their booth. Meimei insisted on placing the little yellow duckling hairclip in his hair, and so Lin Mu could only brace himself and allow her to do so.

As such, with a little yellow duckling hairclip, Lin Mu sat stiffly at the back of the booth and watched as Lu Rong dealt with the customers. Almost everyone who came over would pay attention to his hair, whether intentionally or not, then they would hold back a smile and purchase a couple of items.

In the end, Lin Mu surrendered himself to despair—he sat there like a mascot, allowing Meimei to show off her "talent" on him.

It's just a wig anyway. Lin Mu was fairly philosophical about it.

Chen Meihua tied his hair into two plaits, fixing them using hair ties with pink little crystals. Humming along to a song, she seemed as though she was doting on her child.

When the sky turned dark, paper lanterns were hung on both sides of the booth.

Lu Rong collected the money they earned today. Taking an account book, he wrote on it and pushed it over to Lin Mu. "Where's your brother?"

Lin Mu thought about the age old saying of how people who confessed would receive lighter punishments, while those who refused would be dealt with severely. He mustered up his courage to tell Lu Rong the truth, but when he saw Lu Rong's doe-like eyes, it was as though he lost all his judgement. Bowing his head, he signed hesitantly, "He wasn't free..."

There was no ripple of emotion in Lu Rong's gaze. It was like a snowflake on the body, melting away in a few seconds. He wrote, "I thought he would come with you."

Lin Mu did not want to bring himself into the conversation, and so could only sign, flustered, "I thought you dislike him?"

Lu Rong's forehead twitched. He wrote, "I never disliked him."

Lin Mu could not help but hold his breath when he saw this.

"Then, do you like him?" After a pause, he continued signing, "My brother likes you very much."

Lu Rong remained silent.

Lin Mu pretended that he was not affected by his response, and his fingers continued moving, "My brother is a very nice person."

Lu Rong was speechless.

Unabashedly, Lin Mu Lin Mu continued to praise himself. "You'll know when you're friends with him. He's extremely good to his friends!"

Lu Rong bit his lip, and his eyes twinkled with amusement. He wrote in the book, "I know."

Lin Mu blinked. He saw Lu Rong added more words to what he wrote.

"But we're different." Lu Rong stopped writing; he did not seem to know how to go on. After a long time, he drew a line across the sentence.

Lin Mu opened his mouth, but Lu Rong suddenly raised his head. Looking at Lin Mu, he clumsily, slowly moved his fingers.

"No one will always be nice to Meimei and me for no reason." As soon as he knew Lin Mu got it, he put down his hands, clenched his fist, and placed it on his knee. A while later, he raised it again and knocked on the crook of his arm.

Lu Rong signed, "Eventually, he would get tired."

In a daze, Lin Mu sat aside and waited for Lu Rong to pack the booth up. Meimei added more things to his hair again, but he was not paying any attention. When Lu Rong returned after packing up, seeing Lin Mu, he revealed a tiny smile, amused.

"Meimei, don't make trouble." Lu Rong was very tall. His neck was half-bent as he studied Lin Mu's face. "*Jiejie* doesn't look nice anymore."

Chen Meihua seemed to be appalled at the three words "doesn't look nice." She acknowledged him obediently and no longer added any more things to Lin Mu's hair.

Lin Mu was embarrassed. He reached out, trying to remove the ornaments on his head. However, the moment he tried, the clip of the wig tugged at his real scalp, and he hissed in pain.

Lu Rong caught hold of his hand.

"Let me do it," he signed.

As such, Lin Mu sat there obediently.

Lu Rong was extremely good at dealing with hair—his fingers were like the feathers of a bird's wing; even though it was just a wig, Lin Mu could not help reddening slowly.

After Lu Rong removed the flowers that were randomly placed on Lin Mu's head, he untied the two plaits. The boy's hand drifted through Lin Mu's hair to his neck, gently sweeping his hair to his shoulder.

Lin Mu touched his hair, discovering that the little yellow duckling hairclip was still there.

This time, Lu Rong did not use sign language. He looked at Lin Mu, smiling as he said, "It's very cute, it suits you very much."

SILENT HEARTS

Skirts ❹

Skirts

When the alarm went off on Monday morning, Lin Mu had a strong urge to skip school for the first time in his life. During breakfast, Lin Zhao found out that he still had yet to tell Lu Rong the truth, even keeping it from her over the weekend.

Lin Mu chewed on his toast. As usual, the siblings had woken up for school at 6 AM. Lin Yanlai was preparing breakfast in the kitchen, and Lin Zhao signed sternly at her brother across the dining table, "You're really a little liar!"

Silence lay on Lin Mu, as he knew that he was at fault. He took a new piece of toast and smeared jam on it, handing it to Lin Zhao. "Don't scold me anymore, have breakfast first."

Lin Zhao took the toast, but continued scolding him, "You'll get into trouble sooner or later. I'm not going to clean up your mess for you!"

"Clean up his mess?" Lin Yanlai carried a plate of poached eggs over, and then asked Lin Mu, "Did you provoke your sister again?"

Lin Mu nearly rolled his eyes. "How would I dare provoke

her?"

Gulping his milk down, he signed at Lin Zhao and Lin Yanlai, "I'm leaving now, there's a morning recital today."

Kunqian had the tradition of morning recitals for students. In such a high-pressure study environment, students would be selected to recite certain texts from memory. As a good student, Lin Mu was rarely selected, yet neither did he dare to slack off and skip the memorization.

When he arrived at school, it was only a few minutes after seven. There were already more than a dozen people in the class—including people like Sun Hai who came early to compare homework answers.

"Didn't you already call me last night to ask about it?" Lin Mu took out his workbook and checked his answers. "You still don't understand how to do it?"

Sun Hai checked his answers while grumbling, "With the way you process the question, how could it be explained clearly over the phone?"

Isn't it because you're stupid? Lin Mu thought to himself.

Looking at the door, he saw Xu Yilu enter the classroom.

He called out, "Little Heron."

Xu Yilu looked towards Lin Mu's voice. Holding his white cane, he could only vaguely make out shadows. He gave a big grin, greeting, "Good morning."

Lin Mu ran over to help him, but Xu Yilu pointed outside. "Dopey is here; he says he needs to borrow a textbook."

Cao Zhan was standing outside their class, poking his head in and looking around. When he saw Lin Mu, he said, "I-I'd like to borrow your language textbook."

His voice was a little loud, attracting the attention of many students. Many greeted him as well, calling him Dopey.

Cao Zhan had taken a shine to the nickname 'Dopey'. His face would light up with a bright smile to anyone called him by the nickname.

Lin Mu took his language textbook and handed it to him. He could not help asking, "Didn't Auntie pack your schoolbag this morning?"

Cao Zhan was born into a wealthy family, and they could be compared to An Jincheng's family. The clothes he wore and the bag he carried were all recognizably expensive brands.

Lin Mu heard that Cao Zhan's father ran a gaming company with a truely impressive scope of business, even collaborating on projects with X-cent and A-X. His mother was a genius as well, but to take better care of Cao Zhan, she had given up her career to be a housewife.

"I wanted to pack it by myself," Cao Zhan admitted honestly. He was a little disappointed. "I had checked many times before coming to school, but when I looked for the textbook just now, I couldn't find it."

Lin Mu frowned. His expression became a little grim as he thought about how Cao Zhan's classmate bullied him.

"Is Jiang Tianhe there?" He asked.

Cao Zhan nodded.

Lin Mu clicked his tongue. "Tell him to stay back after school. I'll meet him at the basketball court."

Cao Zhan remained silent and thought for a while, seeming to ponder over Lin Mu's words. Finally, he shook his head and replied earnestly, "I'm not going to help you tell him that. You're going to fight him, aren't you? You can't do that, it's wrong to fight."

Lin Mu was speechless.

On the first day of class, Lu Rong was late, as Chen Meihua threw a tantrum, refusing to get out of bed. She cried for a long time, and after coaxing her to get out of bed, he still had to prepare breakfast. By the time he hurried over to the school, the morning recital session was almost over.

There were some special circumstances among the first-year students every year. Hence, Chu Lin personally came to supervise and inspect them in person. Today, she was wearing a pair of three-inch heels. One classroom after another, she patrolled the corridor, her heels clicking distinctly on the ground.

Lu Rong froze a little when he bumped into her. Bowing his head slightly, he greeted, "Good morning, Chu-*laoshi*."

Chu Lin nodded. She glanced at Chen Meihua and spoke warmly, "If there are any issues, let your form teacher know, don't be embarrassed and bear with it alone."

Lu Rong replied softly, "Thank you, Chu-*laoshi*."

Chu Lin was not a verbose person; she gestured at Lu Rong to enter the classroom. The boy had been arranged to sit all the way at the back, and there was even a seat specially prepared for Chen Meihua.

Mo Xiaoxiao looked up from her textbook, flicking her eyes curiously at him.

Lu Rong shot her a quick glance without a word. Pulling his grandmother along, he sat down.

Nothing much happened during their four classes in the morning, except that Chen Meihua had to go to the washroom after every lesson due to her age. As it was not convenient for Lu Rong to go to the female washroom, Mo Xiaoxiao would accompany Chen Meihua. On the third trip, Li Zi suddenly came over and took the job.

"I'll accompany Meimei this time." Her hair seemed to be a little shorter than before. Her face was very small, her features highly defined and even a little sharp, and she tended to be rather expressionless.

Mo Xiaoxiao clearly admired her greatly. She loved making friends, and she really wanted to become good friends with Li Zi. "Sure, sure, let's go together."

As such, the three "girls" went hand in hand to the washroom. Since it was not convenient for Lu Rong to follow along, he could only lean against the classroom door and wait for them to return.

Social interaction among students of sixteen or seventeen years old was actually not that simple. Lu Rong was standing there quietly, yet no boys in the class took the initiative to speak with him. After the three days of military training, along with the weekend, the twenty-odd boys in the class were like male wolf cubs dividing their territory, gathering in cliques and ostracizing others.

Even if no one spoke to him, Lu Rong did not feel awkward or uncomfortable. He did not feel that making friends was something necessary. He had Meimei, and no matter how energetic young people were, taking care of an Alzheimer's patient was still emotionally and physically draining.

No one would be willing to be friends with troublesome people, and Lu Rong was unconcerned about the entire matter. He looked across the flower beds on the first floor and saw a few second-year students gathering in groups on the basketball court.

Lu Rong watched them for a while, then looked down again, staring at his fingertips.

"Lin Zhao" came into his mind, the image of "her" wearing a small yellow duckling hairclip.

Although the twins were almost identical, the differences between them were pretty stark if one looked closely.

Their eyes, their lips, the shape of their ear lobes, and even their scent.

Lu Rong was a little surprised by himself for being able to remember their differences so clearly. Frowning as he took a deep breath, he ran his hand across his hair.

Mo Xiaoxiao and Li Zi had come back with Chen Meihua.

Lu Rong took his grandmother's hand, asking her, "Did Meimei say thank you?"

"Yes, I did!" Granny smiled happily. "Meimei even sang a song! Everyone says Meimei sings really well."

Mo Xiaoxiao praised her too, "It really sounds beautiful. You should sing more to us, Meimei."

Lu Rong asked Li Zi, "She didn't give you any trouble, did she?"

"No." Li Zi remained expressionless. She looked at Lu Rong, speaking suddenly, "We met the upperclassman from the last time."

Lu Rong did not understand. "Who?"

Mo Xiaoxiao was a little excited. "Lin Mu, it was Lin Mu!"

Lu Rong closed his mouth, not saying a word.

Li Zi said, "Meimei called him *Jiejie*."

Lu Rong sighed, "Meimei got the wrong person."

"I don't think so," Li Zi answered indifferently, "as soon as she called him *Jiejie*, that upperclassman agreed very quickly, scooting over to help us."

Lu Rong did not know what to say.

When Sun Hai realized that Lin Mu had been going to the washroom on the first floor between every period, he looked at him with a deeply suspicious and probing gaze.

"Is there a pretty first-year girl you're interested in?" Sun Hai finally could not resist asking at lunch.

Kunqian had two large canteens along with a small one. Due to their intensive study schedule, most third-year students would not choose to eat in the canteens. The ones who had time to stay there to eat and chat were mostly the first and second-year students.

Lin Mu was one of the most popular students of the second year; he had always been surrounded by friends. Whether disabled or not, they all enjoyed hanging out with him. Usually, whenever he occupied a long table, he could chat with anyone from the top of the table until the end.

Cao Zhan sat next to him, carefully picking the mushrooms out from his bowl.

Lin Mu glanced over and reproached him, "You have to eat everything, you can't be picky about food."

Cao Zhan pursed his lips reluctantly, then slowly put the mushrooms back.

Since Xu Yilu was using his own bowl and utensils, there was no need to worry about him.

"All you can think about is pretty girls." Lin Mu fiddled with his chopsticks, smiling lazily. "Can't I just be giving a helping hand?"

Sun Hai was baffled. "Who are you helping?"

Lin Mu did not respond. He looked up and saw a new group of people coming into the canteen. Due to the way she walked, Mo Xiaoxiao was immediately noticeable.

"Hello, *xuezhang*!" The pretty girl they were talking about was now here. She really was very lovely and sweet, and as Lin Mu shot her a smile, his eyes also shifted towards Lu Rong who was behind her.

Lu Rong was holding Chen Meihua's hand. His eyes still had the same expression, like pebbles deep in water. He looked at Lin Mu, aloof, and only gave a small nod,

A good-looking junior is so hard to deal with, Lin Mu thought in resignation.

Sun Hai and Cao Zhan had some impressions of these new students, especially Lu Rong. With just a few photos taken from far away, he was able to push ahead of Lin Mu and An Jincheng, becoming the best-looking boy in school. Seeing him at close distance now, Sun Hai felt as though jealousy was running through his veins.

While Mo Xiaoxiao and Lu Rong went to get food, Lin Mu made space, arranging for Chen Meihua to sit down next to him. Cao Zhan seemed a little curious about Alzheimer's patients, and he kept sneaking looks at Meimei.

"You don't like mushrooms?" Pointing at Cao Zhan's bowl, Chen Meihua asked suddenly.

Cao Zhan nodded, speaking softly, "Mushrooms smell bad."

Chen Meihua identified with him. "Meimei doesn't like them either."

Cao Zhan was delighted. Just as he was about to pick the mushrooms out again, he saw Lin Mu watching him.

Cao Zhan paused.

Unclear if his words were directed at Lin Mu or Meimei, he said seriously, as if he were taking a pledge, a stern expression written all over his face, "I'm a good child, I can't be picky about my food."

Chen Meihua looked at him. Copying him, she repeated, "Meimei is a good child too, Meimei also isn't picky about food."

Done, the two of them exchanged a nod, clenching their fists in encouragement.

Lin Mu watched their entire conversation, extremely amused, and Sun Hai felt that this pair of old lady and young man had a very good tacit understanding going on, as they were pretty similar. No wonder they could get along.

By the time Mo Xiaoxiao and Lu Rong returned with food, Cao Zhan and Meimei had already become good friends. Lu Rong seemed a little surprised, but he did not say anything. Holding the bowl, he prepared to feed his grandmother.

However, this time, Chen Meihua was not very cooperative. She wanted to eat by herself.

"Meimei doesn't need your help." Chen Meihua turned her head away, pointing at Cao Zhan. "Meimei wants to be like him."

Cao Zhan deliberately tried to maintain as perfect an eating posture as he could.

Lu Rong had no choice but to hand over the bowl to Chen Meihua, reminding her, "Don't spill the food."

Chen Meihua agreed, and began imitating Cao Zhan's motions as she started eating. However, it was not long before a clump of rice fell onto the table. As such, Lu Rong could only stop eating and help her clean up. When he was halfway through, he suddenly saw Lin Mu's hand.

The boy's fingers were long, slender, and fair, and his fingernails were smooth and clean, shiny and round. Lin Mu picked up the rest of the rice, smiling at Lu Rong.

"You should go ahead and eat," he said, "I'll take care of Meimei."

Lu Rong did not move. Very naturally, Lin Mu reached out and held Lu Rong's palm, picking the bits of rice from it and placing them on his own. He urged the younger boy, "Hurry up and eat."

Lu Rong opened his mouth, speaking quietly, "There's no need... It's too much trouble for you."

"It's no trouble at all." Lin Mu's answer came very quickly. He nudged Lu Rong's shoulder, his tone a little stubborn, "Eat first."

Xu Yilu was the slowest to finish his food among them, but no one would speak a word of it, and waited patiently for him while chatting away. When Xu Yilu was done, Lin Mu helped him clear his tray.

Xu Yilu extended his white cane, holding onto Lin Mu's shoulder from the back. Carrying Chen Meihua's bowl, Lu Rong turned back to look at the two people.

Mo Xiaoxiao was a little envious. "Lin Mu-*xuezhang* is really nice."

Lu Rong did not respond. He heard Mo Xiaoxiao sigh, "I remember his sister is a deaf-mute too... No wonder he's so good at taking care of people."

Few moments had passed before Lu Rong broke his silence, shaking his head. "No."

"What?"

"That's who he is," he replied placidly, "it has nothing to do with Lin Zhao."

Jiang Tianhe had received the message about meeting at the basketball court in the evening for a challenge. When Lin Mu left his classroom, he saw Jiang Tianhe trying his best to present a cool front, leaning against the wall of the corridor. His uniform was slung over his shoulder, his legs crossed, and he looked as though he was running for the best-looking rogue in the school.

These days, there seemed to be something wrong with An Jincheng—he had persisted with going to the special education class every day. Following behind Lin Mu, a frown immediately appeared on his face as soon as he saw Jiang Tianhe.

Although there was no way he could beat these two people in terms of academics, in the ranking of the most famous students on Kunqian's forum, Jiang Tianhe held steady at position three.

Girls had always paid more attention to good looking boys. With his rebellious bad boy character, Jiang Tianhe too had fans and followers.

"With your stature, are you sure you can play basketball?" Jiang Tianhe made a pre-emptive strike, eyeing Lin Mu. He laughed, "I'm afraid you'd be crying to that little deaf girl in a bit."

Lin Mu raised a brow. Crossing his arms, he said, "Not only can I play basketball, I can also beat the crap out of you. However, I don't know who you'll be crying to later."

Jiang Tianhe had no response to that.

He truly hated Lin Mu's sharp tongue. However, he knew it was unwise to make his move in the corridor now, with An Jincheng standing there and watching them. The three people's relationship was actually very well established, a triangle where none of them saw eye to eye with each other. As such, no one was willing to start a fight in front of the other, afraid that a situation would occur where someone else would gain the benefit, while they themselves would be at a disadvantage.

However, this time, An Jincheng did not seem willing to keep out of trouble and remain as the pretty wallflower Young Master An.

"Basketball?" An Jincheng was expressionless, as though he was just asking a casual question. "How many are playing?"

Lin Mu had a strong urge to tell him that they were playing one-on-one, and to not involve himself in this. However, Young Master An was not the obedient sort that would listen. The three people stood in the corridor, pitted against each other, and the news had long spread through the school forum. Everyone was interested in this piece of gossip.

"Wow, the two of them have always been at odds with each other. Why do they suddenly seem to be in agreement?!"

"Forget about these two, what is Jiang Tianhe doing?"

"I'm shocked! Jiang Tianhe could probably take the two of them in a fight, right?"

"No one believes in the wallflower?"

"Who's the wallflower?"

"It's exactly what it is. The standard of nicknames coming out from this forum has gone into the toilet. The Prince of the Night Forest? I can't believe you fangirls even came up with something like that."

"As if you boys are any better. If Lin Zhao were to find out that her fanboys have been calling her 'Fairy Zhaozhao' in the forum, do you believe she would change her name the very next day?"

"..."

Cao Zhan watched as the "Fairy Zhaozhao" next to him closed the forum page and ran her fingers through her hair coolly, her face expressionless.

Cao Zhan decided to try making up for it. He wrote on the scrap paper, "I think Fairy Zhaozhao sounds very nice."

Lin Zhao shot him a winsome smile, picking up the pen and adding a sentence below, "The Prince of the Night Forest isn't too bad as well."

Cao Zhan did not know what to say.

Lin Mu had originally thought that he might not be able to beat Jiang Tianhe in basketball, but he would definitely not lose to him in a fight. Arranging to meet on the basketball court to play basketball was only for show, as Lin Mu was actually going to just beat the person up one-on-one. However, his plan fell through when An Jincheng poked his nose into their business. Eventually, he could only give up his initial idea and play basketball, as they "planned."

There was no way to play basketball with just three people, and so during the last half hour of the self-study session, they managed to get seven more boys from their classes to play a game. First-year and second-year teachers were not as strict as the third-year teachers, and they were even supportive of ending the self-study session thirty minutes ahead of time in the name of exercising. Mr. Yang had volunteered to be the referee, and the thin, old man changed specially into Phoenix Suns' No. 13 jersey, standing on the court with a whistle in his mouth and his hands on his hips.

Sports had never been the elite class's forte, but Sun Hai, this ex-bully, could be considered half a sports student. Seeing An Jincheng rolling up his sleeves, Lin Mu felt that this person was really trying too hard to put on a cool front.

An Jincheng was secretly referred to as a pretty wallflower of a young master by his schoolmates, and on the forum, they directly called him the wallflower—implying that he would not perform well in the area of physical activity. Lin Mu, too, did not believe that An Jincheng would make a successful transformation into a young and sporty character, but in the end, the situation ended up being a slap in his face.

From midcourt, Lin Mu passed the ball to Sun Hai; Sun Hai aimed the ball at the net, but after some time, he still did not shoot. Near the sideline, An Jincheng raised his hands. Sun Hai could only grit his teeth and pass the ball to him, then watched as Young Master An coolly performed a jump shot, gaining them three points.

With one eyebrow raised, Lin Mu whistled.

An Jincheng was starting to perspire, but he was still unlike others. Looking closely, his collar was still clean and neat, and his voice was indifferent as he said, "You might as well pass the ball to me rather than Sun Hai. At least I can get the ball in."

Speechless, Sun Hai felt insulted.

Although Class Three had Jiang Tianhe, the others around him mostly seemed impressive but lacked in real ability, used to swaggering about based on Jiang Tianhe's name alone.

Just like Lin Mu, Jiang Tianhe had originally planned to fight him under the pretense of playing basketball. He did not expect that the class representative of the top class would come and put his foot in as well. Now, they had no choice but to only play the game seriously, even restraining themselves from being too aggressive—the referee would blow his whistle when fouls or other aggressive actions were noted.

More and more students gathered by the courtside. In the end, students from Class Three and the elite class were all there. An Jincheng turned and looked towards the sides of the court, and Lin Mu had to call out to him a few times.

"Stop looking at the courtside." Lin Mu knocked his head with the ball. "We're about to win. Who are you looking for?"

An Jincheng shot him a quick glance, feigning casualness as he asked, "Where's your sister?"

Lin Mu looked at the crowd as well. Not seeing her, he shrugged. "She's probably not back from Go yet."

An Jincheng closed his mouth, not saying any more. They had long outscored Class Three greatly, and with ten minutes left, Lin Mu challenged Jiang Tianhe arrogantly.

"Let's make a deal if you lose." Lin Mu again darted his way through the people guarding him. By the time Jiang Tianhe rushed towards him, it was too late. He could only watch as Lin Mu passed Sun Hai the ball, and the latter performed a lay-up shot.

Jiang Tianhe was so angry that he wanted to hit his teammates and then beat up Lin Mu. This loss was too embarrassing, yet he could only accept it. With just him and four other useless people, even if he were the superman of basketball, there was no way he could win.

"You sure like to fight on others' behalf," Jiang Tianhe could only taunt Lin Mu verbally, "you sissy."

This was not the first time Lin Mu had been called a sissy, and he had long been unbothered by it. "Only kindergarten children would use this as an insult."

Jiang Tianhe was wordless.

He thought Lin Mu would make him promise to never bully Cao Zhan again, but in the end, after the match, Lin Mu had left him in suspense instead.

"It's not like I can't beat you in a fight." Lin Mu pointed at Jiang Tianhe. "If you ever bully Dopey again, I'll kick your butt for sure."

When the match ended, Mr. Yang made the two teams shake hands. With a dark expression, Jiang Tianhe ground his teeth.

The so-called "promise" was thus owed for the time being.

With the end of the basketball game, the forum once again descended into bloodshed. Someone created a few threads on the forum in which the images captured during the match were uploaded, and these threads were focused mainly on "The wallflower is actually so manly!" and "We should change Lin Mu's nickname from 'The Prince of the Night Forest' to 'the Knight of the Night Forest'!"

"Oh please, a knight is not much trendier than a prince!" This was one of the most liked comments on the thread.

Lin Zhao did not watch the match, purely because she did not want to get involved with the crowd. Lin Mu went to pick her up after school, bumping into Lu Rong who was about to head upstairs.

The first-year special needs students were soon about to begin their evening self-study sessions. Lu Rong was bringing Chen Meihua to familiarize herself with the special education classroom.

When she saw the siblings, Chen Meihua called out without thinking, "*Jiejie!*"

Lin Zhao and Lin Mu both froze simultaneously.

A while later, Lin Zhao forced a smile at the grandmother and grandson.

Although Lin Zhao had previously said that she would not clean up the mess Lin Mu made, she still could not bear to sell her brother out at this critical juncture.

"You're not going home yet?" Lin Zhao signed at Lu Rong. "Is Granny visiting the classroom?"

Only after signing did she remember that she should have used Chen Meihua's nickname. Next to her, Lin Mu was in deep despair, rubbing his forehead as he tried to conceal his emotions.

Lu Rong did not seem to register the mistake. He signed back simply, "We'll return home once we finish seeing the classroom."

Lin Mu quickly asked, "Do you want me to take you there?"

Lu Rong looked at him and nodded without much hesitation.

Lin Zhao sighed in relief, hurriedly signing that she would leave first.

Lin Mu brought Lu Rong and Chen Meihua upstairs, continuing to help his "sister" patch up the lie. "She still has to attend Go sessions, so she's quite busy."

Lu Rong's gaze fell on his face and said noncommittally, "Is that so?"

Lin Mu's smile was a little stiff, and he could only brace himself and continue weaving the lie. "Didn't you attend the bazaar during the weekend together? My sister even brought home a little yellow duckling hairclip, it's quite nice."

Lu Rong smiled a little. Walking with Lin Mu to the entrance of the special education classroom, Lu Rong turned around. Bending his neck slightly, he suddenly asked, "Do you like the hairclip?"

Lin Mu fell into a daze for about a second. There seemed to be something grasping at his heart, and it took him some time before he could rearrange his expression and speak nonchalantly, "I think my sister looks quite cute with it. Did Meimei make it herself?"

Lu Rong looked at him for some time, and he then gave a very faint smile.

"I made it by myself," he said, "didn't your sister tell you?"

A lie was sometimes a trap in itself. Lin Mu clearly remembered that Lu Rong had mentioned it was Chen Meihua who made the hairclip, but he had to pretend that this was the first time he was hearing it, and so shook his head innocently.

Lu Rong did not ask any further questions. Pulling his grandmother's hand, he brought her around the classroom. Arranging a couple of desks and chairs, he also let her meet some of her new "classmates."

"Most of them have gone home already." Cao Zhan was waiting for his mother, Ji Qingwen, to pick him up, so he had not left yet. He recognized Lu Rong's face, and so took the rare initiative to speak to him. "Everyone will be here tomorrow."

Having had lunch together, Meimei and Cao Zhan discovered that they shared a common enemy—mushrooms—and thus they had formed a revolutionary friendship in this war.

Lin Mu noticed Lu Rong was still wearing his own clothes, and some thoughts crossed his mind, "You haven't had your uniforms measured?"

Lu Rong nodded. "They'll start tomorrow."

His eyes moved to Lin Mu's shirt. "Was it warm?"

Lin Mu did not catch his drift. "What?"

Lu Rong bit his lip, quietly saying, "When you were playing basketball."

Lin Mu finally understood. "You were watching?"

Lu Rong did not admit it, but neither did he deny it. He only reached out, flicking Lin Mu's collar lightly. "It's damp."

Lu Rong's fingers were cool to touch, and his scent was not that of soap. Lin Mu could not recognize it, but he thought that it smelled very good.

The male uniform of Kunqian had a white shirt, and most students would order two sets and wear them on rotation. At night, Lin Mu rubbed at the sweat stains on his collar, even looking closely at it. Lin Zhao came out from her Go room, glancing at him while walking past, and she was baffled.

She signed, "What are you looking at?"

Lin Mu could only say, "I'm looking to see if the collar is damp."

"Of course it'll be damp after sweating. Are you stupid?"

Lin Mu had no reply.

All the first-year students would be measured for their uniform together in turns, during the period for the self-study sessions. Mo Xiaoxiao looked at the sample photos, noticing that the uniform for girls was a short skirt, and she suddenly became nervous.

Lining up behind her, Li Zi glanced at her.

When it came to Mo Xiaoxiao's turn, abruptly, she spoke to the person taking measurements with a low voice, "I... I'm getting pants. "

Holding the measuring tape, the person froze. She watched as Mo Xiaoxiao bend over and roll up the leg of her pants, and immediately understood.

"This is nothing," said the tailor with a smile. "There's a third-year boy who lost his left arm, but in the summer, he still wears a short-sleeved shirt."

Mo Xiaoxiao did not speak, and hesitation seemed to enfold her.

The tailor placed the measuring tape across her shoulders, taking her measurement as she persuaded her, "All girls look very nice in skirts."

She looked at Mo Xiaoxiao, "How about this. I'm going to take two measurements for you. Later, you can choose whether you'll prefer to wear pants or skirts."

After having his legs measured, Lu Rong spread his arms open. The tailor exclaimed in wonder, "Oh wow, every part of you is so long."

The boys around him cracked up in laughter, and plenty of girls looked over, yet Lu Rong's expression remained bland. He left the area after the measurements were taken, sitting by the side with Meimei. Mo Xiaoxiao and Li Zi had their measurements taken already as well, and the two were talking with each other.

"You don't want to wear a skirt?" Li Zi asked Mo Xiaoxiao.

Mo Xiaoxiao looked conflicted. "I've never worn a skirt in front of so many people before."

Then, in a whisper, she continued, "I do own some skirts, sometimes I'd wear them secretly at home."

Li Zi's facial features were on the aloof side. "Just wear them if you like them, don't think about so many things."

Mo Xiaoxiao was tempted after hearing what she said. With a slight blush, she asked, "What if I don't look nice in it?"

"How can you not look nice?" Li Zi looked at her seriously, then turned to ask Chen Meihua, "Does Meimei think she'll look nice?"

Chen Meihua's expression was very solemn. She looked at Mo Xiaoxiao. "Girls are the cutest when they wear skirts."

Mo Xiaoxiao laughed. She was still a little shy about it, feeling worried over many things.

Just as Li Zi was about to speak again, Lu Rong stopped her by shaking his head.

"You don't have to care about what we think," Lu Rong told

Mo Xiaoxiao. "It's your right whether to wear a skirt or not, you don't have to care about what others think."

The uniforms needed some time before they were ready, and Mo Xiaoxiao was awaiting her new uniforms with eager anticipation. Li Zi saw her secretly looking at shoes to match the skirt, seeming as though she wanted it to fit her prosthetic as well.

Lessons did not stop them from discussing the length of Mo Xiaoxiao's skirt. Mo Xiaoxiao even drew a sketch, feeling that she had made a smart choice as she told Li Zi, "I asked them to make the skirt a little longer for me."

Li Zi looked down, patiently asking, "How long will it be?"

Mo Xiaoxiao gestured at her prosthetic. "It'll be a little below my knee, concealing where my limb is fitted into my prosthetic. It'll look better."

Li Zi's eyes were gentle. "That's so cool. You'd look just like a cyberpunk."

Mo Xiaoxiao burst into laughter and showed Lu Rong her sketch as well. Before Lu Rong could see it properly, the drawing was snatched out of his hand by his grandmother.

The three "girls" gathered together, discussing about skirts. Lu Rong stared at them, resting his head in his hand. All he could hear were the girls chattering away, but he did not find it noisy, and he could not help but smile.

Lin Mu, too, was eagerly anticipating the first-year's new uniforms. His relationship with Lu Rong currently seemed to have finally improved. A good-looking junior was truly not easy to deal with, but with enough time, a relationship could still be built.

Lin Zhao usually spent the evening self-study sessions at the

Go institute, whereas Lin Mu would tutor Cao Zhan in the special education class, as well as make use of every bit of available time to talk to Lu Rong. In truth, they did not share many common topics; they were in different grades, and so they could not discuss their homework. However, Meimei loved talking to Lin Mu, stubbornly calling him "*Jiejie*."

Lu Rong corrected her a few times, but, upon realizing that it was useless, he eventually gave up.

Lin Mu believed that his acting ability was off the chart, and he continued patching up his lies confidently. "My sister and I are twins. It's very normal for Meimei to mistake me for my sister. It's not just me saying this, a lot of people have mistaken us for each other before too."

Lu Rong's eyelashes were very long. When he focused on someone, his eyes seemed filled with emotions, and easily made one's heart soften. Even Lin Mu would sometimes feel that lying to Lu Rong was a great sin he was committing.

"Lin Zhao and you don't look alike at all," Lu Rong said calmly. His words sounding deliberate, he added, "I can differentiate between the two of you."

Lin Mu was a little tentative. "R-really?"

Lu Rong gazed at him in silence. Suddenly, he reached out and pinched Lin Mu's earlobe. "This is different."

Lin Mu covered his ear. His mouth fell open, his ears reddening.

Lu Rong suddenly laughed. "Why are you blushing all of a sudden?"

Lin Mu naturally was not able to explain why. He did not want to keep talking about Lin Zhao with Lu Rong, but if he did not talk about her, he did not know what else they could talk about.

As time went by, the two people continued chatting like this. Lin Mu would find a conversation topic, and Lu Rong would spend most of his time listening. He often needed to pause and take care of Meimei, and during moments like this, Lin Mu would wait quietly by the side.

Unable to think of something to say, Lin Mu would often end up looping the conversation back to Lin Zhao, praising her for her skills at Go, how many wins she had during her competitions, and how many sessions she did as a mentor. During the conversation, Lu Rong listened very seriously, and Lin Mu could not tell if it was because he was listening to him, or because of the topic.

Once, after listening to them, Xu Yilu could not help but ask Lin Mu when Lu Rong was not around. "Why do you keep talking to him about your sister? Does he like her?"

Lin Mu froze, then immediately denied it without thinking, "Of course not. The two of them met each other during the community sessions; they're just good friends."

But right after Lin Mu finished, he found that his words were utterly absurd. He was the one who attended the community sessions and eventually met Lu Rong, and he was also the one who believed that they were good friends, but in the end, it was all done under the name of Lin Zhao.

Xu Yilu could not see, but his hearing was very sensitive. Chuckling, he said, "You say they're both good friends, but why do I feel that the two of you are closer to each other?"

Lin Mu could only say abashedly, "Well, look how enthusiastic I am, always trying to fire up the conversation."

There was not much busy work to do during the evening self-study sessions for the special education class. They had a special education teacher present, so if any of the students had any questions, the teacher would guide them along with one by one. When Cao Zhan finished stumbling through his homework, he decided he wanted to play on his phone.

"What would you like to do?" Lin Mu asked.

Cao Zhan thought for a while, and finally decided to go on the school forum.

Lin Mu then opened the school forum page for him.

Lin Mu did not pay much attention to their school forum. This was due to the posters being anonymous, and with the nature of the school, there would occasionally be some malicious posts appearing. Although moderators quickly removed any posts that discriminated against the special needs students, Lin Mu would feel very upset when he saw even one of such posts.

Lin Mu had to hand it to Cao Zhan for liking to browse the forum. But on second thought, some of the thread titles were simply enigmatic insinuations. With Cao Zhan's ability, he might not have been able to understand them.

Just like now, he had tapped into a post titled, "Some of the girls in our school are really very brave." There was only a photo attached to it; it was Mo Xiaoxiao bending down and trying on a pair of shoes. It was evident that this photo had been taken secretly, only revealing her rolled-up pants.

"Who took this photo? What was this girl thinking about? She wants to show off her legs? But this leg is a fake one."

"I remember there's a special needs student in Class Five of the first years, with a prosthetic right leg?"

"She's in the class next door, I can see her every day. She really wants to wear the uniform skirt?"

Only then did Cao Zhan realize that something was wrong in this forum thread. After some hesitation, he left a comment, "Why can't she wear a skirt?"

Someone replied to him immediately.

"Are you joking? After seeing such a leg, wouldn't you get a nightmare?"

The post on the forum was deleted very quickly, and no one knew if Mo Xiaoxiao had read it.

The new uniforms were issued, and Mo Xiaoxiao now owned a checkered skirt that was a little longer than standard. The day she received it, she looked at it for some time, then carefully tucked it into her bag.

On Sunday, Li Zi could no longer hold herself back from calling Mo Xiaoxiao. The girl did not have a mobile phone, and when Li Zi called her at home, the one who picked up was Mo Xiaoxiao's mother, Cai Liyun.

"Oh, it's Li Zi!" Cai Liyun's voice sounded energetic. She was not highly educated, and she mainly worked as a housekeeper now. If she was not working at her employer's place, she would be working part-time in food-delivery. Taking care of her daughter alone was hard, but she rarely complained. "Xiaoxiao is studying, I'll get her."

Li Zi waited patiently for a while. She heard the sound of flip-flops across the floor, and Mo Xiaoxiao soon picked up.

"Hello?" There was not much of a change in Mo Xiaoxiao's voice. Cai Liyun was still next to her, and the woman said, "Ask Li Zi to come to our place to play.

Mo Xiaoxiao smiled, telling her OK. On the line, she asked, "Did you hear that? My mom asked you to come over to my place."

Li Zi made a faint sound of acknowledgement. After a pause,

she continued, "There's a flag-raising ceremony tomorrow, remember to wear your uniform."

Mo Xiaoxiao froze, a little uncertain. "You called me just to tell me this? I know that."

Li Zi hummed in response. She wondered if she should ask Mo Xiaoxiao to wear her skirt. After a bout of silence, she asked with feigned casualness, "Have you tried on the skirt? Does it fit?"

"It fits well!" Mo Xiaoxiao seemed very happy. She thought about it for a moment, then added, "My mother thinks I look very nice in it."

Li Zi finally laughed. She said earnestly, "I feel that you'll definitely look very nice in it as well."

That night, Cai Liyun helped Mo Xiaoxiao iron her skirt. Humming to herself, she hung up her daughter's school skirt along with her school blouse. Looking at it for a long time, she could not stop herself from smoothing out some small wrinkles from it.

Mo Xiaoxiao left her room to get a drink of water. When she saw the skirt, she paused.

"You'll be able to wear it tomorrow." Cai Liyun was clearly even happier than her. "I've shined your shoes too; they'll match very well with your skirt."

Mo Xiaoxiao did not speak. It seemed as though she wanted to smile, but before her lips could curve up, her eyes reddened first. Looking downwards, Mo Xiaoxiao spoke, a beat later, "Mama, I won't be wearing the skirt anymore."

Cai Liyun got a shock. She grasped her daughter's hand, pulling her into her arms, coaxing, "Why are you crying? If you don't want to wear the skirt, then we just won't wear it. I'll take your pants out."

Mo Xiaoxiao nodded. She wiped her tears away, but she was also reluctant to let go of the skirt. Twisting her fingers, feeling conflicted, she looked at the skirt, then looked at her own leg.

Cai Liyun did not know what happened in school to make her daughter suddenly refuse to wear the skirt. She was unable to come up with anything that could comfort her daughter, and so she could only look at her face, speaking with a pained heart, "No matter what you wear, in my eyes, Xiaoxiao is the best-looking. My daughter's leg is nothing to be ashamed about at all."

Mo Xiaoxiao shook her head. She clasped her arms around Cai Liyun's neck, and spoke after a moment of silence, her voice muffled, "I also don't think that there's anything to be ashamed about of my leg."

She sniffled, speaking in a very soft voice, "But I'll still be scared."

Li Zi arrived very early on Monday morning. She first sat in the classroom and waited. But after a while, she was tired of waiting and decided to stand at the classroom door instead. Lu Rong took a few glances at her, and finally could not resist asking, "Are you going to pick her up at the school gate?"

Li Zi gave him a quick glance, her response sounding indifferent. "How I wish I could just go to her house and help her put on the skirt."

Lu Rong lowered his lids, smiling a little. "Don't be so nervous. Maybe she didn't even see it."

"Good things never come easily, but bad things will always happen. My intuition has always been very accurate."

Just as she finished speaking, Mo Xiaoxiao appeared around the corner of the corridor.

Simultaneously, both Lu Rong and Li Zi looked towards the girl's lower body. They did not see that pretty, new checkered skirt, but a pair of black school trousers like the boys.

Li Zi stood there stiffly. Her fists clenched tightly, and her tiny face was grim.

Mo Xiaoxiao looked up. She seemed a little startled when she saw them and averted her gaze in guilt. Taking some time to muster her courage, she finally put on a smile and greeted, "Good morning..."

Lu Rong frowned. He looked up, sighing faintly. "Morning."

Li Zi did not speak.

Mo Xiaoxiao scratched her head. She was not the type to hide or conceal anything. Reaching out and grabbing Li Zi's arm, she swung it slightly, her voice was a little ingratiating, "I thought about it... and I still think that I should wear pants."

After a pause, she continued quietly, "I'm quite cowardly, I'm afraid that someone will talk about me on the forum again."

Li Zi felt as though someone had poured boiling water down her throat. Feeling both ashamed and indignant, her eyes reddened. Covering her eyes with her hands, she was unwilling to look at Mo Xiaoxiao, and it took her some time before she spoke hoarsely, "Don't be scared, I'll change to pants as well."

Mo Xiaoxiao grinned, "What nonsense are you saying? Your legs are so nice. You look amazing in a skirt."

Crossing her legs, Lin Zhao sat in her seat. As she skimmed through the school forum, her phone vibrated a few times—Lin Mu sent her a text.

"We're having the flag-raising ceremony with the first-years today." Lin Mu's text was succinct. "Help me look at the uniform of the girl with the metal leg."

Lin Zhao tapped swiftly on her screen. "Why doesn't the school allow us to check the IP addresses? What is that scoundrel Zhong He thinking? That son of a bitch!"

Lin Mu was speechless.

Lin Zhao was probably the only one who dared to criticize their own principal like this. She rarely attended culture class, so she rarely suffered through Zhong He's torment, and thus she dared to be so insolent. Even someone like An Jincheng wouldn't want to truly offend Zhong He.

Everybody knew that Kunqian's Chu Lin was famous for being sharp-tongued but softhearted—a tigress on the outside, yet extremely gentle towards her students, especially the ones with special needs. In comparison, Zhong He was the truly severe one, only thinking about the school's profits and any potential upcoming development for it. He was the reason why there was such an intense studying environment in the school—he ruled with an iron fist, and never understood how to be humane.

Even after cursing out Zhong He, Lin Zhao did not feel any better. When the bell for the ceremony rang, Cao Zhan pulled at her before she finally stood up.

The classes were lined up neatly. The first-year classrooms were located on the ground floor, and the students made their way to the sports ground, then followed by the second-year classes coming from a level above. As the third-year students were studying for the university entrance examinations, they were allowed to skip the ceremony.

The elite class of the second year stood right in front. Lin Mu was about to sprain his neck, yet he still could not see where Lu Rong's class was. Suddenly, his phone vibrated in his pocket. Taking it out, he saw an emoji Lin Zhao sent him.

Lin Zhao:【Angry!】

Lin Mu: "You saw her?"

Lin Zhao: "She's not wearing a skirt."

Lin Mu: "..."

Lin Zhao: "I'm so pissed off! Why was the post deleted so quickly! I want to argue with that scumbag! From dawn til dusk and from dusk til dawn! Let's see if I can't curse him out to death before he does the same to me!"

Oh, come on, there's no way somebody can be cursed out to death, Lin Mu thought to himself.

He kept his phone in pocket, turning his head to see Sun Hai watching him.

"Where's the girl with the metal leg?" Sun Hai asked him anxiously.

Lin Mu thought about it, then answered, "She's wearing pants."

Sun Hai's eyes widened, and a moment later, he swore indignantly. "Fuck!"

Lin Mu, too, shared his sentiments. Today, it was An Jincheng speaking on the podium, but he was not interested in listening. His hand fiddled with his phone in his pocket for some time before he took it out and sent Jiang Tianhe a text.

"You finally have a chance to pay back the promise you owe me." After sending the text, Lin Mu seemed a little worried, and so he sent another message. "Don't think about denying the fact that you owe me one. We made a deal on that day, and whoever who denies it doesn't have a dick."

A while later, Jiang Tianhe's reply came, and it was only a line of ellipses.

"You have to run around the sports ground and shout, 'I, Jiang Tianhe, don't have a dick!'"

Perhaps Jiang Tianhe's wrath was ignited by that. He typed for a long time and a reply finally came: "What the fuck do you want me to do?!"

Feeling a bit bitchy, Lin Mu responded, "Well, I just wanted to make sure that you remember about owing me a promise."

Jiang Tianhe was wordless.

During a break between classes, Li Zi came alone to the second floor.

School had only just started, and it was rare for a pretty first-year junior to take the initiative and look for a second-year student. Many people in the corridor all stared at her, but Li Zi ignored them all. Still, it could be seen that she was a little nervous. Standing at the door of the elite class for a while, she finally seemed to make up her mind. Grabbing the person walking through the door, she asked, "May I ask if Lin Mu-*xuezhang* is here?"

The whole class was hooting when Lin Mu walked to the door. Without looking back, he waved at them to stop. "Don't make a fuss out of nothing, or I'll beat you all up."

Li Zi was a little shy when she saw him, her expression a little stiff. "Hello, *xuezhang*."

Lin Mu raised a brow, smiling. "Hello, *xuemei*."

Li Zi did not know how to react for a moment. Perhaps she did not expect that Lin Mu would be so polite. With a little hesitation, she lifted her lids, glancing up at Lin Mu, weighing things over before asking, "*Xuezhang*, are you able to track IP addresses?"

Lin Mu understood right away. "You're doing it for Mo Xiaoxiao?"

Li Zi nodded, her voice cold as ice, "I want to know who posted the photo on the forum."

Lin Mu watched her for a little while, before shaking his head. "The moderators of Kunqian's forum are all teachers, and they won't allow us to track the IP addresses. Besides, what are you going to do if you find out who the person was? Are you going to make them apologize to Mo Xiaoxiao?"

Li Zi bit her lip, remaining silent.

Lin Mu sighed, continuing, "Furthermore, the person who uploaded the post was just one of them, and there were others commenting as well. There may be more people holding such malice than we thought. Are you going to dig them out one by one?"

Li Zi looked up. She was not the type of girl who cried often, but her eyes had started to redden. Calmly, she said, "No matter how many malicious people there are, none of them have the right to take away Mo Xiaoxiao's freedom to wear skirts."

Lin Mu looked at her and suddenly, he cracked a smile. Taking out his phone, he opened his WeChat and handed his phone over to Li Zi. "You're right. So, let's come up with an idea together and let Mo Xiaoxiao wear a skirt again."

Lin Mu set up a WeChat group. For now, there was only Xu Yilu, Sun Hai, Lin Zhao, Cao Zhan, Li Zi and himself in it. When Sun Hai was added, he was a little baffled. A second later, the name of the chat was changed to "Skirts."

Sun Hai sent a string of ellipses to the group chat. "What is this group for? Something artistic?"

Li Zi typed and typed, but in the end it was Lin Mu who sent a voice message first. "Little Heron is here, so let's try to use voice messages as much as possible. My sister will be the exception, since she types super fast."

Lin Zhao sent a custom emote, asking if Lin Mu wanted to die.

Lin Mu sent another voice message. "This is why WeChat is so great and convenient! It has speech-to-text support."

Lagging behind a little, Cao Zhan sent a text. "What are we going to do?"

Lin Mu responded, "Something big. Li Zi-*xuemei*, come, tell us."

Li Zi explained Mo Xiaoxiao's situation to the group. As a matter of fact, she did not understand why Lin Mu had added so many people to this chat. At the start, she had only felt that Mo Xiaoxiao admired Lin Mu quite a bit, and as the latter was someone popular in the school, he might be able to find out who sent the photo, or even console Mo Xiaoxiao as well. However, this upperclassman did not behave as expected but seemed instead to want to blow up this matter, and no one knew what was going on.

Lin Mu sent a message, "Even though we can't track the IP addresses, we can't just let things go so easily. We can't have it out with them, but we should at least make sure Mo Xiaoxiao can happily put on her skirt, right?"

Hearing that it had to do with this matter, Sun Hai immediately perked up, sending a long chain of exclamation marks. "We're all here for the girl with the metal leg! Tell us, what are we going to do?"

Unable to restrain herself from being a spoilsport, Lin Zhao sent, "Stop being so impulsive. You can't just shout '*Jiejie* is here' without any plan. We still don't know what we'll be doing."

Lin Mu replied, "It's not '*Jiejie* is here', it's '*Gege* and *Jiejie* are here'. We don't discriminate between genders here."

Cao Zhan's reaction was the slowest, and naturally, he was the last to reply. His text was also a repeat of others. "Then what are we going to do?"

For a moment, a thought had crossed Li Zi's mind, but she did not know if she should say it out.

It was as if her mind and Lin Mu's were connected. He took the initiative in asking her, "Li Zi-*xuemei*, do you have something good in mind? Let's discuss it."

"*Xuezhang*," Li Zi typed slowly. Editing the message several times, she finally sent it out. "Are you willing to... wear a skirt?"

Lin Mu was stunned.

The next day, Jiang Tianhe was suddenly added by Lin Mu into a WeChat group called "Skirts." Completely bewildered, he looked at it a few times, then left the group with no hesitation.

Lin Mu was left speechless.

Jiang Tianhe was again added to the group.

This time, Lin Mu struck first and took the upper hand. "If you leave the group chat again, you're going to run around the sports ground and shout that you don't have a dick!"

Jiang Tianhe was so angry he could vomit blood. "Come out, let's fight!"

"Are you sure about that? You really won't be able to beat me, and if you lose to me again, you'll owe me another favor."

Jiang Tianhe dared not make a sound again. He actually had never fought directly with Lin Mu before, but he was aware of Sun Hai's ability to fight. Sun Hai had been infamous as a bully in junior high, yet Lin Mu had beaten the crap out of him and even made him his loyal lackey. Thus, it was reasonable for Lin Mu to claim that he was good at fighting.

"As long as you help with this matter, the debt you owed during the basketball match will be wiped clean," Lin Mu started negotiating. "You don't want to run around and shout that you don't have a dick, do you?"

The force Jiang Tianhe exerted when he typed could even be felt through the phone. His messages either only had exclamation marks or there was no punctuation at all. "What exactly do you want!!"

Lin Mu sent a ":)," then said, "Jiang Tianhe, let's wear skirts together~"

Jiang Tianhe was speechless.

In truth, it seemed much more acceptable to wear a skirt than to run around the sports ground and yell that he did not have a dick. As for the reason, the boys' logic was basically, "As far as crossdressing goes, the only difference is in never doing it and in doing it all the time."

Jiang Tianhe did see the photo of Mo Xiaoxiao on the forum as well. He had been ready to spew out all the vulgarities he had learned in his lifetime towards the person who replied to Cao Zhan, but the post had been deleted too quickly, and he had no choice but to swallow them all down.

When he saw Lin Zhao cursing out the uploader in the group chat, it was as though Jiang Tianhe had found someone just like him. They ended up venting about the person for half an hour.

After they vigorously vented their frustrations, Lin Zhao ended up sending a thumbs up.

"Don't bully Dopey," she said, "and we'll be bros."

Jiang Tianhe replied, "I'm the only one who can bully Foolish. No one else is allowed to do so."

Cao Zhan was speechless.

Jiang Tianhe said, "Foolish, you must wear a skirt too."

Cao Zhan was not repulsed by wearing one. He felt that it was a good thing as long as he could help, and so he obediently agreed.

Lin Zhao tagged Sun Hai. "You're not wearing one?"

Sun Hai almost blacked out in response to being tagged by his goddess. For her sake, he could even cut his own throat! So he too joined the team, "I'll wear it!"

Lin Mu thought that things were coming along well. They were now a group of crossdressers.

But surprisingly, the matter of "wearing a skirt" did not end here.

Jiang Tianhe had a group chat with his lackeys. Since their boss had to wear a skirt, his loyal lackeys too had to do so, and they would bravely lead the way. As such, Jiang Tianhe formed another chat with the entire Class Three, with Cao Zhan as the admin, and Lin Zhao as the overall planner. Not only did the twenty-odd boys in the class joined in, the girls responded positively as well, offering up their skirts.

Cao Zhan's mind could not move fast, but he was very earnest in everything he did. Surprisingly, his needlework was excellent. The physique of boys was much wider than girls, and thus the skirts had to be modified. Cao Zhan quickly used all the free time he had between classes to help everyone secretly modify their skirts. With such a big development in Class Three, the classes next door naturally heard about it as well. One by one, more and more people came asking about it, and the matter spread like a fire.

During the second-year committee meeting, An Jincheng was questioned by several class representatives. Therefore, he had no choice but to look for Lin Mu.

"We're running an event, something like *'Gege* is here.'" Lin Mu no longer held Young Master An with as much enmity. He also did not want to offend him, and so explained nicely, "If even boys can wear skirts, of course Mo Xiaoxiao would be able to wear them. We're just simply looking at the situation like that."

As An Jincheng remained expressionless, Lin Mu was not confident in his reaction. "Young Master An, couldn't you just turn a blind eye to this and not tell the teachers?" His tone became a little softer, negotiating, "If the scoundrel Zhong He were to find out, we won't be able to carry out our plan."

An Jincheng glanced at him and suddenly asked, "When are you doing this?"

"Any time. We'll probably do it on a Monday when we all have to participate in the flag-raising ceremony."

An Jincheng paused to think over, and then spoke with his indifferent voice. "You'll be speaking on the podium next Monday. What do you think about standing there in a skirt?"

Lin Mu did not know how to respond to that.

He was a little alarmed, and prickles had crept over his scalp. Haltingly, he said, "There's no need..."

"The effect would be best if you did it." An Jincheng cut him off, looking very determined. He sounded very business-like as he spoke sternly, "Since you want to do it, you must do the best you can. If you're just going to do it sloppily, you might as well not do it at all."

Lin Mu was left wordless.

An Jincheng turned his head towards him, his pretty face pleasing to the eye. "Do you have any more skirts? Give me one."

When Lin Zhao saw that An Jincheng had been added to the group chat, she was not very happy.

When he joined, he immediately gave a rundown of the plan, saying that all five class representatives of the second year had

discussed it already. They would try to get all the boys to participate, and every class was doing their preparations, waiting for
Lin Mu to speak on the podium next Monday.

When An Jincheng finished talking, the group chat fell into
silence. A while later, Li Zi broke the silence with a text, faltering, "Would we be kicked out of school... if we blow things up
like this?"

An Jincheng felt absolutely no sense of crisis even though he
was stirring up trouble like this despite his role as the leader of
the school committee. "It's because there's so many people involved, that's why everyone will be safe." He responded calmly.

Lin Mu responded, "...You're safe, but I'm the leader of this
thing!"

An Jincheng replied, "You took first place in the final examinations. Zhong He wouldn't make things difficult for you."

Lin Zhao suddenly asked, "Are you wearing a skirt too?"

For a long time, there was no response from An Jincheng.

Lin Mu responded on his behalf. "He'll be wearing one."

"Oh." Lin Zhao continued asking, "Want to wear mine?"

Just as Lin Mu was about to type that Lin Zhao's skirt was his
to wear, he heard something dropped heavily on to the floor. An
Jincheng bent down in a fluster to pick up his phone. Since it was
just a revision class, Mr. Yang made light of it and only gave him
a small reminder, "Study properly, don't play with your phone."

"He dropped his phone and was found out by Mr. Yang." Lin
Mu kindly helped An Jincheng respond. "*Jie*, your skirt is mine to
wear, don't just give it away randomly."

Lin Zhao replied with an "Okay" emoji.

An Jincheng, who just retrieved his phone, was left speechless.

Lu Rong noticed that Li Zi and Lin Mu had been very close

recently, but he did not say much about it. Instead, Chen Meihua was the anxious one, and she kept asking Li Zi why she was always looking for "*Jiejie*."

"I want to see *Jiejie* too." Chen Meihua kicked up a fuss during break. "Meimei hasn't seen *Jiejie* for many days already."

Lu Rong could only quietly persuade her, "*Jiejie* is busy. Meimei has to be good; we can't cause any trouble for *Jiejie*."

Chen Meihua was unconvinced. "But why does Li Zi get to go, and Meimei doesn't?"

Lu Rong had no choice but to call Li Zi over. The girl acted mysteriously, pulling the two of them out of the class, deliberately avoiding Mo Xiaoxiao.

"Okay, so, this is the secret," Li Zi specially reminded Chen Meihua. "Make sure to keep the secret from Mo Xiaoxiao until next Monday, okay?"

Chen Meihua's eyes went wide, looking very solemn. "Meimei understands, Meimei won't say anything." She even clasped her hands over her mouth.

Lu Rong was a little stunned. He did not seem to believe it, and he confirmed it once again, "Is Lin Mu really going to wear a skirt on the podium?"

Li Zi nodded. "This is what *xuezhang* is planning."

A few faint wrinkles appeared on Lu Rong's forehead. His mouth opened and closed a few times, looking as though he wanted to say something, only to swallow it down as he thought it was inappropriate. In the end, he asked Li Zi, "Do you have Lin Mu's WeChat contact?"

When Lin Mu received a friend's request on WeChat, he thought it was an advertisement. Lu Rong's profile photo was very plain and simple, it was Chen Meihua's photo with a mobile number added to it.

His signature was: Alzheimer's patient, if she's lost, please contact: 138XXXXXXX

Lin Mu hurriedly accepted his friend's request. Mulling over it for some time, he took the initiative and sent a greeting, "You have a mobile?"

Lu Rong only responded after some time. "Yes, I bought it a very long time ago, an old model, just in case Meimei wanders away."

Lin Mu fell silent. This topic was a little too heavy. Lin Mu regretted mentioning it, but fortunately Lu Rong didn't seem to mind.

"You're going to wear a skirt while speaking on the podium?" Lu Rong typed.

"Li Zi told you so?"

"Yeah." Lu Rong typed for a long time before sending another text: "You're really very enthusiastic."

Lin Mu was unable to decipher the meaning behind his words. After thinking it over, he decided to tease Lu Rong instead. "I'm even more enthusiastic towards you."

A while later, Lu Rong asked, "How so?"

"Look how nice I am to Meimei."

"That's to Meimei, not me."

Lin Mu's fingers grew a little hot. Tapping on his screen, he edited his message multiple times before sending it out. "I can accompany you to the washroom too."

"... I'm not a little girl."

Lin Mu laughed, slowly typing, "I know you're not."

The secret event of "*Gege* is here" was in full swing. Lin Mu was so busy that he was unable to see Lu Rong, but they did chat regularly on WeChat.

Every day, he would take photos of the boys in skirts and send them to Lu Rong. Often, the entire screen would be filled with a hairy leg, and Lin Mu would even ask him to guess whose leg it was.

"...I don't know any of the other boys other than you."

Lin Mu answered his own question, "It's Sun Hai hahahahaha."

The boy in question had no idea he had become their topic of conversation. Wearing the skirt, he even felt quite coquettish. He walked back and forth as if he were on a catwalk, causing others to start jeering at him.

Xu Yilu had a skirt too. His legs were fair and smooth, and after he put it on, all the girls in the class went crazy.

"Where's your skirt?" Lu Rong texted.

Lin Mu took a photo and sent it to him, "It's Lin Zhao's."

The two of them seldom talked about Lin Zhao these days, but whenever she was mentioned, the feeling of guilt would arise in Lin Mu again.

"Do you want my sister's WeChat?" Lin Mu asked, "Since you two are such good friends, do you want me to send it to you?"

He sent Lin Mu a string of ellipses, and only after some time, he finally added, "No."

Lin Mu felt as though he got snubbed, but he was also secretly delighted.

"Oh," he responded.

Ever since Mo Xiaoxiao wore pants to the flag-raising ceremony on the first week, she had seemed rather listless. She would still spend time with Lu Rong and Li Zi, as well as accompany Meimei to the washroom. Yet when she waited by the door, her eyes would always fall upon the other first-year girls in skirts.

Chen Meihua came out from the washroom. Seeing Mo Xiaoxiao gazing at the checkered skirts, she also joined her. "Xiaoxiao should wear a skirt."

Mo Xiaoxiao forced out a smile. "I don't look nice in a skirt."

Chen Meihua frowned, shaking her head. "Who said that?"

Mo Xiaoxiao didn't know either. Sometimes, malice was like a net—it could be just an ordinary sentence to the person weaving the net, yet to someone else, it was an enormous, terrifying net, clinging to them and suffocating them, striking fear into their hearts.

Behind that photo, how many people thought the same way, and how many people agreed? Mo Xiaoxiao felt as if she were a prey captured in the net, and at any moment, she would be devoured by malice. Her photo had been secretly taken, she had been commented on casually, and all this only happened because she was different from others, because she was missing a leg.

However, none of them knew that it was only by paying the price of her leg, was she then able to continue living. None of them knew that her father had sacrificed his own life and left the world to save her, the girl who had lost a leg.

No one liked listening to grievances and misery. Ever since Mo Xiaoxiao lost her leg, she understood this sentiment even more. She was afraid of the contempt behind the malice.

For her, it was enough that she herself understood that there was nothing to be ashamed about her missing leg.

During the flag-raising ceremony on Monday, Li Zi deliberately stood in line next to Mo Xiaoxiao. Mo Xiaoxiao turned to look at her.

"Xiaoxiao," Li Zi said suddenly. "Let's hold hands."

Mo Xiaoxiao did not know what she wanted, but she still held out her hand so they could clasp their hands together.

The second-year classes also arrived at the sports ground. With the boys walking in an odd manner, they attracted the eyes of the crowd.

Several first-year students started whispering to each other. "Did the second-year students change their uniforms? Why does it seem like the boys' pants don't fit?"

Mo Xiaoxiao too could not refrain from looking over, and Li Zi squeezed her hand lightly.

The girl's sharp eyes were surprisingly soft, and she whispered, "Lin Mu-*xuezhang* is going up on stage."

Mo Xiaoxiao looked up. Sure enough, she saw Lin Mu walking up the podium. His pants were very loose, and it seemed like there was something stuffed in it, with how the area around his buttocks bulged out.

Zhong He and Chu Lin were both standing below the podium, and all the teachers were gathered by the side as well. At first, the content of Lin Mu's speech was just like usual, but it changed sharply towards the end.

"Everyone should know Kunqian's motto." Holding the microphone, Lin Mu straightened. "Kindness, Courage, Equality, Love."

Mo Xiaoxiao recited silently along with him, and her eyes inexplicably reddened.

Lin Mu looked down at the students. He suddenly gestured, and all the second-year boys simultaneously bent down and started to remove their pants.

The first ones to notice something wrong were the teachers. However, by the time they wanted to stop them, it was too late—too many students were removing their pants, and they were too fast. In only a couple of seconds, most of the second-year boys were dressed in the checkered skirts they wore inside their pants, revealing many hairy legs. Jiang Tianhe and Sun Hai were even standing right up in front, hairs on their legs ruffling in the wind.

"Mo Xiaoxiao, are you seeing this?" Standing on the podium, Lin Mu took off his pants. He wore a skirt underneath, completely ignoring the dark expression of the principal, Zhong He.

Mo Xiaoxiao was struck dumb. The entire sports ground burst into activity, and many first-year students took out their phones to capture shots of their upperclassmen.

"Mo Xiaoxiao." Lin Mu smiled.

"*Gege* and *Jiejie* are here," he said loudly.

The entire crowd shouted along, cheers of "*Gege*" and "*Jiejie*" resounding everywhere.

Everyone was yelling at Mo Xiaoxiao's name, and Li Zi wrapped an arm tightly around her trembling shoulders.

Lin Mu said, "Don't be afraid, Mo Xiaoxiao."

His smile was even brighter than the blazing sun. "You're the most beautiful metal-legged girl, and you have the coolest leg in the world."

SILENT HEARTS

05 The Labor
Society of
The Demerit Kings

05 The Labor Society of The Demerit Kings

Lin Mu took the lead, standing in the principal's office, and all the second-year boys were still in their skirts as they left the sports ground. Seeing their bare legs standing in a row, Chu Lin really wanted to laugh, only managing to hold it back with great effort.

Zhong He took a few deep breaths. He was not very old, looking to be in his early forties. His hair was still very thick, and he wore a pair of gold-rimmed glasses. The bottom half of his face, because of his thin lips and sharp nose, looked a little unkind. Although his suit was well-ironed, there was still a faint smell of cigarettes and alcohol left from the night before.

Lin Mu held his chin up, refusing to look at the principal, and his neck was unbent.

"You all sure know how to kick up a fuss," Zhong He sneered as he adjusted his glasses. He calmed down after saying that. "Are you looking to be expelled?"

Lin Mu did not respond, and An Jincheng was standing next to him. Despite being the ringleaders, they both had excellent grades, and hence, this was a great headache.

Zhong He always knew that Lin Mu was not some law-abiding student. If he was unruly, it would have be fine if he was a bad student—in that case, the teachers wouldn't need to worry about him. However, the problem was that Lin Mu was not a bad student.

Not only was he not one, his sister, Lin Zhao, was a professional Go player with a very promising future ahead of her. In Kunqian's annual school newspaper, as well as the school's public image, Lin Zhao was basically a living mascot.

The more outstanding the twins were, the greater the benefits they were able to bring to the school. At the same time, the trouble they caused was harder to solve.

When a good student made a mistake, teachers could not hold double standards, and the student had to be punished. Therefore, not only did Lin Mu and An Jincheng receive a demerit each, they had to clean up the school's outdoor swimming pool for a semester as well. Their performance would be evaluated at the end of the semester, and their demerits would be wiped off if Zhong He was satisfied.

Cao Zhan and Xu Yilu managed to escape any punishment as they were declared to have no autonomy over the matter. The two of them at first wanted to share in the punishment, but after getting reprimanded by Chu Lin, asking them if they were in a hurry to seek trouble for themselves, they stopped arguing and fell silent.

On the other hand, Sun Hai and Jiang Tianhe were old hands at receiving punishments. Having been declared as accessories to this matter, they did not receive any demerits, but they also had to clean the school's indoor basketball court for half a semester.

Everyone looked as though they were not afraid of getting

punished at all. It made Zhong He's eyes hurt when he looked at them.

"Go back to your classes." The way Zhong He waved them off was as though he disdained them for being dirty. Looking at their bare legs, a vein in his forehead pulsed, and he gritted, "Change out of your skirts!"

The event "*Gege* is here" had created too big a stir, and some students even posted the videos on the school forum. As the moderators had to keep removing some of the more radical posts, they decided to draw a stricter line, banning any discussion on the appearances and dressing of disabled students.

When Lin Zhao changed the name of the group chat to "The Labor Society of The Demerit Kings," Lin Mu and An Jincheng dared not offer their opinions. Li Zi added Mo Xiaoxiao and Lu Rong into the chat too.

Mo Xiaoxiao took a photo of herself wearing the school skirt, revealing her metal prosthetic below the knee, and added a shy emoticon to the image.

"Does it look nice?" She asked.

Before anyone else could speak, Sun Hai's message popped up. "I'm up for it! I'm coming! I don't even have a drop left in me anymore."

The chat was left speechless.

Is he a fucking pervert?! everyone wondered.

From then on, Mo Xiaoxiao alternated between pants and skirts. Although she liked wearing skirts, pants were still more convenient. Her final conclusion was that she would just wear whatever she liked.

After the name of the group chat changed, it became a chat

for Lin Mu, An Jincheng, Jiang Tianhe and Sun Hai to report on their work. The four of them were really very pitiful, having to go to work halfway through their evening self-study sessions, and other people couldn't even help them either. Once, Cao Zhan secretly helped Lin Mu out with his cleaning, but someone saw and reported it to Zhong He. On the next day, the scoundrel Zhong He gave them an extremely enigmatic speech over the school's broadcast, making them all thoroughly disgusted.

"Is that scoundrel Zhong He married?" Lin Zhao could not help asking in the group chat.

Lin Mu replied, "He's definitely not."

Lin Zhao responded, "How do you know?"

Although it was just words, Lin Mu's disdain for Zhong He was clearly revealed in his tone. "His suits aren't too bad, but he stinks too heavily of cigarettes and alcohol. Even if he had a wife, she definitely would have run away from the smell."

Sun Hai continued, "That scoundrel's busy flattering various bosses for sponsorships and investments. Look at how many more projects Kunqian has this semester. Moral and ethics education? This scoundrel has basically fallen into the pit of seeking wealth and benefits."

In the eyes of the students, Zhong He's reputation was the lowest of the low. Not only did he like nitpicking on all sorts of insignificant and disgusting rules of the school, he often used students as a tool to boost the school's reputation. Olympiad examinations, science conferences, competitions, awards, anything—as long as the students participated in such events that brought glory and honor to the school, he would trumpet it all around, announcing it in various newspapers, singling them out and displaying their achievements across the doors of Kunqian. Even Lin Zhao's successes in Go were not spared. Through some unknown connections of Zhong He, the media even included the name of Lin Zhao's school in their articles, turning it into free advertising for Kunqian.

While reading the chat, Lin Mu rolled up the legs of his pants and changed into a pair of slippers. Today, he would be cleaning up the pool alone, as Young Master An was attending a school committee meeting. It would be An Jincheng's turn tomorrow.

Kunqian had two swimming pools, one indoors and one outdoors. There was a contractor hired to maintain the indoor swimming pool. As for the outdoor pool, it was rarely used, and it was quite troublesome to clean it. Holding on to a long water hose, Lin Mu walked by the side of the pool, pinching the mouth of the hose and spraying water at the leaves and mud on the tiles. The pool was surrounded by a wire fence about the height of a man, and the fence had already turned rusty.

The pool was just next to the sports ground, and the cleaning was done during the evening self-study sessions. Thus, there were many students playing basketball, as well as couples strolling around the sports ground, pretending that they were exercising. Since Lin Mu was one of the most popular boys in school, passersby often took the initiative to greet him.

It was in the middle of September, but the sweltering heat of summer had yet to dissipate. After cleaning for a short period, Lin Mu was completely soaked in sweat. He undid a few buttons of his school shirt, rolling up his sleeves to his shoulders, and revealed a rather exquisite display of lean chest muscles.

After washing the tiles for some time, Lin Mu heard someone shouting "*Jiejie*."

Chen Meihua was standing outside the fence, her smile as

bright as the sun.

"How did Meimei come here?" Lin Mu put down the hose, opening the gate in the fence.

The old lady wanted to come in, so Lin Mu reached out to help her. Today, Chen Meihua wore a dress printed with little daisies, and on her feet were a pair of sandals decorated with glittering plastic butterflies.

Noticing that Lin Mu was looking at her shoes, Chen Meihua stuck her foot out. She asked, sounding pleased like a little girl, "Does it look nice?"

Lin Mu nodded. "Meimei is the prettiest."

He looked around and could not help asking, "Where's Lu Rong?"

Chen Meihua said, "Little Deer has gone to buy candy."

Lin Mu coaxed patiently, "Little Deer has gone to buy candy, but why didn't you go with him?"

A crafty look appeared on Chen Meihua's face. "Meimei secretly ran off to find *Jiejie*."

Lin Mu could pretty much guess what had happened. He sent a text to Lu Rong and stayed with Meimei by the pool. Afraid that the old lady would slip and fall, he found a bench for her to sit, instructing her, "Meimei cannot run around here. If you fall, it will hurt a lot."

Meimei seemed a little scared when she heard the word "hurt." She sat obediently on the bench, hugging her knees and not daring to move.

Lin Mu continued washing the walls of the pool. Seeing her unfading frown, Lin Mu was a little confused. "Is Meimei afraid of water?"

"Yes," Chen Meihua answered in a small voice. "Don't let the water hit Meimei."

Lin Mu moved the water hose away. "Don't be afraid, I won't let the water hit Meimei."

Chen Meihua nodded, but suddenly shook her head again. She spoke vaguely, "You won't, but others will."

She seemed to recall something, and after a long time, she continued, "Last year, at Little Deer's old school, someone sprayed Meimei with water."

The sun was painfully scorching. Holding onto the water hose, Lin Mu stood where he was. His back was covered with sweat, soaking through his shirt entirely. Lin Mu suddenly remembered that, after he first heard the story of Sun Hai, Lu Rong had written, "You can even become friends with someone who bullied you."

At that time, he did not know why Lu Rong would write something like that, but Lin Mu felt that he could understand now.

Chen Meihua dared not get closer to the pool, and her eyes were fixed on the water hose in Lin Mu's hand. Lin Mu bowed his head, thinking, then looked up and asked her, "Does Meimei want to play?"

Chen Meihua asked him cautiously, "What are we playing with?"

"Let's play with water."

He shoved the water hose in Chen Meihua's hand and pointed at himself. "Meimei can spray water on me. The weather is too hot, I want to wash my hair."

Chen Meihua's eyes rounded, seeming to be a little in disbelief. The fear in her was obvious, and she slowly lifted the water hose with a trembling hand. Lin Mu bent his neck over, standing there without moving. After some time, he finally felt the cool water flowing over his head.

"Does it hurt?" Meimei asked while spraying at his hair.

Lin Mu closed his eyes, letting the water flow across his face. Chuckling, he spoke, yet sounding a little low-spirited, "It doesn't hurt."

Chen Meihua was happy when she heard him saying that it did not hurt. Reaching out, she combed through Lin Mu's hair, washing it for him, as though she had learnt it from someone. She could not help saying, "Your hair is so soft."

Feeling the warm and rough hand in his hair, Lin Mu fell silent for a moment before asking, "Have Meimei ever helped Little Deer wash his hair?"

Chen Meihua's actions paused. She tried very hard to recall, and in the end, she said regretfully, "Meimei cannot remember anymore."

Lin Mu didn't say much after that, waiting patiently for Chen Meihua to wash his hair. The old lady later got into the fun of playing with water, spraying it everywhere. Lin Mu did not dodge the spray, but taught Chen Meihua how to pinch the mouth of the water hose and direct the spray towards the mud on the tiles.

When Lu Rong arrived, he saw his grandmother and Lin Mu squatting down and playing with water. Chen Meihua was holding the water hose up to wash Lin Mu's face.

Lin Mu did not realize that there was now another person around him. With his eyes closed, he asked as he no longer felt any water on his face, "Is my face clean now?"

No one responded.

A few rough fingers gently stroked across Lin Mu's eyelids, eyelashes and eyebrows. Drawing a circle, they stopped somewhere near the bridge of his nose.

Lin Mu opened his eyes reflexively.

Lu Rong was pretty much cupping Lin Mu's cheek in his hand. Then, as if nothing had happened, he took his hand away.

"Don't go along with Meimei making trouble," Lu Rong said. When he stood up and looked down, he could see into Lin Mu's gaping collar. Soaked with water, the shirt was a little translucent, clinging onto the lines of Lin Mu's back. The view from this angle was really too delightful, revealing a sight of the unlimited splendor of youth.

Yet Lin Mu was not aware. He stood up, brushing his wet fringe back and saying casually, "Since Meimei likes it, just let her play."

He tilted his head and smiled, asking Chen Meihua, "Are you still afraid of water now?"

The old lady did not disappoint him, saying loudly, "Meimei is not afraid anymore!"

Lu Rong stood in silence. He seemed resigned, looking like he had no other choice but to go along with them.

Lin Mu still had to finish cleaning up the pool, and Lu Rong and Chen Meihua accompanied him. With candy to eat, the old lady did not want to speak anymore; she had only a few teeth left, and thus, she had to eat it carefully.

The evening sun was still shining brightly. Chen Meihua could not stand the heat and moved to sit in the shade, but Lu Rong remained standing by the pool.

Afraid that it would be too hot, Lin Mu asked him to go into the shade.

Lu Rong shook his head. "It's fine."

After a pause, he continued, "I'll stay with you."

Lin Mu was a little delighted. Just as he was about to finish up, an idea crossed his mind. "Later we'll fill up the pool, and we can wash up in it together."

Lu Rong bit his lip. "This is a swimming pool."

Lin Mu did not feel that there was anything wrong with what he said. "Let's swim together then. Come on, we're both guys, you don't have to be shy."

Lu Rong did not know what to say to that.

Lu Rong could not understand where Lin Mu got his courage to say that. Why didn't he say anything like "You don't have to be shy," when he'd been pretending to be Lin Zhao?

The little liar seemed to be convinced that he'd managed to deceive Lu Rong, too. As such, Lu Rong just went along without trying to expose him, only periodically making a few rather pointed remarks. Lin Mu would then try to patch up his lies even more, and before he could fully patch one up, he would have to work on patching up another. For some reason, Lu Rong found it amusing yet also a little pitiable.

The swimming pool was quickly filled. The evening self-study session had also ended, and students from the first and second year were all dismissed. They made their way past the sports ground in a flurry.

Lin Zhao sent him a text, informing him that there was an evening match at the Go institute. Lin Yanlai would pick her up later, so she told Lin Mu to go home by himself. Looking at his phone, Lin Mu thought for a moment, then asked Lu Rong if he wanted to leave together.

"We're all living in East Zone anyway." Lin Mu wiped his feet clean and put on his shoes, his hair still dripping with water.

It made no difference to Lu Rong, but Chen Meihua was very happy. She wanted to eat ice cream, and she kept talking about it.

The three of them left the school together to take the subway. On Chen Meihua's neck was a card—proof that she was an Alzheimer's patient. Although her peculiar behavior was monitored by Lu Rong, it still attracted the attention of others.

Lin Mu chatted with her, only speaking with Lu Rong occasionally. The latter was the silent type, and it was rare of him to take the initiative in starting a conversation topic.

"Which part of East Zone do you live in?" Lin Mu asked.

The area was big and located next to the business park. Overall, housing there was not expensive, and there were many shopping areas. Lu Rong told him the location of his home, and Lin Mu smiled, "We live very close to each other."

Chen Meihua said that she often bought ice cream from a supermarket near them. Lin Mu wondered if it could be Luo Yu's store, and his guess was soon verified after asking her the name of the store.

"I know the boss very well." Lin Mu felt a pride of being well-connected. He told Lu Rong, "Later on, I'll treat you guys."

Lu Rong gazed at him, neither agreeing nor disagreeing.

Two trains arrived at the same time, and a lot more people got on. Protecting Chen Meihua, Lin Mu had been squeezed towards the side of the door. With an unyielding posture, Lu Rong stretched his arm out, pressing his hand against the wall next to Lin Mu's head.

Lu Rong stood head and shoulders above others, and half his head was beyond the upper handrail. Together with his very attractive appearance, many people were stealing glances at him.

Lu Rong noticed Lin Mu looking up at him. He lowered his gaze, his expression very patient. "There's quite a lot of people," he said, "bear with it for a while."

The two people stood very close to one another. The train stopped at a station, and the doors opened. People rushed to get out, and Lu Rong wrapped an arm around Lin Mu's shoulders reflexively, pulling him into his arms. Lin Mu turned his head a little, his chin resting on Lu Rong's shoulder.

Lu Rong continued embracing him, only letting go when the passengers had exited.

A slight blush could be seen on Lin Mu's face, his voice faltering, "It's a little warm..."

Lu Rong seemed to smile. He stroked Lin Mu's sweaty forehead, and as though he was comforting him, he quietly said, "We'll be arriving soon."

He was right; it took just a few more minutes to reach their station. The three of them took Exit Four, and with Lin Mu leading the way, they walked to Luo Yu's store.

The boss was carrying her son, sitting behind the counter. When she saw him, her eyes sparkled as she asked, "Where's Lin Zhao?"

Lin Mu feigned jealousy and spoke a little unhappily, "You only remember my sister, do I not exist?"

Laughing, Luo Yu called him a slick weasel. When she saw Chen Meihua behind him, she was a little surprised. "Granny is here too?"

Lin Mu corrected her, "She's Meimei."

Luo Yu smacked him lightly. "So disrespectful!"

Lu Rong was the last to enter the store. He gave Luo Yu a nod; she immediately understood and asked, "White Rabbit?"

Lu Rong let Chen Meihua picked the ice cream she wanted. The old lady clapped her hands, repeating "White Rabbit" a few times happily.

Lin Mu chose two Binggrae popsicles and passed one to Lu Rong, but Lu Rong seemed a little hesitant.

"Quick, my hand's aching." Lin Mu sure knew how to put on a show.

As such, Lu Rong could only take it from him.

Lin Mu smiled. "Hurry up and eat it, don't wait until it melts."

Lu Rong tucked the wrapping paper around the plastic shell, pulling the tab open and putting it in his mouth.

Chen Meihua was the quietest when she was eating. She was afraid of the heat, and so she stayed in the store while Lin Mu and Lu Rong sat down next to each other on the bench outside.

The sky finally darkened a little, leaving only the golden-red glow of the setting sun. Luo Yu's store was located at a corner of an intersection. Across it was a residential community, and on another side was a small commercial zone. The roads were not wide, with parasol trees planted along the sidewalk, and the faint chirps of cicadas could be heard.

Lin Mu had stopped sweating. He sat next to Lu Rong, feeling the gentle breeze of the late evening across his face and the sweetness in his mouth.

Lu Rong had his head tilted back, sucking on the popsicle as his throat bobbed elegantly. It was a little challenging to reach the bits of ice inside the plastic tube, and Lu Rong frowned slightly.

"Just squeeze it out," Lin Mu taught him, "like this."

Lu Rong copied his actions, but it ended up overflowing from the tube. The syrupy sweet ice dripped onto his hand, flowing down to his wrist. Afraid that it would become sticky and difficult to clean up, Lu Rong quickly licked at his hand and mumbled a thanks.

Lin Mu could not help but laugh. "Why are you always so polite?"

Lu Rong licked across his wrist, tasting both sweet and salty. His silence brewed for a while before he spoke, "You shouldn't have taught Meimei to play with water. You're too nice to her."

He paused a moment, and then continued, "Not everyone will be so nice to her."

Lin Mu was still eating the popsicle, but it did not stop him from grumbling, "Who cares about others? As long as I'll always be nice to you guys, isn't that the only thing that matters?"

Lu Rong lifted his lids. His face was expressionless, yet a little ridicule could be found in his eyes. He said, "Don't make everything sound so simple. Meimei isn't your grandmother."

Looking at Lin Mu, Lu Rong inhaled deeply. "And neither do you have any obligations to me."

Lin Mu received a red packet sent by Lu Rong through WeChat—the money for the "White Rabbit" ice cream and the Binggrae popsicle. Sitting in his living room, he could not restrain himself from kicking the coffee table in front of him. In the end, the pain was so great that he could not make a sound; hugging his toes, he huddled pitifully on the couch.

Jiang Wan came in and saw this scene. Baffled, she asked, "What craziness are you dealing with this time?"

Lin Mu's voice was feeble: "I hurt my foot..."

His mother had no sympathy at all. "Use some iodine on it and it'll be fine, why are you being so delicate?"

Lin Mu was speechless.

Jiang Wan might be a little unconcerned, but at least Lin Yanlai behaved more like a father—after he finished cooking, he asked Lin Mu to remove his sock so that he could take a look. His skin was not broken, but his toes were a little swollen. "Why are you so careless?" The father asked.

Lin Mu did not speak, feeling both angry and resentful. He desperately wanted to blacklist Lu Rong, but he was afraid that he would not be able to add him back later, and thus he remained conflicted and reluctant.

The red packet notification was still on the screen, looking all lonely and pitiful. Lin Mu stubbornly refused to accept it.

In the end, when the red packet was automatically sent back the next day, Lu Rong and Meimei again came to the swimming pool where Lin Mu was.

"What do you want?" Through the rusty wire fence, Lin Mu's face was long as he looked at Lu Rong. He felt that having just argued with the other party and having yet to reconcile, it would be an affront to his dignity if he seemed too friendly.

Lu Rong seemed unbothered by his attitude. "Meimei wants to play with water."

An Jincheng was present today as well. He looked at Lu Rong, then looked at Lin Mu. He did not know why these two people were at a deadlock, and so he walked over and opened the door.

"Come in." An Jincheng's face seemed as though it belonged in the Wong Karwai-directed film, *In the Mood for Love*. Looking down, he said indifferently, "Be careful of the slippery floor."

Lin Mu was usually the one who spoke a lot; neither An Jincheng or Lu Rong were talkative people. As Kunqian's number one wallflower, it was rumored that when An Jincheng said a sentence to the common folk, he would need to wash his mouth ten times, and he was as cold and aloof as a frozen chicken on Mount Everest.

But right now, the most talkative Lin Mu refused to speak, and the three boys crouched awkwardly by the pool.

Chen Meihua dared to play alone with water now. An Jincheng handed the water hose to her, and the old lady smiled and thanked him. Raising the hose, she swung it here and there.

Lin Mu persisted in the one-sided war with Lu Rong. He refused to look at him, and he forcefully scrubbed at the tiled steps with a stern expression, remaining silent. An Jincheng felt that the atmosphere surrounding the two people was not quite right. At first, he did not want to meddle in their affairs, but after some time, this pervasive awkwardness made him antsy.

A hardly seen sight, An Jincheng tried to find a topic of conversation and asked Lin Mu, "Have you finished your homework?"

The relationship between him and Lin Mu was much better than before, and so Lin Mu did not leave him hanging. "Yeah, I finished it."

An Jincheng continued asking, "What's your answer for the second question in the math homework?"

Lin Mu did not take too long to answer. "Square root of two."

An Jincheng frowned. He was not very happy with this offbeat answer. Before he could utter another word, on his other side, Lu Rong suddenly asked, "*Xuezhang*, does Kunqian have any extra classes during the weekend?"

For the Jiangnan students who had to face immense studying pressure, from primary school until high school, weekends never existed for them. Working adults had the 9-9-6 system of working hours—working six days a week from 9 AM to 9 PM; meanwhile, students were left with the 7-0-7 system of studying hours—studying seven days a week from 7 AM to midnight. Kunqian was a semi-private school, and their passing rate was a benchmark for other schools. Extra classes were held every Saturday and Sunday until three or four in the afternoon, and they allowed students to self-study until 6:30 PM before they closed the school doors.

An Jincheng could not only just speak to Lin Mu. As such, he looked at Lu Rong, "Extra classes will start in October. If you can't keep up with your studies, you can register for the classes."

It was not compulsory for special needs students to attend the extra classes. Furthermore, East Zone held community sessions every week for the handicapped, and Lu Rong may not be able to attend classes weekly.

Lin Mu glanced over to Lu Rong intermittently. His question was directed at no one in particular, his tone inflectionless, "You're afraid of not being able to catch up?"

Lu Rong did not look at him and replied calmly, "My studies are so-so."

They fell into silence again.

An Jincheng, trapped between them, did not know what to do.

A few minutes later, something seemed to have fritzed out in Lin Mu's brain. He asked An Jincheng, "When are the Olympiad examinations this year?"

An Jincheng was a little uncertain. "It's probably at the end of the year. Just take it easy with the competition before the winter break, the focus should be on the one during the summer holidays."

Lin Mu nodded. Suddenly, Lu Rong interrupted, "Is there a science fair competition for the first-year students?"

This time, An Jincheng answered in the affirmative. "There is, but you'll have to check with Miss Chu when it's held."

Lin Mu asked unexpectedly, "Are you going to participate?"

It was not sure who Lu Rong was directing his answer to, and his tone was casual as well, "I'm only just asking."

For a moment, An Jincheng felt like he was an electrical circuit resistor controlling the flow of current from both sides.

The superficial conversation continued for a while, and the resistor An Jincheng could no longer bear it anymore. He quickly finished cleaning up half the pool, then found an excuse and left, leaving Lu Rong, Lin Mu, and Chen Meihua behind to stare at the pool.

Naturally, Chen Meihua did not notice that Lu Rong and Lin Mu were at odds. After playing with water, she went to eat her candy quietly under the shade of a tree.

Lin Mu discovered that Chen Meihua, to some extent, had her own schedule. Whatever she did was based on her schedule, and nobody could stop her from doing so. Of course, this would work only when her condition was stable. When her condition was unstable, she would do things like secretly running off to look for Lin Mu, causing Lu Rong to be unable to find her.

Half of Lu Rong's attention always had to be on his grandmother. The look in his eyes was deep, and when he focused on someone, the person would feel as though they were very important.

While scrubbing at the pool, Lin Mu sneaked glances at him. After countless glances, their eyes finally met.

That focused and intense gaze tickled Lin Mu's face like a feather.

Lin Mu did not avert his eyes. With a complicated expression, he sighed, as though he could only let Lu Rong be.

"Don't guard against me like a thief," Lin Mu said. "I have Lin

Zhao, and I know how to take care of others."

Lu Rong's brows creased. A moment later, he only made a small ambiguous sound of acknowledgement.

Lin Mu continued, "I'm not like others." He paused, seemingly about to give an example of how he was different. However, feeling that that would be too deliberate, he could only say, "You'll understand after some time."

Thinking for a while more, Lin Mu laughed and added, "After all, time reveals a man's heart."

Lu Rong did not speak. He lowered his lashes, and his gaze slid away from Lin Mu's face. Lin Mu walked a few steps forward. Standing in the pool, he rested his arms by the edge, and looked from below, up at Lu Rong's face.

"Little Deer," Lin Mu called out to him, "promise me."

Lin Mu actually also was not sure what he wanted Lu Rong to promise him, but as long as the boy looked at him, casually agreeing to it, he would no longer be at odds with him.

A good-looking junior is truly difficult to deal with, Lin Mu again exclaimed to himself.

But fortunately, it's very easy to persuade me, Lin Mu added in his mind.

Lu Rong reached out, pulling Lin Mu up from the pool. The boy's palm was not soft and tender, but firm and warm. He helped Lin Mu pull the leaves out from his hair, and Lin Mu bent his head down, asking, "Are there any more left?"

Lu Rong said no, and Lin Mu started smiling as he filled the pool.

They stayed there until the evening self-study session was about to end. Lin Zhao too had returned from the Go institute.

She came over to pick her brother up. From outside the fence, she signed, "Are you done?"

Lin Mu moved his fingers swiftly, "I'm done."

He turned to ask Lu Rong, "Do you want to leave together?"

Lu Rong nodded. He pulled Meimei up, quietly speaking to her.

Frankly speaking, Lin Zhao was a little apprehensive of Lu Rong—Lin Mu had been extremely friendly to him when he was pretending to be her. Yet, as herself, she was very distant and estranged. She never exuded the sort of warmth that was innate to Lin Mu.

Lu Rong greeted Lin Zhao as well. Though he was not as enthusiastic as before, he could still be regarded as friendly. His deep gaze, however, now seemed to have some unknown implications. When their eyes met for a moment, Lin Zhao had the feeling that she was completely exposed.

Yet Lin Mu did not notice anything at all, even trying to pull the two closer. "My sister has always kept the little yellow duckling hairclip you gifted her."

Lu Rong glanced at Lin Zhao before returning his gaze to Lin Mu. His voice was gentle as he said, "Is that so?"

With a stiff face, Lin Zhao did not respond.

That little yellow duckling was actually in Lin Mu's drawer. She had to admire her brother's acting, to dare lie to Lu Rong so grandiosely.

"Meimei and I have made a lot more things," Lu Rong suddenly said. "There's an event next week, have you heard about it?"

His question seemed directed at Lin Zhao, yet Lu Rong was not signing; obviously, he was talking to Lin Mu.

Lin Mu blinked his eyes, assuming that he was just the messenger. Naturally, he asked on behalf of Lin Zhao, "What event?"

Lu Rong answered blandly, "A picnic in the park."

He looked at Lin Zhao again, asking "Are you going?"

Lin Zhao could not read his lips as Lu Rong spoke too fast. She shot Lin Mu a baffled look, but her brother was facing the complete opposite direction.

"Of course she's going." Lin Mu did not hesitate before agreeing. Only after saying that did he remember something, and signed at Lin Zhao, "There's a community outing this week. I told him that you'd be going too."

Lin Zhao was speechless.

SILENT HEARTS

06 He Still Doesn't Know A Thing

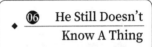

06 He Still Doesn't
Know A Thing

Lin Zhao's current emotions could probably be described to be like pebbles in a ravine, like a reef under the sea. It was a feeling of hopeless resignation, an awareness that things were uncontrollably moving in a worse direction.

The crux of the matter was extremely baffling, and she could not understand what exactly was going through Lin Mu's head.

"When are you going to tell him the truth?" Lin Zhao signed, asking. "You can't continue like this."

Because of Lu Rong, Lin Mu had agreed to go without any hesitation. But now, facing Lin Zhao alone, he was starting to feel a faint sense of regret. This made him feel both ashamed and conflicted—he had done wrong to his sister, and he was also afraid to face Lu Rong.

"I'll definitely tell him this time." Lin Mu felt that he had probably made up his mind about eight hundred times already, and at the same time, he had also backed out at the critical moment about eight hundred times too.

Lin Zhao did not really believe him, but she still helped Lin

Mu apply his makeup and wig. She felt as though she was an ac-
complice, and her expression was serious.

"If I knew things would be like this, I wouldn't have let you
take my place right from the beginning." Lin Zhao signed. She
looked at the makeup on her brother's face, and continued signing with immense guilt, "I'm really a genius, to have made you up
to look so pretty."

Lin Mu was left dumbfounded.

The association of handicapped people had been established
for many years in East Zone, and they would normally have about
two slightly larger-scale events every month. The previous bazaar
and the outing this time were to allow everyone to interact and
to build relationships, so they had attracted many participants.

The picnic's location was set at the wetland park in Xiangcheng District. It was finally nearing the end of summer, and the
weather was a lot cooler. This time, Lin Mu was dressed in a long
chiffon skirt. He had a lace choker tied around his neck, and a
wide-brimmed straw hat with wide brim covered half his face.

Teacher Ma looked a little surprised when he saw him. Ob-
serving him from top to bottom, the teacher signed, "Did you
grow taller again?"

Lin Zhao was quite tall, and when she wore heels, her height
could even surpass quite a few boys. However, ever since their
first year in high school, Lin Mu showed a likelihood of gradually
becoming taller than his sister.

Lin Mu maintained his aloof character and gave a casual wave.
Following behind the group, he waited for a while and saw Lu
Rong and Chen Meihua walking from a distance away.

The old lady noticed him very quickly.

"*Jiejie!*" Chen Meihua was carrying a red bunny backpack, and she waved at Lin Mu. Lu Rong cast his eyes over, and when his gaze fell onto Lin Mu's face, it paused there lightly.

"Good morning," Lin Mu smiled as he moved his fingers demurely, making sure that he would not expose himself.

Lu Rong looked at him a while, so long that Lin Mu was about to be unable to maintain his smile any longer, before finally smiling back.

"Good morning," he replied.

The association had chartered a bus. Afraid of getting carsick, Chen Meihua sat at the front, while Lu Rong and Lin Mu sat behind. When the two of them moved through the aisle, Lu Rong deliberately stepped aside, intending for Lin Mu to sit by the window.

Upholding the principle of "ladies first," Lin Mu did not stand on courtesy. After sitting down, he took off his hat and placed it on his thighs.

Lu Rong took out a notebook.

Lin Mu watched him write a question, "Are you warm?"

Lin Mu signed, "I'm not, it's pretty cool today."

Lu Rong continued writing, "Let me know once you start perspiring."

Lin Mu did not understand. "Why should I let you know?"

Lu Rong was looking down at first, but upon registering Lin Mu's question, he looked up a little, glancing at him. "Your makeup would melt when you start perspiring. Aren't all girls quite worried about this?"

Lin Mu blinked. He seemed to have understood, but also not, and so he could only sign back vaguely, "Got it."

East Zone was not far from Xiangcheng District. Although the traffic was a little heavy, it only took half an hour to reach the destination. Teacher Ma even specially prepared a little tour guide flag; he stood at the front, leading everyone in somewhat orderly lines.

The wetland park was enormous, over 133 hectares in size. There were fishponds and rivers, and long wooden bridges criss-crossed across the park. The group had come at a very nice time, as the lotus flowers had yet to fade. Blue stretched across the sky, contrasting against the pink and white lotus flowers.

Lu Rong and Lin Mu followed behind the group.

Chen Meihua would often stop and crouch by the bridge to look at the lotus flowers, and so Lu Rong and Lin Mu could only stop and wait for her. Gradually, they drew further from the main group.

Teacher Ma ran back and forth a few times, and finally some-one in front shouted, "Don't disturb the young couple on their date, let them have some time to themselves!"

Embarrassed, Lin Mu looked at Lu Rong subconsciously. How-ever, the other person was watching his grandmother and showed no reaction to those words. Teacher Ma could not help but tease, "What a good-looking pair. It's very normal for you to start dat-ing."

Only then did Lu Rong look towards Lin Mu.

"No." It was unclear what exactly he was denying. The boy bowed his head, speaking to Chen Meihua, "Meimei, let's go. We'll go look at other lotus flowers."

Chen Meihua stood up obediently and went to hold Lin Mu's hand. "Jiejie, let's go together."

As Lin Mu had no choice but to maintain his character as a quiet and aloof young beauty, he pretended that he did not hear a thing and walked beside Lu Rong.

The path was very long, and one bridge came after another.

Sometimes, it was only wide enough for two people to walk abreast, so Chen Meihua walked with Teacher Ma in front, while Lu Rong and Lin Mu followed behind.

As it was not convenient to write while walking, and Lin Mu was pretending that he could not speak, there was a fair bit of silence between the two. When they reached a spot to admire the scenery, they were both looking separately at the view, and they were unable to communicate.

Lin Mu could not hold himself back anymore, and so he signed, "Shall we find a place to sit?"

Lu Rong hesitated for a while. Chen Meihua was again crouched on the end of the bridge; she was looking at a dragon-fly, seemingly entranced.

"Let's go there," Lu Rong signed clumsily.

Lin Mu would naturally be fine with anywhere. He followed Lu Rong to the bridge, and they sat down on the ground not too far from Chen Meihua. Having walked for a little too long, Lin Mu forgot to pay attention to his current character setting, and sat down very boldly with his legs spread apart.

Speechless, Lu Rong stared at him for a moment before abruptly reaching out and tugging his skirt down.

Lin Mu gave him a questioning look.

This time, Lu Rong did not sign. With an indifferent, quiet voice, he said, "Your underwear was showing just now."

For the next half an hour, Lin Mu sat properly, hugging his knees. Halfway through, Lu Rong turned back a little to buy some drinks, and brought a cup of lemon tea for Lin Mu.

Even the way Lin Mu drank was very ladylike.

Lu Rong seemed to smile a little. On his book, he wrote, "There's no need to be nervous, no one else saw it."

Lin Mu thought that it was even more dangerous for Lu Rong to have seen it.

However, there was nothing he could do about Lu Rong having seen his underwear. Lin Mu had always been good at following good advice. He relaxed a little and watched Meimei reach out to try touching a lotus plant.

Lu Rong supported his grandmother, allowing Chen Meihua to touch the flower.

"Do you want to touch it?" Lu Rong turned his head and asked Lin Mu.

Lin Mu did not think too much about it. He went over, and Lu Rong wrapped an arm around his shoulders like an embrace, holding onto his arm.

The tips of Lin Mu's fingers brushed past the lotus leaf.

He found it very interesting. Tugging at it lightly, the lotus leaf swayed daintily very much like a beauty's fan.

"It's cool to touch," Lin Mu pulled his hand back, signing happily at Lu Rong.

Lu Rong smiled subtly, not saying a word.

Another group of people came to the bridge. Lu Rong pulled Chen Meihua up, about to give way. Lin Mu stood up as well, and upon raising his head, he noticed a very familiar face.

Xu Yilu stood very close to them. Today, he was wearing his special glasses. Staring at Lu Rong for a long time, he finally asked uncertainly, "Is this Little Deer?"

Lu Rong was also a little surprised to bump into him. Before he could react, Xu Yilu turned his head and stared at where Lin Mu stood. With an even more uncertain tone, he mumbled to himself, "Lin... Mu?

Xu Yilu was actually not very confident whether he had recognized them correctly or not. His left eye was diagnosed to be at Category 2 for blindness, and his right eye Category 3. When he wore those special glasses, at a very close distance, his right eye could make out silhouettes. Xu Yilu had simply recognized the people based on height, and that was also the reason he managed to guess correctly.

Eyes could sometimes be deceiving. However, like what Lin Mu said before, Xu Yilu's heart could always see more clearly than the eyes of many other people.

Due to his uncertainty, Xu Yilu wanted to lean in even closer. Suddenly, someone blocked his light—Lu Rong now stood in front of him.

"It's not Lin Mu." Lu Rong's voice was inflectionless; not much emotion could be heard from it. He said, "It's Lin Zhao. Our East Zone community has an event today, and we're here to play."

Xu Yilu blinked. Suspicions arose in his heart. However, he thought about how his eyes were not good, and that Lu Rong could definitely see better than him. How could Lu Rong possibly fail to recognize her?

As such, he nodded. Xu Yilu smiled in the direction where Lin Mu stood and greeted him with Lin Zhao's name.

It had been mentioned before that there was no logical manner that a blind person and a deaf-mute person could communicate with each other, but Xu Yilu and Lin Zhao had managed to cultivate an extraordinary tacit understanding between the two of them.

Lin Zhao was also able to lip read if the speed was not too fast. As such, as long as Xu Yilu was a bit more careful, Lin Zhao was able to understand what he had said.

Hence, Lin Mu could only bite the bullet, reaching out and holding Xu Yilu's hand.

Xu Yilu was surprised.

Again, he turned to stare at Lin Mu uncertainly. After some time, he could not help but ask, "Why are you so tall today? Are you wearing heels?"

Lu Rong looked down, his eyes falling on Lin Mu's feet. A glance, and he looked back up and spoke expressionlessly, "Her heels are a little high."

Lin Mu was speechless.

He was wearing a pair of low-cut sneakers today. It was really a farce to say that he was wearing heels in the first place.

Xu Yilu showed an enlightened expression. He was no longer feeling doubtful and nodded, "No wonder."

Lin Mu could not say a word, and he just muddled along with the conversation. Deceiving himself, he pretended that he did not hear anything.

Xu Yilu had come to the park with a similar association from his district. Their association had only been set up recently, and they did not have many participants. Today could be considered the first time the association had tried to gather the people in their district for an outing so that they could interact with each other. Now that the two groups had bumped into each other, they decided to walk around the park together.

Chen Meihua was not familiar with Xu Yilu, mainly because there were only so many people and things she could remember. She had to interact with things for a long time before she could have an impression of them.

Now that there was another person added to their little group, the interaction between Lu Rong and Lin Mu was reduced even further. Seeing how Lu Rong had to take care of the three people alone, Teacher Ma decided to help him out, and he signed at Lin Mu, "Lin Zhao, why don't you walk with me?"

Lin Mu froze a little. He turned to look at Lu Rong. Lu Rong was waiting with Chen Meihua for a boat to travel around the lake, while Xu Yilu was standing next to Lu Rong, holding his white cane with one hand while Lu Rong supported his other arm.

Teacher Ma was still trying to persuade him. "It's fine to be apart for a while. Everyone will have to get into a boat, so why don't you come sit with us?"

In the end, Lin Mu could only nod and follow him slowly.

It finally came to Lu Rong's turn to get into a boat. He first helped Chen Meihua board, arranged a space for Xu Yilu, a only to not see Lin Mu when he turned around. Standing up straight, he looked around and finally saw Lin Mu queuing up behind Teacher Ma on another pier.

Seated on the boat, Xu Yilu asked, "What's wrong?"

Lu Rong crouched down and clasped Xu Yilu's and Chen Meihua's hands together. "You guys wait here for a while. Meimei, be good and sit still. I'll bring *Jiejie* over."

Hearing that "*Jiejie*" was coming, Chen Meihua nodded vigorously. "I won't move, hurry up and bring *Jiejie* here."

Xu Yilu laughed. "Don't worry. I'll hold onto Meimei. Hurry up and come back."

Lu Rong did not waste any more time. He turned and walked over to the other pier next to him. Teacher Ma had already boarded, and he was holding out his hand towards Lin Mu.

Lin Mu lifted his skirt. He bent over, and just as he was about to take a step, someone caught his arm from behind.

The straw hat on his head nearly fell into the water. Lu Rong caught it with his other hand as he helped Lin Mu straighten up, then placed the hat back onto his head.

"She's with us." Lu Rong looked at Teacher Ma from above, saying, "There's no need to trouble *laoshi*."

Teacher Ma looked a little astonished. He seemed a little shocked, and it took him some time to stammer a reply. "A—alright."

Lu Rong held onto Lin Mu and walked back together. Many people on the boat were looking at them, and good-natured teasing was directed at them both.

Lin Mu held onto the hat on his head. His ears were very sharp, and he naturally heard all the teasing.

Without looking back, Lu Rong led Lin Mu all the way to the pier and helped him into the boat. When Chen Meihua saw Lin Mu, she was thrilled, calling out loudly, "*Jiejie*, sit with me!"

Lin Mu smiled at her.

It was a boat for four—two on each side, facing each other.

Lin Mu and Chen Meihua sat at the front of the boat, while Lu Rong and Xu Yilu sat at the tail end. Lu Rong was the only one who was pedaling the boat, and he made it seem very easy.

Chen Meihua kept playing with the lotus flowers and leaves around the boat. As Xu Yilu was basically unable to see them, he touched them even more meticulously.

The water in the lake was cool to touch. Lin Mu bent over the side of the boat, drawing his fingers through the water. Small fish swam past, kissing his fingertips. The surface of the lake was lush with lotus leaves, their rootstalks peeping out from the water, swaying gently in the wind. The blossoms were charming, shyly hiding among the leaves, and they could only be seen properly when the leaves were pushed apart.

Lin Mu looked at them for a while. When he raised his head, his eyes met Lu Rong's. The boy's forehead had broken out in sweat from pedaling the boat, and a bead rolled down the side of his face, falling onto his collar.

Lin Mu took out a pack of tissues from his bag. He leaned over slightly, wiping Lu Rong's sweat for him. Due to him standing up, the boat swayed a little. Lin Mu nearly lost his footing, and he supported himself on Lu Rong's shoulder in his anxiety.

Surprised, Lu Rong held his waist. Pursing his lips together, he said in a low voice, "Be careful."

This position made Lin Mu's face flushed red. It took him some time before he could finally calm down and wipe the sweat off Lu Rong's brow.

However, it became clear that the sweat could not be wiped away in just one move.

Finally, Lu Rong could not help but reach out and hold onto Lin Mu's fingers.

"Just like this is enough." His expression seemed as though he was suffering a little. He said, "There's going to be more sweat even after you wipe it anyway."

Lin Mu could only return to his seat awkwardly. Pretending as though nothing had happened, he turned his head here and there. Many people on other boats were happily snapping photos, and so Lin Mu took out his phone as well. Turning on the camera, he snapped photos of the lake, the lotus flowers and the huge swaths of green lotus leaves. When he turned back, Lu Rong's face appeared on his screen.

Lu Rong's gaze was very substantive, piercing right through the lens and falling onto Lin Mu's face.

He did not seem to mind that Lin Mu had his phone directed at him. He raised his eyebrows a little, his long eyelashes sweeping down before lifting back up again, and he looked straight at Lin Mu.

The stare made Lin Mu's hand tremble, and he tapped on the shutter.

Hearing the sound, Lu Rong suddenly smiled and asked Lin Mu, "Did you get a good shot of me?"

Lin Mu put down his phone. His ears burned, but still he pretended that nothing had happened. Turning his head, he saw Xu Yilu's expression, looking both interested and strange.

Xu Yilu had probably been listening for quite some time. As his vision was poor, his eyes shifted in confusion between the two people. He was not the sort that was very interested in gossip, but everyone loved being on the sidelines watching a good show.

Only after Lin Mu calmed down did he feel that he had revealed a little too many flaws just now. Lu Rong did not sign, and Lin Mu could use the excuse that Lin Zhao could read lips. However, it happened too many times, and Lin Mu could not remember exactly how many times it occurred. If he was actually Lin Zhao, she could not have managed to read Lu Rong's lips correctly every time.

The sun was blazing by noon.

Xu Yilu and Lu Rong had both brought along an umbrella each for shade, on the boat, they opened the umbrellas up. Due to the heat, Lu Rong pedaled for a while and then stopped, letting the boat drift gently by itself.

Lu Rong and Lin Mu did not speak again. However, Xu Yilu was still rather curious, his eyes wandering between the two people until the boat reached the shore. Lu Rong then started to help them all out of the boat.

Lin Mu was the last to step back onto the shore. He saw Lu Rong holding out his hand towards him, and hesitated for some time before placing his hand in Lu Rong's palm. The boy's palm was dry, and his strength was astonishing. It seemed as though Lu Rong did not manage to control his strength when pulling Lin Mu over, and so Lin Mu stumbled forward. Reaching out with his other arm, Lu Rong incidentally wrapped it around Lin Mu, and the older boy essentially fell into his arms.

Slightly shocked, Lu Rong probably did not expect that would happen. After a moment of silence, he said, "Please excuse me."

This time, Lin Mu was not looking at his face, and he could only pretend that he did not hear.

Standing by the side, Xu Yilu had a look of anticipatory eagerness on his face. He clearly was unable to see anything distinctly, yet he looked just like a middle-aged woman watching a midnight soap opera.

For the rest of the walk, Lin Mu was not sure if it was his misconception, but there seemed to be a lot more physical contact between Lu Rong and him.

Perhaps due to being used to taking care of Chen Meihua, Lu Rong was very meticulous and considerate when doing anything. He bought drinks for them all; he was able to remember that Xu Yilu preferred something sweet, and Lin Mu liked tea, preferring it cold. Lu Rong was extremely diligent, and he did not grumble in the slightest when running back and forth. What Lin Mu saw the most during this walk was Lu Rong's back—always so tense, as though he was shouldering something heavy, looking both strong and powerful.

When they were nearly done visiting the park, everyone gathered for a break. Chen Meihua wanted to go to the washroom, and so Lin Mu accompanied her.

"I'll come along as well." Holding onto his white cane, Xu Yilu stood up.

Lu Rong wanted to follow, but Xu Yilu waved him off. "I can go alone; you should rest for a bit."

Lu Rong did not continue insisting. He sat on a park bench, reminding his grandmother, "Meimei must be obedient, and don't cause *Jiejie* any trouble."

Chen Meihua nodded firmly. "Meimei knows."

The washroom was a little far. Lin Mu helped Xu Yilu along as he led Chen Meihua there. Halfway, Xu Yilu suddenly turned and spoke to him leisurely, "Lu Rong's pretty nice."

Lin Mu had a bewildered look on his face.

Xu Yilu was not bothered by whether Lin Mu understood what he meant. He continued, "He likes you, right?"

Lin Mu was astonished.

Xu Yilu seemed as though he was watching some youth idol drama, his smile shining brightly. "It must be, he's really too nice to you. Did you not notice it at all?"

Lin Mu was completely shocked.

When Lin Zhao came back from the Go Institute, she discovered that her wig and dress had been thrown casually onto the floor of her room. Narrowing her eyes dangerously, she picked up the wig and went to knock the door of the room next door, suppressing her anger for the time being.

Lin Mu only opened the door after a long bout of knocking. His face was listless as he looked at his sister.

Frowning, Lin Zhao raised her hands, showing the items she

was holding. "How many times have I told you not to throw my clothes casually about?"

Lin Mu hung his head, signing perfunctorily, "Sorry, I've just came back, I'm a little tired."

Lin Zhao asked, "It wasn't fun?"

"It was," Lin Mu moved his fingers. He thought for a moment, then continued, "I'll wash your dress for you now."

Lin Zhao actually had no intention for her brother to wash her dress, but the other person clearly seemed like he was looking for something to do, and so she let him be.

The chiffon dress had to be soaked first. Lin Mu squatted in the washroom, and Lin Zhao squatted down next to him, signing, "Did you admit the truth today?"

Lin Mu was in a daze, and it took him some time before he registered the question. "No... but there's no longer a need for it."

Lin Zhao signed a question mark.

"In the future, you'll go as yourself. I'm not going anymore."

Lin Zhao was baffled. "Why?"

Lin Mu thought about it, his expression a little complex. "It seems like Little Deer likes you. It's not appropriate if I continue taking your place."

Lin Zhao felt as if a meteorite had hit her in the head, crashing through her skull. On her face was written, "what nonsense are you saying," but Lin Mu did not seem to think there was anything wrong with what he had just said. He was still immersed in his own thoughts, and feigning as though he was unbothered, he patted Lin Zhao on the shoulder. "You don't have to consider me at all. If he says he likes you, you don't have to do anything overboard. Just treat him a little nicer, he's really a good boy."

Lin Zhao naturally would not believe her brother's bullshit about Lu Rong liking her. Arriving at school on Monday, she waited for the evening self-study session to confront Lu Rong. In the end, after waiting for a very long time, Lu Rong and Chen Meihua did not appear in the evening.

In the group chat she shared with Li Zi and Mo Xiaoxiao, she sent a message. "Where is Lu Rong?"

Mo Xiaoxiao was also in the special education class. When she saw the message, she looked around her. Realizing that Lu Rong was not there, she too found it strange. "He seems to be absent from quite a few self-study sessions already. Have you seen him, Li Zi?"

Li Zi's reply came in a while later. "He has been bringing Meimei to the sportsground, they should be talking a walk."

Lin Zhao thought about it and remembered that the swimming pool Lin Mu had been cleaning was just next to the sports ground. Her mood became increasingly more complicated, and she felt that this excuse of taking a walk was very fishy. As such, she stood up and gestured at Mo Xiaoxiao, signaling that she was going out.

Today, An Jincheng still felt as though he was a resistor. He thought the two people should have already made up, but for some reason, there was once again a conflict between the two people on Monday. However, this time, it seemed one-sided on Lin Mu's side—no matter what Lu Rong said to him, his responses were very obviously perfunctory.

If Young Master An had noticed it, Lu Rong definitely registered it as well.

After speaking a few more times to Lin Mu, Lu Rong frowned slightly as he asked in a quiet voice, "What are you angry about?"

Guilty, Lin Mu dared not look at him in the eyes. He answered falteringly, "I'm not angry... Why aren't you attending the self-study session?"

Lu Rong replied faintly, "Meimei wants to play with water."

"Oh," Lin Mu said insipidly, and suddenly he changed the topic. "My sister didn't go to the Go institute today."

Lu Rong did not catch the drift. While raising a brow, he asked doubtfully, "So what?"

Lin Mu shot him a quick glance, thoughts like "Why did you come here to waste your time instead of cultivating your feelings with Lin Zhao in class?" welling up within him, causing his mood to turn sour. He then came to a realization that he was feeling jealous, and he started to wonder who the target of his jealousy was.

At first, Lin Mu had summed up his emotions to having a sister complex. As a little brother, he did not want to see his older sister in a relationship. However, he quickly discovered that even if the person Lu Rong liked was not Lin Zhao, he would also not be any happier.

He could only sigh silently, feeling that the worries of youth were really too complicated and powerful, His heart felt barren, and yet aflame, both like the rain in a desert, and the winter snow in spring.

Seeing that Lin Mu did not speak, Lu Rong gradually felt anxious, and he asked again, "What's wrong?"

In a dilemma, Lin Mu finally spilled it out. "I know that you... umm, something about Lin Zhao. You don't have to worry about me, really."

Lu Rong could not understand what Lin Mu was trying to say. Just as he uttered a word, An Jincheng suddenly interrupted.

"What did you guys say about Lin Zhao? What's wrong with her?"

Lin Mu wanted to clarify everything, but he suddenly caught sight of Lin Zhao standing outside the fence with the corner of his eyes, and her arms were crossed. She was not looking at him, only signing at Lu Rong, "Come out, I have something to say to you."

Lu Rong's brows creased. He glanced at Lin Zhao, then at Lin Mu. The brother was crouching by the pool with his head down, refusing to look at him.

"Wait for me here," Lu Rong spoke after a pause. Although he did not really understand what was going on with Lin Mu, he still quietly spoke, coaxing him, "Don't be angry with me anymore, alright?"

SILENT HEARTS

He Had Once Thought About Ending It All

07

═══

┌─────────────────────────────────────┐
│   ◆   **⑦**   He Had Once   │
│   Thought About Ending It All   │
└─────────────────────────────────────┘

Beyond the rusty fence stood two people. Lin Zhao's back was against the fence, and Lin Mu could only vaguely make out Lu Rong's face.

An Jincheng stopped cleaning as well. He stared at them, his expression a little inscrutable.

On the other hand, Lin Zhao was quite calm. She was thinking about how she could clarify everything without casting any doubt upon Lin Mu's identity.

Lu Rong waited for a while, then took the initiative to start the conversation, signing, "Is there a reason why you're looking for me?"

Lin Zhao looked at him. She frowned, then looked carefully at him again.

If things were just as what Lin Mu said, that this person liked her, then his attitude today was a little too cold for having just spent a day in the park together over the weekend.

Lin Zhao was unlike Lin Mu, who was as much of an idiot in romance as a blockheaded straight guy. Standing in front of her,

Lu Rong's face was indifferent. His was a little too handsome and good looking, and he seemed a lot more mature than other boys his age. When he looked at others, his eyes always seemed to be covered with a layer of fog, deep and impenetrable.

For some reason, Lin Zhao was certain that this person absolutely had no interest in her at all.

"My brother seems to have misunderstood something," Lin Zhao moved her fingers quickly. She glanced at Lu Rong, continuing, "Xu Yilu misunderstood as well."

Lu Rong blinked. He went through his memories, finally recalling Xu Yilu's motherly expression at the end of the day in the park and realizing what it meant. This was obviously a huge misunderstanding, and Lu Rong felt both helpless and amused.

He could not resist looking back at the swimming pool.

Lin Mu did not expect that Lu Rong would suddenly turn his head over. Caught in the act, Lin Mu averted his eyes in embarrassment and guilt.

Lu Rong looked at him a little while more before turning back. He thought for a moment, then signed at Lin Zhao, "Don't say anything, I'll tell him myself."

Lin Zhao raised a brow. Although she was not sure what Lu Rong had in mind, she believed in the principle that the less one spoke, the fewer mistakes they would make. Now that the misunderstanding had been clarified, it was no longer her business.

Done with the conversation, Lu Rong returned alone to the pool. An Jincheng was unable to decipher anything from Lu Rong's expression, and became a little anxious. He stood up, walking towards him, only to turn back halfway. In the end, he still could not help himself. Standing near Lu Rong, he asked, "What did you and Lin Zhao talk about?"

Lu Rong never expected that An Jincheng would be the first

to ask. Pondering for a moment, he said, "Nothing much, it was about the self-study session for the special needs class."

Lin Mu heard him, and he turned to look at Lu Rong a little doubtfully. Lu Rong happened to be looking over too. Their eyes met, and Lin Mu was the first to look away.

Hearing the answer, An Jincheng seemed a little relieved. He watched as Lin Zhao walked away. The sports ground was huge, the red running track surrounding the green grass. The girl's silhouette was slender and tall, and against the red and green, she looked like a swaying flower.

An Jincheng stared at the sight for some time, then suddenly said to Lin Mu, "You clean up the rest, I'll take my leave first."

Lin Mu was unable to deal with Lu Rong already, and so naturally could not be bothered with what the wallflower was going to do. He picked up the hose An Jincheng was using, spraying the pool as though nothing was bothering him as he sneaked a look at Lu Rong.

The latter was still looking straight at him, and with no awkwardness, he crouched down by Lin Mu.

The two people did not speak at all. Of course, Lin Mu did not believe that Lin Zhao came to talk to Lu Rong about the self-study session. However, if he were to ask now, it would make it very obvious that he had something to hide.

Fortunately, Lu Rong took the initiative to speak: "I don't like your sister that way."

Lin Mu did not expect him to say it so directly. His mouth fell open, and he stammered for quite some time, "R—really..."

Lu Rong looked at him, and he suddenly asked, "Just now, you were angry with me over this?"

Lin Mu did not know how to respond.

Lin Mu refused to admit that he was angry and throwing a small tantrum, and Lu Rong also did not press him. After they finished washing the pool, they brought Meimei back with them, and naturally, they left together.

Lin Zhao had become very busy of late. She still had to go to the Go Institute in the evening, and she was usually picked up by Lin Yanlai.

"There have been a lot of strangers outside your school these days," Lin Yanlai told his son when picking up Lin Zhao. "Be careful when going home."

The location of Kunqian was a little far, and there were also quite a number of other schools near it, both good and not so good ones. A few years ago, there had been a case of bullying occurring outside the school compounds, and it had only been settled after the police were called down.

Lin Mu was not the slightest bit worried. "Nothing will happen to me."

Lin Yanlai indeed was not very worried about his son. He left with Lin Zhao, while Lin Mu returned to look for Lu Rong.

Meimei was standing at the school gates, sucking on a lollipop Lu Rong just bought for her. When she saw Lin Mu walking over, she took out a new one from her pocket.

"Candy for you, *Jiejie*," Chen Meihua said.

Lin Mu accepted it with a smile. He glanced at Lu Rong, but the other boy was looking into the distance.

"What are you looking at?" Pulling the wrapper off, Lin Mu placed the lollipop in his mouth. He followed Lu Rong's line of sight, only to see a number of unfamiliar faces loitering around the convenience store near the school. However, since he did not know them, Lin Mu would not go and provoke them.

Lu Rong withdrew his eyes. He glanced at the lollipop stick

hanging out of Lin Mu's mouth and said indifferently, "Nothing."

Lin Mu thought about it and tried to put Lu Rong at ease. "There's a lot of schools around here, and the shopping street is nearby too, so there are always all sorts of people hanging around. However, don't worry. Kunqian has a discipline committee set up by the teachers, and the students are all pretty safe."

Lu Rong nodded, noncommittal. He seemed to not be bothered by such matters, taking up Chen Meihua's hand.

"Let's go," he told Lin Mu.

Sure enough, a few days later, the teachers started patrolling outside the school in shifts, headed by Chu Lin. Cao Zhan even sent a photo in the group chat of the Demerit Kings.

"Did something happen recently?" Li Zi asked in the chat.

Mo Xiaoxiao was not surprised. "The first-year students have just started, and many of them had specially applied to enroll into Kunqian from other schools. For example, Lu Rong and I came from schools that were rather problematic, and so trouble tends to follow easily."

Lin Zhao had been protected too well since she was a child. Other than Sun Hai in junior high, she had pretty much never experienced bullying. Finding it bizarre, she asked, "The junior high bullies will even follow you to your new high school?"

"It's hard to say." Mo Xiaoxiao attached a sighing emoji. "Some people are extremely nasty."

Lin Mu scrolled through the chat after class, his expression very stern. He again recalled the unfamiliar faces he saw over the past few days and called out to Xu Yilu who was sitting in front.

"Little Heron," Lin Mu asked, "can you ask your housekeeper to pick you from school for now?"

To train Xu Yilu's independence, he had been coming to

school alone. However, it was now troubled times, and Lin Mu felt that they should just play safe.

Xu Yilu had heard about the bullying incident before as well. Without much hesitation, he agreed. Of course, while chatting with Lin Mu, he recalled what he thought he discovered about Lin Zhao and Lu Rong, and he wanted to share the gossip.

"That day, when we went to the park, Lu Rong was awfully nice to your sister!" Xu Yilu was very professional as a witness to a show, narrating every detail meticulously. "Are they dating?"

It would have been fine if Xu Yilu did not bring it up, but the moment he did, Lin Mu felt that gossip and rumors were really too harmful. Not only was Xu Yilu enjoying his popcorn, he was even trying to get him to join in!

"It's impossible between the two of them," Lin Mu could only personally refute the rumor. However, as he could not declare that he was the one who went to the park, he could only gloss over it, "Don't let your imagination go wild."

Xu Yilu was not particularly convinced. "I'm not imagining things, I heard it myself that day! Lu Rong sounded so very gentle, and your sister even helped him wipe his forehead!"

Lin Mu was at a loss for words.

He could only say, "You didn't see anything, don't talk nonsense!"

Xu Yilu's expression was extremely stern. "I can't see, but my heart is like a clear lens!"

Lin Mu thought, *stop thinking that you're a lens, you're just like a girl with a microscope chasing after her idol, it's too terrifying!*

The microscope boy Xu Yilu really gave Lin Mu a headache, and the pairing he shipped was problematic as well. Yet he was

very into it, refusing to listen to any persuasion, and whole-heart-
edly devoted himself to the OTP he believed to be real.

Lin Mu himself was also quite worried about it.

Lu Rong and Lin Zhao might not be together now, but what if
they really ended up together in the future?

When he came to this realization, Lin Mu also discovered that
he did not seem to have any qualifications to involve himself in
the future of Lu Rong and his sister.

As such, Lin Mu remained in this inexplicable awkwardness.
Meanwhile, Lu Rong continued treating him like how he always
did.

They were actually a lot closer than how they used to be when
school had just started. They would clean the pool together, as
well as have lunch together. Four more people now joined Lin
Mu at lunch—Li Zi, Mo Xiaoxiao, Lu Rong and Meimei.

It was rare to see the people of different grades eating together
in school. Even more so, most of the people occupying their table
were very good-looking. Although they only spent that thirty
minutes in the canteen, the splendid sight had become a hot topic of discussion on their school forum.

Meimei was now very unwilling to let Lu Rong feed her. She
was now revolutionary buddies with Cao Zhan, and both of them
tended to spill food on the table. Jiang Tianhe would sometimes
make sarcastic remarks towards Cao Zhan, but Cao Zhan ignored
him, and there was nothing Jiang Tianhe could do about it.

Lin Mu helped Lu Rong clean up the rice Chen Meihua scattered on the table.

The rice grains were a little sticky, and it was not easy to pick
them up if they were left there for too long. Lin Mu carefully
picked them up, and just as he was scraping at some grains of

rice, Lu Rong's finger suddenly extended towards him.

He was helping him to scrape the other side.

The rice grains were too small, and their fingers, whether intentionally or not, would often bump into each other. Lin Mu could not help but look at Lu Rong.

Lu Rong had his head bent down. His fringe covered his forehead, only revealing his straight and high nose bridge. Finally, the rice grains stuck to his index finger.

Lin Mu pulled his hand back, his ears burning. "I'll throw them away."

Lu Rong glanced at him. Without saying a word, he picked up Chen Meihua's bowl and walked with Lin Mu to the bin.

Cao Zhan hurried after them.

"Lin Mu," Cao Zhan called out. "I need tutoring."

Lin Mu emptied the plates, answering casually, "Sure. You have half a day of classes on Saturday. I'll tutor you after that?"

Everyone knew that in Kunqian, there were half-day tutoring sessions on the weekends. Cao Zhan was unable to catch up in his studies, and naturally fell behind in every class. Lin Mu wanted to help Cao Zhan, and he casually asked Lu Rong, "Do you want to join us?"

Lu Rong did not answer; he seemed to be considering it.

Lin Mu was inexplicably eager. He quietly said, "You can bring Meimei along... It's only for an afternoon. It's important to master the basics in the first year. Trust me, I'll never lie to you."

Lu Rong bit back a smile when he heard Lin Mu say that he would never lie to him. He glanced again at Lin Mu, giving a nod and answering, "Sure."

With this agreement, Lin Mu rummaged through his belongings and dug out all his first-year notes when he was home.

Working with great enthusiasm, he did not even notice that Lin Zhao returned.

The elder sister watched as her little brother jumped up and down busily, feeling a little scornful. When he was nearly done, she finally signed, "What are you doing?"

"I'm looking for my notes, I'll be tutoring Dopey on Saturday afternoon."

Lin Zhao was expressionless. "Dopey is in his second year, just like you."

Lin Mu could only come clean. "Lu Rong will be there too."

Lin Zhao was a little uncomfortable. if this situation progressed any further, a problem would definitely crop up. Putting aside the issue of her brother cross-dressing to meet the other party, what was going on now? He had stopped cross-dressing already, and yet they were still meeting each other to study? The relationship between the two was really very close, did Lin Mu not find it odd at all?

Of course, there was no way she could clarify this with Lin Mu, but holding it back made her feel a sort of discomfort as well. As such, she could only change the topic by beating around the bush. "I heard that something happened on another street a few days ago. A new student from No. 3 High school bumped into some hooligans. The teachers from Kunqian are unable to cover that area during their patrol. Be careful when you're going to school on Saturday."

"What can happen to me?" Lin Mu was completely unworried. He flexed his arms, saying, "When has your brother ever lost a fight?"

Half a semester had gone by, and the rankings for the midterm examinations were out. Once again, Lin Mu stood steadily at the top of the list, and he was praised by Mr. Yang when he handed the papers out.

However, despite all the praise, Lin Mu still had to complete the punishment he received.

After November, the weather was getting a lot colder. When Lin Mu left his house on Saturday, he remembered to wear a jacket. In the group chat, he reminded Cao Zhan and Lu Rong to bring along their examination papers. By the time he arrived, both Cao Zhan and Lu Rong were already waiting for him in the special education classroom.

Someone had pushed two desks together, so Meimei could also sit down next to Lu Rong. The three of them looked like good, obedient students waiting for class to start, and when they heard Lin Mu enter, they all turned their heads towards him.

Lin Mu was a little tickled. He asked, "Have all of you eaten yet?"

Lunch was not provided for the morning tutoring sessions, but the school canteen remained open. Students could just swipe their lunch cards for food.

Cao Zhan hurriedly raised his hand. As though he was answering a question in class, he spoke loudly, "Yes!"

Lin Mu nodded. He put down his bag and started pulling books out from it.

No one had expected that he would bring even more books than they usually used in class. One book was placed on the table after another, and other than the second-year books, there were also first-year books, as well as workbooks. The blue covers of the workbooks had all curled up from heavy use, and the notes inside were cramped and tidy.

Cao Zhan started to become afraid, faltering as he spoke, "There are so many..."

Lin Mu said, "It's not like I'm asking you to finish them all by this afternoon."

Cao Zhan was quite upset. "I didn't even manage to pass a single subject this time."

Flipping through the books, Lin Mu paused. He held back his smile. "How many marks were you away from passing?"

Cao Zhan pulled his exam paper out. His scores were actually not that bad, and he only needed a couple more marks to pass. Lin Mu silently grumbled that the teacher was too strict—Cao Zhan could have gained at least a few more points if they were a little more lenient.

Lin Mu peeped at Lu Rong through the papers. The other boy was spinning his pen around. Lin Mu coughed, knocking on the table. "Where's yours?"

Lu Rong glanced at him, and then somewhat reluctantly took it out of his desk.

Looking over, Lin Mu saw the marks scribbled in red.

His grades were actually fine, and not as low as what Lin Mu was imagining. Lu Rong had managed to scrape a pass in four subjects, and he did quite well for the three main subjects.

"For a paper of 100 marks, this result is still salvageable," Lin Mu commented. "However, you will be taking exams of 150 marks in your second year, and this result won't be good enough."

Lu Rong pressed his lips together. He knew that Lin Mu was the top student among the second years. The results had been announced over the school broadcast, and it was hard for anyone to avoid hearing about it.

After looking through the papers, Lin Mu did not waste any more time. He placed a few other papers in front of the two people, resting his chin on his hand and smiling. "Come on, try working on these papers first."

The biggest issue with Cao Zhan was not his intelligence; it was his ADHD and his inability to focus. After going through half the paper, he started to get restless.

"I want to play with my bamboo-copter," Cao Zhan said as he looked cautiously at Lin Mu, "just for a little while."

Knowing his problem, Lin Mu nodded. "You can only play in the classroom, okay?"

Cao Zhan grinned.

A strange whistle came from him, and he rolled the stick of his bamboo-copter hard. Lin Mu watched him run around with it for a while. Seeing that Cao Zhan was fine, Lin Mu let him be, and Chen Meihua looked on curiously from the side.

She said, "Meimei wants to play too."

Lu Rong had yet to finish his paper. He thought about it, and said quietly, "Meimei can't run too fast, okay?"

Chen Meihua nodded. "Meimei will definitely run slowly."

Lu Rong sighed, "Go ahead."

Chen Meihua was delighted. Standing up, she started running with Cao Zhan.

They ran around the classroom—from the podium in the front to the blackboard at the back, and then from the blackboard back to the podium. Cao Zhan's whistles were very restrained, and Meimei giggled along behind him.

While teaching Lu Rong, Lin Mu was a little distracted by the noise. He pointed at a question, repeating it twice, and Lu Rong finally could not help but look up at him.

"I understand this question already," he said.

Running past the desks, Cao Zhan shouted, "Fly—!"

Lin Mu forced himself to focus. "What's the answer?"

Chen Meihua ran past, laughing as Lu Rong gave the answer.

Lin Mu could not hear him clearly, and so he asked, "What?"

Lu Rong's lips were in the shape of an equal sign. However, this sign disappeared quickly.

He said something that was unrelated to the paper or the schoolwork.

He asked, "Why are you being so nice to me?"

This time, Lin Mu heard it very clearly.

Cao Zhan was still playing with his bamboo-copter, and Chen Meihua was chasing after him, laughing. As Lin Mu was thinking about how he should respond, the bamboo-copter suddenly landed on his head.

Lin Mu was stunned.

Lu Rong reached out and removed the toy. He rolled the stick between his palms, and again, it flew up high.

Cao Zhan was extremely delighted, calling out, "How amazing!"

Lu Rong reminded Meimei to run a little more slowly.

He did not mention the question again but turned back and continued working on the paper. Lin Mu remained silent for a moment, then he could not help asking, "Are you still coming next week?"

Lu Rong did not look up. Still writing, he said, "I'll come as long as you want me to."

Chen Meihua was the first to tire out. The old lady sat on her seat, catching her breath. Lu Rong packed up his books, waiting for Cao Zhan and Lin Mu.

The sky had turned dark. When the four people left the school, the surroundings were cold and quiet, and Cao Zhan was a little scared.

He said, "Let's take the subway together."

The school was located about five hundred meters from the subway station, and they needed to go through an underground passageway to get there. Lin Mu remembered that some of the lights in it were broken, and it was dim and dark within.

Lin Mu consoled him, "Don't be scared, we'll walk together."

"I'm not scared," Cao Zhan immediately refuted, but his actions were the complete opposite of his words. "I want to hold hands."

Lin Mu had no other choice. Before entering the underground passage, he took Cao Zhan's hand.

Chen Meihua was also very scared, and she held onto Lu Rong's hand. Lin Mu looked over, only to see Lu Rong watching him.

"You want to hold hands too?" Lin Mu asked. It was as though he had been possessed.

Lu Rong did not say yes or no, but Lin Mu felt a sudden warmth surrounding his left hand—Lu Rong's fingers were interlocking with his.

As the four people were hand-in-hand, no one seemed to find it strange.

Cao Zhan again squeezed towards Lin Mu. With nowhere else to go, Lin Mu's arm was pressed snugly against Lu Rong's. Their fingers were interlaced, their palms like iron welded together.

It was not a very long path.

Lin Mu's thoughts were muddled.

He walked along the dark underground passage, all the way to where there was light, but Lu Rong still never let go of his hand.

Before he went to bed, Lu Rong did a final check on the gas

stove, then went to Chen Meihua's room.

They lived in the oldest area in East Zone. It was a house with a front yard that his parents had left behind. Lu Rong's father had been a businessman, and when he made some money, he bought quite a number of shops. Later, Lu Rong's parents passed on, leaving only him and his grandmother behind.

The Lu family was not one with many relatives. Hence, after his parents passed, there was no messy family drama about fighting over inheritance or other similar matters. At that time, there were no issues with Chen Meihua's health. She was able to take charge of the family and take care of her young grandson.

For her convenience to move freely about, Chen Meihua's room was on the ground floor. Ever since she was diagnosed with Alzheimer's, her temper and intelligence were like that of a twelve-year-old girl. Her room was painted in a pastel pink color, and her bed was piled with all kinds of soft toys.

When Lu Rong went into her room, she had yet to sleep, looking through her new picture book.

"Meimei has to turn the lights off now." Lu Rong sat by his grandmother's bed, tucking her into bed. "We have to go to school tomorrow."

"Mn," Chen Meihua acknowledged him. Her head was bowed, still reading her book. A moment later, she seemed to recall something, and suddenly said, "Don't take too many sleeping pills, okay?"

Lu Rong froze. He kept quiet for a moment before speaking, "I haven't been taking any recently."

Chen Meihua finally lifted her head, looking at him. Quietly, she asked, "Really?"

Lu Rong nodded. "Really."

Chen Meihua smiled.

Due to the incident where a student from No. 3 High School had been harrassed outside the school grounds, there was an increase in the number of teachers patrolling around Kunqian. Chu Lin even personally stood by the road, watching out for students arriving and leaving the school.

Xu Yilu was seated at a convenience store entrance a little further away, waiting for his mother, Song Wenjuan, to pick him up. Perhaps to compensate for his poor vision, his hearing was extremely sharp. The size of the store was about 20 square meters, and he was able to clearly hear whatever people inside said.

"The incident with No. 3 High School seems to have been done by someone who used to be from X Junior High." The person sharing the secret did not hide anything, and they seemed to be a little proud that to know this insider information.

Another person's voice was astonished. "X Junior High? That's madness. I heard that something big had happened there a couple of years back, and someone nearly lost their life."

"Really?"

"You bet. One of the parties even enrolled in our high school. You know that boy who brings his grandmother to school every day?"

Xu Yilu frowned. Groping about, he extended his white cane. He tapped around with it, slowly making his way through the source of the conversation.

"Was it really so serious that someone nearly lost their life..." The person who started the topic seemed a little scared. They quietly asked, "What happened exactly?"

The other person seemed to be recalling their memories before answering uncertainly, "I think it didn't happen to the boy, but to his grandmother. She was pushed into the river by the biggest bully in the junior high, and she nearly drowned."

After cleaning the pool, Lin Mu was getting ready to leave; Lu Rong and Chen Meihua were already standing outside waiting for him. The weather was getting colder, and Lin Mu shivered as he climbed the steps. He could not help but grumble, "That scoundrel Zhong He sure knows how to torture people... If it snows before the semester ends, and the pool freezes, how are we going to clean it?"

Lu Rong saw how his fingertips were frozen red and quietly said, "Give me your hands."

There was a questioning look on Lin Mu's face. He did not think much about it, and extended his hands.

Lu Rong looked down. His palms were very hot, and he rubbed them against Lin Mu's hands.

Lin Mu was surprised.

Lu Rong asked, "Does it feel warmer now?"

Lin Mu shamelessly said, "A little while longer."

Lu Rong's eyes swept past his face. He seemed to smile a little and continued rubbing his hands.

Chen Meihua was wearing a coat. Due to her age, she was afraid of the cold. However, she loved to dress up; on her head was a fashionable woolen beanie.

Lin Mu spoke to her as Lu Rong warmed up his hands.

"Jiang Tianhe bullied Cao Zhan again today," Chen Meihua complained to Lin Mu. "He scolded Dopey, saying that he was stupid, and he even wanted to beat him."

Lin Mu seemed to find it amusing. He asked Lu Rong, "Did he really hit him?"

Lu Rong shook his head. "No, he didn't."

Lin Mu understood, and he was not surprised. Smiling at

Chen Meihua, he said, "Meimei, don't worry. Jiang Tianhe won't hit anyone."

Cao Zhan was originally waiting for his mother to pick him up. However, when he saw Jiang Tianhe at the school gates, he was a little angry, and so decided to go somewhere a little further to wait for Ji Qingwen instead.

Chu Lin was standing by the road. Seeing him walk a little further away, she loudly reminded him, "Be careful, come back if you meet anyone you don't know."

Cao Zhan nodded obediently. "I know, Miss Chu."

Behind Jiang Tianhe was a group of people. The moment they saw Cao Zhan, they started making a ruckus, even wanting to chase after him, only to be called back by Jiang Tianhe.

"You're so noisy." Jiang Tianhe kicked the butt of one of his lackeys. He pulled his earphones out from his bag, swinging the cable. Impatiently, he said, "All of you, go home now, back to your families. Don't stir up any trouble."

He then ignored them all and followed Cao Zhan to the other side of the street.

Jiang Tianhe truly was not going to bully anyone. This was his way home, and he stayed a long distance away from Cao Zhan.

Cao Zhan was really not very clever, and he often got lost as well. When he came to an unfamiliar place, he would take all sorts of turns. Soon, Jiang Tianhe did not see him anymore. His brows knitted, and he scolded softly, "Stupid idiot."

Unfortunately, Cao Zhan could not hear him.

He stood in a dark alley between two malls, staring blankly at the group of people gathering at the end of the alley.

A man with hair bleached yellow was the first to spot him. He yelled, "What are you looking at?!"

Cao Zhan trembled. Without thinking, he hugged his school-bag tightly, his eyes falling to those people's feet. There seemed to be some people kneeling there, and a boy wearing an unfamiliar school uniform was filming the scene with his phone.

"Hurry up, take your money out." There was a tall boy behind the yellow-haired boy. His back faced Cao Zhan, and he kicked the people on the ground. "Forget about the bunch of poor kids in No. 3 High School. No. 6 must have some money, right?"

The yellow-haired boy looked at Cao Zhan with narrowed eyes, then suddenly nudged the boy with the phone. "Look at his uniform. Is that Kunqian?"

The person filming looked up. He studied Cao Zhan carefully, then started to laugh. "It really is. They've been clamping down pretty hard recently, and we've been unable to get our hands on any one of them. Imagine, we spent so much effort for nothing, only to have the prey walk here himself."

The tall one seemed to not have heard them, and he was still kicking the two people on the ground. Hearing the cries, Cao Zhan could not endure any longer. He raised his voice, his words trembling. "Y-you shouldn't hit people."

Surprised, the yellow-haired boy seemed to have heard a joke. "What did he just say?"

The boy filming fiddled with his phone.

Cao Zhan thought that he really did not hear him. He took a few steps closer, speaking earnestly, "You shouldn't hit people. Hitting people is wrong, and the teachers will scold you."

Everyone was speechless.

The tall boy finally turned his head around. He pushed past the two people in front of him, moving closer to Cao Zhan.

Kunqian's uniform was unique. Unlike the usual sporty style of other schools, the boys' uniform was a shirt and pants, with the school's badge embroidered on the arm. Due to his special needs student status, a badge stating that he was intellectually disabled hung around Cao Zhan's neck.

The tall one suddenly reached out, yanking off Cao Zhan's badge.

"An idiot, and yet he still wants to save others." The tall boy raised his hand, slapping the badge against Cao Zhan's face. "Helping out others in need, are you trying to be a hero?"

Jiang Tianhe never thought that Cao Zhan would be so unlucky to meet those bullies, and he even took the initiative to meet them head-on, being a busybody and bringing trouble unto himself.

Cao Zhan was not severely beaten. He was a child of a wealthy family, which was evident in the brand of his bag. After being held onto the ground by the yellow-haired boy, the other two people began to rummage through his backpack.

Jiang Tianhe arrived at the wrong time—they were not done yet.

Bumping into two Kunqian students in a row, the yellow-haired boy was delighted. He eyed Jiang Tianhe, but felt that this person was not someone he should provoke easily.

Cao Zhan's expression spelled despair when he saw him. He even had enough determination to turn his head away, ignoring him.

"Yo," the boy with the phone squatted on the ground, asking, "you guys know each other?"

Cao Zhan's brain really did not work too well. At a time like this, he still denied it stubbornly. "He's a bad person, he always bullies me in school. I don't know him at all."

Jiang Tianhe did not know how to react to that.

The yellow-haired boy burst into laughter. Perhaps he took Jiang Tianhe as one of them, and thus threw a friendly arm around his shoulders. "Are there a lot of idiots in your school? Call some out and let us have some fun with them?"

Jiang Tianhe looked steadily forward as he spoke calmly, "Are you done? If so, just let him go."

Losing interest, the yellow-haired boy pursed his lips. He looked through Cao Zhan's phone, ignoring the missed calls and scrolling through his photo album.

At a certain point, the yellow-haired boy's finger stopped moving on the screen. He whistled, his tone frosty, "That person seems to be living pretty well, huh?"

The tall boy stopped rummaging through Cao Zhan's bag. He turned his head around, sweeping his eyes over Jiang Tianhe and Cao Zhan as he asked, "Who?"

"Who else?" The yellow-haired boy held the phone out, displaying the screen. He laughed. "Lu Rong and that damn old woman."

"Here." The yellow-haired boy crouched down, pulling Cao Zhan's head up by his hair and patted his cheek with his phone. "Idiot, we'll let you go. Just bring this Lu Rong here tomorrow with his grandmother."

No matter how stupid Cao Zhan was, he knew how to differentiate between good and bad. Bad people should not interact with good people, and this was a simple logic that he could understand.

"I don't want to." Cao Zhan shook his head. "You snatch money from other people and beat them up, you're all bad people. If Lu Rong comes, he will definitely be beaten up. He cannot come."

His head hurt from his hair being pulled, and his words were a little incoherent, but they could still be understood. The yellow-haired boy had no patience, and this provocation caused him to swell up with rage. He exchanged his hand for another, and just as he raised his arm, someone suddenly caught his wrist from behind.

"Get your hand off him." Jiang Tianhe stared at Cao. Even lying on the ground. His anger had turned his eyes bloodshot, and a vein pulsed prominently on his forehead. "Also, don't call him an idiot. You're the fucking idiot, get it?"

Jiang Tianhe was not Cao Zhan, and he had already informed Chu Lin before coming over. According to his original plan, there was no need for him to be a hero; all he had to do was wait for help to arrive and deal with these hooligans.

However, the situation changed rapidly. Seeing someone grabbing the fool's hair and pressing him down to the ground, the heroic warrior in his head burst out of him.

Cao Zhan was dumbfounded watching this fight of one versus three.

Not because of how impressive Jiang Tianhe was, but because Cao Zhan had not expected that he would be so badly beaten.

The tall one and the yellow haired boy did not hold back on their hits, their first punches already drawing blood. Pressing his nose, before Jiang Tianhe could steady himself, a kick from the yellow haired boy left him on the ground.

"I thought he'd be much better than this." The boy filming held his phone up, laughing non-stop. "Turns out, he's just a weakling."

At first, Cao Zhan did not react. He was still shocked over how Jiang Tianhe was being beaten up. Finally, he caught up with the situation, and he lunged over onto Jiang Tianhe, shielding him from the tall one and the yellow haired boy as he shouted, "Stop hitting him!"

Protecting his head, Jiang Tianhe tried to push Cao Zhan to the side. Just as the yellow-haired boy was about to give them a few more kicks, Chu Lin's roar came from the entrance of the alley. "Stop, all of you!"

Cao Zhan sobbed, holding onto Jiang Tianhe and refusing to let go. The yellow haired boy and the tall one fled, dragging along the other boy who was still filming.

Jiang Tianhe pushed himself up, wanting to chase after them. Cao Zhan refused to let him go. "You're bleeding already!"

Jiang Tianhe's response was not very nice. "Let go! If not, I'll hit you!"

"You won't be able to win me in a fight!" Now, Cao Zhan was not the slightest bit afraid of him. Clumsily, he wiped at the blood dripping out of Jiang Tianhe's nose, his tears pouring down his face.

"You're not impressive at all," Cao Zhan complained.

Jiang Tianhe had no response to that.

"You've always been so fierce to me, a—and you always bully me."

With a dark expression, Jiang Tianhe forced his words through gritted teeth. "Shut up!"

It took a few moments before Cao Zhan finally recalled the phrase he wanted to use. Crying as he hiccupped, he stammered, "T—this is called—it's called 'impotent rage'!"

Jiang Tianhe was dumbfounded.

Chu Lin called the police. With the aim of "killing all and sparing none," she did not plan on letting any single one of the bullies off. Jiang Tianhe was brought back to the infirmary in Kunqian, and Cao Zhan's mother, Ji Qingwen, had also arrived. With great ceremony, she thanked Jiang Tianhe for being a good Samaritan, and she seemed as though she was about to present him with a silk banner.

Jiang Tianhe blushed a bright red from the praises, cotton wool still stuffed in his nose. The school doctor asked him to lift his head and saw blood still seeping out through the cotton wool.

The police collected the evidence to file on record. Both Cao Zhan and Jiang Tianhe needed to make a statement, and when one of the policemen saw the bruises on Jiang Tianhe's face, he smiled, praising and calling him a young hero.

Jiang Tianhe had no choice but to accept the compliment.

This matter definitely had to be publicized positively, and Jiang Tianhe was commended the next day through the school broadcast system. He tried to conceal and hide his face, but many people still came asking.

His lackeys could not wait to brag about it to the world.

"Our boss is certainly that impressive!"

"It was 1 vs 10!"

"Injured? So what if he was injured? Go fight ten people yourself and see! Your arms and legs will definitely be broken!"

"Our boss only has such a small injury on his face!"

Jiang Tianhe wanted nothing more but to seal their mouths shut. As for Cao Zhan, who knew the truth, he did not let it slip.

However, Lu Rong came over during the afternoon break.

With Chen Meihua, he stood outside the door of Class Three. Jiang Tianhe, who was sitting at the back, paused when he saw him, then kicked Cao Zhan's chair in front of him.

A beat slow, Cao Zhan looked up. When he saw Lu Rong, his

eyes rounded as he said, "Ah."

"What are you ah-ing about?" Jiang Tianhe stood up impatiently. He tugged at Cao Zhan. "Let's talk outside."

Cao Zhan and Lu Rong could not be considered familiar with each other, but he was familiar with Chen Meihua. Their friendship was deep, the sort that would hold each other's hands when they meet. He still remembered what the yellow haired boy and the tall one said yesterday, and he looked cautiously at Lu Rong, "You know them?"

Lu Rong was rather expressionless. He said succinctly, "We were junior high classmates."

Jiang Tianhe folded his arms, a rare solemn expression on his face. "Exactly how big is your enmity for them to come looking for you even in high school?"

Cao Zhan also wanted to ask this question. Since Jiang Tianhe asked it first, he hurriedly nodded. "They're really fierce, don't go looking for them."

Lu Rong looked at him. "Even if I don't look for them, they'll come to me."

Jiang Tianhe frowned. "Why?"

Lu Rong did not answer.

Cao Zhan consoled him, "Miss Chu has called the police already. They'll definitely be able to catch the bad people. By then, you don't have to be scared anymore."

Jiang Tianhe laughed. "What's the point in catching them? They're only just sixteen, and they did not snatch a lot of money, their only crime was bullying students. They won't be sent to juvie, and even if they were kicked out of school, they'll only be more audacious and unbridled. By then they'll be able to find you at any time." He rattled everything off like a machine gun, then asked again, "Why would you have any interactions with people like that in the past? Did they bully you?"

"They bullied Meimei." Chen Meihua, who had been playing with her beanie, suddenly looked up. On her wrinkled face was a slightly naïve expression, and her voice was soft and weak. "They bullied Meimei, then asked Rongrong for money. If Rongrong gave them the money, they wouldn't bully Meimei anymore. Rongrong was small, and he couldn't win them in a fight. Later on, they asked for more and more money. Rongrong could not give it, and they pushed Meimei into the river."

"Meimei doesn't like water." The old lady hugged herself, sniffling a little pitifully. "The water is too cold."

Some pasts could not be recounted, but also could not be forgotten.

In junior high, Lu Rong would carry a lot of money on him. It hadn't been for spending, but for "offerings" to those who had malicious intentions towards him.

He'd reported it to the teachers before, and he'd fought them as well, but these methods had all been useless.

Those people hadn't been afraid of getting kicked out of school. The one threat they'd used against him the most was, "It's even better if we're kicked out. We'll be able to stay outside your house every day and play with that old woman."

However, Lu Rong could not withdraw from school. Not only could he not withdraw, he had to study hard as well. He had to take Chen Meihua away and leave that bog. He wasn't alone; he had his grandmother. Even when fighting, he hadn't dared to give his all. If something happened to him, what would happen to Meimei?

The day Chen Meihua had been pushed into Hucheng River had been the coldest day of the winter. Even in the south of China, the rivers were nearly frozen. Lu Rong had rushed to the riverbank, not even hesitating before he'd jumped in to save her. When he'd resurfaced with Chen Meihua, a sudden thought had crossed his mind—he might as well just die with his grandmother like this.

In the piercing cold water, he'd looked up at the people who had been making fun of him.

Again and again, he'd wondered if it would be better if he just died like that.

His grandmother would no longer suffer from the disease; she would no longer lose control of her most basic faculties.

Every day, he was fearful of going to school; he was tired of trying to find his grandmother; tired of fighting; and tired of enduring both ridicule and disdain.

He was unable to see anything good, or anyone nice.

He was bogged down in the mud, getting dragged down, never able to climb back out.

When the water level had reached above his nose, Lu Rong had finally been dragged up on shore by several people. Chen Meihua had been both cold and scared, crying so hard that she could not breathe. She had not known that she'd nearly just died in the river with her grandson.

Lu Rong had lain on the shore for a very long time. Finally, he'd stood up, carrying his grandmother on his back.

That night, snow had begun to fall. Carrying Chen Meihua on his back, Lu Rong had walked aimlessly. He'd walked for very, very long time, not knowing where he should go. In the end, he'd been brought back to a police station by a police patrol.

After the incident blew up, the school had finally taken anti-bullying measures. Lu Rong had experienced a rare tranquility for the last half of his semester. He'd gotten into Kunqian, and then he'd brought Meimei to the community sessions for handicapped people in East Zone during the summer holidays.

Lu Rong never bumped into those who bullied him in junior high again.

But occasionally, he would still think about dying.

He would think about the ice-cold river and the endless road that snowy night.

Until later, when he'd met Lin Mu, who'd been dressed up as Lin Zhao.

The hot summer breeze had blown across his face. There'd been shadows cast by trees and cicadas chirping noisily.

Seated on a bench, that person had smiled at him. He'd then held his hand out, waving his fingers before tapping lightly on his forehead twice.

"Not anymore," he'd signed at Lu Rong.

SILENT HEARTS

08 The World
Is Limitless

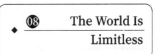

08 The World Is Limitless

Regarding the bullying incidents outside of school, even with police involvement, it was not easy for the case to be decided. Just like what Jiang Tianhe said, these people were sixteen and under-aged, and the amount of money they had taken was less than the punishable amount. Even with the bullying, the injuries of their victims were not severe to the point that they could be charged with battery. As such, all the police wanted to do was to calm the matter down.

However, Chu Lin was unwilling to let it go just like that.

The police suggested a compromise, arranging for auxiliary police to patrol the area. For this, Kunqian called for a meeting among the schools, assembling all the heads to consult over this issue of bullying. However, the attitudes of each school were very obviously different, and from start until end, everyone was in a stalemate.

Chu Lin exploded in Zhong He's office, and Zhong He was helpless as well.

"You can't expect all teachers to be like you, seeing every student as their child." Zhong He adjusted his glasses. He was very perceptive and open-minded. "For the school to only be responsible for the students' safety within the school, it is in accordant to the rules. Coming to school and leaving the school are the responsibilities of the students and parents, this is also not wrong. "

Chu Lin shot him a look, taunting him, "This is what you think too, right?"

Zhong He did not speak. He was not angry, only saying, "We have a lot of students and teachers, we'll definitely find another way."

Anger flared up within Chu Lin, and she responded rather rudely, "What way?"

Zhong He drank his tea, his voice calm. "Fighting and matters like this, isn't it just strength in numbers?"

Chu Lin was speechless.

Every school had its good and bad students. As the principal, this was something Zhong He was very certain about. He cared about reputation and the benefits that came along with it, and of course he liked to preach to students about collective achievements. During every morning exercise, he would preach; during every week's flag raising ceremony, he would preach; and this could also be seen from how the school held all sorts of events every month. Zhong He developed the school like a business, instilling education and culture into them like force-feeding a duck. This was also why the students did not like him.

In Lin Mu's words, studying was already like being in the depths of hell, yet such a school culture still had to be forced upon them with such great effort. Students were human beings, not robots. There was no reason for students to slog for the school without getting paid.

However, what most of the students did not realize was that over the years, Kunqian's school culture had been subtly instilled in everyone. When the school was in peril, the students knew that their unity was their strength, and they were willing to give their all to come out top.

The school first contacted the parents. For parents of special needs students, they would try their best to pick them up if they could do so; for those who could not, Chu Lin tried her best to arrange for teachers to send them home. With An Jincheng as the representative, the students too formed themselves into groups. The usual disharmony on the school forum had also vanished. Everyone had the mindset that "the only ones allowed to bully our students are us, not students from other schools." The school board had posted a message about travelling safely, and, every day, the ordinary students could apply to be a volunteer and partner with special needs students or any other students who wanted a buddy walking to and from school.

The biggest group came from Class Four of the first-year students, who came and left school together. The boys took charge of accompanying the girls. They set a location to gather, and they were very orderly.

As this momentum grew larger, becoming a very eye-catching scene, the topic of "travelling safely" was reported on the city's newspapers. Zhong He, of course, would not give up this chance for free publicity, and he also pushed out more recommendations and advertisements for the school. Naturally, the school spirit was now on the rise as well, and Kunqian became even more famous throughout the city.

The group chat of the Demerit Kings also heard about these matters. During this period, Cao Zhan did not go to school and back home alone, but was accompanied by his mother, Ji Qingwen. Jiang Tianhe even received a silk banner that had been personally ordered by Ji Qingwen, and he no longer dared continue stirring up trouble in class. After all, his weakness was in the hands of Cao Zhan, and he still wanted his dignity!

Lin Mu was very vicious, kicking him when he was down. "You really fought ten people by yourself? You're that impressive?"

Jiang Tianhe had no reply.

"It's understandable that you got beaten so badly, really." Lin Mu continued digging at him leisurely. "I'd also have problems fighting ten people myself."

Jiang Tianhe roared in the chat. "Fight them first before saying anything! Useless!"

Cao Zhan sent an image: "impotent rage.gif."

Jiang Tianhe exploded. "Where did you get this reaction image from?!"

Lin Mu responded, "Hahahahahahahaha!"

Lu Rong sent Lin Mu a private message after class. "How did you know Jiang Tianhe can't fight?"

Lin Mu's reply came quickly. "I've known since the first time we played basketball. His lower body is too weak, he's useless."

"And your lower body is strong?"

Lin Mu gloated, "Watch carefully, and you'll know!"

Ever since Xu Yilu heard about what happened to Lu Rong in junior high, his gaze towards him was unknowingly filled with care and concern. Unfortunately, his vision was poor. No matter who he looked at, it was as though he was looking at air. Other than his eyes lingering on a spot for a slightly longer time, not much emotion could be deciphered from them.

Of course, he was also very enthusiastic about gossip, automatically adding Lin Mu into a gossip chat of two.

"You must tell your sister about this." Xu Yilu had unshakeable faith in the "Zhao-Lu" pairing he shipped, conscientiously doing what a fan would do. "Let Lin Zhao console Lu Rong properly."

The first time Lin Mu heard about the incident. he was naturally furious. He wanted nothing more than to drag out the yellow-haired boy and the tall one who had beaten up Jiang Tianhe, then teach them what the rules were, and what it meant by propriety and decency! However, with Xu Yilu stirring the pot, Lin Mu was still angry, but also amused, finding it both funny and annoying.

"Don't tell anyone else about this," he reminded the little heron. "He might be embarrassed about it."

Xu Yilu nodded, his expression saying that he would protect his ship with all his life. "Of course I won't go around spreading it, it's nothing good to share."

Lin Mu snorted, his expression was icy as he spoke through gritted teeth, "I have to find these people out."

Xu Yilu got a shock. "Why are you looking for them? Don't fight, even Jiang Tianhe couldn't beat them. You'd definitely get beaten up."

Lin Mu responded, "Jiang Tianhe is Jiang Tianhe. It's expected that he can't beat them. How can I ever lose to them?"

Xu Yilu blinked, clearly not convinced.

"I have Sun Hai as well." Lin Mu found an excuse to stop Xu Yilu. "Don't worry, I won't let them find trouble for Lu Rong anymore."

Xu Yilu considered it. He seemed to find it reasonable, and he exuded the aura of having discovered that Lin Mu was also a fan of the "Zhao-Lu" ship. "That's right! You have to protect Lin Zhao and Lu Rong well! I will keep supporting you!"

Lin Mu was left speechless.

The "travelling safely" movement had, within a couple of months, becom one of Kunqian's customs. Seeing its effectiveness, other schools in the area also followed, and the results were excellent.

Now, Lu Rong travelled with the fixed group of Lin Mu, Sun Hai and Jiang Tianhe. Mo Xiaoxiao and Li Zi were with some other boys from their class, and they would periodically update each other in the chat of Demerit Kings.

"Someone seemed to have seen the yellow-haired boy," Li Zi sent a message in the chat after school, attaching the location.

Having been beaten up by them before, Jiang Tianhe replied with no hesitation, "Just avoid them."

Sun Hai was unbothered. He looked at Lin Mu, who had already opened the map on his phone and was looking at the location.

Sun Hai asked after a moment, "What do you want to do?"

Lin Mu was expressionless, his tone indifferent, "Nothing."

Sun Hai choked. "You're going out to look for trouble?"

Lin Mu eyed him, speaking leisurely, "What if I say yes?"

Lu Rong was currently buying candy for Chen Meihua in the convenience store. The weather had now turned cold, and so he did not allow his grandmother to eat any more ice cream. Because of this, Meimei had thrown a few tantrums.

Jiang Tianhe glanced at Lu Rong, a little disapproving. "Meimei is here, don't stir up trouble."

"You think I'm you?" Lin Mu said frankly. He raised his chin towards Lu Rong. "You guys stay with him; I'll go look for them. If Little Deer asks where I am, just tell him I have something on and had to leave first. Be careful of what you say, don't leak anything out."

Done speaking, Lin Mu turned on his navigation app. The location was five hundred meters away, and he would definitely still be able to catch them even if he walked there.

As soon as he left, Sun Hai panicked. He sighed loudly, "I'm scared he can't handle it alone. You stay here, hide it from them!"

Jiang Tianhe was left all alone, not knowing what to do.

How was he going to hide this?! Lu Rong was in the group chat too! Did the blood rush up into these two people's heads and shut off their brains?!

In terms of *wuxia* novel tropes, Lin Mu was now out to seek revenge.

The navigation app was fairly accurate, leading him to a KFC along a busy street nearby. Entering the restaurant, Lin Mu's eyes swept across the tables, and he saw the yellow-haired boy and the tall boy sitting in the dining area.

Thanks to the police who provided the images of the bullies after Jiang Tianhe was beaten up, he was able to recognize them immediately. Kunqian did not care about their privacy in the slightest, putting up posters and images of them on the school noticeboard, asking all the teachers and students to remain vigilant.

The yellow-haired boy was very garish looking. His eyes lingered on Lin Mu's Kunqian uniform, then turned to speak to the tall boy. Lin Mu walked to the counter and ordered a large coke and medium fries, then lifted the tray with a hand and sat next to the two of them. Not too long later, the boy who was previously filming the incident also arrived.

Lin Mu sat there motionless. He twiddled a french fry in his hand, removing the lid of his cup with another hand.

The yellow-haired boy said something to the tall boy, and the boy filming suddenly took his phone out, secretly aiming it at Lin Mu. Drinking his coke, Lin Mu looked over deliberately.

He asked, "Why are you taking my photo?"

The boy holding up his phone froze, probably not expecting that Lin Mu would discover what they were doing so quickly. However, he had the yellow-haired boy and the tall one here as backup, and there was no need for him to feel guilty at all. With a devil-may-care attitude, he asked, "So what if I took your photo? Are you a superstar? Am I not allowed to take any photos?"

Lin Mu pointed at him, speaking indifferently, "Delete it."

The boy with the phone frowned, as though he was not used to people speaking to him like that. His expression was dark as he said, "What if I won't?"

Lin Mu gave a small smile. Without saying a word, he poured his coke over the boy's head.

There were not many people in the KFC, so their actions did not garner much attention. After emptying his cup, Lin Mu behaved as though nothing had happened, returning to finish the rest of his fries.

"Are you deleting it?" He calmly asked again. "If not, I'll throw your phone away."

The scene descended into silence.

From the side, the yellow-haired boy finally spoke up. "You're pretty good-looking, yet your temper's really bad."

Lin Mu finally looked directly at him. He again smiled, saying, "I do have a pretty bad temper, but at least I'm better than you. Your heart is just too filthy."

By the time Sun Hai arrived, Lin Mu and the three people were no longer in the KFC. It was not difficult to find them along the busy streets. There were only a few alleys around the area, and as a bully himself, Sun Hai naturally was aware which location was best to teach others a lesson.

He quickly went through the alleys and finally found them at the end of one with an abandoned pond.

Lin Mu's schoolbag had been tossed to the side, and his sleeves were pushed up above his elbows. The boy with the phone was still holding it up, but his face was covered in tears. It seemed like he was being forced to film, and while filming, he was crying.

The yellow-haired boy was kneeling, holding his schoolbag above his head. Signs of crying could be seen on his face, but perhaps he thought it was too shameful, so he had already stopped.

Lin Mu was not done yet. Grabbing the head of the tall boy, he shoved it into that disgusting pond. No one knew how many days the water had been lying stagnant there. Even standing a distance away, Sun Hai could still smell the stink.

"Is it cold?" Holding the boy's head down, Lin Mu asked. "Do you know what it's like to fall into the water now? I'm already very kind to you, letting only your head get wet."

He seemed a little regretful, saying, "Do you know how cold it was when you guys pushed Meimei into the river? It's now just barely autumn, so the water is still warm. You can lie inside a little while longer."

The yellow-haired boy quaked. He secretly put his schoolbag down, wanting to run away. It was as though Lin Mu had eyes in the back of his head, and he spoke coldly, "If you dare move a single bit, I'll make you drink up all the water in this pond."

The yellow-haired boy froze, not daring to say a word.

Sun Hai did not like to talk much when fighting, but that was not the case for Lin Mu. A long time ago, when he beat up Sun

Hai, his tongue had been even more vicious than his fists. Sun Hai had been taught a lesson in both in flesh and in mind, and it was as though Lin Mu was training the future successor of socialism.

Lin Mu dragged the tall boy out of the pond. That person was a head taller than Lin Mu, but right now, his face was swelling from various punches. Although his expression was stiff, traces of crying could still be seen.

Sun Hai nearly could not bear to continue watching this scene.

Lin Mu made the three people kneel in a row. The hands of the boy with the phone were trembling, and he received a glare from Lin Mu. "Hold your phone steady, don't miss a single moment out."

The boy began to cry softly again, but Lin Mu ignored him.

"Know that you're wrong now?" Standing up straight, Lin Mu looked down at the yellow-haired boy. "Tell me, what did you do wrong?"

The yellow-haired boy spoke hesitantly, his voice as loud as the buzzing of a mosquito. "I shouldn't beat up other students... I shouldn't take their money... I can't bully the aged, the sick, or the handicapped..."

Lin Mu said coldly, "Louder."

The yellow-haired boy quivered, repeating everything he just said at a louder volume.

Lin Mu turned to look at the tall boy. "What about you?"

The tall boy remained silent. Lin Mu smiled before asking, "You want to be beaten up again?"

Sun Hai thought that this person was quite stubborn. Looking at him carefully, he then realized that the boy had actually started crying again. Kneeling on the ground, the tall boy wiped his eyes as he cried, sobbing, "Y-you hit m-me t-too hard, it's t-too painful... I... I want to call the police..."

Lin Mu waited for his sobs to quieten down a bit before he slowly said, "You want to call the police? Do you think the police will arrest me?"

He crouched down, staring at the yellow-haired boy and the tall one, his voice sounding even-tempered. "When you asked Lu Rong for money, and pushed his grandmother into Hucheng River, did you ever think that the police will come arrest you?"

The yellow-haired boy and the tall one did not answer.

Lin Mu smiled mockingly. "You did think of it. It's just that you knew that the police can't do anything to you."

He pointed at himself. "The same goes for me."

"You're all actually well aware of it, and because of your awareness, you can be this audacious, this impenitent." Lin Mu stood up. He looked down at the three people, expressionless, and spoke clearly, "You all know that what you've done will not cause any loss to you, and so you can happily go around trampling on others, worry-free. You are really disgusting."

Next to them, Sun Hai sighed. He turned around, only to freeze, then turned back to Lin Mu with an expression of wanting to alert him, but not knowing how to do so.

Unaware, Lin Mu signaled for the boy with the phone to capture how the other two people looked like currently, and then asked him to send everything to his phone. Finally, he waved his phone, speaking calmly, "The recording of everything you said today, and the beatings you received, is now with me. If you dare come seek trouble with any Kunqian students again, I'll post it online." A pause, then he continued, "Don't appear in from of Lu Rong again. I'm underaged as well, and I wouldn't be charged with murder, understand?"

The yellow-haired boy and the tall boy curled up, trembling. Obviously, Lin Mu was not joking, and naturally, they did not dare retort.

"From now on, I'll always be with Lu Rong. He'll be able to see an even greater world out there, and don't even think about trying to drag him back down into the bog." Lin Mu put his phone away, tucking his hands into his pockets. He stood, the light behind him, childish pride on his face.

He raised his chin, smiling. "He's mine. Don't ever think about harming him."

The things a person said when trying to be heroic tended not to go through much thought. Lin Mu realized that his words had been a little too cringy, and had too much of a delusion of grandeur within.

However, words spoken aloud were like spilt water. He was someone who would pay attention to momentum, and so he maintained his zealous air.

On the other side, Sun Hai's eyes were nearly cramping up with the amount of signaling he was trying to do. When Lin Mu looked at him, he was baffled, but after turning around, he realized Jiang Tianhe was here too.

Jiang Tianhe had previously been bullied by the three people kneeling on the ground, and currently, he was feeling elated and pleased with the situation. He probably never paid attention to Lin Mu's ambiguous words.

Lin Mu's neck was becoming stiff from turning. He finally noticed Lu Rong and Chen Meihua, and his ears started reddening involuntarily.

Lu Rong was expressionless. He glanced at the people in a sorry state, who had been taught a severe lesson, then calmly looked towards Lin Mu. In the south of China, once the weather became colder, it would always be accompanied by a few days of continuous rain. Having not seen the sun for the past few days, Lu Rong's skin had turned more fair, forming a great contrast with his dark eyes and long eyelashes.

As he did not know how much Lu Rong had heard, Lin Mu gave a few embarrassed coughs and feigned unconcern. "I just casually taught them a small lesson. They'll definitely not dare to come seek us out for trouble next time."

Lu Rong watched him for a moment and smiled imperceptibly. He hummed in acknowledgement, then asked, "Shall we go?"

Lin Mu naturally could not wait to go. He urged Sun Hai and Jiang Tianhe to leave as well, but Jiang Tianhe was still taking photos, a little reluctant to leave. Sun Hai landed a kick on Jiang Tianhe's buttocks. "Let's go!"

Entering the subway station, the group split into two. Sun Hai and Jiang Tianhe took the same line, while Lin Mu followed Lu Rong and his grandmother back to East Zone.

He kept wondering exactly how much Lu Rong heard throughout the entire journey, but he never managed to muster up the courage to ask. When they left the subway, Lu Rong suddenly stopped, and from behind Lin Mu came the beeping of the doors, signaling that they were about to close.

Lin Mu was puzzled.

Lu Rong turned around. The station was broadcasting a warning that the train was leaving soon, and to take note of their safety.

Their surroundings were a little noisy. Other than the beeping signal, there was also the racket of the train preparing to leave the station.

Lu Rong opened his mouth. Lin Mu could not hear him, and so asked, "What?!"

Behind them, the train whistled, moving off with a shrill sound. The spinning lights were reflected in Lu Rong's clear eyes.

"I'm yours, Lin Mu." He smiled, and said quietly, "I'm forever yours."

A long while later, Lin Mu was still muddle-headed. After saying those words, Lu Rong had behaved as though nothing significant had happened. Halfway home, their paths had separated, and Meimei had even waved goodbye. Until the moment he fell asleep, Lin Mu was still thinking about what Lu Rong meant. However, before he could understand it, the next day, Lin Zhao discovered that he had again been in a fight.

"You really make people worried." This was Lin Zhao's first time wearing a down jacket since the weather grew colder. Today, she hadn't let Lin Yanlai drive her but had instead decided to go to school with her brother. "You troublemaker."

Lin Mu signed at her, "I didn't lose."

Lin Zhao was angry. "Am I afraid that you'd lose? I'm afraid you'd beat someone to death!"

Lin Mu did not know how to react to that.

In the chat of Demerit Kings, Jiang Tianhe had posted a few shots of the bullies on the ground. Seeing them like this did make one feel gratified, but Cao Zhan was still worried.

"Are you sure you're okay?" He purposely came to Lin Mu's class before the morning exercise to ask him that. "They're really good at fighting."

Lin Mu spun in a circle, letting Cao Zhan see him clearly. Laughing, he said, "I'm really okay, and they're not that good anyway."

Xu Yilu naturally heard about Lin Mu's astonishing battle record as well. As a secret, conscientious fan of the "Zhao-Lu" ship, he truly admired Lin Mu's dedication towards his sister's romance.

Today, Lin Mu was too lazy to keep Xu Yilu from randomly shipping people. He could only hope that Xu Yilu would see the light as soon as possible so that he would not be left disappointed and upset.

After the morning exercise, just like usual, the principal Zhong He said some words. Somehow, he had managed to hear about the incident as well, and again enigmatically disparaged certain students for wanting to display their heroism. However, at the end, he turned the topic around, saying, "There is clearly strength in numbers, but if you insist on doing it alone, losing the fight will be a loss of dignity for Kunqian!"

Standing in the crowd, Lin Mu pursed his lips, grumbling, "I won, didn't I..."

Many people standing around knew that he was the target of those words, and laughter resounded all around. The first years were not standing too far away. Through the crowd, Lin Mu turned to look at Lu Rong. Lu Rong happened to look over as well, and their eyes met through the indistinct faces. Something close to a smile was on Lu Rong's face, and there was only Lin Mu in his eyes.

Near the end of the semester, the second years would be split into liberal arts and STEM streams. However, this did not have much of an effect on Lin Mu's class, as 99% of the students chose the STEM stream.

Jiang Tianhe and Cao Zhan chose the liberal arts stream. Lin Zhao was the exception, and it did not matter to her which stream she chose.

During the weekends, Lin Mu continued tutoring Lu Rong and Cao Zhan. The four of them were now a fixed team. Habitually, Cao Zhan would become restless halfway through the lesson, and would want to play. Chen Meihua played with him, and Lin Mu let them be. Resting his chin on his hand, he pointed at the questions in the practice book and asked Lu Rong to work them out.

Lu Rong's head was half-bowed, and their foreheads were nearly pressed together. At the start, Lin Mu did not notice it, and so he was seriously explaining the solutions to Lu Rong. Only when there were a few times when Lu Rong's fringe brushed across his forehead did Lin Mu then realize they were a little too close.

As such, Lin Mu choked midway through his explanation. Lu Rong waited for a while and could not help looking up at him.

The tips of Lin Mu's ears were burning. He leaned back a little, with no other choice but to repeat from the start again.

Lu Rong did not say anything. After listening to the explanation, he worked on the question, and Lin Mu sneaked a look at him.

Halfway through, Lu Rong suddenly spoke without lifting his head. "Don't stare at me."

Lin Mu was a little deflated. "I didn't... Hurry up and write."

Lu Rong swapped to another piece of paper. The tip of his pen tapped on the paper for some time, and he was a little helpless. "I've lost my train of thoughts, could you repeat it again?"

Lin Mu could only do so.

This time, Lu Rong finally finished the question by himself.

Cao Zhan and Meimei were still making a ruckus, running all

over the classroom. The two of them were very noisy, but it did not distract the two who were working on homework questions. However, for some strange reason, Lin Mu still occasionally got distracted during his explanations.

He would sometimes stare at Lu Rong's sleeves. That was probably a jacket that had been worn for a very long time, lint clearly gathering around the threads. When Lu Rong was working on the questions, his fingers that were not holding onto a pen would twiddle unconsciously. They were long and slender, his fingernails neat and clean, and there were a few calluses that came from doing housework.

Lin Mu remembered the time where their fingers were interlocked with each other, and the feeling of their palms clasped together. Lu Rong's hand had been rough and warm.

Perhaps Lin Mu had been staring for too long, so Lu Rong placed his hand under the desk and asked quietly, "Are we still going through the questions?"

Lin Mu returned to his senses, calmly saying, "Let's take a break."

Lu Rong bit his lip, smiling softly.

Recently, Lu Rong had been smiling a lot more. His smiles were not big; they were small and faint, as though he was concealing his delight. When Lin Mu saw him smile, he could not help but smile as well.

At that moment, Cao Zhan ran over to them, pointing out of the window. "It's snowing!"

Lin Mu looked out in astonishment.

It was a light snowfall, snowflakes drifting down gently. It did not clump up, melting even before landing on the ground. Chen Meihua pressed herself against the window, and her breath fogged up the glass in circles. Clenching her fist, she stamped a mark on the window as she giggled non-stop.

Lin Mu looked at the snow, then turned around to discover Lu Rong watching him.

"Do you want to go out and take a look?" Lin Mu asked.

Lu Rong shook his head. "There's no need."

A while later, a thought came to his mind, and he said solemnly, "You're better looking than the snow."

After the last paper for the end-of-semester examinations was done, the second-year students were like goats released from their pens, bounding about in delight. There were only twenty-odd days for the winter holidays, and when the results were released, no one cared, as they were all eagerly waiting to celebrate the new year.

The Go institute Lin Zhao attended ended later. All the professional Go players had good relationships with each other, and they gathered to have a year-end party. The institute was different from a school, having a little more social activities among them. Lin Zhao was the youngest attendee, and so her entire family had accompanied her to the party.

Other than posting examination results in the school itself, Kunqian also mailed every student's result slips to their homes. When the rankings came out, Lin Mu's name again reigned at the top.

However, he was not very concerned about his own ranking. Instead, he cared more about how many subjects Cao Zhan had passed.

"I passed three subjects this time!" Before the school day ended, Cao Zhan proudly took his papers, showing them to Lin Mu and sharing the good news. "Language, history, and geography!"

These three subjects were the sort that one could pass if they spent the effort to memorize what was being tested. This time round, Cao Zhan's essay was still that of a primary school level, but it was fluent, and the emotions in it were moving.

Lin Mu was obviously even happier than him. The two exclaimed in excitement for some time, then Cao Zhan said that they should go look at the first years' rankings.

Lin Mu really wanted to go, but he was afraid that Lu Rong's results would not be good, and so hesitated because he did not want anyone to be embarrassed. But in the end, Lu Rong was the one who first mentioned his own grades.

The day before the winter holidays, the two people had agreed to go home together. There were nine subjects to be taken in the first year, and they were not yet split into science or arts streams. While waiting for the subway, Lin Mu was still looking through Lu Rong's papers.

His average score had increased by over ten points. Although the total score was not high, it was already a pretty decent score.

"Do you want to come over to my place before the new year?" Lin Mu worried over his studies like a mother. "We'll go through your papers, and I'll help you with your sciences."

Lu Rong thought for a moment before speaking, "I'm afraid Meimei would be troublesome."

"What's so troublesome about Meimei? It wouldn't be a problem with us taking care of her together."

Lu Rong smiled. "I still have to go for the community sessions. Ma-*laoshi* has come asking a few times already."

Lin Mu blinked, only remembering now that there was still this issue. Up until today, he had still yet to tell Lu Rong about him dressing up as Lin Zhao, and this was a potential hiccup in their relationship.

Perhaps because of his guilt, after getting into the subway, Lin

Mu did not really dare speak to Lu Rong. Previously, he had even seriously told Lin Zhao that he would never attend the sessions again, but now, he was starting to regret it. There were more than twenty days of the break, and their friendship had finally warmed up. What if it cooled down again?

Lu Rong did not know what he was thinking. After keeping the papers, he held Chen Meihua's hand and exited the subway. Today, his grandmother was dressed in a flower-print jacket, her silver hair bound up with a silver hairpin.

She looked at Lin Mu, then looked over to Lu Rong as she whined, "Meimei wants to go to *Jiejie's* house too."

Lu Rong was a little resigned. "*Jiejie* is very busy."

Lin Mu hurriedly said, "I'm not busy... Why don't you come over when you're not attending the sessions?"

Lu Rong glanced at him, seemingly unable to reject him, and he quietly agreed.

On one end, Lin Mu had just set a date to meet Lu Rong, and on the other, Sun Hai and Jiang Tianhe refused to let him off easily. Ever since the bullying incident, although Jiang Tianhe still maintained his character of impotent rage, he was a lot more civil to Lin Mu.

Sun Hai's main objective was to copy his holidays homework. For this, he also invited Xu Yilu and Cao Zhan. However, those two people were good little children, and no matter how difficult their homework was, they insisted on finishing it by themselves.

Thinking about the number of people coming over to his house, Lin Mu's head began to hurt. As for Lin Yanlai and Jiang Wan, they were very welcoming. They had always been very liberal parents, afraid that their children would be lonely. They believed that it was good to have more people around, and that children should play together.

Because of her unique situation, Lin Zhao did not have much holiday homework to complete. Once the break started, she stayed at home, practicing Go. In one afternoon, she saw her brother walking back and forth, in and out several times, and when she went downstairs to take a look, what faced her were familiar faces crowding the living room.

Jiang Tianhe and Sun Hai were playing on Lin Mu's Nintendo Switch that had been connected to the television, happily swaying their limbs and swinging the controllers. When Lin Zhao came down, they did not even notice her. Their attention had been completely sucked into the game, and they were one with the machine.

Cao Zhan was here too, waving when he saw Lin Zhao. Lin Mu brought over a plate of fruits, and when he noticed his sister, he signed, "You're done with your Go practice?"

Lin Zhao responded, "I'm taking a break."

Lin Mu handed a plate of strawberries to her, then went to take some drinks. Xu Yilu had brought along a braille book and was currently reading it, looking a little bored. Lin Zhao walked over and ruffled his hair.

"Where's Lu Rong?" Lin Zhao asked Lin Mu. "Didn't you say he was coming?"

Lin Mu signed back, "He should be on the way."

He thought for a moment, then added, "I'll go and pick them up, are you OK staying here with them?"

Lin Zhao waved him off. "Go ahead."

She was a little scornful. "The things you boys play with are really very boring."

Lu Rong had the navigation app in his phone open, only stopping when he arrived at the entrance of the estate. Confirming the address once again, he tightened his hold on Chen Meihua's hand.

"You must be good when we're at *Jiejie's* house." He looked at his grandmother, speaking seriously, "You can't run around, and you must tell me when you want to use the washroom, understand?"

Chen Meihua answered obediently, "Meimei understands."

Lu Rong held his little finger out. "Let's pinky swear."

Chen Meihua pouted, reluctantly hooking her little pinky with his. Before they separated their hands, Lin Mu suddenly appeared at the entrance.

"There you are." He was not wearing a jacket. There was a distance from his place to the entrance, and the weather was cold. The tip of his nose had reddened a little.

Lu Rong stared at the blooming red for a little while before asking, "Are you cold?"

Lin Mu smiled, "No, I'm not."

His breath condensed in the air as he spoke, like a goldfish blowing bubbles. It was quite adorable.

Lu Rong could not stop himself from lifting his hand to touch Lin Mu's lips and the tip of his nose.

Lin Mu was a little startled, but he did not dodge. Unconsciously, he closed his eyes. Lu Rong's palm was burning hot, and it felt very warm pressed against the lower half of his face.

"I brought a gift," Lu Rong said quietly. "It's pastries."

With both his mouth and nose covered, Lin Mu's words were a little muffled. "You bought them from Huang Tian Yuan? What time did you start queuing?"

Lu Rong did not answer. Thinking that there would only be the three of them in the house later, he was afraid that Lin Mu would be bored, as well as that he himself would be nervous. So, he brought it along in hopes that the atmosphere would not be as tense. However, the moment Lin Mu opened the door, Sun Hai was standing right on the porch, immediately noticing the bag in Lin Mu's hand.

"Wow, it's Huang Tian Yuan!" Sun Hai was very excited, coming over and taking the bag. "You can only buy this if you start queuing very early in the morning! This *xuedi* sure is considerate!"

Lu Rong was dumbfounded.

When Chen Meihua saw Cao Zhan, she exclaimed in delight, shouting, "Dopey!"

"There's quite a bit of people here, please don't mind it." Lin Mu looked at Lu Rong, a little embarrassed. "There's no need to restrain yourself, make yourselves at home."

Lu Rong bit his lip. Giving Lin Mu a somewhat aggrieved look, he kept quiet for some time before giving a neutral acknowledgement.

Upon Lu Rong's arrival, the little team of homework copiers and tutees was immediately set up, and Jiang Tianhe handed the game controller to Lin Zhao. Xu Yilu did not need tutoring, and so he sat on the couch with his braille book. Chen Meihua followed along, sitting there obediently eating the strawberries. The rest of them gathered around the dining table, and they even looked quite serious and formal. Lu Rong was the only junior there, with a more aloof sort of personality. Other than Lin Mu, he was not very familiar with the rest of the group, having just spoken maybe a few sentences to them before.

Lin Mu took his homework out, and Sun Hai and Jiang Tianhe fought over it before finally deciding to copy it together. Cao Zhan and Lu Rong were going through their exam papers, and the two of them huddled closely together with Lin Mu. Cao Zhan was even half-sprawled across the table, his head nearly brushing under Lin Mu's chin.

Lu Rong gave him a look. Unable to stop himself, he said, "Move a little away."

"Oh." Cao Zhan no longer tried to push himself forward.

Lin Mu pulled out a few pieces of scratch paper, explaining the questions to the two people. His explanations to Cao Zhan took longer, and often he needed to repeat himself several times. However, Cao Zhan still seemed to not understand, and in the end, he could only rely on memorization to complete the algebraic derivatives questions. When Lu Rong finished going through his paper, Cao Zhan had yet to even be halfway done.

"Shall I take the pastries out?" Lin Mu noticed that Cao Zhan's attention had started drifting away, obviously wanting to go play instead. He stood up. "Let's share them together?"

During periods of festivities, queuing was required to purchase anything from Huang Tian Yuan, and this was even more so the case for the days before the eve of the Chinese New Year. It was difficult to get one's hands on these New Year goodies, and Lu Rong did wake up very early in the morning to go squeeze in a crowd of old ladies to buy them. While plating the pastries in the kitchen, Lin Mu discovered that there was only one portion of *Dingsheng* cake available, and he was reluctant to place it on the plate. Hardening his heart, he decided to just stuff it in his mouth and eat it himself. Turning his head around, he saw Lu Rong standing at the doorway, looking at him.

With the *Dingsheng* cake in his mouth, Lin Mu was stunned, looking embarrassed having been caught red-handed.

Until Lu Rong took the plate from his hand.

Lin Mu awkwardly removed the *Dingsheng* cake from his

mouth, explaining, "There was only one piece..."

Lu Rong tilted his head at him. "You like it?"

Lin Mu nodded. One of Huang Tian Yuan's famous pastries was their *Dingsheng* cake, and Lin Mu's family would buy it every year for the Chinese New Year. However, as the little brother, there was no way Lin Mu could snatch it from Lin Zhao.

Without saying anything, Lu Rong walked out with the plate. The people outside distributed the pastries among themselves, while Lin Mu hid in the kitchen, finishing up the *Dingsheng* cake and wiping his mouth clean before coming out.

Jiang Tianhe and Sun Hai stopped copying and started to fight over the pastries. Jiang Tianhe was truly unable to win in a fight; his sturdy and muscular limbs were a waste on him. Only his emotions managed to fulfill the characteristics of a bully, and the moment he needed to supplement it with physical actions, his whole image would crumble. The others all laughed as they watched them horse around. Lin Mu laughed along until Lu Rong, next to him, suddenly reached out and wiped the corner of his mouth.

Lin Mu gave him a questioning look.

After wiping one corner, Lu Rong wiped the other. With lowered lids, his gaze was intense. "I see crumbs."

Lin Mu stood there obediently, raising his chin. "Are there any more left?"

Lu Rong said no, but he did not remove his hand. Cupping Lin Mu's face, it was not sure what he was looking at.

Only when Xu Yilu's white cane suddenly came between the two of them did Lin Mu avert his eyes, but his head was still tilted up.

Realizing that there were people in front of him, Xu Yilu too froze. Looking carefully, he then asked uncertainly, "Lin Mu? What are you doing?"

Lu Rong let go, and Lin Mu could only explain, "There was something on my face, so Little Deer was wiping it away."

"Oh." Xu Yilu nodded. He found it strange. Why was Lu Rong always with Lin Mu? Where was Lin Zhao? Should they not be cultivating their feelings instead?

However, it was only a thought, and he could not ask these questions directly. Only when Lu Rong walked away did he quietly gossip with Lin Mu.

"Are there too many of us here?" Sensing something, Xu Yilu asked. "Lu Rong seems a little unhappy."

Lin Mu was not that sensitive, but after thinking about it, he was not sure either. "Is he?"

Xu Yilu's eyes widened, asserting himself, "I think so."

The two people's thoughts headed in different directions, but for some inexplicable reason, the thoughts still managed to merge together in a spot. After Xu Yilu's reminder, Lin Mu, too, felt that there were a little too many people, and he started to think about how he could meet Lu Rong alone next time. There would at most be Meimei with them, and no one else.

The group of friends stayed until evening, and Lin Mu again went in and out, sending them off. Finally, when walking Lu Rong to the entrance, he felt a little reluctant.

"What will you be doing during the Chinese New Year?" Lin Mu asked.

Lu Rong thought for a moment. "I'll just be taking meals with Meimei at home. We don't have many relatives, so we don't really go visiting."

Lin Mu had many relatives, but their reunion dinner was usually eaten at home. Lin Mu wanted to ask when Lu Rong would be free during the Chinese New Year period, but he felt that it was too girlish of him to keep clinging onto him.

In the end, they did not manage to speak much before Meimei started making noise about wanting to go home. Dejected, Lin Mu returned home. Lin Zhao caught sight of his expression, signing at him, "What's that look on your face? Are you guys the cowherd and the weaver?"

Lin Mu ignored her insinuations that he and Lu Rong were star crossed lovers. The Goddess of Heaven that stood between the cowherd and weaver of myth existed also between Lu Rong and him. In fact, there were multiple Goddesses of Heaven standing between them; just look at the entire house full of goddesses today! It made Lin Mu angry just thinking about it.

On Chinese New Year's Eve, Jiang Wan did not need to work, and she prepared gifts and huge red packets for her children. Early in the morning, Lin Yanlai accompanied his wife to purchase New Year flowers such as Chinese crabapple blossoms, kumquat blossoms, moth orchids, and money plants. The potted plants took up half the space in their living room.

After getting out of bed, Lin Mu was feeling rather lazy. The chat of Demerit Kings had now been changed to the chat of the Limitless World. An Jincheng was distributing red packets in it, and the normally decent people in the chat were now shamelessly kneeling down and calling him Daddy.

Lin Zhao managed to snatch one too, and she was the luckiest one of all. Lin Mu leaned over, taking a look, and spoke enviously, "You sure have an affinity with him."

"What affinity is this?" Lin Zhao found it hilarious. She patted

227

her brother's head. "It's the New Year, why are you unhappy?"

It was not that Lin Mu was unhappy, but he was concerned about how Lu Rong and Chen Meihua would be spending the night of the Chinese New Year's Eve, to the point where even his reunion dinner was no longer delicious.

Distractedly watching the New Year's Gala program on television, Lin Mu could no longer remain still. Selecting a pot of moth orchids and grabbing some sparklers, he pulled on his scarf, hat, and gloves and headed out of the door.

Sitting with her daughter on the couch, Jiang Wan finally took a look at him, asking, "It's already late at night, where are you going?"

Lin Mu replied casually, "A friend's home."

After reminding him to be careful on the road, Jiang Wan no longer paid attention to him.

Lin Mu carried his bicycle out from the basement, then discovered that the world outside had started snowing.

The contrast of the dark night made the snowflakes seemed even whiter. The streets were empty, and the lights stood a few meters apart from each other, reflecting sections of the street in loneliness.

Lin Mu rode his bicycle. The pot of moth orchids was settled in the front basket, its red flowers swaying as snowflakes landed softly on the petals.

He held his hand out to shield the flowers, afraid that the red blossoms would freeze and wilt before they reached their recipient.

Due to the wind and snow, Lin Mu did not cycle fast. Only after arriving at his destination did he feel that it was a little rude of him to have come running over without any warning. As such, carrying the flowers, he stood outside Lu Rong's door and hesitated for a long time before mustering up the courage to knock.

It took a while for the person inside to come out.

Even many years afterwards, Lu Rong would still remember the thrill he felt opening the door that night.

Lin Mu was standing in the snow outside his door with a festive pot of moth orchids in his arms.

The red petals were dusted with white snow, adorned with translucent crystals, looking both elegant and adorable.

Lin Mu held the flowers out to him, as though he was offering him his passionate heart.

"Here's wishing you good fortune," he smiled, "Happy New Year."

SILENT HEARTS

⑨ **The Dawn
of Spring**

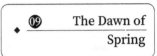

09   The Dawn of
          Spring

Orchids were delicate and difficult to take care of. The pot of flowers Lin Mu had gifted was not very big, but it was growing very well, two blooming blossoms each with exquisite petals. That night, he was not able to stay too late. The two boys accompanied Chen Meihua to play with the sparklers, then Lin Mu cycled home in the dark and snowy night.

It was a busy period around the Chinese New Year. For the next few days, the Lin family was visiting their relatives, and it was as though Lin Mu and Lin Zhao were participating in a visiting tour among all their aunties and uncles. Every day, Lu Rong would send Lin Mu photos of the flowers on WeChat, and Lin Mu saved them all. When the photos were viewed together, not many differences could actually be seen between them.

Right before school started again, it was another round of hectic homework copying. Now, Sun Hai had a formidable competitor, Jiang Tianhe, fighting with him. Furthermore, due to his poor foundations, Cao Zhan reported at Lin Mu's house almost every day. Lu Rong also came with Chen Meihua a few times, but unfortunately, Lin Zhao and Cao Zhan were there every time; one acting as the Goddess of Heaven preventing the cowherd and weaver from seeing each other, and the other as the magpie bridge helping them meet each other.

The days went by speedily. Time slipped by unnoticed, and the new school semester was about to start.

During this semester for the second-year students, there was an increase in the pressure for them with regards to studying. Only after a few days of classes, they had to go through a general examination. Apart from that, Kunqian also emphasized greatly on school events. Except for the third-year students who were given a special exemption, it was compulsory for both the first and second-year students to show great enthusiasm towards the events.

The students naturally grumbled and complained, but this time, Lin Mu had a rare show of acceptance towards it. He was once again the top student during the general examination, his rank above An Jincheng firm and steady. Thus, a new post appeared on the school forum in the new semester thread—"The Years When Young Master An Was Suppressed By The Prince of The Night Forest."

There was a cold spell in March, but the moth orchids in Lu Rong's house were still growing very well. East Zone had organized many more community sessions, but because of her Go finals, Lin Zhao did not attend. After requesting to be excused through official channels, Lin Mu also no longer needed to dress up as a girl and attend the sessions on his sister's behalf anymore.

To be honest, Lin Mu was actually a little regretful about it. He wanted to apply as a volunteer to help out, but he was afraid that he would accidentally expose himself in front of Lu Rong and the others.

At the end of the day, when it came to this matter, Lin Mu became a scaredy-cat. He felt that he had deceived Lu Rong, and he was afraid that once the truth came to light, the other boy would be angry with him.

In April and May, all the teachers and students of Kunqian became even busier. First was the school's cultural event. This year, the first and second-year students organized the event together, holding an event fair with each level in charge of separate sections. As the representative of the second-year students, An Jincheng had to hold meetings during the lunch break. Two representatives from each class attended, and a total of twenty-odd people gathered in the canteen at noon. Lin Mu was one of them. After being forced to switch to another table for lunch, he could only see Lu Rong and Chen Meihua from a distance.

As the representative of the special needs students, Xu Yilu was seated next to Lin Mu. Although his eyes could not see clearly, he could still notice the person next to him frequently turning his head around, seemingly very distracted. As such, Xu Yilu could not help but ask, "What are you looking at?"

Lin Mu glossed over it. "Nothing."

Xu Yilu gave him an unconvinced stare.

Lin Mu reached out, turning Xu Yilu's head around. Then, the moment he turned away again, he noticed Lu Rong's gaze darting through the crowds, falling onto him.

An Jincheng just happened to call Lin Mu's name. "Do you have any opinions on the suggested activities?"

Lin Mu could only look back and ask, "What are the activities?"

An Jincheng looked down at his notes. "Maid cafe, *hanfu* garden party, flea market, a showing of an old movie, an anime display, a game show..."

He paused halfway through his recital, his face very beautiful but expressionless. "These are the activities that would mainly be done by the first-years."

Lin Mu was a little shocked. "So many already? Then what are we doing?"

An Jincheng seemed as though he was looking at a useless teammate. "How would I know?"

Lin Mu stared at his face.

An Jincheng narrowed his eyes slightly, an ominous premonition coming over him. Conflicted, he asked, "What are you looking at?"

Lin Mu spoke solemnly, "We can organize a character tutoring class, called 'Let's Go, Pretty Boys!' We'll offer all students a one-on-one, heart-warming tutoring session, how about that?"

An Jincheng did not know what to say to that suggestion.

Somehow, this suggestion was approved by everyone else. An Jincheng's expression was extremely dark, yet he had no stand for objection. The first-year juniors were all very excited, hinting that with Lin Mu and An Jincheng headlining this activity, they would definitely support them.

Compared to An Jincheng's mannerisms of being a precious young master, Lin Mu was a lot more easy-going. After deciding on the activities, he had already claimed the name of the King of Pretty Boys for himself. Spreading his arms out, he imitated the mannerisms of a wickedly charming, overbearing CEO, pointing at his juniors. "If you want to book a slot with me, best do it early. My business will definitely boom, and I won't be available if you're too late."

The girls covered their faces and screamed, and the commotion was so loud that even the tables nearby could hear them. Lu Rong raised his head, looking over, and Mo Xiaoxiao turned red from excitement after looking at her phone.

"Lin Mu-*xuezhang* really knows how to play!" She could not help gossiping with Li Zi. "Our class leader has announced in our class chat that the upperclassmen will be organizing a pretty-boy tutoring class, and Lin Mu-*xuezhang* will be the headliner! There's definitely going to be so many people wanting to book an appointment with him!"

Lu Rong pressed his lips together, looking a little surprised. He suddenly asked, "He's the headliner?"

Li Zi smiled. "This is the forum's Prince of the Night Forest. With his face, it would be such a waste if he's not the headliner."

Lu Rong did not speak. Lowering his eyes, he helped Chen Meihua pick up the rice grains that had fallen on the table. A moment later, he again raised his head and look over at Lin Mu.

The latter did not sense his gaze at all; the boy was being praised to high heavens by the crowd around him, his smile bright and radiant.

Lu Rong stared at Lin Mu's smile for some time, finally averting his gaze expressionlessly.

The moment the activity of the year two's top class was decided, it was immediately announced on the school forum. Lin Zhao immediately changed the name of the group chat to "Pretty Boy Tutoring Class," and right after that, Jiang Tianhe sent a vomiting emoji.

Sun Hai was upset, yelling in the chat, "Why are you vomiting?! The activity your class chose isn't any better!"

Class Three had decided to hold an astronomy research session of some sort, something that sounded extremely unpopular. It was speculated that there would be barely anyone willing to go take a look.

"What about Xiaoxiao?" Lin Zhao typed into the chat. "What is your class organizing?"

Mo Xiaoxiao's reply came a while later. "We're doing an anime and manga cosplay event, it's nothing new."

Scrolling through the chat, Lin Mu happened across this message. Considering it for a moment, he then sent Lu Rong a private message.

"Who are you cosplaying as?" He asked.

Lu Rong's reply came very quickly. "I haven't decided yet, but Meimei will be Lulu, The Flower Angel."

Lin Mu could not help but laugh when he imagined how she would look like. "It suits her very well."

No reply came from Lu Rong, but the application indicated that he was typing. Waiting for some time, Lin Mu still had yet to see a text, and he found it a little odd.

"During the event, come look for me to play." Since he did not receive a reply, Lin Mu took the initiative to send an invitation.

Lu Rong finally sent a reply. "Won't you be very busy?"

Lin Mu frowned, feeling that the other boy's tone was a little strange. However, after pondering over it, his slightly obtuse character did not understand the issue, and he could only unconsciously try to pander to Lu Rong. "What are you thinking about? If you come, how can *Gege* not dote on you first?"

Lu Rong's reply came after a pause. "Then, would *Gege* agree to only dote on me alone?"

Lin Mu felt that he was completely done for. Lu Rong only

needed to say a few words to him, and he would immediately turn giddy, and his heartrate would speed up. Spring had yet to arrive, but he was already in heat!

Lu Rong seemed to be waiting for his response, giving off a calm and steady feeling. With a red face, Lin Mu retyped and edited his reply for a long time before sending it. "When have I doted on others? I'm even nicer to you than I am to Lin Zhao."

After sending the message, Lin Mu was too embarrassed to read Lu Rong's response. He kept his phone away, distractedly waiting for the event committee members to assign their tasks.

"The outfits have already been ordered." The committee member was very enthusiastic, her expression looking as if she was determined to make the event as big as possible. "Lin Mu, send us a photo of yourself. On that day, we'll print it out and hang it on the door of the classroom!"

Lin Mu was not willing to do it. "Why is it only mine? What about An Jincheng?"

The committee member chirped, "Both of you have to do it, don't even think of running away!"

An Jincheng was wordless.

Although he felt a little aggrieved at being forced to "sell himself," the event, having already been confirmed, could no longer be changed at the last minute. An Jincheng supplied his photo in mortification, and it was hung grandly on the door.

Other than the two of them, Sun Hai and Xu Yilu were also assigned to "entertain customers." The classroom was being well-decorated, looking just like a parlor. All they had left was to wait for the next day to arrive, and they would be able to start their business and receive guests.

There were many students staying after school hours the day

before the cultural fair, and Lin Mu was one of the last to leave. He was a little disappointed at not having received any messages from Lu Rong. However, when he arrived at the school gates, he saw two familiar figures standing there, hand-in-hand, seeming to be waiting for him.

Lin Mu ran over in a hurry.

Chen Meihua waved at him, smiling to the point where it seemed her eyes had almost disappeared. She nagged, "Slow down! Slow down!"

As soon as Lin Mu stopped in front of them, she jumped up and hugged him.

Lifting up the old lady, Lin Mu spun her in a circle. He then looked at Lu Rong. The boy was not smiling, but his eyes were bright as they focused on Lin Mu's face.

"Are you cold?" Lin Mu asked.

Lu Rong shook his head. He had an enormous scarf wrapped around him, but he bowed his head, taking it off and wrapping it around Lin Mu's neck instead.

Half of Lin Mu's face was covered. The scarf was imbued with the warmth from Lu Rong's neck, and the scent of some un-known brand of soap wafted into his nose.

"Let's go home." Lu Rong tilted his head down slightly to look at Lin Mu with a faint smile.

Lin Mu's voice was muffled within the scarf. "What are you smiling about?"

Lu Rong did not answer him, but before entering the under-ground passageway to the subway station, he held his hand out to Lin Mu. "Meimei is afraid of the dark."

Lin Mu gave a puzzled look.

Lu Rong looked at him, his voice was calm. "I'm afraid of the dark, too."

This was the second time they were walking hand-in-hand together.

Fortunately for Lin Mu, half of his face was concealed, and so others could not see how red he was. This time, Lu Rong did not interlace their fingers together, only holding his hand loosely. When he saw the subway station, he let go.

On the subway, Chen Meihua stood between the two people. Using her as a shield, Lin Mu sneaked a look at Lu Rong, and when the boy looked over, he quickly averted his gaze.

Once they arrived at their station, the three people would have to separate. After suppressing his thoughts through the entire journey, Lin Mu finally gathered up his courage and asked Lu Rong, feigning unconcern, "Are you coming to our class tomorrow?"

Lu Rong glanced at him. "You should be very busy tomorrow."

Lin Mu hurriedly said, "If you come, I'll be busy with you then."

Lu Rong smiled. He did not speak, but he reached out and adjusted the scarf around Lin Mu's face.

As always, Zhong He would make a speech before the start of the event. Today, he was dressed in a rare casual outfit, instead of his usual three-piece suit, and he looked a lot younger than usual.

The students were very enthusiastic, and the scoundrel Zhong He did not make any enigmatic remarks to mock some of the activities held by the classes. He emphasized to everyone about having fun, as well as highlighting the hard work that the class representatives had put in. Sharp-eyed students noticed that there were several reporters around the sports ground, and so they were aware that Kunqian would again occupy a space on the newspapers tomorrow.

At first, Lin Mu had thought that no matter how busy it got, he would still have time for himself. In the end, things became so unexpectedly busy that he did not even have the time for a breather.

The main issue that he was also a class representative, and he needed to patrol the school grounds during the first half of the cultural event. Finally, he managed to make his way to the first-year's Class Five, and Mo Xiaoxiao was standing at the door in cosplay, holding onto a sign.

The girl's prosthetic limb was decorated with the flair of the character she was portraying. When she saw Lin Mu, her eyes brightened, and her smile was incandescent. "Lin Mu-*xuezhang*!"

The upperclassman nodded his head reservedly. "Where's Lu Rong?"

Mo Xiaoxiao had been standing at the door, welcoming guests the entire morning. Other than Lin Mu, who was very eye-catching, she could not remember any other faces she saw. As such, she tried to recall for some time, then said uncertainly, "He might be inside...?"

Lin Mu poked his head into the classroom, realizing that he had been far too optimistic. The classroom was dark and filled with all sorts of characters jumping and moving around. There was no way to identify anyone.

Mo Xiaoxiao said weakly, "... There are too many people here today."

Unable to see Lu Rong, Lin Mu was clearly reluctant to just let it go. Just as he was thinking if he should squeeze into the crowd to look for him, he suddenly remembered that he was wearing his outfit for his class activity.

Mo Xiaoxiao gave a compliment at the perfect timing. "*Xue-*

zhang, you're really handsome today!"

Lin Mu sighed, not giving up. "If you see Lu Rong, remember to tell him that I'm looking for him."

Mo Xiaoxiao nodded vigorously.

The crowd was so huge that even phone signals were affected. Lin Mu had no choice but to use the most ancient way of passing messages to find Lu Rong. Standing outside the classroom door for a short while, he was quickly called back by the year two committee. After finishing his patrol, he then returned to his classroom, bumping into Xu Yilu, who was preparing to "entertain guests."

"Lin Mu?" The two boys were wearing the same outfit. On the little heron, it gave off an aura of an obedient scholar. "Lu Rong came looking for you just now."

Lin Mu nearly blacked out, barely able to catch his breath. He hurriedly asked, "When did he come?"

Xu Yilu thought for a moment. "About half an hour ago."

Lin Mu desperately wanted to wail to the heavens. Just as he was about to head downstairs again, a class committee member came running out from the classroom.

"Headliner!" Lin Mu was caught and dragged inside. "You can't just let Young Master An entertain guests alone!"

At that moment, An Jincheng already had a pile of papers in front of him. Like an instructor with a frosty appearance, he was sitting behind the desk with his arms folded as he watched the students work on their papers. If they ever made a mistake, they would have to endure Young Master An's harsh and vicious critique. Lin Mu began to suspect that the students who selected An Jincheng were all masochists.

"Where's Sun Hai?" Lin Mu was still struggling.

The class committee member said heartlessly, "The customers complained that he's too ugly."

Lin Mu was left with nothing to say.

Chen Meihua was wearing the frilly, puffy dress of LuLu, The Flower Angel; on her head was a flower wreath woven by Lu Rong. Like a butterfly, she flitted from the second floor to the first.

As there were too many people, Lu Rong was afraid that she would get separated, so he held her hand at all times. Browsing around for a little while, Chen Meihua remembered Lin Mu. "Where's *Jiejie*?"

"*Jiejie* is too busy, we'll look for him later when he's free."

Chen Meihua was not very happy. "But *Jiejie* promised to accompany us."

Lu Rong tried to distract her. "Then, shall we go look for Dopey?"

Chen Meihua was very good friends with Cao Zhan, and so she was naturally willing to oblige. The two of them headed to Class Three, discovering that the person sitting by the door receiving customers was Jiang Tianhe.

Without thinking, Lu Rong looked up at the signboard above the door.

Jiang Tianhe's temper immediately flared up. "What are you looking at?! Just go in if you want to, get lost if you don't!"

Lu Rong was unable to hold his smile back. "Is your class not afraid that you'll chase everyone away?"

Perhaps Jiang Tianhe felt that what he said was rubbish, and he rolled his eyes as he opened the door for them.

The Astronomy Research Institute sounded very grand, but

upon entering, it was basically people lying down and watching stars. As for the "stars," they were of course fake, created by tiny lightbulbs stuck onto the ceiling in the shape of constellations. However, it was still very pretty.

Cao Zhan had a table to himself to display his craftwork. Among them was a leather keychain with stars on it, and its stitching was very meticulously and delicately done.

When Chen Meihua saw him, it was like the reunion of old friends that had not met in years, and they chattered away for a long time.

Lin Zhao was present too. In front of her was a Go board. Next to it was a sign, and on it was written, "The Secret of The Stars."

"Welcome, sir." Lin Zhao raised her arm expressionlessly. In her hand was another sign, and on this one was written, "Let's play Gomoku!"

A professional Go player lowering herself to play Gomoku, it was a great honor for ordinary folks. It would be rude of Lu Rong to refuse, and so he sat down across Lin Zhao, randomly placing a black piece at the center of the board.

With great seriousness, Lin Zhao put a white piece down.

Lu Rong placed another black piece.

Lin Zhao glanced at him, picking up a pen and writing on the sign, "Have you looked for Lin Mu yet?"

Lu Rong nodded, and then waved his hand. The gestures meant that he had done so, but he was unable to find him.

Lin Zhao gave a look of comprehension. She thought for a moment, and then she wrote another note, "I'm going to look for him once I'm done with the Gomoku session. Do you want to come with me?"

Besides Lin Zhao, Cao Zhan too was also very eager to find Lin Mu. In the name of the cultural event, he had brought along many various handicrafts he made himself. Among them was a card wallet he sewed for Lin Mu. He had been wondering when he could present it personally to him.

"Which one does Meimei like?" Cao Zhan asked.

Usually, Chen Meihua was not very interested in anything that was not bright or glittery. However, there was a little leather bunny that she liked very much, and so she pointed at it. "This, it is very nice!"

Cao Zhan generously hung the bunny on the little bag she was carrying. "Here, for Meimei then."

Chen Meihua grinned delightedly. She could not resist showing it to Lu Rong, and the boy stroked her hair, asking, "Did you thank Dopey?"

The old lady quickly turned her head, saying loudly, "Thank you, Dopey!"

Cao Zhan also replied in a loud voice, "You're welcome, Meimei!"

Perhaps Jiang Tianhe found them too noisy, and he poked his head in front of the door, scolding, "What're you guys doing?! Yodeling at each other?!"

Lin Zhao could not hear their conversation, but she seemed to guess what was going on. She resigned from the Gomoku game, gesturing at Lu Rong to go with her. Cao Zhan followed them as well, planning on going with them.

"Are we going to look for *Jiejie*?" It was clear that Chen Meihua finally remembered again what her main objective was.

Lu Rong raised his index finger, pressing it to his lips and shushing her. He whispered, "Meimei cannot call him *Jiejie* in front of others. Remember, we've made a promise about this before."

There were not many visitors in Class Three, and Jiang Tianhe could not be bothered to continue working at the front of the "shop" anymore. As such, a group of people made their mighty way to Class One.

It was already past noon, yet An Jincheng and Lin Mu's "business" was still very busy. Young Master An was basically blazing a trail—no matter how stern and harsh he was, there were still people eagerly queuing up to be scolded and criticized by him.

When there were fewer visitors, the class committee member would assign Xu Yilu to solicit clients at the door. Lin Zhao and friends happened to come over during one of these lulls, and the only thing missing from the "Zhao-Lu" fan Xu Yilu was the tattoo of "Zhao-Lu is real" across his face.

After scolding a batch of people, An Jincheng's anger had yet to abate, but when he looked up and discovered Lin Zhao standing in front of him, his rage immediately became stuck in his throat. He coughed and coughed, finally speaking in a hollow voice, "Wel-welcome..."

Lin Zhao did not manage to read his lips. Frowning, she leaned a little closer. Her face drew in too quickly, and An Jincheng leaned back unconsciously. Lin Zhao blinked, not understanding his reaction.

As soon as Lin Mu saw his sister, he signed at her, "Come over to my table."

Lin Zhao pointed behind her. "Lu Rong's here."

Lin Mu was surprised. Sure enough, he saw Lu Rong walk in with Chen Meihua. The boy was expressionless when he saw him, only pressing his lips slightly together before he bowed his head and spoke to his grandmother.

Lin Zhao was not here to seek tuition from Lin Mu. After reuniting Lu Rong and Lin Mu, due to her communication problem, she thought that she had nothing else to do here and was about to leave. But just as she stood up her, An Jincheng suddenly moved his fingers quickly, asking, "Do you have any topics you need help on?

Lin Zhao got a shock. Hesitantly, she raised her hand, signing, "You know sign language?"

An Jincheng glanced at her, only to look back down again. Feigning casualness, he signed, "I just happened to pick it up."

Lin Mu had no time to pay attention to what was happening next to him. His eyes were glued to Lu Rong's face as he and Meimei sat across from him. Lin Mu could not help saying, "I even went downstairs specially just to look for you, but Xiaoxiao said you weren't there."

Lu Rong's eyes were fixed on Lin Mu's face as well, as he gave a simple acknowledgement.

Lin Mu licked his lips, asking, "Where have you been?"

Lu Rong said, "I took a trip to Class Three."

Lin Mu smiled, "Little Heron said you came by looking for me."

Lu Rong cast a sidelong glance at him. "But you weren't here."

Lin Mu spread his palms open. "I'm here right now."

From the door, the committee member shouted that time was almost up. Lin Mu poked his head out, arguing for more time. The member did not seem very happy about it, arguing back, "There are a lot of people queuing outside, no one's allowed any backdoor deals."

Lu Rong again watched Lin Mu for a little while more. Just as he was about to stand up, Lin Mu caught hold of him. "I'll go down later to look for you?"

Lu Rong neither agreed nor disagreed, only saying, "I won't disturb you for now."

Next, Cao Zhan entered, even bringing along a pile of workbooks with him. Jiang Tianhe was there too, just like a little hanger-on.

With no choice, Lin Mu could only tutor Cao Zhan as he watched Lu Rong and Chen Meihua leave the classroom.

The April evening gradually grew longer. After 5 PM, the crowd attending the cultural event slowly diminished. Lin Mu did not have the patience and mind to sit down for the debrief of their class event. He did not wait for the committee member to stop him, yanking off his tie and running out of the classroom.

Rushing through the corridor, he nearly knocked down Xu Yilu, who was on his way back to the classroom. After steadying the white cane in his hand, Lin Mu looked down to see a branch of peach blossoms in Xu Yilu's hand.

"The peach blossoms have bloomed?" Lin Mu asked in delight.

Xu Yilu smiled. "They've bloomed right outside the building. You want to take a look?"

Lin Mu crumpled his tie into a ball. Feeling deliriously happy over a peach blossom, he raced down the stairs, skipping some steps. He made a turn, and saw Lu Rong standing on the steps below.

The boy raised his head, his face a little startled.

Lin Mu did not slow down, and the other boy opened his arms without thinking, catching him with an embrace.

"T—the peach blossoms are blooming." Lin Mu tugged at Lu

Rong's collar, so nervous that he stammered a little.

Lu Rong did not let go. Like carrying a child, he wrapped his arms around Lin Mu's waist, looking up at his face.

"The peach blossoms are blooming!" Lin Mu repeated.

Lu Rong smiled. "I know."

"Spring knows too," Lin Mu suddenly said.

Lu Rong blinked. Softly, he asked, "What does it know?"

Lin Mu lowered his head, looking into Lu Rong's eyes as he said quietly, "Even the spring knows I'm falling for you."

To Lin Mu, liking someone was like the sun shining on the beach, a hermit crab finding its shell, and waves washing over it; it was like being in the hottest summer day, a cool rain pattering upon the leaves of a banana tree, the constant sound a lullaby.

His feelings could not be concealed, just like how the spring could not conceal the blooming of the peach blossoms.

While carrying Lin Mu, Lu Rong's eyes reflected a tiny version of him. Lin Mu patted his shoulder, signaling that he wanted to be put onto the ground.

"Didn't you want to see the peach blossoms?" Lu Rong asked.

Lin Mu smiled at him. "I've already seen them."

Holding back a smile, Lu Rong gently put Lin Mu down. Just as he was about to say something, behind them came a person.

Li Zi was probably wondering why two big guys were blocking the staircase, so she casually asked them why.

"I came to find Lu Rong," Lin Mu explained openly. "It's nothing much, I just wanted to tell him that we'll leave together later."

A crease appeared between Lu Rong's brows and he seemed

a little resigned. Turning to glance at Li Zi, he then quietly told Lin Mu, "Meimei and I will wait for you."

Unfortunately, going home together was nothing but a dream. In reality, Lin Mu was trapped by work.

The cultural event concluded with immense success. Their class was the best in "business," and so they were naturally asked to stay back by Zhong He to face the media. Photos were taken and interviews were done, and Lin Mu and An Jincheng were forced to work. Their expressions were both completely dark, and yet they could not just wash their hands off the matter and leave.

Lin Mu had no choice but to send a text to Lu Rong, telling him to leave first and not wait for him.

The boy did not reply.

By the time Lin Mu done with all the interviews, the streetlights were already coming on.

Someone would be picking An Jincheng up, and Lin Zhao had long left with Lin Yanlai. Alone, Lin Mu packed up his bag and ran downstairs, only to nearly collide with someone sitting by the staircase.

There were only a few wall lamps lit on campus at night. The dim yellow glow cast shadows everywhere. Chen Meihua seemed to have fallen asleep, her head resting on Lu Rong's shoulder.

Afraid that he would wake her up by being too loud, Lin Mu subconsciously held his breath. Lu Rong turned his head around, his face half-shadowed, giving further definition to his straight nose and long eyelashes.

"You're done?" He asked in a low voice.

"Yeah." Lin Mu looked at him. "Why didn't you leave first?"

Lu Rong glanced over. "We agreed to go home together."

Lin Mu held back a smile. At this moment, Chen Meihua woke up blearily. With his back facing her, Lu Rong crouched down, and the old lady clambered onto his back obediently.

"Do you want me to carry her instead?" Lin Mu asked.

Lu Rong did not answer. With one hand supporting Chen Meihua, he held his other hand out to Lin Mu. "Give me your hand."

Lin Mu teased lightly, "Are you afraid of the dark again?"

Lu Rong did not answer. He tightened his grip around Lin Mu's fingers, tucking his hand into his palm.

Spring came too quickly, and, as a city in the south of China, the flowers all bloomed gloriously. Although Lin Mu did not confess his feelings on impulse, he was still quite nervous about what exactly Lu Rong felt for him.

As a youth in the throes of his first love, he was impassioned and ardent. Sometimes, he felt that the entire world loved him, and other times, he was afraid that his beloved would scorn him.

For the next few days, Lu Rong's attitude towards Lin Mu did not change. They still had lunch together in the canteen, and they would exchange looks across the distance during the evening self-study sessions.

When the photos taken of the cultural event were published, the school forum again exploded into a discussion on the most handsome boys in school.

"The Prince of the Night Forest is just as handsome as usual." The photo posted happened to be of Lin Mu, dressed up for his class activity.

It did not take long before there were a thousand comments on the post. Even after twenty pages, there seemed to be no stop to the discussion.

"It's not just him, did you guys see Young Master An?"

"Young Master An is truly a beauty, but he's too cold and aloof. This is the style of the beauties in our school. It's easy to offend them, and it's exhausting appreciating their beauty, you understand?"

"You guys have been talking for so long, but why hasn't anyone mentioned Lu Rong from the first year?"

When Lin Mu saw this comment, he finally was a little interested. Scrolling on his phone, he browsed casually and realized that the discussion seemed to have gone a little off track.

"Lu Rong is pretty handsome, but he's not suitable as a boyfriend."

"And the Prince of the Night Forest is?"

"He's better than Lu Rong. The Prince looks more friendly, and he should be quite easy to talk to."

"That's because you've never tried talking to him before. When Lin Mu ignores someone, he's just like his sister."

"It's not only because of this reason," the person who said Lu Rong was unsuitable to be a boyfriend replied. "His grandmother is an Alzheimer's patient."

"It's not that I'm prejudiced, but to take care of this sort of patient, Lu Rong probably is unable to have a relationship with someone ordinary, and he himself doesn't have the time nor energy too. Last semester, there were some girls who confessed to him, and they were all rejected with similar reasons. Therefore, compared to the Prince and the Wallflower, having a relationship with Lu Rong is the most unlikely out of all."

During the physical education class, Lu Rong accompanied Chen Meihua, sitting by the side of the sports field. Chen Meihua's emotions were a little out of control, and she was throwing quite a tantrum. Lu Rong was a little tired, but he could not ignore his grandmother and walk away, so he sat there quietly next to her.

"Do you want some candy?" When Chen Meihua quietened down, Lu Rong asked her softly.

The old lady shook her head listlessly. "No... Meimei wants to drink water."

Lu Rong frowned. He would have to go to the little shop in school to buy water, but he could not leave Chen Meihua here alone. As such, he coaxed, "Then would Meimei come along with me?"

Chen Meihua pursed her lips, looking rather unwilling. However, she still stood up in the end.

They walked slowly. The shop was located in the canteen, and there were not many people there when they arrived. Lu Rong let Chen Meihua pick a bottle herself, only for her to start throwing another tantrum very quickly.

"I don't want to buy water anymore!" The old lady's voice was so loud, causing quite a ruckus and drawing the eyes of the people around them. "You just think that Meimei is troublesome!"

Lu Rong caught her flailing hands, afraid that she would accidentally hit herself. Holding back his temper, he said, "I never thought that Meimei is troublesome. What would Meimei like to drink? How about a yoghurt drink?"

Chen Meihua burst into tears. She was feeling both miserable and wronged, and it seemed like everything upset her. More and more people started gathering around, and she was scared.

Lu Rong hugged her tightly.

None of the spectators seemed to have any intention of helping, all standing there as though they were watching a show. Lu Rong did not expect anyone to understand the situation, but he still felt uncontrollably ashamed and embarrassed.

Chen Meihua was still crying. Lu Rong gently patted her back, trying to comfort her.

They crouched at the door of the shop, blocking the door. Someone walked over, and Lu Rong instinctively wanted to apologize. He attempted to pull Chen Meihua up to give way, only for that person to first hug Meimei.

"Time to break this up, what are you looking at?" Lin Mu's voice sounded rather impatient. "What's there to look at? Have you never seen a dementia patient before?"

Lu Rong raised his head. Lin Mu had his chin raised up, and he was not looking at him.

"Don't go around talking nonsense." Lin Mu pointed at the people still watching. "For all you know, you might also have dementia when you're older. Alright, that's enough, disperse now."

When Lin Mu was done speaking, he hugged Chen Meihua and turned around. His fingers gently brushed past the corners of the old lady's eyes. "Meimei, why are you crying? The little princess isn't pretty when she cries."

Chen Meihua seemed to feel extremely aggrieved, sobbing as she refused to let go of Lin Mu. Coaxing her with a smile, he looked up and saw Lu Rong watching him. Lin Mu could not resist winking at him, then feigned righteousness as he asked Lu Rong, "Tell me, why did you make Meimei angry?"

Lu Rong sighed. It was not clear who his words were directed to as he softly said, "I was wrong."

Chen Meihua refused to talk to him.

Lin Mu could only continue putting on a show. "Meimei, you see, he knows he's wrong. Don't be angry with him anymore, alright?"

"No." This time, Chen Meihua was not so easily coaxed. "He doesn't like Meimei anymore."

Lin Mu burst out laughing. "How could Lu Rong not like you anymore? He definitely likes you the most."

Chen Meihua was not convinced. She turned to look at her grandson, asking him doubtfully, "Do you really like Meimei the most?"

Lu Rong smiled. He thought it over seriously, then asked, "Can Meimei be the person I like second-most?"

Chen Meihua was not angry that she was relegated to number two. Instead, she asked curiously, "Why am I the second?"

Lu Rong looked at Lin Mu, saying quietly, "Because there's someone else I like the most now."

Chen Meihua's tantrum subsided. On the way home, she kept asking who was the person Lu Rong liked the most. Of course, Lu Rong refused to tell her.

Lin Mu bought three bottles of vitamin-fortified milk. After drinking it, Meimei seemed to have forgotten about the matter. Perhaps the milk was too tasty.

"Who is the person you like the most?" Lin Mu phrased the question deliberately.

Lu Rong said, "Even spring knows, so how can you not?"

Biting his straw, Lin Mu's heart was filled with joy and delight. He then said, "Let's start dating."

Lu Rong looked at him, finally releasing a laugh that somehow also sounded like a sigh. It seemed as though he was happy, but helpless as well.

One-sidedly, Lin Mu was like a child who had received an award. He did not feel that there were any difficulties or awkwardness in liking Lu Rong. In his eyes, even Meimei with her Alzheimer's disease was adorable.

Liking Lu Rong made him feel like a superman, and nothing

could stop him.

During the evening self-study session, the second-year students again had a monthly test. As Xu Yilu's situation was a little special, he had a little examination room to himself, and the time given to him was also longer than the rest. Lin Mu was in charge of collecting the papers, and after he was done with his test, he waited outside the room Xu Yilu was in. Upon noticing him, the invigilator gave him a nod.

Leaning next to the window, Lin Mu watched Xu Yilu who was touching his paper. Gazing at the scene for a while, he then turned towards the special education class. Cao Zhan was also done with his test, and he was speaking with Meimei dispiritedly. The moment Lin Mu's face popped up, Chen Meihua immediately noticed him.

"You didn't do well?" Lin Mu asked through the window.

Cao Zhan was unhappy. "I'm definitely going to fail again."

"It's alright, even passing one subject is already an improvement."

Cao Zhan sighed, as though he was old and aged. "When I was doing the questions, I found them very difficult. Why am I so stupid?"

"You're just occasionally a little dopey, how can that be called stupid?" Lin Mu laughed. He reached out, ruffling Cao Zhan's hair. Looking up, he found Lu Rong watching him.

Tilting her head up, Chen Meihua spoke to Lin Mu. "Are we going home together today?"

Lin Mu deliberately asked her, "Is it Meimei who wants to go home with me, or is it Lu Rong who wants to go home with me?"

Chen Meihua answered obediently, "We both want to."

Lin Mu laughed until his belly ached, and Lu Rong could only change the topic.

"Are you not going to collect the papers?" He asked.

Lin Mu stretched his neck, taking a look. "They're not done yet."

He coyly asked, "Want to accompany me and wait for a little while?"

Lu Rong was a little doubtful. Finally, he compromised, quietly saying, "I can only stay with you for five minutes. Meimei cannot be left alone."

Forget about five minutes. To Lin Mu, even a few seconds were also an opportunity. Before leaving the classroom, Lu Rong gave Chen Meihua a few reminders repeatedly, then accompanied Lin Mu to the door of the little examination room. The invigilator was surprised to see Lu Rong.

"Why did you kidnap a junior here?" The teacher joked.

Lin Mu was not embarrassed at all. "The junior came to help me collect the papers."

"You sure know how to boss people around."

Xu Yilu had already finished his paper, and he was checking it now. Hearing Lin Mu's voice, he could not help but turn towards his direction. Only after he submitted the paper did he realize who was standing next to Lin Mu.

"Lu Rong?" Xu Yilu was astonished. "Why are you here?"

Lu Rong said, inflectionless, "I came to keep Lin Mu company."

"Oh." Xu Yilu found it rather odd. Lin Zhao should also be in the special education class at this hour too, but why did Lu Rong follow Lin Mu here to collect the papers...? The "Zhao-Lu" fan Xu Yilu had a vague sense of crisis, feeling as though his ship was about to collapse.

After collecting all the papers, Lin Mu had to go to Mr. Yang's office. Meanwhile, Lu Rong was about to return to the special needs class with Xu Yilu. While leaving, he took advantage of the departure of the invigilator as well as the empty room, suddenly reaching out and catching Lin Mu's wrist.

Lin Mu was caught off guard. His hand, holding the papers, trembled, and pages scattered across the ground.

Lu Rong instinctively crouched down to help him pick everything up.

The papers were stacked like snow, layers and layers upon each other. Lu Rong lifted his eyelashes, looking at Lin Mu.

"Hurry up and pick them up..." Lin Mu was the first to turn shy. He busied himself with picking the papers up, then sneaked a peek at the person in front of him. Lu Rong's hand was hidden under a few papers, and their fingers were interlaced together.

"What are you guys doing?" Standing at the door, Xu Yilu had been waiting for some time. Although he was wearing his special glasses, his vision was still blurry. He could only vaguely surmise that something had dropped, and both Lin Mu and Lu Rong were crouching on the ground, picking them up.

However, they had been crouching there for a long time; why were they not done yet?

Lin Mu's hand, holding Lu Rong's, had long turned sweaty. He first let go, and when Lu Rong finally tidied up all the papers, he took them back.

"I dropped the papers." Lin Mu's voice could be considered calm, and he asked a random question. "How was the test?"

Xu Yilu gave him a suspicious look. "It was fine... Don't mess up the papers, okay?"

"How is that possible? Hurry up and return to your class."

Xu Yilu could not shake off the feeling that Lin Mu was feeling guilty over something, but he had no evidence for that. He then turned towards Lu Rong, but with his poor vision, he could not see anything.

Glancing over Lin Mu, Lu Rong then turned and spoke to Xu Yilu, "Let's go."

Walking back to the classroom, Xu Yilu kept pondering over how the papers could have suddenly fell for no reason. Even when he was back in the class, he still could not understand why, while Cao Zhan and Chen Meihua took the initiative to greet him.

"Is Lin Zhao here?" Coming back to his senses, the first thing Xu Yilu did was to worry over the development of his ship.

Cao Zhan looked around, answering honestly, "Yes, she is here. Zhaozhao just came back from the Go institute."

Xu Yilu nodded with satisfaction. Just as he was thinking about how to persuade Lu Rong to cultivate his relationship with Lin Zhao, Chen Meihua suddenly piped up. "We'll be going home with *Jiejie* later!"

"*Jiejie*?" The radar of the "Zhao-Lu" fan instantly lit up. Excitedly, he asked, "Are you talking about Lin Zhao and Lu Rong?"

Chen Meihua frowned, objecting unhappily. "Not Lin Zhao, Lin Zhao is not *Jiejie*."

Xu Yilu paused, and he was at a slight loss, "Why is Lin Zhao not *Jiejie*?"

"Anyway, it's not Lin Zhao." Chen Meihua did not seem to understand it herself. It was as though she was on the opposite side of a shipping war, and she said sternly, "Little Deer belongs to *Jiejie*, not Lin Zhao. You can't snatch him away!"

Over at Mr. Yang's office, Lin Mu rearranged the papers again.

He was a little anxious to leave, and during the process, he could not resist looking at the time on his phone, confirming that there were still a few minutes until the bell would ring.

Mr. Yang glanced at him a few times, and the teacher finally could not help but ask, "Why are you in such a hurry? You have a date?"

Although the studying environment in Kunqian was intense and there were a lot of school activities, the school was actually not very strict about the students being in relationships. This was especially the case for top students like Lin Mu, so the teachers would all close an eye to such matters. Moreover, Mr. Yang was the sort of form teacher who was close to his students, and he could also tease and joke with them occasionally.

"I want to go on a date too," Lin Mu grumbled, "but there's too much homework."

Mr. Yang feinted, pretending to punch him. "You're much too free."

Lin Mu dodged, declaring, "It's not a date, we're just going home together."

Mr. Yang scolded him, laughing. Recently, his bald spot had been expanding even more, and he barely had any hair left on the front part of his head. Every day, he needed to spend a long time to comb what hair he had left nearly. Now, he again took a comb out from the drawer of his desk in the office to tidy his hair. While combing, he chased Lin Mu away. "Go now, go now, go home earlier!"

Lin Mu of course agreed quickly. He grabbed the last few minutes before the bell and returned to his classroom for his bag. Without waiting for the bell to ring, he ran straight to the special needs class.

Several passers-by thought he was waiting for Lin Zhao, and

in fact, Lin Zhao herself thought that her brother would be going home with her.

"We'll go home together next time." Lin Mu had no qualms about embarrassing his sister. "I've promised to go home with Little Deer today."

Lin Zhao did not know what to say to that.

With her fingers, she swore at him, then jabbed his shoulder hard. "Now that you're hooking up with a good-looking junior, you don't want your sister anymore?"

Lin Mu's fingers moved leisurely. "What nonsense. I'm not hooking up, I'm making friends."

Lin Zhao's response was a roll of her eyes.

SILENT HEARTS

The Date

⑩   The Date

Mr. Yang's words did give Lin Mu a reminder. Although Lin Mu had confessed his feelings to Lu Rong and thus they were technically in a relationship, other than going home together after school, they did nothing that was remotely similar to a date. While they secretly held hands, Lin Mu was even more nervous than Lu Rong, completely losing the imposing manner he should have as a upperclassman. It really felt as though he was being led around by this good-looking junior of his.

The first to confess was Lin Mu, and the one to suggest dating was also him. But why, at the end of the day, did Lu Rong seem to be more equal to the task than him?

However, wanting to go on a date was really not that easy.

Every weekend, Lu Rong would attend remedial on Saturday, and Meimei had to attend the community sessions on Sundays. Looking at the situation, if not for Cao Zhan's tutoring sessions on Saturday afternoon, where Lin Mu could use this excuse and hang out with Lu Rong, forget about dating, they might not even be able to see each other during the weekend at all.

But he could not dress up as Lin Zhao again to attend the sessions, right? Lin Mu was in despair. He still had yet to confess his deception; did he have to continue deceiving him?

Besides, he was the one dating Lu Rong, not Lin Zhao.

Pondering over it for a long time, Lin Mu still could not come up with any good ideas. As such, during the tutoring session on Saturday afternoon, Lin Mu was a little distracted.

Cao Zhan and Chen Meihua were again running around the classroom, making a ruckus. Now, when Lin Mu saw them, it was as though he was looking at two huge gooseberries, their presence so undeniably strong that they could not be ignored.

First-year students did not need to complete as many papers, and Lu Rong's workbooks were the ones given by Lin Mu. In this aspect, Lu Rong was very serious. He would finish all the assigned work, and when his answers were wrong, he would highlight them and repeat them a few more times. As long as it was something Lin Mu emphasized on, he was willing to memorize it all.

With such a hardworking student, the tutor dared not slack off.

Resting his chin on his hand, Lin Mu watched as Lu Rong worked on the questions, his head bent over the books. The tip of Lin Mu's finger drew back and forth across Lu Rong's book, and finally, Lu Rong could not help but raise his eyes, looking at Lin Mu in helplessness.

"Are there any other questions you don't know how to do?" Lin Mu deliberately asked.

Lu Rong seemed to find it amusing. "No, not yet."

Lin Mu leaned in closer. "Let's talk, then?"

"I'm not done."

Lin Mu clicked his tongue, a little grumpy. "You're so serious."

Lu Rong did not speak. He extended his legs, hooking around Lin Mu's chair and abruptly tugged it closer. The two of them sat across the desk, their legs intertwined as though they were hugging.

Lin Mu was left frozen.

Lu Rong's face was so close that Lin Mu only needed to tilt his head down to touch it.

His eyelashes were annoyingly long, half-concealing his eyes that were like the reflection of the moon on a lake.

"I know what you want to do." Lu Rong whispered. He glanced over at Cao Zhan and Chen Meihua who had run to the back of the classroom. Tilting his head suddenly and taking advantage of the moment when no one was paying attention to them, Lu Rong gave a swift kiss to the tip of Lin Mu's nose.

Lin Mu immediately covered his nose, swearing. He felt as though that he had been taken advantage of, but he also seemed to have gained a benefit out of it.

After the kiss, Lu Rong's attitude was as though it was nothing special. He lifted his head, asking Chen Meihua to run slower, and be careful not to trip. Under the desk, his legs were still hooked around Lin Mu's chair, with no intentions of letting go, and his inner thighs were pressed against the boy's knees.

After running about, Cao Zhan seemed to be tired as well. He returned to his seat, before realizing that the positions of the two people were a little strange. Neither clever nor perceptive enough, Dopey asked with great innocence, "Why are the two of you hugging the desk??"

The expression on Lu Rong's face did not change. "The legs of this desk are a little wobbly, so holding on to it will make it more stable."

Cao Zhan was easily convinced. He had only passed one subject during the monthly test, and he had yet to finish going through the questions. As such, he could only continue to let Lin Mu tutor him.

However, as the explanations went on, Lin Mu kept getting stuck. He did not seem very focused, and he kept repeating himself.

"... Bring this over to A, then move it to the right, and the answer can be calculated." Lin Mu spent quite some time scribbling the equations down on the scrap paper, and Cao Zhan was completely confused looking at it.

Chen Meihua exposed them. "Everyone is not very serious. The teacher's going to get angry."

Expressionlessly, Lu Rong said, "The teacher himself isn't very serious either."

Lin Mu cast him a side-eye glance.

Chen Meihua did not understand. Even if her IQ were added to Cao Zhan's, the total value would still not be very high. Their attention quickly shifted to something else, and they started giggling and fooling around again.

After Lu Rong finished his questions, Cao Zhan was then forced by Lin Mu to finish going through his paper. When the four of them left the school, the sky had already turned dark. Chen Meihua requested a cold drink from the corner store, so Lu Rong went to buy it for her.

When Lu Rong was paying, Lin Mu secretly asked the old lady, "Is Meimei attending the community session tomorrow?"

Chen Meihua nodded obediently, "Yes, Meimei is going there to draw."

Lin Mu thought for a moment, then coaxed her, "Would Mei-mei want to draw with me tomorrow?"

Uncertain, Chen Meihua tilted her head. "Is *Jiejie* not going to the session to draw with Meimei?"

Lin Mu could only say, "I cannot go any more... So, would Meimei want to go out and draw with me?"

Chen Meihua seemed to only be interested in drawing. Whether she was going to the community sessions, she did not care at all, and she clearly preferred to be with Lin Mu. As such, when Lu Rong returned with the drink, she started making a fuss about not attending the community session tomorrow.

Lu Rong was a little surprised. He glanced at Lin Mu before asking his grandmother, "Where would you like to go then?"

Chen Meihua did not have a scheming bone in her body, and she immediately sold Lin Mu out. "*Jiejie* says he's bringing me to draw tomorrow. I want to draw with *Jiejie!*"

Lin Mu was dumbfounded.

Lu Rong suppressed his laughter and turned to Lin Mu. "Where would you like to go?

Lin Mu responded guiltily, "I haven't decided yet... Meimei wants to draw, so anywhere is fine, right?"

Lu Rong sighed. He reached out suddenly, grasping the back of Lin Mu's neck softly. "If you want to go on a date, just say it. Don't use Meimei as an excuse, or I'll be upset."

Lin Mu seemed to really worried that he would anger Lu Rong. He did not dare to mention the date again, and only until they were about to separate at the subway station did Lu Rong confirm the next day's itinerary with him.

"I've already texted Ma-*laoshi*, requesting to be excused." Lu Rong kept his phone, looking at Lin Mu. "Let's go to No. 2 Library. It's closer to us, and Meimei can draw there too."

How could Lin Mu dare to be up to any tricks now? Whatever Lu Rong said, he agreed to them all with no argument.

Chen Meihua did not know what was going on. Thinking about how she would be going out to draw with Lin Mu tomorrow, she was delighted and cheerful, just like a young girl.

"We'll see you tomorrow!" Chen Meihua held out her hand, wanting to cross pinkies with Lin Mu. "You must draw with Meimei!"

Lin Mu smiled as he crooked his pinky with Meimei's. "I'll definitely draw with Meimei."

After getting Lin Mu's assurance, Chen Meihua was very satisfied. On the way home, she had been talking about drawing with Lin Mu. As for Lu Rong, he was very quiet. Only when they arrived home did Chen Meihua look up at her grandson. "Is Rongrong unhappy?"

Chen Meihua continued asking, "Don't you want to go out and play with *Jiejie*?"

Lu Rong pressed his lips together. He crouched down, helping Chen Meihua remove her shoes. Holding onto one of his grandmother's feet, he slowly said, "I want to go out and play with him, but I have to take you with me."

Chen Meihua's expression was a little muddled. A little sorrowful, she said, "You don't want me to play with *Jiejie*?"

"No," Lu Rong denied. However, after a moment of hesitation, he gave a self-mocking smile. "I don't want him to be too nice to anyone, not even you."

Lu Rong looked at his grandmother, speaking a little solemnly. "Lin Mu is different, so I'll get jealous, I'll get angry."

A pause, and then he asked, half in jest, "Meimei, can you understand that?"

Chen Meihua naturally could not understand, and Lu Rong held no expectations as well. He was aware that there was no way he could have a healthy, perfect, or proper emotional concept towards relationships. This was especially so after Chen Meihua fell sick, and Lu Rong found it very difficult to go through an entire day properly, either with himself or with the world.

In the past, he had come across people who said they liked him, but after some time, their feelings became a superficial burden. However, was Chen Meihua not another type of burden?

Lu Rong loved his grandmother, but he also hated her. Pity, sympathy, shame, loathing—they all were present in what was left of the feelings he had inside him.

It was heavy, pressing down on his back which he dared not bend.

In his hardest days, he never thought about kneeling and crawling down the rest of the road. He had taken so much effort, carrying Chen Meihua on his back for such a long time. Having walked down such a long road like this, there was no way he was going to give up.

And now, in the middle of Lu Rong's journey, it seemed as though Lin Mu, bathed by light, was walking towards him.

He was the sudden, cheerful utopia, and he was the silver lining in the clouds.

Lu Rong was unable to think of any better phrases to describe him. Everything seemed too shallow, too insipid and dull, just like himself.

The noisy chirping of birds broke through the dawn. Lu Rong was not in the habit of snoozing. He woke up very early, and instinctively scrolled through last night's chat with Lin Mu.

Looking at it for some time, he headed downstairs to prepare breakfast. Chen Meihua was still asleep, and so Lu Rong did not wake her up, heading to the kitchen alone.

By the time the eggroll was ready, his grandmother was also awake. It was never known when her Alzheimer's disease would play up. Chen Meihua could be her adorable, girlish self, and in the next second, she could turn into a hysterical, unreasonable old lady.

This was the fifth time clothes were thrown onto Lu Rong's face. A wooden button smacked into the corner of his forehead. Pressing against the injury, Lu Rong suppressed his temper, speaking resignedly, "If Meimei doesn't put on her clothes properly, she won't be able to go out and draw."

Chen Meihua's hair was in a mess, and she was very upset. "I don't want to draw any more!"

Lu Rong looked at her, speaking a little sternly, "You've already promised *Jiejie* that you'd go."

Chen Meihua immediately choked back her tears when she heard the word "*Jiejie*." Thinking for a moment, she seemed to find the option of going out with Lin Mu more alluring, and so she feebly said, "Meimei wants to get dressed now..."

Lu Rong released a breath of relief. Sitting by the bed, he dressed his grandmother, plaited her hair, washed her face, and coaxed her to brush her teeth. Finally, through a mix of persuasion and threats, he made her finish her breakfast.

Over in another place, Lin Zhao found out that Lin Mu was going out today. Early morning, she watched as he selected his clothes, fussing about with his hair, her expression a little enigmatic.

The siblings signed at each other in front of the full-length mirror.

"You're going on a date?" Lin Zhao asked.

Lin Mu was currently trying on his shoes. Although it was almost May, it was not warm enough for short sleeves. He chose a pair of Dr. Martens boots, and, after tying his shoelaces, he shifted about, studying himself. "I'm going to the library with Meimei and Lu Rong."

Lin Zhao's fingers moved in his direction. "You're instigating others to skip the community sessions."

Lin Mu was unbothered. "It's just this once. Besides, how many times have you skipped it?"

Lin Zhao rolled her eyes. She had skipped quite a lot of sessions, but Lin Mu had dressed as her and attended on her behalf. So, technically speaking, she never skipped a single one.

As for Lin Mu deceiving Lu Rong... Lin Zhao no longer had any expectations that he would confess. Furthermore, Lu Rong also did not seem conflicted over it, but as for why he was not conflicted... Lin Zhao looked at the foolish Lin Mu, letting out a silent sigh.

Before leaving, Lin Mu especially reminded Lin Zhao to attend the community session, saying that she had to go there to experience the warmth of humanity.

Lin Zhao had long been numb to such warmth. Impatiently, she urged him out of the house. "Scram."

No. 2 Library was located within the Xiangcheng District. It had only been recently built, and it also came with a children's library. Recently, the library had been organizing art events for children and youth, such as creative arts that involved the use of sand, finger painting, and clay. There were various kinds of activities available, beyond the simple pencil drawings.

Chen Meihua had always wanted to come, but the association could not organize such an event for her alone. As such, this time Chen Meihua could have been considered to have gained a benefit from Lin Mu's feelings for Lu Rong. Catering to what Chen Meihua liked, Lin Mu finally found an opportunity to invite the grandmother and the grandson out alone.

When Lu Rong arrived, Lin Mu was queuing.

He was standing alone in a group of children ranging from the age of six to ten. A boy in front turned to look back at him, his frowning face looking very serious.

"How old are you?" The boy was obviously unhappy. "If you're above the age limit, you can't play."

Lin Mu cocked a brow, speaking shamelessly, "Who said so? Is there an age limit stated on the brochure? I'm also a youth, you can't stop me."

Like an adult, the boy folded his arms. He raised his head, struggling to meet Lin Mu's eyes. "It's all children here, and you're so old. There must be a problem!"

...I'm still a youth after all. Why is this child making me sound so old? Kids these days really can't speak nicely! Lin Mu thought to himself.

A little girl queuing behind Lin Mu poked her head out, speaking reasonably, "*Gege* is a high school student, so he can join too. Don't be unreasonable."

Lin Mu nodded, copying the little girl and repeating, "Don't be unreasonable!"

The little boy was speechless.

The children in front shifted forward, and the queue was like a line of ants. Lin Mu was tall and long-legged; the children both in front and behind him in the queue only reached his waist. Even so, he was not embarrassed in the slightest, standing proudly and openly, even arguing with a parent who wanted to cut the queue and take over the spot of the boy in front.

After that, the little boy no longer judged him, and even started chattering away with him. The little girl behind Lin Mu too piped up like a little bird, and Lin Mu was a little overwhelmed. When he looked up, he saw Lu Rong standing a slight distance away, holding Chen Meihua's hand.

"*Jiejie!*" When Chen Meihua saw him, her eyes crinkled up with mirth, almost disappearing into her face. She shrugged off Lu Rong's grip, running towards Lin Mu. Without thinking, Lin Mu spread open his arms, catching the old lady.

Lin Mu saw the butterfly hairclip on Chen Meihua's head and smiled. "Meimei is dressed very prettily today."

Chen Meihua was delighted, tilting her head to show off her hair. "Little Deer tied my plaits."

The way she addressed Lu Rong was very random. When she could not remember his identity, she would call him Little Deer, and when she did, she would call him Rongrong. Occasionally, she would make a mistake, and call him Zhengnian.

It had taken Lin Mu some time to figure out how this worked, and now he understood that, currently, Chen Meihua was not viewing Lu Rong as a grandson.

Subconsciously, he looked up over to Lu Rong. The boy was expressionless, and there was a glaring red mark on the corner of his forehead.

Lin Mu frowned. Reaching his hand out, he wanted to touch it, but Lu Rong dodged.

"What happened?" Lin Mu had yet to put his hand down.

Lu Rong did not dodge him again but lowered his head, letting Lin Mu touch it.

It was a little swollen.

"I was hit in the morning." Lu Rong's voice was calm. After a pause, he continued, "Don't touch it anymore."

Lin Mu seemed not to have heard him, and his fingers were thus caught. Lu Rong lifted his lids, his eyelashes concealing half his eyes. Smiling slightly, he sighed, "Don't touch it anymore, it's quite painful."

The old lady queued among the children, accompanied by Lu Rong and Lin Mu, one on each of her side. Their heights were too conspicuous, and the little children queuing up could not help but keep turning to look at them. Hence, Lin Mu could only hold onto the little boy's head in front of him and turn him to face forward.

"Queue properly," he said.

The little boy refused to obey. "With your age, you can draw, but the granny cannot."

Lin Mu clicked his tongue. "Why do you have so many opinions? Granny isn't granny, she's Meimei. She's the same age as you."

The boy sucked in a deep breath, his eyes widening. He looked at Chen Meihua, clearly not convinced.

In order to let Chen Meihua draw, Lin Mu had contacted the person in charge of the studio beforehand. The other party was very understanding, and so when it came to Chen Meihua's turn to enter, after confirming her name on the list, she was allowed to enter.

The little boy queuing in front was dumbfounded. With no guilt, Lin Mu continued lying to the child. "See that? Meimei is also a little child. You can't call her granny, got it?"

Muddleheaded, the little boy nodded. He opened his mouth, cautiously greeting Chen Meihua, "Meimei."

The three of them sat down at a long table. Lin Mu went to the tools area and gathered a pile of kinetic sand and paint of all colors. He helped Meimei roll up her sleeves, and the old lady clapped her hands excitedly, eager to start playing with the sand.

Although these were meant for children, Lin Mu was curious too. He also started playing with the kinetic sand, and after a while, he realized that Lu Rong was just sitting there.

"You're not going to try anything?" Lin Mu picked out some paint, handing it over to Lu Rong. "It's easier than drawing, just paint whatever you like."

Lu Rong pressed his lips together. He was even taller than Lin Mu, and he seemed a little cramped in the seat meant for children. His legs were folded up, his knees almost to his chest.

Instead of picking up the paint Lin Mu was holding out to him, he said, "I don't know how to paint."

"Just try it even if you don't know, it's fun."

Lu Rong hesitated for a moment, but still shook his head. "It's fine, you go ahead."

Lin Mu pursed his lips reflexively. Being rejected too often clearly made him upset. Today was a rare chance for them to come out and play together, and he did not want to argue with Lu Rong over such a small matter.

Chen Meihua played happily alone, and after going along with her for a bit, Lin Mu too started feeling bored. Lu Rong looked at him, asking suddenly, "Do you want to drink something?"

Lin Mu glanced at him. "Are you going to buy something?"

Lu Rong smiled a little. He had a bag on his shoulder, and Lin Mu realized that it was quite heavy when Lu Rong placed it down. Like Doraemon, the boy started taking out all sorts of drinks from his bag.

"I prepared them for you." Lu Rong's voice was a little low. He bowed his head, rummaging through his bag as he spoke. "I have water, milk tea, fruit juice, and soft drinks. What would you like?"

Lin Mu licked his lips, suddenly cheering up. Suppressing his smile, he asked, "Anything else?"

Lu Rong didn't respond. Instead, he twisted the bottle of milk tea open and handed it to Lin Mu, then picked the bag up again.

"Is it heavy?" Lin Mu asked.

Lu Rong shook his head. "No."

Lin Mu still wanted to continue talking to him, but next to him, Chen Meihua's kinetic sand seemed to have fallen onto the ground. Without any warning, the old lady burst into tears.

Lin Mu could not drink the milk tea anymore. He quickly coaxed Chen Meihua, but it did not seem to have much effect. After some time, Chen Meihua's crying grew louder, so loud that the children around could not help but look over.

Instinctively, Lu Rong began to apologize. He tried to grab Chen Meihua's shoulders and stop her from making a ruckus. However, the old lady flung her hands unexpectedly, and paint ended up splashing onto Lin Mu's clothes.

Lin Mu was shocked silent.

Lu Rong's expression finally changed. He caught Chen Meihua's wrist, berating her, "Keep quiet!"

Scared, Chen Meihua hiccupped, looking at Lu Rong with tearful eyes.

Without a word, Lu Rong took away all the art tools in Chen

Meihua's hands, standing and pulling her up, then walking to-wards the door of the studio. Lin Mu hurriedly ran to the staff to explain the situation, and afraid that Lu Rong would already be a distance away, he chased after him.

As the old lady was being dragged along, they were not mov-ing quickly. She probably knew that she was in trouble, so her cries had quietened down. Lu Rong brought her to the sink in the garden outside, turning the tap on and washing her hands.

The old lady started crying again, struggling. "It hurts! You're holding me too tightly!"

Lu Rong's expression was cold. He ignored her, until Lin Mu reached out and turned the tap off.

"You're holding her too tightly." Lin Mu frowned, seeming to blame Lu Rong. "Don't be so fierce, be gentler with Meimei."

Lu Rong jerked his head over. The corners of his eyes were red, either from anger or from being wronged. He then bowed his head, as though trying to conceal his face, and stood to one side, giving way.

Chen Meihua was still crying. Lin Mu had no choice but to bend down and first coax Chen Meihua to wash her hands. Then, he heard Lu Rong say, "Take your sweater off first, wear mine in-stead."

Lin Mu chuckled. "It's just some paint, it's fine."

Lu Rong stubbornly stared at the streak of paint across the collar of Lin Mu's sweater.

Lin Mu tilted his neck away, exposing the area. "Why don't you wipe it off for me instead?"

Most of the paint had splashed onto Lin Mu's clothes, but some had stained Lin Mu's neck too. His skin was very pale, and some of his veins were visible. Lu Rong wetted a piece of tissue paper, carefully dabbing Lin Mu's skin clean. When he reached Lin Mu's collarbone, Lin Mu could not help but giggle a little, complaining that it tickled.

"Are you treating me like a girl?" Lin Mu said helplessly. He looked at Lu Rong with the corner of his eye, his phoenix eyes charming. "You're so gentle."

Lu Rong's eyelashes swept up and down. "Your skin here is softer than a girl's."

Lin Mu sounded jealous. "Why, you've wiped many girls' skin before?"

Lu Rong answered after a moment, "You're the only one."

After a pause, he added, "And Meimei."

Laughter quaked through Lin Mu's body, and his neck shivered too. Lu Rong stared at it for some time, then reached out and placed his palm on Lin Mu's Adam's apple.

Lin Mu gave him a questioning look.

"You're beautiful here."

His hand moved slowly, stopping at Lin Mu's collarbone. "Here as well."

Lin Mu coughed, the tips of his ears flushing red. "Where else am I beautiful?"

Lu Rong gave a fleeting smile. He said quietly, "I've yet to see other parts of your body, so I can't make a conclusion now."

Lin Mu was struck dumb.

Chen Meihua finally washed her hands obediently, and stopped crying as well. Whenever her disease played up, she would tend to make a huge ruckus, but once it was over, she would be like wilted grass. Now, she sat on a bench inside the library, a little bleary.

Lin Mu finally felt relieved, while Lu Rong seemed to be used to this. From his bag, he took out a lunchbox, prepared to feed her.

"Shall I buy a set of art tools for Meimei?" Lin Mu suggested as he watched her eat. "She seems to like them very much."

Lu Rong paused slightly, then shook his head and rejected the offer. "There's no need. She never likes things for too long, it'll be a waste of money."

Lin Mu did not give up. "We'll just get a set, maybe she might continue?"

Lu Rong wanted to feed Chen Meihua some more, but she shut her mouth tightly, refusing to eat anymore. He could only put the lunchbox down, looking at Lin Mu seriously. "My grandmother is an Alzheimer's patient. She's sick, and she's not like other healthy people. I know you have no prejudice, but she's different from Lin Zhao, different from us, she's different from everyone else."

Lu Rong's tone softened, asking, "Lin Mu, can you understand?"

"I've been taking care of her for the past four years, ever since I was twelve. Every day, once I open my eyes, she would cry and make a fuss. She would forget who I am. She would leave the house, but forget how to come home. Out of the 365 days in a year, half my time would be spent looking for her. From the police station, from the resident's committee, from strangers, I would have to bring her home." Lu Rong paused for a moment, then continued abruptly, "When you asked me to paint just now, I know that it's out of kindness. I want to oblige you, but I can't."

"I can't have time for myself, to do my own things, and to do what I like," Lu Rong said. "Because I know that these are things that I cannot afford to want."

Lin Mu opened his mouth. He was a little befuddled, and he

stammered, "I—I didn't want to argue with you, I..."

"Hear me out," Lu Rong interrupted him. He seemed to be thinking about how he should put his points across. After a long time, he slowly said, "Just like what happened just now, as long as you're with me, such incidents will always happen."

Lin Mu said anxiously, "I'm not scared, don't..."

"Don't break up with me." Lu Rong's voice was a little loud, and a slight hoarseness could be heard.

Lin Mu was startled, but it was too late to cover Lu Rong's mouth. The people around them looked over curiously, and Lin Mu decided to just cover Lu Rong's face, not allowing them to see him.

Only Lu Rong's eyes were exposed. It was as though within them were the ripples of a lake, lapping at Lin Mu's heart.

He said, "I can't afford to want anything, but I still want you. So, don't be angry with me because of Meimei, and don't break up with me."

Lu Rong lowered his lashes. He spoke cautiously, just like a little deer, "Lin Mu, you have to know, I will love you with all my heart."

Chen Meihua's dementia did not play up again for the rest of the afternoon. However, she was very lethargic, and she was easily distracted. There were many things that she was interested in, but her interest never last long. In the morning, she was still very eager about the arts session, but in the afternoon, she was completely disinterested in it.

The library was not suited for noise and ruckus. Due to Chen Meihua's unstable emotions, Lu Rong and Lin Mu dared not stay in the library for too long. As such, they brought the old lady to Rencai Park, which was nearby, for a stroll.

With the nice weather, many people were walking their dogs, and dogs both big and small were sprinting all over the place. Chen Meihua was a little scared, timidly hiding behind Lu Rong.

"Does Meimei want to hold my hand?" Lin Mu asked her.

Chen Mei thought about it and felt it was a good idea. She grabbed Lu Rong's hand with one hand and slid the other into Lin Mu's.

The three of them were all hand-in-hand, the old lady separating Lin Mu and Lu Rong.

Lin Mu tried to hold himself back, but he failed. Softly, he muttered, "I'm holding your hand indirectly."

Lu Rong glanced at him, seemingly wanted to laugh. Sometimes he felt that Lin Mu was killing him—bringing him flowers on a snowy winter night, confessing his feelings in spring, and now, he even saw the three of them holding hands so romantically.

Lin Mu himself too found it a little too mushy, but despite so, he was still very happy. The three of them strolled around the park until the sun was about to set, yet Lin Mu and Lu Rong had no intention of going home. It was only until Meimei started fussing about, saying that they had to go home when the sky was dark. Lin Mu very much wanted to send the both of them back all the way home, but he was stopped by Lu Rong at the subway station.

"School's starting again tomorrow," Lu Rong said. "You've been tired out today, go back home earlier and rest."

All Lin Mu could think of was about how he was not tired, that he still could, and wanted to continue. However, looking at Lu Rong's expression, he knew that there was no room for negotiation, and so he could only agree obediently.

Standing at the platform, Lu Rong looked at Lin Mu for a

while before suddenly asking, "Will there be a sports meet next month?"

Lin Mu calculated the days, then nodded his head. "June will be the last sprint for the final examinations, so the meet has to be held by May."

In a low voice, Lu Rong said, "Don't sign up for too many events on that day."

Lin Mu looked puzzled.

Lu Rong smiled. He said, "Let's have a date."

For exceptional students like Lin Zhao, they did not participate much in the sports meets. However, with such a "villainous" principal like Zhong He, who liked to put students to work, he could always come up with new ideas to torture them, glorifying it as improving the friendship between students.

When Lin Zhao was assigned to the cheerleading team, she thought it was some kind of prank, but when she went there she found out that it was really just that. Furthermore, she did not need to worry about not being able to hear, as someone else would stand in front and lead the cheers while she only had to follow from the back.

"Not only have I been assigned something like this, Little Heron is also a sportscaster," Lin Zhao's fingers signed agitatedly. "He can't even see exactly how many people are on the track. How is he going to commentate?!"

Lin Mu thought for a moment. "Maybe they're just finding something for him to do?"

Lin Zhao was expressionless. "Then, what's with Cao Zhan being a member of the disciplinary committee? With his brains, who can he discipline?"

Cao Zhan looked completely muddled, and he clearly did not

understand what was going on. He only felt that being part of the disciplinary committee sounded pretty cool, but he had no idea what he was supposed to do.

"With regards to the committee, An Jincheng should be there to guide you," Lin Mu patiently explained. "Just follow him, and you'll be fine."

"Oh," Cao Zhan said, and then he asked, "Lin Mu, what events are you participating in?"

Last year, Lin Mu was basically a decathlon athlete, participating in all events that he could participate in. Other than some events where his results could not compare to those of sports students, he was basically the most eye-catching person on the track that day.

Lin Mu blinked. He suddenly straightened up properly, placing both his hands nicely on the table.

Lin Zhao, who saw his actions, gave a questioning look.

Cao Zhan was extremely baffled.

And Xu Yilu, who had no idea what had happened from beginning to end, looked completely confused.

Lin Mu gave a reserved, fake cough, speaking delicately, "I'm really not that good at sports, so I just randomly signed up for a 400m run."

Xu Yilu's astonishment lasted for a couple of seconds. In complete disbelief, he asked, "When did you turn into Little Sister Lin?"

Of course, another person who was extremely unhappy with his lack of participation in the sports meet was An Jincheng.

The sports meet was basically a competition among classes, with points awarded, and it was a day for honor. The elite class was full of studious people, but when faced with anything physical, most of them were like quails. If not for Lin Mu and An Jincheng taking one of the top three positions in all the events, the points for their class would probably have been at the bottom of the barrel. This year, Lin Mu had decided to not participate at all, leaving a mess for An Jincheng to handle.

"Fine, forget about the participating in the events. Are you not even bothering about the official duties that need to be done during the meet?" When An Jincheng was holding the meeting to discuss the sports meet, Lin Mu was pretty much slacking the whole time.

Kunqian's sports meet was different from other schools. The entire process was ran by students themselves, and the teachers were completely hands-off. From arranging the location, the timing of the events, the drinks, snacks, banners to even the first-aid tents, they were all managed and decided by the students.

Their studying life was busy, and it only became busier when such events were going on. All the students in the school were bustling about the entire day, and the class committee members were even busier. From morning until night, from the front stage to the back, the discipline and the logistics had to be watched over tightly.

Lin Mu was very sheepish when facing An Jincheng. His eyes darting all over the place, he gave an excuse, "I haven't been feeling well recently... I think I won't be able to deal with the sports meet..."

An Jincheng had an expression of "are you treating me like an idiot." He said coldly, "You have to make a choice between taking care of the performance, or the logistics. Everyone has something to do, you cannot slack off."

Lin Mu too knew that he could not avoid this, but he did not want to be busy the entire day as well. Making his calculations, he finally decided with great difficulty that he would take charge of the logistics.

"We need helpers for logistics, right?" Lin Mu asked. Towards this, he was quite enthusiastic. "Shall we ask the first-years to help?"

The beautiful Young Master An gave him a strange look, unable to resist asking, "Why are you so enthusiastic about the first-year students? Tell me the truth, are you dating some first-year girl?"

Lu Rong's class was located on the first floor, all the way at the end of the corridor. It happened to be their afternoon break, and everyone had returned to their class after lunch, reading or resting. Mo Xiaoxiao had signed up for the girl's high jump event, and she was the only special needs student who would be participating in the sports meet as an athlete.

"Do you have to change your prosthetic limb that day?" Li Zi looked at Mo Xiaoxiao's leg curiously.

Mo Xiaoxiao was wearing a skirt today, and she stretched her leg out with no embarrassment, showing it to Li Zi. "My mom has already checked it out for me. Did you guys watch 'Kingsman: The Secret Service'? It's just like the limb of the beautiful villain in it."

Li Zi whistled. "Cool..."

Lu Rong listened to them chattering away, his attention shifting a little away from Chen Meihua. Lin Mu just sent him a text message, saying that he was coming down to mobilize students for the sports meet, and so Lu Rong could not help but look towards the window. The moment he turned his head, he saw Lin Mu's face appearing right outside. Lin Mu's face was very close to him, almost plastered against the glass.

Lu Rong gave him a questioning look.

He was sitting by the window near the back door, and at that moment, the class had yet to discover this new arrival.

Lin Mu took a look around, before his eyes returned to Lu Rong's face.

Smiling, he winked, pursing his lips through the glass.

Lu Rong was speechless.

Mo Xiaoxiao happened to look up after showing Li Zi her leg. With no hesitation, Lu Rong reached out, placing his palm against the window, covering the lower half of Lin Mu's face.

As such, Lin Mu's "kiss," through the glass, landed accurately onto his palm.

SILENT HEARTS

⓫   The Sports Meet

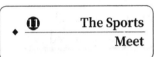

◆   **⑪   The Sports
Meet**

Standing behind Lin Mu, An Jincheng gave him a look of disgust as he watched him press his lips to the window. Lin Mu even made a kissy sound, as if there weren't other people around.

An Jincheng and Lin Mu both were notorious figures of the school. They only stood by the backdoor for a few minutes, and many of the students in Class Five soon noticed them. Lin Mu was too embarrassed to keep his lips pressed against the glass, so he walked through the door, even pinching Lu Rong's face when he walked past him.

Lu Rong was left speechless.

Lin Mu did not use much force, so his pinch was more like flirting. An Jincheng frowned, glancing at Lu Rong, seeming to disapprove of how Lin Mu was behaving like a playboy. "Don't get all touchy-feely with the underclassmen."

Why are you being so uptight? I'm only just touching my husband, Lin Mu thought.

Of course, he couldn't say this aloud, and Lin Mu gloomily kept his thoughts to himself. An Jincheng went up to the podium to speak. He was basically the epitome of aloofness, a coldly attractive man, and so he had tons of die-hard fans. Once he started talking, the emotions of the kids in front of him were all stirred up by his sweet-talk, and they wanted nothing more than to fulfil his requests.

Lin Mu deliberately sat at the back. He was very near Lu Rong, and he leaned over, whispering into his ear, "Don't listen to him... It's all grunt work and physical labor. Run as far as you can away from it."

Lu Rong looked at him with lowered lashes, quietly asking, "Then why are you in charge of logistics?"

Lin Mu spoke resignedly, "I have no choice. As a member of the student committee, I have to lead by example. However, I only signed up for one role this year."

He winked gleefully. "Logistics isn't that busy. When I'm free, we can play truant and take Meimei out to play."

Next to them, Chen Meihua heard him and happily repeated, "Out to play, to play!"

Lin Mu held a finger up, pressing it to his lips and shushing her. "This is a secret, so Meimei can't tell anyone, alright?"

Li Zi was now the assistant class representative, and thus she had to participate. As soon as the assignments were allocated, Lu Rong took the initiative to ask her if she needed any help.

"Meimei and I can work on some banners to cheer the class on," Lu Rong explained. "If we find something for Meimei to do, she will be happier."

Li Zi was certainly happy to hear that. After recording down all the materials needed, she added Lu Rong's name to the logistics team, and it just so happened to be right under Lin Mu's name.

Lu Rong eyed that list a couple of times, and did not say a word.

It was a busy period for both the first- and second-year students. As Lin Mu was in charge of logistics, every class had to report their progress to him. Sometimes, they even had to trouble him to seek out materials like red silk fabric, ribbons, and plastic trumpets. When funds were running low, he needed to find Chu Lin or Mr. Yang to get approval for more money. Lin Mu was as busy as a bee, spending the entire week running around the school.

In all this preparation, he didn't even have time to have lunch with Lu Rong and the others. After his morning classes, he had to hang the banners on the sports ground, so his lunch was delivered to him by Lin Zhao instead.

The elder sister's heart ached for the younger brother, and she signed, "Can't you just slack off?"

While eating, Lin Mu signed, "It'll be done within the next few days, and then I'll be able to be more relaxed on the day itself."

Lin Zhao did not understand. "What do you have in mind for that day?"

Lin Mu raised a brow. "I'm not telling you."

Lin Zhao wasn't baited by him trying to keep her in suspense, and she then informed him that her group was short of cheerleading uniforms.

Lin Mu asked, "How many?"

Lin Zhao thought for a moment. "About three to four sets. I have to bring a wig that day too."

Lin Mu was baffled. "Why are you bringing a wig?"

Lin Zhao gave a mysterious smile. "There's a little first-year boy in the cheerleading team, we'll be getting him to put on the wig and dance."

Lin Mu was speechless. He didn't really understand how his sister had cultivated such strange interest in looking at cross-dressing boys. He completely had no idea that he was the instigator of the whole matter.

It was quite easy to settle the issue of the cheerleading uniforms. Kunqian had an aerobics club, and the cheerleading uniforms this time had been provided by them. However, they still needed a few sets more. Lin Mu reported the number required to Chu Lin, and they waited for the factory to deliver them.

When the uniforms were delivered, Lin Mu then went to monitor the contingent parade of the athletes from all classes. An Jincheng was already seated on the podium, looking extremely haggard from the work.

The aloof beauty was just like a flower that had not been watered, its petals drooping and its colors fading. Even when he saw Lin Mu, he could not be bothered to put on any airs, his greeting a simple raise of his chin.

"There are only three days left." It was not sure if Lin Mu was consoling An Jincheng or himself. "We just have to endure a little longer, and it'll all be over."

An Jincheng nodded feebly. Lin Mu noticed that the cheerleading team was entering the sports ground from the other side. It seemed like they were about to rehearse. Suddenly, Lin Mu asked, "Has my sister told you?"

Question marks appeared all over An Jincheng's face. As it had to do with Lin Zhao, he was a little curious. "About what?"

Lin Mu pointed towards the sports ground. "She joined the cheerleading team."

An Jincheng looked confused.

The boy did not seem to believe him, stiffly turning his neck towards where Lin Mu was pointing. An Jincheng was a little myopic, and he unconsciously leant forward, pushing himself closer to see a little more clearly.

Lin Mu continued pointing her out for An Jincheng. "Do you see her? There, right in the front row. Her high kick is pretty on point."

An Jincheng was struck dumb.

Strong, rhythmic music pulsed through the air. This was also the first time Lin Mu discovered that Lin Zhao had quite a talent for dancing. Throwing her arms out and kicking her legs, she followed the tempo perfectly and looked great doing so. As she could not hear the music, Lin Zhao's eyes were focused the entire time on the person leading the steps. However, she was really outstandingly beautiful. It was as though there was a spotlight shining on her, and everyone's eyes were all drawn towards her.

Lin Mu was very entertained, but An Jincheng's expression only got darker and darker.

Finally, unable to hold himself back anymore, he spoke frostily to Lin Mu, "You agreed to let them perform like this?"

Lin Mu could not understand why An Jincheng was suddenly so angry, and he joked, "Isn't this good? Look at how charming, bright and energetic they are. What are you unsatisfied with?"

An Jincheng was silent, clearly unable to say anything against it. However, he seemed unwilling to give up. His face reddening, he opened his mouth, then closed it. Repeating this a few times, he finally forced out, "The skirts... They're too short."

Lin Mu thought he had heard wrongly. He turned back again, looking at the cheerleaders' skirts. They were not long, but they were almost knee-length. Furthermore, the girls were all wearing safety shorts underneath the skirts, and there was completely no risk that they would expose themselves.

Pondering over it, Lin Mu came to a sudden realization. Acting as though he found out An Jincheng's little secret, he gloatingly hooked his arm around An Jincheng's neck, whispering into his ear, "Tell me the truth, your girlfriend's one of the cheerleaders, right? You just don't want her to kick her legs up for everyone to see?"

An Jincheng did not know what to say to that.

Lin Mu's question was very direct, but he had no expectations that Young Master An would admit to it. Once Lin Zhao's rehearsal was over, she was summoned over by her brother, and the two of them communicated with each other, one on the podium and one on the ground.

"Help me find out which of the cheerleaders is An Jincheng's girlfriend." Lin Mu did not conceal his movements from the person next to him as he signed.

However, Lin Zhao knew that An Jincheng understood sign language. She glanced at An Jincheng, perplexed, before signing, "Why do you want to know this?"

Lin Mu signed back sloppily. "He thinks your skirts are too short, and he's getting all jealous and possessive over it."

Lin Zhao was speechless.

Completely exposed by Lin Mu, An Jincheng seemed to be considering if he should just come clean. With an aloof expression, he stood there, motionless. Although Lin Zhao was a little doubtful, she did not think much about it. Facing the two boys, she lifted her skirt up directly, signing, "We're wearing safety shorts."

Lin Mu laughed uproariously, pretending to object, "Put your skirt down!"

An Jincheng stood there like a statue. He dared not look at the girl's pale, slender legs. His ears were a bright red, and he hastily turned to face another direction.

Lin Zhao pursed her lips, putting her skirt down unconcernedly as she signed, "I'm going to the Go institute later, Ninth Dan Li is coming to play a game later."

Lin Mu nodded, signaling that he got it. Before she left, Lin Zhao gave An Jincheng a look. The boy seemed to be feeling awkward over something, refusing to show his face the entire time.

The the twins' attention seemed to have been diverted. Lin Mu ignored An Jincheng's sudden bout of inexplicable temper, leaning alone on the railing of the podium and looking down. The contingent for the first-year students happened to be making their way onto the sports ground, and Lin Mu immediately caught sight of Lu Rong at the back.

Lu Rong lifted his head, his eyes meeting Lin Mu's. The latter grinned at him, and Lu Rong only looked away after a long time.

When the contingent had passed him by, Lin Mu was still reluctant to pull his gaze away. For now, he could not leave either, and so he could only continue watching.

When things got busy, three days would pass in the blink of an eye. Making use of every bit of time he had, Lin Mu met Lu Rong a few times, one of which was when they even worked on banners together. Li Zi had brought the materials, and Chen Meihua excitedly took the initiative to request to work on it.

Under normal circumstances, it was impossible for the two boys to be alone together. Other than Chen Meihua, Cao Zhan, Xu Yilu, and Mo Xiaoxiao were all here as well. These days, Lin Zhao was either at the Go Institute or with the cheerleaders. An Jincheng was responsible for inspecting the sports equipment, and he had specially brought Jiang Tianhe and Sun Hai around with him for the past few days. Standing there like bodyguards, the two were in charge of keeping up a front for the wallflower.

In principle, Cao Zhan's situation was unique. He could not focus on anything for too long, but as long as the matter had something to do with craftwork, he was no longer interested in playing.

Dopey had a pair of skilled, deft hands. Cutting cloth, sewing, embroidery, these were all things he was very good at. Even Lin Mu was extremely amazed by him, and he had asked Cao Zhan in private about it a few times.

"I just like it..." Cao Zhan thought about it, feeling a little frustrated yet very earnest. "These are the only things I know how to do, and so I kept doing them."

Lin Mu looked at the motifs he embroidered on the red banner. There seemed to be no repeated ones, and he could not help but click his tongue in admiration.

Even Li Zi and Mo Xiaoxiao came over to take a look. They recalled Cao Zhan's leather craftwork that was displayed during the cultural event in his class, and the reddish-brown little leather bunny that was currently still hanging on Chen Meihua's school bag.

"Dopey, you must be a genius!" Mo Xiaoxiao did not hold back on her enthusiasm, showering Cao Zhan with praise. "My mom told me before that some people may be mentally deficient, but they can excel much more than ordinary people in other matters. This is absolutely the case for Dopey!"

Although Xu Yilu was unable to help with the work, he could still help keep inventory. Laughing, he said, "Dopey's only a little slower than others."

Cao Zhan nodded vigorously. "Yes, yes. Just a little, a little."

Chen Meihua's fingers were not as deft as Cao Zhan's, but she also liked doing such craftwork. Together with Lu Rong, they produced quite a sum. Taking the opportunity when no one was paying attention to them, Lin Mu whispered to Lu Rong, "Did you sign up for this after seeing that I'm in charge of logistics?"

Lu Rong glanced at him, and he did not admit it. "It's Meimei who wanted to join."

Lin Mu was not convinced. "You didn't?"

Lu Rong did not answer, instead taking a plastic trumpet and packing it. Lin Mu raised his arm, bumping it against Lu Rong's shoulder. Lu Rong turned away, bumping Lin Mu back.

They were behaving just like children, bumping into each other for a long time. Seated next to them, Xu Yilu felt his desk moving, and he could not help asking, "Lin Mu? What are you guys doing?"

Lin Mu's arm was caught by Lu Rong. Unable to free himself, he could only feign ignorance. "Nothing... We're just playing around."

Li Zi and Mo Xiaoxiao were probably used to it, and so they were unconcerned about what they were doing. Only Xu Yilu felt that they were too suspicious. After all, he was the "Zhao-Lu" fan with a magnifying glass, and before anything could happen to his ship, he must first stand on guard at the front line.

While working on the banners, Chen Meihua tried to convince him. "Little Deer and Mumu have a perfect relationship, they both like each other!"

As Lu Rong had repeatedly emphasized to his grandmother about how to address Lin Mu, so Chen Meihua could finally remember to no longer call Lin Mu "*Jiejie*" in front of other people.

As a fan of the other pairing, Xu Yilu's notions about this "perfect relationship" and "like" were innocent and straightforward. In his eyes, it was extremely normal for this pair of "brothers-in-law" to share a good relationship, and this good relationship proved that he was on the right ship!

Xu Yilu choosing the wrong ship to support could be concluded as the biggest misunderstanding of the year. Now, with Chen Meihua constantly arguing with him, the shipper Little Heron was not lonely in the slightest.

Only after horsing around for quite some time did Lin Mu and Lu Rong then complete the logistics work. They really had no regards for others around them, and, near the end, even Cao Zhan picked up on it, asking them in curiosity, "Why are the two of you always sticking together?"

At that moment, coincidentally, Lin Mu happened to be hugging Lu Rong from behind. His chin was on Lu Rong's shoulder, and their cheeks were pressed to each other. In such a position, where they could kiss each other if they just turned their heads, Lin Mu finally noticed how flirtatious they were behaving. Lin Mu was not the brazen sort, and with Cao Zhan's question, he tried to clamber off Lu Rong's back, only for the boy to suddenly grab his arm.

Lin Mu got a shock, and he said quietly, "Everyone's looking."

There was no change in Lu Rong's expression. He did not let go, as if he did not care how the people around them were looking at him.

Cao Zhan was a little envious. Whining to Lin Mu, he said, "I want to cling to you too."

Before Lin Mu could respond, Lu Rong spoke up first. "No, you can't."

Cao Zhan blinked, unconvinced. "Why?"

There was still not much of an expression on Lu Rong's face.

He spoke, though nothing could be more obvious, "Because Lin Mu is mine alone."

Cao Zhan's intelligence was no higher than that of Meimei, so naturally, there was no way he could understand the implication behind Lu Rong's words. He always had a good relationship with Lin Mu, and he relied on him greatly. It was not wrong at all to call him Lin Mu's tail, with how he so readily followed after him. Now, he felt that Lu Rong was bullying him, so he stared at Lin Mu with his lips flattened, feeling greatly aggrieved.

Lin Mu felt guilty from his stare, but right now, it was a critical moment. A human's innate instinct was to choose hoes before bros. Even as he berated himself, Lin Mu reveled completely in bliss. With a peace of mind, he leaned against Lu Rong's back.

The logistics were nearly done. The few people worked together, counting them all once before placing them at the storeroom below the podium on the sports ground. On Friday, Lin Mu would be the one in charge of watching over the storeroom, and when the things were needed, each class would send a representative here to check and collect them.

Things looked very simple. But when it came to the actual day itself, Lin Mu realized that he had been too naïve.

Once the parade was over, just like usual, standing on the podium Zhong He went on and on. In front of the storeroom, the class representatives formed two lines, collecting water bottles and energy bars, as well as the insufficient banners and trumpets.

Holding onto a clipboard, Lin Mu kept track as he distributed the items, becoming a little dizzy towards the end.

The surroundings were noisy, and Lin Zhao even brought some of the cheerleaders there to collect their outfits. They were performing more than one dance, and so they gathered in the store-room during the break in the middle. Once everyone was nearly gone, Lin Zhao took out the wig, gesturing at Lin Mu's head.

"Don't disturb me." Lin Mu was busy with the list he just recorded. "Where's that underclassman of yours?"

Lin Zhao fluttered her fingers at him. "He suddenly felt un-well, and he's no longer performing. I brought my wig for noth-ing."

Lin Mu thought, *if it was for nothing, then let it be! Why was she trying to shove the wig onto his head?!*

But it was only grumbling. Lin Mu could not spare a hand to stop his sister's prank. The other girls were also intrigued, and they gathered around, putting the wig on him, even tying it up into a princessy hairdo. Lin Zhao took a photo when they were done.

"You two really look almost identical." One of the cheerleaders was so surprised that she could not help exclaiming.

Lin Mu signed what she said to Lin Zhao. Lin Zhao was very pleased, signing, "We haven't put on makeup yet, we'll be even more identical after that."

Someone egged her on. "Put some on and we'll see."

Lin Mu was about to turn crazy. He pleaded, "Girls, please let me off, alright?"

When he lifted his head to speak, Lin Zhao quickly dabbed his lips with lipstick.

Lin Mu was stunned.

Lin Zhao swiftly colored his lips, then signed in satisfaction. "It's a Dior limited edition lipstick, both waterproof and trans-fer-proof. It'll make your skin look fairer, and your complexion glow!"

The girls did not stay long. More students came over to collect various items, and Lin Mu was so busy that he did not have time to remove the wig. Some of the students familiar with him all had an expression of entertainment. After collecting their items, they all wanted to take his photo, and had to be chased off quite a few times by Lin Mu before they were willing to go.

When there was finally time for Lin Mu to sit down, someone pushed open the storeroom's door abruptly.

Lin Mu was trying his best to remove the wig, only looking up when he heard the sound. Lu Rong had already entered, and behind him was his classmate. Seeing Lin Mu like this, Lu Rong blocked the door without thinking.

Lin Mu did not know how to react.

Lu Rong clearly did not expect Lin Mu would be dressed up like this. Just as he was about to utter a sound, his classmate behind him urged, "What's wrong, Lu Rong? Get in there."

Lu Rong did not say a word, closing the door and locking it instead.

The classmate left outside was dumbfounded.

Lin Mu's wig could not be removed, and remnants of his lipstick were still apparent. Lu Rong had to glance at his clothes before confirming that Lin Mu was not dressing up as Lin Zhao, but Lin Mu was so guilty that he dared not speak at all. He could only cover his face, deceiving himself, as he refused to look at Lu Rong.

"Lin Zhao dropped by?" Lu Rong asked calmly.

Lin Mu hesitated for a moment, then nodded.

Lu Rong asked, "Why are you covering your face?"

Lin Mu's voice was muffled. He said, "I have lipstick on..."

Lu Rong did not speak. Outside, someone was pounding on

the door, shouting, "Is anyone there? I'm here to collect the water bottles!"

Lu Rong randomly grabbed a carton of Nongfu Spring. He opened the door, and the person outside tried to squeeze in. "What are you guys doing? Aren't you going to let us collect the items?"

Lu Rong shoved some bottles from the box into their arms, blocking the door and not giving way. "Lin Mu is not feeling well. Go back and let the others know."

"He's not feeling well? Then why isn't he going to the medical room?"

Lu Rong was a little impatient. He reached out, grabbing the door and answering perfunctorily, "I'll take him there later. You guys go ahead, don't disturb him."

The people outside left there in silence.

It was not clear how Lin Zhao fixed the wig onto Lin Mu's head. The way it was pinned down, it seemed as though glue had been involved. Lin Mu had been fiddling with it for a long time, and despite the pain on his scalp, he had only managed to remove some of the pins. The more anxious he was, the clumsier he became, and his explanation was not very convincing.

"A boy joined my sister's cheerleading team, and so she brought a wig... In the end, that boy could not participate, and she was bored enough to put the wig on me." Lin Mu did not manage to control his strength, and a tug caused him to hiss in pain.

Lu Rong sighed. A little amused, he came closer. "Don't move, I'll do it."

Lin Mu wanted to dodge. "It's fine..."

Lu Rong caught his wrist.

Lin Mu's guilty conscience popped up again, and he tried to look for something to say. "My sister and I look very much alike, right?"

Lu Rong looked at him.

Lin Mu struggled to come up with words. "Although we look very similar, but there's actually quite a lot of differences..."

"I know." Lu Rong cut him off. He crouched down in front of Lin Mu, tilting his head up slightly. His long lashes were lowered, and as he helped undo the hair that was tied up, he glanced at Lin Mu. "I can tell the two of you apart very well."

Lin Mu froze.

He felt that if he were to continue explaining, it would only become more suspicious. As such, he simply shut his mouth, looking a little despairing.

Lu Rong slowly removed the hairpins one by one from the hair net. Lin Mu sat there; his head bowed. He suddenly remembered that this was not the first time Lu Rong had tidied "his hair" for him. Last time, the boy had also done so with the little yellow duckling hairclip.

Lu Rong seemed to be very skilled at such matters. Perhaps it was because he had been taking care of Chen Meihua for so long.

"Does it hurt?" Lu Rong asked after removing half the pins.

Lin Mu shook his head. "It doesn't... You can speed up, I'm not a little girl."

Lu Rong laughed. "Then why did you let your sister put the wig on you?"

Lin Mu answered embarrassedly, "She likes it..."

Lu Rong fell silent. His fingers slid through the net, lightly caressing Lin Mu's actual hair. He abruptly said, "Your ears are different from your sister's."

Lin Mu looked confused.

Lu Rong tilted his head to the side, looking as though he was studying Lin Mu's appearance seriously. "Your earlobes are slightly larger than your sister's."

Lin Mu stammered, "I-is that so?"

"Mn." Lu Rong smoothly removed the wig. Before Lin Mu could exhale in relief, his chin was caught by Lu Rong.

"The lipstick." Lu Rong's thumb pressed on his lips. A slight force was exerted, and Lu Rong rubbed them lightly.

Lin Mu did not know how to react.

Lu Rong's gaze was lowered, his eyes falling onto the corner of Lin Mu's mouth. There was a slight stain from Lu Rong rubbing the lipstick away. Lin Mu's skin was very fair, and the lipstick stain was like a blossom, blooming right next to his lips.

"The shapes of your lips are different, too," Lu Rong said suddenly.

Lin Mu met his eyes, stunned for a moment. "What?"

Lu Rong again rubbed at his lips, saying, "Your lips are poutier."

Lin Mu's mouth fell slightly open, looking as if he were about to swallow Lu Rong's finger. Lu Rong chuckled, quietly saying, "I can tell you and Lin Zhao apart. I won't mistake one for the other."

After removing the wig and wiping the lipstick away, Lin Mu still looked a little befuddled. Sitting on a pile of mats used for long jumps, he shifted his legs uneasily, and then cautiously probed, "Y-you found out..."

Lu Rong looked up at him, asking deliberately, "What have I found out?"

Lin Mu's cheeks were suffused with red. He stammered, "Y-you found out that... I... Lin Zhao... Umm... And you..."

"Yeah, I knew it." Lu Rong's voice was steady. As though burying it away to destroy all evidence, he tossed Lin Zhao's wig into some obscure corner of the storeroom, then straightened up the box of mineral water he grabbed just now. "I was the one who asked Meimei not to call you *Jiejie*."

Lin Mu nearly lost his breath. Completely ashamed, he desperately wished for a corner to hide, and to bury himself.

When Lu Rong finished tidying everything up, he stood next to the pile of mats, looking up at Lin Mu. "Don't sit so high up."

Lin Mu obediently clambered off.

"You can wear skirts and wigs if you like."

Lin Mu scorned, "Never in my life again!"

Lu Rong smiled.

Lin Mu asked, "Where's Meimei?"

"She's sitting in the stands. Li Zi and Mo Xiaoxiao are with her."

Lin Mu sighed. "I've been too busy; I can only look for you guys in the afternoon."

Lu Rong nodded. "I know."

He suddenly bent over, lowering his head and kissing Lin Mu. The pressure was so light, like the touch of a butterfly, and he then drew away. The two boys faced each other, and Lin Mu saw Lu Rong's eyes, heavy with emotion. Quietly, Lu Rong said, "That's why I came to you instead."

"The lipstick's pretty much wiped off now." Lu Rong stuck out his thumb, rubbing it against his own lips. He said solemnly, "I've been wanting to kiss you this whole time, but I kept holding back."

He raised his thumb, showing it to Lin Mu, seeming a little

pleased. "Look, there's no stain from the lipstick."

Lin Mu was in a daze, unable to grasp that he had just been kissed. By the time he came back to his senses, the door of the storeroom had once again been opened by Lu Rong.

Outside was a queue of people. Lu Rong could not stay for too long, and only accompanied Lin Mu for a while more before he had to go.

"I'm afraid that Li Zi and Mo Xiaoxiao will be overwhelmed." Lu Rong watched Lin Mu update the list. When there were people around, both the boy's eyes and expression were very restrained, like a wound-up tin soldier, aloof and reserved.

Lin Mu was greatly fascinated by these two very different facets to Lu Rong. His eyes were glued to Lu Rong's face, and he wished that he could look at Lu Rong all the time. However, Meimei could not be left alone, and Lu Rong must accompany her.

Classes were assigned to collect their items either in the morning or afternoon. As Lin Mu had to participate in one of the sports events, he had arranged for Sun Hai to take over for him in the middle.

Lin Mu changed into his running shoes and shorts. Taking off his sweater, he revealed a singlet with a bib number on it. When cutting through the track, he noticed that Mo Xiaoxiao was participating in the high jump event for the first-year girls.

When the girl with the metal leg saw him, her eyes brightened. Waving her arm from a distance away, she shouted, "Lin Mu-*xuezhang*!"

Lin Mu waved back, then realized that Li Zi was there too. Cao Zhan happened to be the assistant referee for the high-jump event. Hearing Mo Xiaoxiao's shout, he turned his head over re-flexively.

"Dopey!" Lin Mu ran over.

There was not much skill required to be the assistant referee of the high-jump event. Therefore, this role was quite suitable for Cao Zhan. He was very serious about what he did, recording the scores and checking whether the pole had fallen off. Although the tasks were simple, he was meticulous in his work.

Cao Zhan remembered that Lin Mu was participating in the 400m race, and he provided some insider information. "Jiang Tianhe is participating as well."

Lin Mu asked, "The 400m race?"

Cao Zhan nodded. "He's one of the best runners in our class."

Lin Mu said, "I'm not worried about him, but there's a sports student in Class Five that I'll have to watch out for."

He then glanced at the track, ruffling Cao Zhan's hair. "I'm going to warm up now. Take care, alright?"

Cao Zhan nodded, clenching his fist and raising it towards Lin Mu. "Fighting!"

There were eight lanes on the running track that encircled the field. Lin Mu was number five, and, although it was a high school sports meet, they followed the standard, official format of international races. From the outermost lane to the innermost one, the runners were positioned diagonally. From Lin Mu's spot, he could see Jiang Tianhe on the outermost lane.

It had to be said that, from head to toe, Jiang Tianhe looked very impressive. In the south, the weather in May was already very hot, yet Jiang Tianhe was wearing a full body running suit and a cool pair of spiked track shoes. He was doing his warmups very seriously, and around him were at least five of his lackeys carefully attending to him, pouring him water and massaging his legs. Together with the cheers of all the students on the stands, it seemed as though, before they even started the race, the first place already belonged to Jiang Tianhe.

Lin Mu could not help but shift his gaze towards the other side of the stands, searching. Sure enough, he found Lu Rong and Chen Meihua sitting in the middle.

Compared to her grandson, Chen Meihua's appearance was even more eye-catching. She wore a very modern-styled cheongsam today, and she had a parasol with her. When she saw Lin Mu turning towards them, she waved the banner in her hand.

Lu Rong's body was tilted slightly forward, staring at Lin Mu very seriously.

The latter gave him a thumbs-up. Then, at the call of "Ready," Lin Mu bent down, his hands pressing against the track.

The instant the gun was fired, Jiang Tianhe shot forward.

Four hundred meters was equivalent to one lap around the track, and the experienced runners would not exert all their strength during the first half of the race. Lin Mu controlled his breathing, and his pace for the first two hundred meters was maintained very well.

Usually, there would be others running along during such medium-distance races. Just as he finished half a lap, from the corner of his eye, Lin Mu caught sight of Lin Zhao on the grass running towards him. As Lin Mu's twin, she obviously did not care for her class honor; all she was concerned about was which position Lin Mu would finish in. While running, she signed at him.

Lin Mu could only sign back, "Don't follow me, it's too dangerous! Don't get too close to the track!"

Lin Zhao completely ignored him. "Fighting! Fighting! Quick, run! Someone's catching up!"

Lin Mu could only speed up. He could no longer spare the energy to continue signing to Lin Zhao, but his elder sister was not discouraged. She continued swinging her arms, cheering him on. When Lin Mu made a turn, he glanced towards the field and discovered that it was not just Lin Zhao. Cao Zhan and An Jincheng were also running along the track. Seeing him turn his head, they started cheering him on, desperately urging him forward.

Jiang Tianhe had already fallen to third place. Seeing that Lin Mu was about to overtake him, Jiang Tianhe was so angry that he roared at Cao Zhan, "You fool! Which class are you in?!"

Cao Zhan froze. He seemed to just realize it, and he immediately changed his target, shouting, "Jiang Tianhe! Fighting!"

Lin Mu burst past Jiang Tianhe.

Cao Zhan continued shouting, "Oh no, Jiang Tianhe! Lin Mu has overtaken you!"

Jiang Tianhe was speechless.

Lin Mu was getting closer and closer to the second place. When he was near the podium, Xu Yilu's voice was suddenly heard on the broadcast.

Little Heron's eyesight was really bad, and no one knew how he managed to see anything. However, he started exclaiming loudly over the broadcast system, "Lin Mu! What position are you in? What position are you getting?!"

The finish line was about a hundred meters ahead. It was the final sprint, and Lin Mu did not have the extra energy to answer. Perhaps someone next to Xu Yilu had informed him, and the little heron grabbed the mic, refusing to let go. "Have you overtaken him yet?! Lin Mu, fighting! Overtake him!"

And Lin Mu really succeeded in overtaking the second place.
The crowd was dumbfounded.

What was wrong with the broadcasting in this race?! Was it prophetic?!

When crossing the finishing line, Lin Mu was gasping to the point where he felt his lungs were about to burst. In first place was a sports student who'd been aiming to break the school's record. Lin Mu was very satisfied with his second place, and, after resting for a bit, he went to the table to report his name. Lin Zhao and An Jincheng were already waiting for him there, the two of them even more excited than Lin Mu. Lin Zhao's face was bright red from running, her delight soundless, and she could only move her fingers vigorously to congratulate her little brother.

"Have some water," Lin Mu gestured. "You're even more tired than me."

Next to them, An Jincheng twisted a bottle open and handed it over.

Lin Zhao paused. Without thinking much about it, she took the bottle and handed it to Lin Mu.

Lin Mu carelessly thanked him, tossing his head back and gulping half the bottle down.

An Jincheng had no words.

Lu Rong could not go to the finish line to wait for Lin Mu, as he had to stay by Chen Meihua's side. It was only after the award ceremony that Lin Mu could then move against the crowd towards the stands.

As he shouted for them to give way, he squeezed through, finally making his way over to Lu Rong's side. Removing the gleaming silver medal around his neck, he shoved it into Lu Rong's hands.

"Too bad it's not gold," Lin Mu sighed. He said proudly, "I'll let you take a look."

Lu Rong took an actual look, and he smiled, "It's for me?"

Lin Mu replied, "Not now, it has to be hung up in our classroom for a few days."

It was a bad habit of Zhong He's, a tradition that stemmed from his vanity. After winning an award, it had to be displayed in the class for a few days. No matter how big or small it was, it would still be shown to everyone.

Lu Rong actually was not bothered whether Lin Mu was giving it to him. He re-hung the medal around Lin Mu's neck, and gathered a palmful of sweat.

"It's all red from the sun." Lu Rong looked down, his eyes falling on Lin Mu's neck.

Lin Mu touched it, grumbling, "It's a little sunburnt."

Lu Rong did not speak. He reached out, placing his palm onto Lin Mu's neck as if he were blocking the sunlight and providing Lin Mu with shade.

Lin Mu quietly bent his neck. He suddenly asked, "You didn't participate in any events?"

After a while, Lu Rong answered, "I'm not able to do so."

Lin Mu raised his head.

Lu Rong looked at him. His voice was calm. "During lively events like this, it's all the more important that Meimei doesn't leave my side."

SILENT HEARTS

⑫   **Youth Is···**

⑫   **Youth**
                  Is···

All around them were students cheering with all their might. Only Lu Rong, Chen Meihua and Lin Mu were quietly sitting there, watching the next event. Lu Rong seemed to already be used to it, and it was as though words like "enthusiastic" and "unbridled passion" would never be applied to him.

It was due to his extreme quietness and his extremely reserved aloofness that he had been the odd one out throughout his entire youth.

Since there was no need for Lu Rong to participate in any events, he helped many of his classmates look after their belongings. In such a lively atmosphere, Chen Meihua's illness would rarely play up, and the old lady watched the events with great interest, even cheering on those she found familiar.

For now, there was no need to return to the storeroom, so Lin Mu chose to accompany Lu Rong and Chen Meihua. The back of his neck was a bright, scorching red from the sun, and Lu Rong kept his hand there, trying to help reduce the heat.

Many students were running back and forth from the viewing platform. The moments when there was something tense and anticipatory, hundreds of students would raise their arms, cheering loudly. Lin Mu would occasionally pay attention to the points that his class amassed, as well as their overall ranking. For his class, it was mainly An Jincheng earning the points, and throughout the live broadcast it was the little heron's excited shouts and exclamations. It was not clear how he managed to report the proceedings without being able to see.

Mo Xiaoxiao won fifth place in the first-year girls' high jump event. Although she did not win a medal, she still earned points for her class. During her last few jumps, almost half the students on the field went over to cheer her on, and Li Zi was so anxious that her legs were turning into jelly. When Mo Xiaoxiao was finally done and came down from the mat, she looked just like a hero, limping her way over to Li Zi and hugging the girl who was secretly wiping away her tears.

The two girls supported each other as they returned to the stands. Cheers and whistles erupted from the crowd. Just like a leader making her report, she greeted her classmates reservedly as she took her seat. She had been wearing her prosthetic limb for too long, and she needed to loosen it and rest her limb.

Lin Mu could not help asking her, "Does it hurt?"

Mo Xiaoxiao's face was covered with sweat, but her smile was as bright as the sun. "It's fine, I'm already used to it. It just feels sore when I exercise for too long." She seemed not to be bothered at all, rolling up the leg of her pants and showing it to Lin Mu.

"It can get sweaty here easily, and the prosthetic will slip down. So, I need to control the amount of time I spend exercising, I can't do it for too long."

The amputated end of the girl's limb had many old scars. On first glance, it had quite a visual impact, but once one got used to looking at it, it did not seem so scary anymore. Li Zi tied a small section of bunting onto the prosthetic limb that Mo Xiaoxiao had removed. Later, when she put it on again, it would seem like she now had a leg for cheerleading.

"You should go and play." Mo Xiaoxiao fiddled with the bunting on her prosthetic. She gave Lu Rong a solemn look. "Li Zi and I will help you take care of Meimei, and you can go participate in any event you like."

Lu Rong hesitated, but still shook his head. "I won't trouble you two."

Mo Xiaoxiao's brows slowly knitted together, looking rather unhappy. "We're all friends, don't keep saying things like this. What trouble are you talking about? It's hurtful when you say that."

Lu Rong fell silent and did not refute her. He rarely explained anything to others. Often, when someone criticized him, it was like they were punching a thick layer of cotton, and they would not receive any response.

Mo Xiaoxiao did not want to quarrel with him. After that small grumble, she didn't continue.

Lin Mu's neck didn't hurt as much as before, but Lu Rong still did not pull his hand away.

As the sun slowly started to set, the events of the sports day were finally coming to an end. Lin Mu could no longer stay in the stands, as he had to deal with logistics.

The students broadcasting the events had already returned to their own classes. Zhong He went on stage to give a concluding speech. It lasted for about half an hour, and once it was over, it was time for the classes to clean up the area of the stands they were in. An Jincheng and Lin Mu were in charge of leading a team to supervise and check on the cleanliness after that.

When they were checking on the first-years, Lin Mu did not see any signs of Lu Rong and Chen Meihua.

Li Zi raised her hand, reporting, "Lu Rong brought Granny to the medical office, they'll be back later."

Lin Mu was surprised. "Why did they suddenly go there?"

Li Zi shook her head. "I don't know either... Meimei suddenly said that she was sleepy. Maybe Lu Rong brought her there for a nap?"

Now, Lin Mu had more experience with the behavior of an Alzheimer's patient. He spoke to An Jincheng quietly, "I'll go to the medical office to take a look."

Although An Jincheng was puzzled by how Lin Mu was so conscientious over this matter, he did not stop him. Lin Mu tossed his armband over to Li Zi, asking for her help to check on the rest of the classes while he turned and jumped down the stands, running towards the medical office.

On his way there, he bumped into many people he knew. After throwing out the rubbish, Jiang Tianhe was walking back with Cao Zhan. When Dopey saw him, he shouted loudly, "Lin Mu, where are you going?"

Lin Mu had no time to speak, and he only waved back. He quickly ran past the canteen and the classrooms, only to discover Lu Rong standing by the door of the medical office.

The boy was holding a plastic bag in his hand, and he was a little astonished to see Lin Mu. "Why did you come here?"

Bending over, his hands on his knees, Lin Mu gasped for air. As he wiped away the sweat dripping down his chin, he said, "Li Zi said that you came to the medical office. I was worried that something had happened to Meimei."

Lu Rong understood now. He smiled a little helplessly. "It's nothing, Meimei was just simply tired out, so she wanted to sleep."

Lin Mu was still worried. "She's really just tired?"

Lu Rong nodded. "Yes."

Lin Mu himself did not know if he was feeling relieved or something else, and his body drooped down. Lu Rong opened the door to the medical office, turning sideways and letting Lin Mu enter first before closing the door after him.

Sure enough, Chen Meihua was lying on the bed inside. She was deep asleep, even snoring slightly. Lin Mu looked at her for a little while before turning to face Lu Rong.

"Would you like some water?" Lu Rong took out a drink from the plastic bag.

Lin Mu discovered that he had bought more than one bottle. There were all sorts of choices within, ranging from milk tea to fruit juice.

Lu Rong explained, "Meimei might make a fuss when she wakes up. Buying a few more drinks can distract her by letting her choose."

"What if she doesn't like any of them?"

Lu Rong thought about it, then answered softly, "It'll be fine if I coax her patiently, she'll settle down sooner or later."

Lin Mu stared at Lu Rong, motionless. He opened his mouth, wanting to say something, only for him to feel as though there was something stuck in his throat, and even the tip of his tongue felt dry and bitter.

"Lu Rong," he suddenly called his name.

Lu Rong tilted his head slightly down. His eyes, like the reflection of a lake, fell onto Lin Mu's face, and the two did not speak for some time.

"Don't exhaust yourself all alone." When Lin Mu looked up again, his eyes were a little red. He stubbornly pressed his lips together, and then continued slowly after a pause. "You can rely on me; I can take care of Meimei too."

Lu Rong paused. "I know."

Lin Mu held his breath, keeping quiet.

Lu Rong reached out. He wanted to touch Lin Mu's face, but the latter shifted a little, dodging him, then remained there, stiff and unmoving.

Lu Rong took a step forward. His forehead pressed against Lin Mu's with a little pressure, and Lin Mu had to raise his head a little.

"I like you, Lin Mu." Lu Rong looked into his eyes. "You're so perfect, and you shouldn't be tied down by my burdens. I can't bear to do that to you, and I'm also scared that you'll be unhappy."

Lin Mu frowned. He spoke earnestly, "You're not a burden, and I will not be unhappy."

His face was a little red, and he murmured, "You're my darling, and I want to be with you for the rest of my life."

Chen Meihua did not sleep for too long before she woke up. She tended to be quite grumpy after waking up, and just like Lu Rong had predicted, she started making a fuss. Lin Mu tried to coax her into choosing something she liked to drink as she sniffled and cried. As such, after selecting a bottle of milk tea and drinking some, her cries quietened down.

Once the sports meet was over, the entire population of Kunqian started to settle down for their studies. For the second-year students, the exams at the end of the semester were similar to a mini version of the national college entrance examinations, and it was very useful in showing where the student's foundations were in preparation for their third year.

Besides worrying about his own results, Lin Mu was also worried over Cao Zhan's. During the tutoring sessions on Saturday with Dopey, he felt that he himself was about to turn dopey too.

Cao Zhan himself, however, was not very anxious. With great naivety, he said, "I can get into a university!"

Lin Mu looked helpless. "Jiangsu's exams are famous for being hellish, and you need quite high scores to enter the universities..."

Nevertheless, he asked, "Which university are you getting into?"

Cao Zhan thought for a moment. "The Art & Design Technology Institute?"

"Art & Design?" Lin Mu paused. "Which major?"

Cao Zhan was very happy to talk about this matter, and he spoke with great pride, "Fashion design!"

Lin Mu was a little surprised that Cao Zhan had such a clearly defined goal in his mind. He considered it, then said, "The art college entrance exam is over, but if you submit your score for your culture examinations, you might have a very good chance of getting in."

Other than attending classes normally, Cao Zhan had been spending a lot of time in the art studio, practicing his foundations in art. His mother, Ji Qingwen, was very farsighted. Although what she was doing wasn't quite on the level of opening a brand new path for her son, she had placed her son's interests and specialties first when she planned this out for him.

"Auntie Ji is really impressive," Lin Mu could not help exclaiming.

Cao Zhan gave a big silly grin, nodding. "Because Mama loves me the most, and I love Mama too."

Lu Rong did not join in their conversation. While arranging the study materials in front of her, Chen Meihua would glance over at Cao Zhan. After listening for some time, she suddenly turned towards Lu Rong. "Is Rongrong taking the college entrance examinations too?"

Calling Lu Rong Rongrong meant that she currently remembered Lu Rong's identity. However, it was clear that she did not remember how old her grandson was.

Lu Rong replied patiently, "It's still a long way to go for me."

Chen Meihua then asked, "Has Rongrong entered primary school yet?"

Lin Mu laughed until his mouth cramped up. "Lu Rong has already graduated from primary school."

Chen Meihua was shocked. She studied her grandson carefully, then said, "No wonder, Rongrong is now so tall."

Although it was not yet time for first-year students to be stressed over coming up with a list of schools and majors they wished to join, Lin Mu was quite curious about Lu Rong's future plans. However, the latter seemed to have never given any great thought to this before.

"There's no point in thinking about it." Lu Rong had already changed into the short sleeves' version of the school uniform long ago in May. His body temperature ran high, and he was prone to perspiring. "So, I might as well not think about it."

Lin Mu was rather disapproving. "How can it be pointless? It's better to start thinking about your university choices early."

Lu Rong was unmoved. "We'll see."

He changed the topic, resting his chin on his hand and looking at Lin Mu. "What about you? Which university are you aiming for?"

"It definitely has to be within the province." Lin Mu upheld the principles that he could not go too far away, and he said proudly, "I want to study medicine."

Lu Rong imagined Lin Mu in a white coat. He smiled faintly. "It suits you."

Ever since the talk in the medical office that day, there had been an obvious change in Lu Rong's attitude towards Lin Mu.

He was no longer overly courteous, nor would he reject Lin Mu's request to walk with them every day. Occasionally, the boy would relax his tense shoulders, revealing a softer attitude, and he often made Lin Mu wonder how he could dote on him even more.

"Give it more thought." Lin Mu crouched in Lu Rong's yard, a shovel in his hand for weeding.

Lu Rong had planted many pots of flowers, not because he liked them a lot, but because the flowers could distract Chen Meihua and make her happier when she looked at them.

The moth orchids that Lin Mu gifted him during the New Year had also been transplanted into another pot, and it was growing very well.

With no sense of embarrassment, Lu Rong stated, "I'll only be in my second year next year, so I don't have to think about it so early."

Lin Mu pursed his lips. "It's just two semesters, and the winter and summer holidays would be over just like that. It's not too early for you to start thinking about it now."

Lu Rong's reply was a little perfunctory. "I got it."

Lin Mu seemed to have no way against him, but he was unwilling to give up either. Reaching out, Lin Mu wanted to tug at his hair. Lu Rong tilted his head back, but he did not manage to dodge him, and so he could only catch his wrist. With a little exertion of strength, he pulled Lin Mu into his arms.

Speechless, Lin Mu felt that Lu Rong had learned to be naughty. He gnashed his teeth, "Let go first!"

Lu Rong changed into a sitting position, spreading his legs apart and clamping Lin Mu in between. He hugged Lin Mu's waist, tucking his chin into the crook of his neck, quietly saying, "I'm not as smart as you, I can't think of too many things."

Once Lu Rong put it that way, Lin Mu naturally could not harden his heart and continue pushing the matter. The two of them shared a quiet embrace until they heard from inside Chen Meihua calling out for someone.

Lin Mu nudged Lu Rong's shoulder, urging him, "Let's go in."

Lu Rong made a muffled noise of acknowledgement. Seeming rather unwilling, he let go of Lin Mu.

Lin Mu stood up then bent over, pressing a kiss onto Lu Rong's head.

The end-of-semester exams were held over two days. Due to a Go competition, Lin Zhao did not take the exams. Lin Mu handed his paper in early, and, as soon as he left the classroom, he could not help but call Lin Yanlai to ask about her results.

Lin Yanlai was very amused. "It's only the first day today, how can the results come out so quickly?"

"How is she doing?"

"Pretty well. If she is able to stay within the top ten positions, she should be able to move one rank up. Don't worry about your sister, how are your own exams?"

It was rare that the father would think about his youngest child. After all, Lin Mu had never needed his parents to worry about him—Jiang Wan would even forget about parent-teacher conferences sometimes.

Lin Mu was completely unbothered. He said, "Of course everything's fine for me. Ask Lin Zhao to reply to my messages."

Lin Yanlai scolded, "Why does she need to reply your messages! Your sister's nervous over the competition already! Don't stir up trouble!"

Without the liveliness of Lin Zhao around, as well as it being the exam period, their group chat was dead and stagnant. Even after the exams, when Lin Mu spammed images asking people to come out to play, only a few people responded.

An Jincheng went straight to the point. "How is your sister's competition?"

Lin Mu replied, "She's a young genius national Go player. If she doesn't get the championship this year, I'll let her change her last name to yours!"

An Jincheng did not know how to react to that.

This vow seemed to have been too conceited, and An Jincheng did not respond for a long time. However, Jiang Tianhe could not help himself, and he roasted Lin Mu, "The two of you sure have some sibling-complex."

Lin Mu could not be bothered with him. Turning his head, he discovered that Sun Hai had left the classroom too. The little tyrant had not done well during the mid-term exams, and so he dared not slack off for the finals. Only after the exam ended did he exhale in relief, grumbling to Lin Mu, "If I fall out of the top 20 ranks again, I'll be sent abroad by my family."

For students with good family backgrounds, studying abroad was nothing new. Jiang Wan and Lin Yanlai had also asked Lin Mu once whether he had such intentions, but his reply had naturally been a refusal; there had been no need for him to even consider it.

Next door, Cao Zhan and Jiang Tianhe had long packed up already. Neither of them were able to do well in school without begging others for help, though Jiang Tianhe's grades were slightly better—his goal was to enter a university, regardless of which university it was.

"Little Heron hasn't finished the exam yet." Cao Zhan counted on his fingers. "There's Lu Rong and Meimei as well."

Jiang Tianhe couldn't take this. "Why are you concerned over the first-years? Also, Meimei doesn't have to take any exams, what are you worried about?"

Cao Zhan pursed his lips unhappily, but he was no longer afraid of Jiang Tianhe. After all, this guy wouldn't actually beat anyone up; he would only impotently rage.

An Jincheng had to help the teachers collect the exam papers. Lin Mu and the others stood in a row, leaning against the windows of the corridor like chicks pecking at grains as they waited for him. Their expressions were all the same, and Young Master An felt a little embarassed when looking at them.

Mr. Yang seemed to find it amusing. He said, "You all have a very good friendship."

An Jincheng opened his mouth but said nothing. He was the class representative, and he could not say things like how he was at odds with the common folk.

Finally, replies from the others started streaming in. Li Zi said that she had been comparing answers with Mo Xiaoxiao, and Sun Hai replied, "You guys actually have the courage to compare answers? I wish I could invite Fish Leong to hold a concert for you two; she can sing her song 'Courage'!"

Lin Mu looked at his phone, typing, "What about Lu Rong?"

Mo Xiaoxiao answered, "He hasn't finished yet. Meimei threw a small tantrum, so the teacher gave him some extra time."

Lin Mu thought about it, then he informed Cao Zhan and the rest that he would head down to Lu Rong's classroom.

In the classroom, he saw that Mo Xiaoxiao and Li Zi were still there. They were a little startled to see him. "*Xuezhang*, why are you here?"

Lin Mu smiled. "I've come to take care of Meimei."

The two girls did not doubt him, and quietly called out to Chen Meihua from the back door. Chen Meihua turned around. The tear tracks on her face were evidence that she had just been crying. With her swollen eyes, she looked upset.

Lin Mu poked his head out, and Chen Meihua saw him.

"Meimei," Lin Mu called out to her softly. "Don't be scared, I'm here now."

Chen Meihua was brought out of the classroom by Lin Mu.

The old lady seemed to have suffered a great grievance, and she was crying uncontrollably. As Lin Mu took her out of the classroom, many students next door who had finished their exam looked over. Li Zi and Mo Xiaoxiao formed a small human wall, blocking Chen Meihua from their sight. Lin Mu wiped her tears, coaxing, "Does Meimei want to go out for a walk?"

The old lady sobbed, "W-where are we going?"

Lin Mu said, "The sports ground, basketball court, anywhere is fine."

Chen Meihua hesitated for a moment, but she nodded in the end.

Lu Rong was still working on his exam. He did not have much time left, but as he was very worried, he kept looking out of the classroom. Lin Mu met his eyes, giving him a smile to soothe his emotions.

Lin Mu gestured, pointing at the exam paper. What he meant was, "Answer the questions properly."

Cao Zhan asked in the group chat, "We're all done, Lin Mu, what are you doing?"

With one hand holding onto Chen Meihua, Lin Mu tapped on his phone with the other. "I'm going for a stroll with Meimei."

Cao Zhan responded, "Where? We're coming too."

Lin Mu asked the chat, "What about Little Heron? Has he finished his exams?"

Cao Zhan soon sent a photo over—An Jincheng, Jiang Tianhe, Sun Hai and Xu Yilu were all there. He said, "We'll come and accompany Meimei for a stroll too."

Lin Mu suspected that An Jincheng and Jiang Tianhe had been forced to do so, but since they were coming, Lin Mu could not reject them directly either. He brought Chen Meihua to the basketball court and waited for them. When Cao Zhan and others arrived, the basketball court was thus filled with familiar faces.

Chen Meihua's emotions had stabilized. As she and Cao Zhan were friends of a revolution, from a far distance, they shouted "Dopey" and "Meimei" at each other. Sun Hai got a basketball from somewhere and started tossing it around with An Jincheng and Jiang Tianhe in a very show-off manner.

Xu Yilu was holding onto his white cane. He sat quietly by the courtside, listening to Cao Zhan and Chen Meihua calling out to each other before confirming Lin Mu's position. Giving a smile, he asked, "How was the exam?"

Lin Mu sat down next to him. "Of course it wasn't a problem for me. What about you? Did you manage to finish the questions in time?"

Xu Yilu nodded. "Yeah, I did. Lu Rong isn't done yet?"

Lin Mu watched as Cao Zhan and Chen Meihua played together. Both of them had their palms stacked on top of each other, and they seemed to be comparing who could stack it higher, happily indulging in the fun.

"Meimei had a tantrum earlier, and the teacher gave him more time," Lin Mu said, "so I brought her here, to prevent Lu Rong's exam from being affected."

Xu Yilu frowned. Although he was unable to see what exactly had happened, he could still imagine it. They shared a moment of silence, before Xu Yilu said heavily, "What a difficult life Lu Rong has."

Lin Mu did not deny it. He looked at Chen Meihua, and it was not clear if his words were meant for only himself or Xu Yilu as well. "It won't be the case anymore. I'll be around."

After Lu Rong finished the last question, he submitted the paper in a hurry without checking it. His form teacher could not help but advise, "There's no need to be in such a hurry, there's still some time left."

Lu Rong pressed his lips together before speaking, "I'm afraid my grandmother would be waiting for too long."

The form teacher spoke gently, "Lin Mu-*tongxue* is helping you take care of her, so you don't have to worry. Would you like to check your paper again?"

Lu Rong still shook his head determinedly. The form teacher sighed, no longer insisting.

Perhaps afraid that Lu Rong would be anxious when he could not find them, Lin Mu had already sent him a message, informing him that he was bringing Meimei to the basketball court. When

Lu Rong went over, he discovered that Chen Meihua and Cao Zhan were still playing hand games with each other, and Lin Mu was sitting by the side. The moment Lin Mu looked up, he immediately caught sight of Lu Rong.

"You're done with the exam?" Lin Mu stood up. He was half a head shorter than Lu Rong, and the taller boy looked at Lin Mu with slightly lowered lids, his eyelashes concealing his eyes.

Lin Mu was very concerned over his results. "How was the exam?"

Lu Rong only said it was fine. There were not many people on the court, just An Jincheng and the other two people playing basketball. Xu Yilu could not see, while Cao Zhan and Chen Meihua were very focused on their own game.

Lin Mu blinked, watching Lu Rong take a few steps closer to him. The boy suddenly bent down, resting his forehead on his shoulder.

Frozen, Lin Mu dared not move. The weather was scorching today, and the trees above them provided shade from the sun. The ends of Lu Rong's hair brushed against Lin Mu's neck, feeling a little prickly.

Lu Rong seemed to be resting on him. He did not say a word, and half his face was cast in shadow. When Lin Mu turned his head towards him, he could see that Lu Rong had his eyes shut.

Until Sun Hai called out Lin Mu's name.

"What are you doing?" Sun Hai's voice was very pervasive, almost covering half the court. "Has the little underclassman finished his exam?"

Lin Mu could only shout back, "He's done!"

Lu Rong did not raise his head. He seemed to have smiled, before turning his face around, his lips meeting Lin Mu's neck.

Lin Mu still had his head turned away, speaking to Sun Hai.

Suddenly feeling warm lips against his neck, he did not react at first. It was only when he jerked his head around did Lu Rong slowly pull his lips away from his neck.

Lin Mu was stunned.

Lu Rong seemed to not have much of a reaction after the kiss. He held out his hand, pressing his thumb against the spot where he kissed, quietly saying, "You don't sweat at all."

Despite the shade of the trees above him, the heat from Lin Mu's cheeks spread visibly to his ears. He feigned calmness as he replied, "I don't sweat easily."

There was nothing funny, but it made Lu Rong crack a tiny smile. The lush greenery was reflected in his eyes that seemed as deep as a lake, and his gaze was clear, like scattering rain across Lin Mu.

"They're calling for you," Lu Rong said. "Go ahead."

Sun Hai had called Lin Mu over to play two-on-two, but Lin Mu was not very interested. After playing for a while, he couldn't help but be distracted, looking over to the courtside. Chen Meihua and Dopey were now playing another game, while Lu Rong was seated next to Xu Yilu, and the two looked to be chatting.

An Jincheng ran past him a few times, and finally could not hold himself back from asking, "What are you looking at?"

Lin Mu received the ball, casually tossing it over to the restricted area and asked, "How long are you guys going to play?"

Jiang Tianhe was the one playing the most seriously. He was still fighting with Sun Hai for the rebound ball in the restricted area. After the ball was snatched from him, he was so angry that even his shoes had been kicked off.

Xu Yilu waved at them from the courtside. "Why don't you take a break?"

Wiping his sweat, Lin Mu left the court. Lu Rong happened to be re-doing Chen Meihua's hair. The old lady and Cao Zhan were playing rock-paper-scissors, and once her hair was done, she then claimed she was hungry.

"Meimei wants something cold." The moment Chen Meihua decided she wanted something. she could not wait even a moment for it. She urged Lu Rong, "Little Deer, go and buy something cold."

Lu Rong looked a little stern. "It won't fill your stomach when you're hungry. Choose something else."

Chen Meihua's face puckered up. Pursing her lips, she said, "I don't want! Meimei wants to eat ice cream!"

Lin Mu crouched down, his tone was half-cajoling and half-deceiving as he spoke, "Ice cream is too cold. Would Meimei like to eat something else with me?"

Chen Meihua's attention was attracted by the words "with me" and "something else." She slowly considered it, then asked Lin Mu, "What are we going to eat?"

Lin Mu pulled her hand. "Meimei will know when she goes with me."

It was definitely impossible to bring just Chen Meihua alone. Cao Zhan wanted to follow as well, and since Lin Mu was no longer playing basketball, there was no need for the rest of them to remain on the court. Xu Yilu extended his white cane, his other arm supported by Sun Hai. Jiang Tianhe asked Cao Zhan a little rudely, "Fool, where's your bag?"

Only then did Cao Zhan realize he had left his bag in the classroom.

"I'll go get it." An Jincheng had the keys to the classrooms. He spoke unconcernedly, "Wait for me at the canteen."

The others naturally had no opinions about it. As such, Lin Mu brought Chen Meihua, along with a tail of people, to the little store located in the school canteen.

The end-of-semester exams had just concluded, and there were still quite a number of people inside the store. There were only a few days left before the school holidays began, and it could be seen that the souls of most students had long fled the schoolgrounds.

Young couples no longer tried to hide away like usual. As the summer holiday would last for two months, before this separation began, they had to cultivate their's feelings even more.

Lin Mu really did not buy any ice cream for Chen Meihua. He picked out some cakes, biscuits as well as some low sugar snacks, finally leaving the store with a big bag.

Jiang Tianhe and Sun Hai occupied a long table, and Cao Zhan was seated next to Chen Meihua.

Lu Rong watched as Lin Mu took everything out of the bag. Everyone got a little something, and the old lady got the most. Chen Meihua was just like a pampered little princess, clapping her hands in delight, and then she grabbed onto the box of the cake, refusing to let go.

"You have one, too." Lin Mu pushed another cake box into Lu Rong's hand.

Lu Rong glanced at him. "It's not my birthday yet."

"I know." Lin Mu could not help but smile.

Lu Rong thought for a moment before speaking, his tone very certain. "It's not your birthday today, either."

Lin Mu could not take it anymore. "I'm just buying you a cake. Why are you overthinking it?"

Lu Rong continued staring at him, and Lin Mu could not

stand it. He clicked his tongue, and when no one was paying attention to them, he leaned into Lu Rong's ear, whispering, "Today is the one-month anniversary of when we started dating officially."

Lu Rong did not know what to say.

Lin Mu's expression said it all. "Cake is a must for us to always be together in sweet and harmonious times."

This anniversary trick was something that Lin Mu learned from the girls in the class.

He did not have any dating experience, and his questions could not be too direct. Therefore, after beating around the bush for some time, he received an answer that was also not very direct—an anniversary must be celebrated properly.

As for what an anniversary was, it seemed that anything could be an anniversary—the first time the couple confirmed their relationship, the first time they held hands, the first time they hugged, the first time they kissed... Girls were truly rich in romance and emotions.

Lin Mu even asked Lin Zhao, and as expected, his sister stood out from the crowd.

"An anniversary?" Lin Zhao had been practicing every day before the Go tournament. She thought for a moment, then moved her fingers expressionlessly, "The day I was ranked professionally, and the day I lost a game."

Lin Mu was at a loss for words.

Their closest anniversary was probably the one-month anniversary of starting their relationship. Thinking that the summer holidays were about to start and that they might not be able to see each other every day, Lin Mu wanted to celebrate it to further deepen their feelings. However, his thoughts about this were actually very much like that of a boy, and his way of celebrating it was rather inept, and even slightly perfunctory. However, as he looked at Lu Rong eating the cake, the other boy seemed to be quite satisfied.

The taste of the cake sold in the school was still acceptable, the key point being that there was abundant cream in it. Holding onto a plastic fork, Lu Rong dug into it bit by bit, sending bites into his mouth.

The fork was a little small. If he dug a little too deep, the cream would smear onto his hand. After a few bites, Lu Rong had to stop and lick the cream off his fingers.

After eating half the cake, Lu Rong noticed that Lin Mu was staring, and so he asked, "Do you want some?"

Lin Mu shook his head. "Is it sweet?"

Lu Rong glanced at him, smiling. "It's very sweet."

Lin Mu was delighted. Chen Meihua had finished her cake, and Lin Mu helped her wipe her hands as they waited for An Jincheng to return with Cao Zhan's bag.

The rest of them discussed their plans for the school holidays, and Sun Hai wanted to go for a trip together.

"We'll be in our third year once school starts." Sun Hai was very insistent. "Everyone knows how tough Kunqian is on our studies. Furthermore, Little Heron, Young Master An and I may be going overseas in our second semester. By then, it will be difficult for us to go out and play together."

It was the first time Cao Zhan had heard about Xu Yilu going abroad. Sorrowful, he asked, "Little Heron, you're going overseas?"

Xu Yilu nodded. "I'll be studying overseas, and I'll be treating my eyes there as well."

Jiang Tianhe looked at Cao Zhan, asking, "Fool, you're going overseas too?"

"I'm not." Cao Zhan shook his head. "I'm scared."

An Jincheng raised his chin towards Lin Mu. "You're not going overseas?"

"Why would I?" Lin Mu was baffled. "It's not like I can't study in the country. My sister's a Go player, and China's Go players are the best in the world. If she's not going overseas, there's no way I'm going."

The Lin siblings had always been inseparable. Therefore, when Lin Mu put it that way, no one suspected a thing.

"When will the tournament end?" Sun Hai asked.

Lin Mu said, "In a few more days."

Sun Hai decisively said, "That works! We'll discuss it again a few days later!"

Because of Lin Zhao, the cable television in Lin Mu's house was locked onto the live broadcast of the Go league tournament. Jiang Wan could not fully comprehend it, and as Lin Mu had half a year's worth of foundation in Go, he was in charge of explaining it to his mother.

This year, Lin Zhao represented the Jiangsu team at the Women's Go tournament. Besides being the youngest competitor, her disability had also been mentioned by the media many times.

The most commonly used phrases were things like "disabled in body but firm in spirit," "persistent and undeterred," and "the heavens do not give up on those who persevere." Few actually paid attention to Lin Zhao's skills, only treating her as a gimmick.

In the end, to their surprise, the three people from the Jiangsu team spared no effort, defeating their formidable adversary, the

Shanghai team. As for Lin Zhao, she was like a newborn calf who was unafraid of anything. In the endgame, she won a match with a white piece in a *knock out* fight at the upper right corner, and thus made a good start for the Jiangsu team.

That night, Lin Mu gave Lin Yanlai another call. "How is it going?"

Lin Yanlai sounded very relaxed. "She's in an excellent condition, and she won all her matches today."

"I saw that. I'm asking if those media outlets are now convinced?"

Lin Yanlai paused for a moment, wanting to laugh. "You twins are really exactly the same. After the last match in the afternoon, your sister scolded the interviewing reporter."

It's good that she scolded them. Who asked them to look down on her? Lin Mu thought.

In the midst of Lin Zhao's matches, Lin Mu dared not send her any texts in case of disturbing her. Their end-of-semester results had just been announced, and coming soon after that was their individual rankings. The school also spoke to their parents and gave out their holiday homework. Everything was over in a couple of days, and by then, Lin Zhao was almost done.

Mr. Yang was still reminding the class to stay safe and obey the rules during the holidays. With a textbook blocking him, Lin Mu was sneakily checking the results of the women's Go tournament on his phone. When he saw that Lin Zhao had won the third place, he immediately exclaimed out loud in class.

Mr. Yang's face was dark as he reprimanded him. "What are you making so much noise for?! It's not the holidays yet!"

Lin Mu sat down obediently, and Sun Hai sitting behind him, gave him a few kicks on his chair. Taking advantage of the moment Mr. Yang looked away, Lin Mu turned and gave the boy an "OK" sign.

Sun Hai was completely anxious. Whispering loudly, he asked, "What's OK? How did she do?!"

Lin Mu could not help but scold him, "Are you an idiot?! It's third! Third!"

Sun Hai was speechless.

All the way until the end of the school day, both Lin Mu and Sun Hai had to stand in the corridor, holding their school bags above their heads. After class, An Jincheng brought them their holiday homework.

When the tournament was over, Lin Zhao was promoted straight up to professional second dan. Lin Yanlai and Jiang Wan behaved as though she had passed the ancient imperial examinations, and if not for the ban of firecrackers and fireworks in the city, the two silly parents would have lit them ten days straight.

Even though they did not light any firecrackers, Jiang Wan made an enormous banner and hung it on the roof. When Lin Zhao returned, she stared at that red banner for a long time, her expression extremely entertaining.

Smiling wickedly, Lin Mu signed, "Now that the whole district knows that you've been promoted to second dan, they'll have to call you Lin-*laoshi* when they see you."

Lin Zhao kicked his backside, her fingers moving swiftly, "Then why don't you try calling me that first?"

Knowing that Lin Zhao was back, the name of the group chat was changed to "Extremely Awesome Second Dan Lin." Sun Hai once again proposed to go on a trip together, and no one objected.

To facilitate the discussion, they agreed to meet at the KFC on Guanqian Street. When Xu Yilu arrived, he was not very enthusiastic about it. Hesitating for a long time, he finally asked, "Would it be very inconvenient to bring me along?"

Li Zi and Mo Xiaoxiao were discussing how big a luggage they should bring. When they heard Xu Yilu, they were a little surprised.

Disagreeing with him, Sun Hai spoke, "What are you thinking about? There are so many of us, you think we can't take care of you?"

Xu Yilu hesitated. "It's not just me... There's Cao Zhan, Lin Zhao, Xiaoxiao, and Lu Rong and Meimei as well. They all need to be taken care of, and it would be very inconvenient."

His concerns were not invalid. If they wanted everyone to go, they would need to take special care of Cao Zhan, Lin Zhao, Chen Meihua and Mo Xiaoxiao. Evaluating the situation, it was indeed a little difficult for one person to take care of one individual, not to mention that some people needed more than one person to take care of them.

Xu Yilu did not want to be a burden on others, and he really did not want a fun trip to become tiring and troublesome because of him. They were different from most people, and their friends should not suffer the gaze and criticism from strangers that they usually had to endure.

Mo Xiaoxiao had never considered this before, but now she seemed a little hesitant when she was reminded by Xu Yilu. It was only Cao Zhan who still did not understand. With a puzzled look, he looked at the others who were now silent.

"I don't think that any of you are a burden," Li Zi folded her arms, speaking up suddenly. "Mo Xiaoxiao can run and jump, and for Lin Zhao-*xuejie*, she only can't hear and speak. There's no need to even mention Cao Zhan, no one will find it troublesome bringing him along."

Xu Yilu frowned, turning towards Li Zi.

Lin Mu reached out, pinching his palm. "We have so many strong and capable people here, there's no need to worry that we can't take care of you."

Xu Yilu opened his mouth, but he was unable to refute him.

Jiang Tianhe spoke lazily, "In any case, everyone has to go. Stop struggling over it. It's so expensive, there's no way I'm willing to pay for two shares by myself."

Sun Hai blinked, and suddenly remembered something. He asked Lin Mu, "Where's Lu Rong? Why isn't he here yet?"

SILENT HEARTS

Together

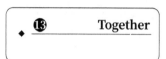

Together

Lu Rong was sitting by the flowerbed in front of the KFC while Chen Meihua was licking an ice cream cone. They had been here for a while, but the old lady refused to go in, saying she had to eat ice cream first. Lu Rong had no choice but to buy her one.

As Chen Meihua grew older, Lu Rong controlled the amount of ice cream and candy she ate. She licked the cone very slowly, and when she was halfway through, An Jincheng happened to appear at the entrance.

"Why aren't you going in?" He pulled the door open, looking at the pair of grandmother and grandson rather expressionlessly.

Lu Rong said, "Meimei isn't finished yet."

Chen Meihua was not bothered by how others felt. She acted as though no one was waiting for her, licking her cone as she swung her legs.

An Jincheng walked over. He crouched down, looking at the old lady with his flower-like face and asked, "Would Meimei like to go in and finish your ice cream?"

Chen Meihua was very determined. "No."

An Jincheng frowned.

Just as Lu Rong was about to tell An Jincheng to ignore her, his phone in his pocket suddenly rang.

Lin Mu asked him, "Where are you?"

"We're downstairs, Meimei is refusing to go in."

"Hold on," Lin Mu said.

He hung up and ran down in less than a minute.

Lin Mu did not seem to mind that Chen Meihua was refusing to go in because of an ice cream cone. He held his hand above the old lady's head, shielding her from the sun as he quietly asked, "Is it hot?"

Chen Meihua did feel a little hot. She was wearing a dress made of a silk-like material today, and her white hair was tied into a bun. Studying the ice cream cone in her hand, she spoke feebly, "Meimei wants air-conditioning."

Lin Mu smiled. "There's air-conditioning in the KFC, does Meimei want to come in?"

This time, Chen Meihua did not refuse, obediently saying that she wanted to.

An Jincheng was very amazed by Lin Mu's ability in coaxing old people. As they went upstairs, he too imitated Lin Mu's tone, trying to coax Chen Meihua. Unfortunately, she did not care much for his sensibilities, and thus was rather indifferent towards him.

Lu Rong followed behind, walking together with Lin Mu. After a long pause, he finally spoke, "It seems that we always have to trouble you."

Lin Mu feigned unhappiness, saying, "I already told you last time, this is no trouble at all."

Now that An Jincheng, Lu Rong, and Chen Meihua arrived, the entire group was present. Sun Hai repeated his suggestion to go on a trip together again, and afraid that Lu Rong might disagree, he repeatedly promised that with so many people around, they would definitely be able to good take care of Meimei.

Lu Rong was still hesitant about agreeing, and he deliberated over it cautiously.

To put him at ease, Lin Mu pressed a hand to his own chest, saying, "You have me."

Lu Rong was a little amused. "Aren't you going to take care of Lin Zhao?"

Lin Mu froze. He reflexively turned to look at his sister. Lin Zhao did not know what they were talking about, and her face was questioning.

Next to them, An Jincheng spoke up. "I can take care of Lin Zhao."

Lin Mu did not think too much about this. It was as if he found his savior, grabbing hold of him and selling his own sister shamelessly. "My sister has no lack of people wanting to ingratiate themselves with her. I'll help you take care of Meimei."

Lu Rong wanted to laugh. He lowered his head, hiding his eyes, and no longer refused.

Due to having an old lady accompanying them, they naturally could not choose a location that was too far away. As such, after excluding some nearby places, Sun Hai decided on Mount Mogan.

"It's one of the top four summer vacation destinations, with a mountain and rivers. How about that?"

Lin Mu looked at the map. "There's no train to get there... Are we going to rent cars?"

Sun Hai's smile became crafty. He fluttered his eyelashes at An Jincheng, standing on no courtesy as he asked, "Young Master An, can we borrow your chauffeur?"

They had a total of eleven people. Together with their luggage, it was best to rent a vehicle for twelve. It would definitely not be cheap to rent a medium-sized tourist bus that could fit all of them.

It was no secret how wealthy An Jincheng's family was, and his family had even invested in an online travel agency. In Sun Hai's words, since they were all going together, there was no need to be standing on courtesy when it came to such a crucial matter!

Now that the transport had been settled, it was also not a problem for the eleven of them to choose a villa to stay in. At first, Lin Mu was a little worried that Lu Rong's pocket money would not be enough, but in the end, it turned out that the boy's true identity was actually a landlord.

"Due to our situation, we also receive some subsidies." Lu Rong had nothing to hide from Lin Mu. "That includes my school fees."

Lin Mu was a little upset. "It seems that there'll be no opportunity for me to provide for you."

Lu Rong could not help but laugh. He explained, "I'm used to saving money, just in case anything happens in the future."

His parents had passed away in an accident, and Chen Meihua's illness was also part of his consideration. Lu Rong had never believed in such a thing as luck. After all, he had never been lucky before, except for meeting Lin Mu.

Less than half a month into the summer holidays and having not seen Lu Rong for over ten days, Lin Mu missed him very much. Even things that couples usually did, like talking on the

phones and sending text messages, were not as easily accom-
plished by them, since Lu Rong had to take care of Meimei.

Alzheimer's patients could not be left alone at any time. Often, Lu Rong would still be on the phone with Lin Mu, and Chen
Meihua's illness would act up. Crying and fussing were like her
daily chores, and if she was not watched properly, she might even
go missing.

Lin Mu could not go over to Lu Rong's house every day. Furthermore, he might not be of help either, as Lu Rong would then
have to worry about him as well.

Lin Mu realized that while learning how to like a person, he
was also discovering that such feelings were not only just sweet,
they could also be sour, salty, and even a little bitter.

Sometimes, due to being unable to distinguish the tastes distinctly, he liked Lu Rong even more for it.

Endurance, tolerance, loneliness, and restraint all turned out
to have no flavor. They were dull and soundless, silent and still,
but so enormous that they were filled with a profound and true
delight.

Lu Rong had his head bent down, speaking to Chen Meihua
next to him. Lin Mu kept his eyes on him, his gaze quiet.

Perhaps they were discussing what to bring along with them.
Chen Meihua said something before Lu Rong raised his head,
looking at Lin Mu.

Chen Meihua followed as well, turning her head around. Like
an innocent child, she asked, "Did Mumu miss me?"

How could he not?

As such, Lin Mu nodded. "Yes, I've missed you. What about
Meimei?"

Chen Meihua grinned, saying that both Little Deer and she had missed him very much.

Calling her grandson Little Deer meant that she did not remember who Lu Rong was to her.

Lin Mu and Lu Rong would not deliberately correct Chen Meihua's faulty memory. She would occasionally remember, and occasionally forget everything. This was nothing uncommon, and they just had to be used to it.

After the conversation, Chen Meihua behaved as if nothing was wrong, cheerily focusing on other matters.

She grabbed Lin Mu's hand. Lu Rong saw it, and he reached out too.

Three hands were clasped together rather awkwardly.

"It's indirectly holding hands," Lu Rong said suddenly.

Lin Mu recalled that during their first date at Rencai Park, they were also holding hands like this. This was also a phrase he had come up with that day, but he did not expect that Lu Rong would use it now.

Perhaps Chen Meihua found this way of holding hands rather interesting. She flipped her hand around, clasping all three hands together, repeatedly claiming that the flowers were blooming. The three hands had turned into blossoms, and their thumbs were all hooked together.

"They're blooming, they're blooming!" She called out over and over again, afraid that Lin Mu and Lu Rong did not hear her.

Lin Mu looked down at the "flowers." His rapidly beating heart pounded fiercely, and his thumb felt as though it was burning up.

The people around them did not notice their actions, and it was not as though they'd be able to hear how fast Lin Mu's heart was racing anyway. Lu Rong and Lin Mu hooked their little fingers together, and they answered Chen Meihua's various unfettered questions perfunctorily. Sun Hai and An Jincheng finally settled on a party villa that could accommodate twelve people, and the cost was acceptable after dividing it among themselves.

"We'll gather at the school entrance at eight in the morning the day after tomorrow." Sun Hai even sent a guide to everyone, in which were listed various must-see destinations at Mount Mogan. Lin Mu glanced through it, discovering that quite a number were places that had blown up online.

"Anyone who has other guides can share them as well." Sun Hai was very democratic as he concluded the end of the meeting. "Everyone must take care of each other, especially with regards to Little Heron and Meimei. We'll split the load among a few people, and we will pay more attention to them."

For such a non-dictatorial group, there was not really a clear division of grouping within themselves. Lu Rong, Lin Mu and Chen Meihua would definitely take part in activities together. Lin Zhao wanted to join as well, but she hadn't expected that she'd been heartlessly sold off by her own brother and that, for some unknown reason, she was arranged to be together with An Jincheng. Sun Hai and Jiang Tianhe took care of Xu Yilu together, bringing along with them Cao Zhan as well. Although Dopey was not very smart, he had no issues with mobility. Li Zi and Mo Xiaoxiao had always been very close both in and out of school, so they would definitely not be separated during such times.

Lin Zhao was still angry with Lin Mu for his selfish behavior of forcing a "marriage" on her. While packing her luggage on the second day, she was still very aggrieved.

"You think I'm troublesome, don't you?" Lin Zhao threw her

clothes into her suitcase as she signed.

Lin Mu could only reply, "How can that be? It's just because I'm afraid that while helping Lu Rong to take care of Meimei, I won't be able to take care of you properly."

In anger, Lin Zhao threw her clothes in his face. Lin Mu pulled them off, folding them nicely before placing them in her suitcase.

"This dress isn't nice, take that yellow dress instead." Lin Mu pointed at her wardrobe, giving Lin Zhao a suggestion.

Lin Zhao looked at him doubtfully, still trying to decide between the blue or yellow chiffon dress. She again asked, "Is the yellow dress really nicer?"

Lin Mu nodded vigorously. "Really. You look great in yellow; it makes you look more fair."

Lin Zhao raised a brow. Few girls could refuse being called pretty, and her mood improved as she handed the yellow dress to Lin Mu.

"I want to bring along my practice guides." Lin Zhao nudged her books, a little hesitant. "Can I bring a Go set along too?"

Lin Mu curled his fingers, tapping at the wooden chessboard. "You can, but it's a little too heavy."

Lin Zhao pursed her lips.

Lin Mu looked at her, then said, resigned, "We'll put it in my suitcase, then?"

Before going to bed, Lu Rong sent Lin Mu a message. It was a photo of two suitcases, one big and one small, next to each other.

Lin Mu typed, "Is the big one yours?"

Lu Rong's reply came very quickly. "It's Meimei's. She has a lot of pretty clothes she wanted to bring."

"My sister has a lot of clothes too. She even wants to bring along her practice guides and her Go set. I'm just like an ox, carrying everything for her."

Lu Rong sent some ellipses over, and after a while, he replied, "I'll help you carry them."

Lin Mu could not help but smile.

The two people did not chat for too long before Lu Rong had to go and make sure Chen Meihua took her medication.

The old lady's blood pressure had been a little high of late, so the hospital had changed her prescription again. Previously, Lu Rong had discovered that Chen Meihua would hide her medicine, then secretly throw them away. As such, now, when she took her pills, Lu Rong had to stay to supervise her.

"Just coax her to eat them. Little girls have to be coaxed," Lin Mu said.

Lu Rong sent a voice message over. "I've coaxed her already. The last time, I lied to her, saying that they were elixir pills, and that once she ate them, she could turn into Chang'e. In the end, in the middle of the night, she pulled her blanket over her and wanted to jump out of the window to fly to the moon."

Hearing this, Lin Mu rolled on the bed with laughter, but his heart began to ache after that. He asked Lu Rong, "So what happened after that? What did you do?"

Lu Rong said, "I lied to her, telling her that the moon tonight was not round enough. Also, she had no rabbits, so she couldn't fly."

Lin Mu was speechless.

Lu Rong said resignedly, "Now, she's fussing about getting a rabbit."

It was easy to settle the matter of the rabbit. They were going to Mount Mogan tomorrow, and Lin Mu heard that there was an organic farm there. They might even have rabbits, and they could buy one and take it home with them.

It actually did not matter to Lu Rong. Now, he was like a crafty parent who would agree to anything first to appease his child, but at the end of the day, he would not abide by his previous promises. Towards this, he felt no shame or guilt.

Fortunately, Chen Meihua's memory was short-term, and she completely forgot about the rabbit the next morning. Waking up early in the morning, she again threw a tantrum. It was only when Lu Rong threatened her about going out that she calmed down, obediently eating her breakfast as well as brushing her hair and changing her clothes.

"Is Mumu coming too?" Chen Meihua could tell the twins apart. She could not remember Lu Rong sometimes, but amazingly, she never forgot about Lin Mu.

Lu Rong carried their suitcases out of the door, locking the gate. He had brought a leash along with him, tying one end to Chen Meihua's waist and the other to his own wrist. "A lot of people are going, including Dopey."

A blank look appeared on Chen Meihua's face, seemingly trying to recall who Dopey was. Finally, she remembered, and she exclaimed in delight.

Lu Rong led her forward, smiling as he asked, "Are you happy?"

Clapping her hands together like a child, Chen Meihua shouted loudly, "I'm happy!"

Although they were not late, Lu Rong and Chen Meihua were the last to arrive. The others were a little astonished when they saw a leash attached to a belt around Meimei's waist. Lu Rong explained, "It's safer like this, I'm afraid we will be separated."

As he had to hold the suitcases with both hands, the reason

for the leash could thus be seen. Lin Mu was a little regretful that he did not go to their house and pick them up in the morning. Lu Rong told him quietly, "You have to help your sister with her luggage, too."

It would have been fine if he hadn't mentioned it, but now Lin Mu could not help rolling his eyes. "An Jincheng came to pick us up early in the morning. You don't know how heavy a Go set can be, he really thinks he's some hunk or something?"

The "hunky" Young Master An turned his head around. His facial features indeed could not be related to the word "hunk" at all, as they could only be described as delicate. His seat was in front, while Lin Zhao and the other two girls were sitting in the back. They were quite a distance apart, and it was not easy for them to communicate.

Sun Hai got a microphone from somewhere. Standing behind the driver, he tested it exaggeratedly. "Ahem, ahem, guys, pay attention, pay attention!"

On the entire bus, only Cao Zhan and Chen Meihua looked at him obediently.

Sun Hai was not embarrassed at all. "Dopey, do you want to sing a song?"

Sitting down, Jiang Tianhe burst out laughing. "What can he sing? Old McDonald?"

Sun Hai clicked his tongue, handing Jiang Tianhe the microphone. "How about you sing then?"

Jiang Tianhe hurriedly raised his chin, scolding him, "Scram."

The word was spoken into the microphone, and it was a little loud. Jiang Tianhe had been rather anxious as he shouted, and his pitch became weird, sounding just like a shrill chicken.

Cao Zhan was heartless, and of course, he was also brainless. He took the microphone over, asking with great sincerity, "Jiang

Tianhe, are you showing off your impotent rage again?!"

Jiang Tianhe froze.

He would probably end up with "impotent rage" engraved on his tombstone.

Everyone on the bus burst out laughing, to the point where even the driver could barely keep the steering wheel straight, and Sun Hai almost wanted to roll across the aisle in laughter. Jiang Tianhe's face was a blushing bright red, and he gritted his teeth, unable to hit anyone.

Xu Yilu felt that it was bad to keep laughing like this. As such, holding onto his white cane, he stood up and asked Sun Hai for the microphone. "I'll sing then."

Sun Hai quickly asked, "What is Little Heron going to sing?"

Xu Yilu refused to tell him. "You'll know once I start."

Holding onto the microphone, his eyes were unfocused. His eyes were fixed on no one, and the scenery outside flew past. The sun shone in through the window, casting light and shadow upon everyone, like an old film projector.

Xu Yilu hummed a melody to himself, his left arm swinging to the rhythm. Then he began to sing:

"Together, our youth goes past.

"Shallow ponds, green grass, and the sun.

"You once said, there was time, and everything should be considered.

"As such, the birds hovered in the sky, and the wind ended among the branches.

"Together, together.

"Our youth goes past, goes past."

Quite a number of them were very familiar with the song Xu Yilu was singing. It was a new song by Ji Qinyang, a famous independent musician. "Together" was marked by the media as a complete return to Ji Qinyang's roots after many years. With the simple and fresh lyrics of the song, its mood evoked the style of his early years.

The boys never cared much about stars, but the girls were very excited as they listened to the song. Although Lin Zhao could not hear, she had an attitude of "I must be excited when everyone else is excited," and so she swayed along with Li Zi and Mo Xiaoxiao beside her.

The microphone made its round, and finally landing in Lu Rong's hand. He held it awkwardly and said after a pause, "I really can't sing..."

Sun Hai snatched the microphone over. His voice was very loud, but he could not carry a tune at all. When he sang, everyone except Lin Zhao covered their ears.

It only took about two hours to get to Mount Mogan from Suzhou, which was enough time for Lu Rong to learn the new song. With his head bowed, he studied the lyrics very seriously. Lin Mu leaned in closely, humming the tune for him.

"When did you learn this?" Lu Rong cast a glance towards him.

While humming, Lin Mu mumbled, "When the song was just released."

Lu Rong pressed his lips together, saying nothing. He returned to study the lyrics, seemingly in a hurry to memorize them. Lin Mu reached out, ruffling his hair as he told him, "Take your time."

Halfway through the journey, Chen Meihua became sleepy. Lin Mu lay her head in his lap, removing his jacket and covering the old lady with it.

They were seated in the last row, and so they could lie across the seats if they wanted to sleep. Lu Rong was still looking at the lyrics, and, feeling extremely bored, Lin Mu leaned his head on Lu Rong's shoulder.

Up ahead, Cao Zhan had fallen asleep as well. His head nodded away, and it ended up on Jiang Tianhe's shoulder. Jiang Tianhe pushed him away in annoyance at first, but he seemed to find it troublesome after a few times. When Cao Zhan's head once again fell onto his shoulder, he finally gave up and let him be.

Li Zi and Mo Xiaoxiao were huddled together, whispering to each other while Lin Zhao quietly studied her practice guide. Sun Hai had his head tilted back, sleeping in an awkward position. An Jincheng turned around, passing a bag of preserved plums to the seats behind.

Lin Zhao had her book raised up. When she saw the plums, she was a little surprised.

An Jincheng held the bag of plums out towards her.

Although Lin Zhao was not at the stage where she would be on guard against his "complimentary attentiveness," she still did not think that they were on close terms enough for such behavior. The knowledge that An Jincheng knew sign language after the conversation during the cultural festival had left Lin Zhao quite astonished.

"Thank you." Lin Zhao put her guide down. She accepted the bag of preserved plums, placing one in her mouth as she asked, "Aren't you going to eat too?"

An Jincheng signed back, "It's all for you."

Lin Zhao blinked. A thought seemed to flash across her mind, but she immediately found it too terrifying. Accepting the plums, she thought for a moment before signing, "Want to play Go?"

An Jincheng did not know how to play Go. Lin Zhao retrieved her Go set from the suitcase, placing it on an empty seat. She reached out, tapping a few spots, and signed expressionlessly, "We'll play Gomoku."

Throughout what was left of the journey, An Jincheng did not win a single round.

When the bus arrived at its destination, Lin Mu saw the chessboard while collecting his luggage, then gave An Jincheng a complicated yet pitying look.

Lu Rong had once played Gomoku with Lin Zhao too, but as they hadn't finished even one round, he was not very sure about where Lin Zhao's standards were. Now that he had seen it for himself, he was rather thankful.

An Jincheng probably did not expect that he would be defeated so horribly. Sitting there, motionless, his mood was a little low. After Lin Zhao tidied up her practice guides, she saw Lin Mu signing at her, "Don't you know how to throw the game?"

Lin Zhao raised a brow, replying neatly, "I did."

Lin Mu was wordless.

No one dared object against Lin Zhao's inclination to see them all as weaklings.

The party villa Sun Hai had booked was a distance away from the scenic spots of Mount Mogan. The villa was quite big, and the group of boys and girls dragged their suitcases in to look at the rooms. The housekeeper had left the keys and a guide to the villa. There were altogether three floors, and the living room on the first floor had a pool table.

"There's a swimming pool outside." Mo Xiaoxiao and Li Zi had gone through the villa. The rooms for the three girls, along with

Chen Meihua's, were located on the second floor, and the empty study room at the end of the corridor was perfect for Lin Zhao's Go practice.

Lin Mu asked his sister, "Did you bring your swimsuit?"

Lin Zhao nodded.

There were only six rooms on the third floor, and two people would have to share a room. Sun Hai took a piece of paper and was ready to draw lots. However, before he could start, Lin Mu took the initiative, stating that he would share one room with Lu Rong.

"It's a bedroom with a king-sized bed," Sun Hai reminded them. "Although the bed is very spacious, are you sure that you'll be fine sharing it?"

Lin Mu glanced at him. "Why? You want to sleep with Young Master An instead?"

Sun Hai's hair stood up on end. "No thanks, I can't afford him."

Lu Rong had already pushed their suitcases into the room. Seeing their underclassman being so proactive, Sun Hai was a little jealous. Feeling conflicted, he could not help saying, "You and I have been buddies for six years, so it's not a problem for me to share a bed with you at such a crucial moment..."

Lin Mu hurriedly interrupted him. "I've got a problem with it."

"What?" Sun Hai was baffled. "What problem?"

Lin Mu's tone was meaningful. "I'm a light sleeper, and I'm afraid you'll be noisy."

Sun Hai felt a little insulted. "How do you know that Lu Rong won't be noisy? Have you slept with him before?"

Lin Mu was left with nothing to say.

He thought to himself, *I'll be sleeping with him tonight! So, leave us alone!*

The villa's kitchen was very well equipped. Unfortunately, among the group of high school kids, few had the ability to cook. As such, when Lu Rong said that he knew how to cook, the remaining ten useless beings looked at him as if he were a saint. Their eyes shone, and they mewled piteously for food.

Lu Rong was extremely amused. "We need to buy some groceries first."

Lin Mu quickly raised his hand. "I'll go with you."

There were seven boys altogether. Except for Cao Zhan and Xu Yilu, who both remained in the villa, everyone else was ready to go to the supermarket to help carry the groceries home. The three girls had already changed into their swimsuits, pulling Chen Meihua along to the swimming pool in the backyard. Lu Rong was very worried about his grandmother, but Cao Zhan stood up straight, puffing up his chest as he said, "Don't worry! I'm here!"

Lin Mu told him, "But you have to take care of Little Heron."

Cao Zhan thought about it and answered earnestly, "I can handle both."

He was not very clever, and his reactions and speech were rather slow. However, his physical abilities were not affected, which could be seen from his craftwork.

Lu Rong said, "If anything happens to Meimei, just give us a call. Do you remember our numbers?"

Cao Zhan nodded. He took his phone out, pointing at it deliberately, showing Lu Rong. "Here's wechat! It can send voice messages! I know how to do it!"

With a smile, Lin Mu praised him, "Dopey is so smart."

Lin Zhao was sprawled by the pool. Sitting next to her, Chen

Meihua was kicking at the water happily. Lin Mu walked over, signing at his sister, "Will you be fine alone?"

Lin Zhao waved him off. In fact, she didn't like how Lin Mu always treated her like glass. It seemed that her whole family had this problem, always handling her with kid gloves.

As Li Zi and Mo Xiaoxiao had been classmates with Lu Rong for a semester, they had already accumulated some experience in taking care of Chen Meihua. Girls were after all more careful, and they almost never left the old lady alone.

"Don't worry about it," Li Zi said firmly. Lin Zhao and she were both beautiful, only of different styles. Her face was small, and her eyes were sharp, making seem as alluring as wisterias. She said, "We'll be here."

The supermarket was not far from the villa, so the five boys decided to go there on foot. There were all sorts of items available in the supermarket, including fresh fruits and vegetables, as well as seafood and meat. Lin Mu assigned each person the items they had to find, and the group split up to search for them.

Lu Rong thought that they should get a small portion of all the types of meat available, and Lin Mu pushed the shopping cart, following closely behind.

While waiting for the meat to be weighed, Sun Hai was the first to send out a voice message calling for help.

"That umm..." He was a little embarrassed. "What do chrysanthemum greens look like?"

Lin Mu made a face. "Don't you know how to search for it online?"

"I did, but looking at the racks, everything looks the same."

Lin Mu was wordless.

After solving the problem of "what does chrysanthemum

greens look like," less than two minutes later, Jiang Tianhe called.

"How much string beans should we buy?" He asked.

Lin Mu said, "Just estimate it."

Jiang Tianhe was a little indignant. "They're all in a bundle. How am I supposed to know how much to get?"

Lin Mu sighed. "Get four bundles then."

Jiang Tianhe grumbled, "You should have just said that earlier."

He hung up immediately. Holding onto his phone, Lin Mu really wanted to swear, only to look up and see Lu Rong watching him.

"Your face is all puffed up." He pinched Lin Mu's cheek, chuckling. "You look just like a pufferfish."

An Jincheng was in charge of getting frozen food and snacks. As long as one was human, they would be able to recognize the words on the packaging.

Finally, these five people gathered at the checkout counter to pay. There were four bags in total, and the largest one was shared by Lu Rong and Lin Mu, each holding onto a handle.

Sun Hai treated everyone to a saltwater popsicle. Lin Mu and Lu Rong fell behind the group.

June was the hottest month in the south. Due to its environment, Mount Mogan was pretty cool, but having to carry the items and walking back, the hale and hearty boys still felt the heat.

Lin Mu had left the villa wearing a UV-protection jacket. On the way back, within a few steps, he removed it, tying it around his waist and leaving him in a wife-beater. His boardshorts were waterproof, and his slippers shuffled along the asphalt road.

The saltwater popsicle melted so fast that Lin Mu had to

stretch his neck out to lick it, afraid that it would drip onto his body.

The back of Lu Rong's T-shirt was already completely soaked, and the rows of bamboo by the roadside cast mottled shadows across his face.

"Wait for a bit," Lu Rong said. Biting onto his popsicle and holding it in his mouth, he reached for the wet wipes in the bag, taking a piece out to wipe Lin Mu's hand.

"Isn't your mouth cold?" Lin Mu took the popsicle out of Lu Rong's mouth. Holding onto two popsicles, he let Lu Rong clean his hands.

Lu Rong's cleaning speed could not match the speed of the popsicles melting. Another drip was about to fall onto Lin Mu's hand, and Lu Rong tilted his head, sucking onto the bottom end of one popsicle.

Lu Rong was so close to him that Lin Mu did not dare to move. Lu Rong's eyelashes seemed to be fluttering right against his heart, taking Lin Mu's soul away with them. Sucking on the popsicle for a bit, Lu Rong licked at it too, the tip of his tongue accidentally swiping against Lin Mu's fingers.

"It's very sweet." Lu Rong did not let go, and it was not sure what exactly he was referring to. "Do you want a lick?"

His face a bright red, Lin Mu did not know what he should be licking. He opened his mouth a few times, but before he could even bend his neck, Jiang Tianhe suddenly turned around, yelling at them, "What are you two doing?! Why are you walking so slowly?!"

Lu Rong looked back, raising his voice, "We're coming."

Standing there stiffly, Lin Mu did not move. Seeing how the

popsicles were still dripping, Lu Rong took the one that had melted more and stuck it into his mouth.

Wordless, Lin Mu had no choice but to lick the one left in his hand. He could not help but grumble, "It's not that sweet."

Lu Rong glanced at him, suppressing his laughter.

Jiang Tianhe and Sun Hai were walking at the forefront. The verdant bamboo trees by the sides of the road stretched continuously onwards. With a bag in his hand, Sun Hai could not stop taking photos. Noticing what seemed to be a cicada on a bamboo leaf in one of his photos, he exclaimed in wonder, calling Jiang Tianhe and An Jincheng over to take a look.

Unwillingness was written across An Jincheng's face, but he did lean in quickly. The three people huddled together, looking for the black cicada.

Lin Mu was also a little curious, and he wanted to go up and take a look. Next to him, Lu Rong suddenly bent down, biting off a chunk of the popsicle in Lin Mu's mouth.

The sweet syrup clung to their lips. The tip of Lin Mu's tongue felt icy and chilly, and his vision was blocked by Lu Rong's face. The popsicle in his mouth felt both cold and scorching at the same time.

Sun Hai called loudly for Lu Rong, probably because the cicada was too high up and they could not catch it.

Composedly, Lu Rong lifted his head, nonchalantly swallowing the icy dessert down.

"What's going on?" He walked over, asking.

Sun Hai pointed at the bamboo leaves above. "Can you reach it? Can you catch it?"

Lu Rong studied the height for a moment, and then shook his

head. "I don't think so."

Sun Hai could only call Lin Mu over, and he was shocked when he saw the latter's face. "What's wrong with you? Why is your face so red?"

Lin Mu could only answer, "The sun's too strong, I'm getting a sunburn."

Sun Hai too felt that it was very warm, but he refused to give up on catching the cicada. In the end, they could only search among the trees, and Sun Hai was finally satisfied after catching a few beetles.

Lu Rong tied a string to the hind leg of one of the beetles, and then tied the other end of the string to Lin Mu's little finger.

The beetle flew forward, pulling at Lin Mu's finger, making Lin Mu raised his hand unconsciously.

Lu Rong suddenly called out to him. "Lin Mu."

Lin Mu turned back, a little nervous. He had his arm raised, afraid that the beetle would escape.

Lu Rong pointed at the beetle, smiling, "You're holding onto the entire summer."

When they returned to the villa, the girls were still playing in the pool. Chen Meihua was holding a small parasol. She was no longer kicking at the water, having found a water gun from somewhere, and she and Cao Zhan were happily shooting them at each other.

Lin Mu cut some fruits, bringing it over. Afraid that Lin Zhao would get sunburned, he brought out a bottle of sunscreen too.

"I've already applied some," Lin Zhao signed.

Lin Mu told her, "Apply it again."

Lin Zhao could only get out of the water and apply the sunblock over her arms, legs, waist and back. Li Zi and Mo Xiaoxiao applied some as well.

"You're not going to come play too?" Mo Xiaoxiao invited him warmly.

Either the girls were truly open-minded, or Lin Mu was no threat to them at all. None of the girls objected to this invitation.

"I won't be swimming; you girls go ahead and play." Although the girls did not mind, Lin Mu felt that he should still avoid any suspicions that might arise. He crouched down by the pool, scooping up a little water and pouring it on his arm. Just when he was about to stand up, he was sprayed right in the face by Chen Meihua.

Lin Mu was stunned.

The old lady giggled. Lin Mu brushed back his wet fringe, coaxing her, "Does Meimei want to change her clothes?"

The weather was too hot. Even with a parasol, such high temperatures were not good for the elderly. Surprisingly, Chen Meihua listened, waving goodbye at Cao Zhan and following Lin Mu into the villa.

Sun Hai and Jiang Tianhe were not in the living room, while An Jincheng was channel surfing on the cable television. He did not notice that Lin Mu had entered, and when he found a sports channel explaining Go, he stopped, no longing switching channels.

Lin Mu looked at the television for some time, baffled. He asked suddenly, "Do you understand it?"

An Jincheng jerked in shock. He turned around, looking a little embarrassed. After some hesitation, he said, "I was just browsing randomly."

Lin Mu held no doubts towards him. He told An Jincheng that he would teach him later, and then brought Chen Meihua upstairs.

Lu Rong finished packing the refrigerator and was about to look for his grandmother. The three of them bumped into each other at the staircase.

"I'm taking Meimei to change her clothes," Lin Mu said.

Lu Rong nodded, and led them upstairs. Chen Meihua's room was located all the way at the end of the hallway. Lu Rong pulled out her suitcase, finding a set of suitable loungewear for Chen Meihua to change into.

"Do you want to change as well?" Lu Rong studied Lin Mu.

Lin Mu looked down at himself. He was dressed in a loose wife-beater, and after being sprayed by the water gun, his collar was soaked, a dark patch around his neck.

"My other clothes are too warm." Lin Mu felt a little lazy. "I'll just wear this."

Lu Rong did not speak. He suddenly held his hand out, inserting it through Lin Mu's loose sleeve. The boy's palm was hot, burning the spot under Lin Mu's collarbone. Momentarily, Lin Mu felt his chest heat up.

Reflexively, Lin Mu grabbed hold of Lu Rong's hand, refusing to let him move. A little anxious, he asked, "Why did you shove your hand in..."

Lu Rong gently tugged at the strap of his wife-beater, saying lightly, "If this part is any looser, your chest would be exposed."

Lin Mu did not expect that.

He was unconvinced. "We're all guys here. Being shirtless isn't an issue, what are you afraid of?"

"I'm not afraid." Lu Rong gave a sigh. He asked, "Do you want to see me shirtless?"

Lin Mu dared not say yes. After all, there were others in this villa. If he could see it, so could the others.

"You should change," Lu Rong chuckled. "When it's dry, you

can wear it again at night."

In the end, Lin Mu changed into a slightly oversized T-shirt. Thinking about what Lu Rong meant by wearing it again at night, his mind spun.

Chen Meihua had to take a two-hour nap in the afternoon. Lu Rong accompanied her, telling her stories.

Afraid of disturbing the pair of grandmother and grandson, Lin Mu headed downstairs first. An Jincheng had his poker face on, seeming as though he was waiting for Lin Mu.

Lin Mu was confused. "What's the matter?"

An Jincheng's exquisite brows creased. However, since he was seeking help, he put up with it. "You just said that you would teach me."

Only then did Lin Mu recall that he had casually offered to teach Young Master An about Go. A little guilty, he sat on the couch in the living room. Watching the explanation happening on the television, he asked, "What do you not understand?"

An Jincheng glanced at the television, answering frankly, "I don't understand anything."

Lin Mu was speechless.

He turned to look at the television, realizing that it was the match between Lin Zhao and Sixth Dan Chen Yu. It was currently halfway through, and a stranglehold was forming at the center of the board. Holding on to a white piece, Lin Zhao dove straight in, alarming the dragon formed by the black pieces on the board. Chen Yu wanted to cut through the gordian knot, as she did not want to be trapped by the top left corner, and the match was now at an impasse.

The explanation of the match was very mysterious and abstract, and Lin Mu could only translate it in layman terms.

Basically, Go was about fighting for territory, and whoever had occupied the most space had the advantage. He explained to An Jincheng the basics of surrounding the opponent, how to capture pieces, and the foundations. As for everything else, if he were to go even a little deeper, there would not be enough time.

"Why don't you get my sister to teach you?" Lin Mu suggested. "It can be a teaching practice, get it? Many professional Go players do hold classes, teaching Go, and she'll definitely be much better than me in teaching."

An Jincheng descended into a short period of silence before asking, "Are there any fees for such lessons?"

"Professional Go players would of course take fees, and good players won't be cheap."

An Jincheng raised his head, looking at Lin Mu. He suddenly said, "How much would your sister cost?"

Lin Mu choked, wondering, *why do these words sound so wrong out of An Jincheng's mouth?!*

Until they finished dinner, Lin Mu was still wondering exactly what sort of sordid things were stored in An Jincheng's superb, clever brain. He naturally would not tell Lin Zhao about An Jincheng wanting to pay her to teach him Go, mainly because even if he told her, Lin Zhao might not agree either.

Back in the room, Lin Mu sent a direct message to Lin Zhao. "How much do you charge for a lesson?"

Lin Zhao's reply came very quickly. "Why are you asking?"

"I'm just curious."

"Last summer, I made enough to buy you a pair of Air Jordans."

After doing some calculations, Lin Mu realized that her lessons were indeed not cheap.

Probably having misunderstood the situation, Lin Zhao asked him, "Are you in need of money?"

Lin Mu said, "Could you give me some pocket money then?"

"I won a prize of sixty thousand yuan in the last competition."

She then added a "rich woman" GIF and proudly continued, "If you're really short of money, your elder sister will support you."

Lin Mu had no answer to that.

After taking a shower, Lu Rong retrieved his freshly dried underwear from the washing machine. It was the first time that he used a washing machine with a drying function, and he had to study it for a while before using it.

Lin Mu's loose, oversized wife-beater was also dry. Thinking that Lin Mu wanted to wear it, he brought it out with him.

The air-conditioning in the room was turned on, but the French windows leading to the balcony was not closed. The evening breeze blew in, and the thin, gauzy curtains brushed against Lin Mu's calves. The latter was sprawled across the bed, his limbs spread, and he was texting someone on his phone.

He saw Lu Rong as well. Blinking, he bounced up from the bed, asking, "You're done showering?"

Lu Rong nodded. Standing up straight, he looked down towards Lin Mu. "Are you chatting with Lin Zhao?"

"How did you know?" Lin Mu held up his phone to him, his tone a little jealous. "My sister makes a lot of money with Go."

Lu Rong shot a quick glance at the screen, not very concerned about how much Lin Zhao had earned. He still had to go downstairs to watch Chen Meihua take her medication, and so he first urged Lin Mu to go and take a shower.

Boys did not need too much time in the shower. The summer was sweltering, and Lin Mu left the bathroom, too lazy to dry his hair. He once again wore the wife-beater from the afternoon, but this time he pulled on a hooded sweatshirt as well.

"Let's go." Lin Mu threw a dry towel over his head. Water was still dripping off the ends of his hair. Lu Rong reached out, patting his hair dry with the towel.

"Done?" Lin Mu could no longer wait, wanting to quickly get it over with. Lu Rong gave him a look, suddenly exerting a little force. The towel, wrapped around the back of Lin Mu's neck, was pulled forward slightly. Since Lin Mu did not have a firm footing, he fell into Lu Rong's arms.

Lin Mu was shocked.

They had quite a difference in height, and Lin Mu's chin rested perfectly on Lu Rong's shoulder. Lu Rong then wrapped his arms around Lin Mu, looking as if he was patting his pet dry with a towel.

Lu Rong said, "We'll go down after we dry your hair."

Lin Mu grumbled, "Then I might as well use a hairdryer..."

"Don't you dislike the heat?"

Lin Mu could only shut his mouth obediently, allowing Lu Rong to dry his hair for him.

Chen Meihua had been thinking about taking the "elixir pills" at night, and she refused to wait alone in the room. When Lu Rong and Lin Mu came down, she had pulled her blanket around her shoulders and was pacing through the corridor. Li Zi, Mo Xiaoxiao and Lin Zhao were not asleep yet, and they were walking around with her.

Lin Mu signed at Lin Zhao, "We'll handle this, you can go to bed."

Lin Zhao replied, "It's still early, I'll practice Go first."

Thinking about how she was working so hard to earn money,

Lin Mu's heart ached. "It's a rare occasion for us to come out and play together, don't practice anymore."

Lin Zhao's fingers seemed as though she was drawing in the air. "Mastery comes from diligence, and waste comes from making merry."

Chen Meihua had to take more than one type of medication, and it took Lu Rong a lot of trouble to coax her into eating them. Chen Meihua asked many questions, and halfway through her medications, she even asked how long more it would take before she would turn into Chang'e.

"Meimei doesn't have a little rabbit yet." Lin Mu replaced her cup of water. "We're going to see the bunnies tomorrow, alright?"

Chen Meihua thought about it. "Can I have a rabbit?"

Lu Rong handed her medication to her. "You can only have it if you take this elixir pill."

Chen Meihua obediently took her medicine. Suddenly, she recalled something, saying, "We also need an osmanthus tree. The little rabbit needs to live under an osmanthus tree."

Lin Mu remembered that there was an osmanthus tree planted in Lu Rong's garden, but it was still a long time before it would bloom.

As though afraid that his grandmother would have more strange requests like "the jade rabbit needed to pound medicine" and "Wu Gang must chop the tree," Lu Rong immediately coaxed her to bed after she finished her medication. This time, Chen Meihua was surprisingly obedient. Perhaps she was also tired, for she soon started snoring lightly after getting into bed.

Once they confirmed that she was asleep, Lu Rong and Lin Mu headed back upstairs together. When going through the door, Lin Mu could not help asking, "Is it always like this?"

Lu Rong froze. When he understood what Lin Mu was referring too, he calmly nodded. "Pretty much."

Lin Mu looked at him, silent.

"Don't look at me like this, it's not that pitiful." Lu Rong smiled.

"I'm not pitying you," Lin Mu sighed. He thought a little, then said, "You're really a very good person."

Lin Mu continued solemnly as he watched Lu Rong, "You're the best person in the whole wide world."

It was not that Lu Rong had never been praised. On the contrary, he was often praised.

His neighbors, his relatives, his teachers, and sometimes even strangers whom he had only met once would praise him for being "filial," "having such a hard time," as well as "being a good child."

Such superficial phrases had mentioned over and over again. They seemed to think that he should be like this, and when others were expressing their kindness, their pity, and their sympathy to him, he should accept them all and be grateful to them.

However, sometimes, Lu Rong would wonder, what exactly did he want?

He wanted to have a complete night's sleep. He wanted to try lazing in bed when he woke up. He wanted to have a full meal with no stress, for it to be in complete relaxation. He did not want people in public to stare at him strangely, and he only wanted to live properly and unashamed.

But now, he was in love with someone, who had just said that he was "the best person in the whole wide world."

It was not praise, nor was it pity, and there was no debate about whether or not he should be like this.

All Lin Mu did was simply place him in the center of his

whole world.

In the middle of the night, Lin Mu woke up groggily. Lu Rong was sleeping next to him, his hands resting neatly on his abdomen.

It was a very orderly sleeping posture, and there was nothing uneasy about it. Lin Mu leaned a little closer, pressing his forehead against Lu Rong's cheek.

Lu Rong woke up.

In the moonlight, he could see Lin Mu's face clearly, and he asked, "Why are you awake?"

Lin Mu quietly replied, "It's a rare occasion for us to be sleeping together. It'd be a waster to sleep the entire night away."

Lu Rong bubbled with laughter. He slid his hand across, resting it on Lin Mu's chest through that oversized wife-beater. The latter's heart was pounding quickly, but the sensation was very gentle, and it made Lu Rong want to be careful.

Lin Mu tilted his head down, pressing his lips against Lu Rong's.

Lu Rong did not move, only watching him silently.

"Your eyelashes are really long," Lin Mu said deliberately. He reached out, playing with Lu Rong's lashes.

Lu Rong obediently closed his eyes.

"Don't always look at me," Lin Mu grumbled speciously after a while. "I'm afraid my heart would beat too loudly. Can't you hear how much I love you?"

SILENT HEARTS

The Light of The Sun ⓮

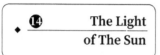

The Light
of The Sun

As they had promised to go to the organic farm the next morning, Lin Mu's simple wish of lazing in bed with Lu Rong for a little while longer had to go unfulfilled.

Lu Rong woke up before six. Lin Mu felt some slight movements on the bed next to him, and soon after, a blanket was pulled over him, up to his waist. The door to the room was very gently closed, then Lin Mu opened his eyes, groping for his phone and glancing at it.

Hugging the blanket, he sat up.

Footsteps could be heard from the hallway outside. Chen Meihua's voice was a little loud. Lu Rong seemed to have said something, and the old lady started whimpering like a little kitten. It carried on for about a couple of minutes, before it finally stopped.

Lin Mu pulled on a T-shirt. As soon as he walked out of the room, he could see Chen Meihua sitting at the dining table in the living room downstairs.

Lu Rong was coaxing her to have her breakfast. With one hand lying relaxed by the side of the table, Chen Meihua was gripping a spoon with the other, scooping at the steamed egg in the bowl. Tilting her head to the side, she said, "Little rabbits eat carrots."

Lu Rong wiped the smears of egg around her mouth. "Keep your voice down, the others are still sleeping."

"Oh." Chen Meihua agreed. She lowered her voice and repeated, "Little rabbits eat carrots."

Lu Rong's voice was very solemn. "They eat green vegetables as well."

Chen Meihua nodded.

Lu Rong continued, "And their poop is like small little balls."

Chen Meihua was stunned.

Lu Rong pointed at the bowl. "Continue eating, you haven't finished yet."

A beat later, Chen Meihua realized that she had just been "bullied" by her grandson. Pressing her lips together, she was about to cry. But before her tears could well up, she saw Lin Mu upstairs.

"Mumu!" She shouted.

Lu Rong turned his head, a little startled to see Lin Mu. "Why didn't you sleep in a while more?"

Lin Mu grumbled, "Without you, I can't sleep."

Lu Rong stood up to get a bowl of steamed egg for him. As they passed each other, Lu Rong suddenly reached out and smoothed the back of Lin Mu's head.

Lin Mu gave him a questioning look.

Lu Rong said, "Your hair's all fluffed up."

There was a large amount of steamed egg, and it seemed like they had been specially prepared by Lu Rong. He brought Lin Mu a bowl, sprinkling some chopped spring onions and a little soy sauce on top before placing it next to Chen Meihua's bowl. Lin Mu sat next to Chen Meihua, and the two of them looked like little children sitting in class, eating eggs together.

It could be seen that Chen Meihua was in a very good mood. Her grumpiness from waking up had vanished, and she finished her egg in delight. Lu Rong helped her with wiping her mouth and combing her hair, then tying her hair up into two plaits, while Lin Mu ate as he watched.

"Shall we wait for all of them to wake up?" Lu Rong asked after Chen Meihua's hair was done.

Lin Mu considered it. He finished his egg, bringing his bowl to the sink and washing it. he said, "No, let's not wait. I'll send a message in the group chat and tell them we're going first. They can join us later."

Lu Rong had to bring Meimei along, and now that the old lady was in a good mood, going to the organic farm would be a little more relaxing. If they were to wait, who knew if Chen Meihua might lose control of her emotions later.

Meimei changed into a flower-print dress, putting on a sunhat and carrying a small crossbody bag. Lu Rong placed a leash inside the bag.

Holding onto Lin Mu's hand, Chen Meihua asked, "Are we going to see the rabbits?"

"Yes," Lin Mu smiled as he walked ahead. The intense heat of summer was not so strong in the morning. Together with the rows of bamboos along the roadside, the shade and the cool breeze made the walk very refreshing.

Lu Rong was looking at the map. Last night, some of them had made a guide on how to get to the organic farm, and so other than it being a slightly further distance away, it was not hard to find.

Lin Mu and Chen Meihua stopped quite a number of times as they walked. Perhaps the old lady was feeling bored, and she started singing along the way. Lin Mu did not understand what she was singing at first, but halfway through, he recognized that the song to be "*Gin no Ryuu no Se ni Notte.*"

Lu Rong was not surprised. "She can understand four languages, and her Cantonese is pretty good too."

Lin Mu was in slight disbelief. "Even with Alzheimer's, she can still remember them?"

Lu Rong shook his head. "It seems like she only remembers when she sings."

Chen Meihua's voice did not sound very aged. During the climax of the song, she even waved her hand along with it. Lin Mu vaguely remembered the lyrics of the song, and he started humming the melody along with her.

The old lady and the youth sang together for some time, and even moved to other songs. However, most of the songs Meimei sang were old songs, and towards the end, songs by Teresa Teng featured more prominently.

By the time she sang "Wine and Coffee," Lin Mu could no longer follow along.

"She had always loved singing, even before she got sick," Lu Rong said suddenly.

Curious, Lin Mu asked, "How old were you then?"

"I was about five or six at that time, still in primary school."

He fell into recollection. Seemingly to remember something happy, he smiled. "She named the dog at home Yuki, which meant snow in Japanese. Its fur was white in color. In winter, we'd start the furnace at home, and Yuki would lie beside it. Granny would hold me in her arms, singing, telling me stories, and coaxing me to sleep."

Lin Mu listened quietly. Chen Meihua was very energetic today, running alone up ahead. Around her waist was the leash, and her song carried far and loud.

Lu Rong's smile gradually faded. "I can always remember what she was like when she was healthy and well. If she'd been given the choice, she would definitely not want to be like this too."

Lin Mu did not speak. His hand was clasped by Lu Rong, and the two walked together hand-in-hand. After a while, Chen Meihua was finally tired from singing.

Lu Rong twisted a bottle of water open, bending down and handing it to his grandmother. Chen Meihua raised her head, asking, "Did Meimei sing well?"

Lu Rong nodded. "Very well."

Chen Meihua smiled brightly. She suddenly said, "Zhengnian said I sang very well too."

Lu Zhengnian was the name of Lu Rong's grandfather. Lu Rong was not surprised at all, and he acknowledged her words softly. Chen Meihua finished drinking her water, then ran off ahead happily.

"Even if she forgets me, she'd never forget my grandfather." Lu Rong looked at Lin Mu, and then suddenly spoke earnestly, "When I'm old, and if I get Alzheimer's as well, I'll definitely not forget you."

Lin Mu wanted to smile, but at the same time, he could not help frowning as well. Kicking Lu Rong lightly, he spat to ward off bad luck. "You won't fall sick, don't jinx yourself!"

The first person to see Lin Mu's message was Jiang Tianhe. Surprisingly, he was the first to wake up. While brushing his teeth, he knocked on all the doors on the third floor, even deliberately shouting "Fool!" when he walked past Cao Zhan's door.

His hair a mess, Sun Hai rubbed his bleary eyes as he yawned. "They've gone ahead already?"

Jiang Tianhe was calling Lin Mu, but the other boy did not answer. He instructed Sun Hai, "Go help Little Heron."

Sun Hai nodded groggily, knocking on Xu Yilu's door.

With his toothbrush in his mouth, Jiang Tianhe swapped his phone to his other hand. This time, Lin Mu finally picked up.

"Hello?" Jiang Tianhe's voice was full of vigor. "Where are you now?"

"We're almost there."

Jiang Tianhe nearly spat out the toothpaste in his mouth. "Are you guys rushing to catch a flight or something?! Why are you in such a hurry?!"

"Is there something in your mouth? I can't hear you clearly."

Jiang Tianhe rolled his eyes. "I'm brushing my teeth!"

As soon as he finished speaking, he saw An Jincheng walking out of his room, looking all clean and neat. The gorgeous youth looked at him, his face full of scorn. "Don't talk while brushing your teeth, it's very disgusting."

Jiang Tianhe was speechless.

Xu Yilu had actually woken up fairly early as well. He was rummaging through his luggage, remembering how Song Wenjuan had packed his outfits. However, something seemed to have messed up somewhere, and the more he rummaged through his belongings, the more he could not find them.

Drawling his words, Sun Hai called, "Little Heron."

Xu Yilu answered reflexively.

"You can't find your clothes?" Sun Hai crouched down next to him. "*Gege* will help you."

Xu Yilu heaved a sigh of relief, hurriedly saying, "I'm looking for a blue T-shirt, my mom put it in a bag."

Sun Hai's vision blurred. "There's quite a number of blue shirts here?"

Wordless, Xu Yilu did not expect this.

Sun Hai simply took them all out, choosing the one that he thought was the nicest looking, and then matched the rest of the outfit according to his own aesthetics. "Hold your arms up."

Sun Hai was actually quite sleepy, but with this task, he was now completely awake. Xu Yilu was small and thin, and Sun Hai felt as though he was taking care of a doll.

Xu Yilu obediently held his arms up, letting Sun Hai help him pull the T-shirt on.

"I'll put on my pants by myself..." Xu Yilu mumbled quietly.

It was not clear if Sun Hai had heard him. He lifted Xu Yilu's legs one by one, pulling his pants on for him.

Xu Yilu sat down, feeling a little awkward.

Sun Hai tidied up Xu Yilu's hair with great earnestness, as it had been messed up when the T-shirt was tugged over him. Extremely satisfied, he said, "It's perfect, you look devastatingly handsome!"

When Lin Zhao woke up, Li Zi and Mo Xiaoxiao were already eating steamed egg in the dining room. As their aloof, fairy-like upperclassman descended down the stairs, like an immortal floating down to earth, the two underclassmen's eating manners became a lot more elegant.

Lin Zhao would bring a writing pad with her when she interacted with others.

"Good morning." Her handwriting was beautiful, but it was

not delicate in the slightest. "How did you sleep?"

Initially, the two underclassmen were looking at her through an extremely thick, beautifying lens. After all, she had so many titles to her name, and she had such an ethereal appearance as well. Too many people held Lin Zhao in extreme respect, and few were close to her.

However, in less than a couple of days, this lens was completely shattered.

As Lin Zhao had been focusing on Go since primary school, she seemed to be completely a step away from earthly desires. It was not because she was cold and aloof, but because she did not fit in normal society. Together with her physical disability, this "incongruity" became something even more concrete, forming a barrier between her and the world.

The first time Li Zi found out that Lin Zhao was a little different was when they were chatting about stars and idols.

For girls their age, as long as they came in contact with things to do with the entertainment industry, they would tend to have a few idols they really liked or preferred. Therefore, when Lin Zhao asked what an idol was, Li Zi thought it was strange, but she still patiently explained the concept to her.

"Someone you are a big fan of?" Lin Zhao pondered over it.

Mo Xiaoxiao even showed her Ji Qinyang's photo, writing her question earnestly. "He's handsome, isn't he?"

Lin Zhao took a look, nodding.

"Does *xuejie* like him too?" Li Zi too wrote her question.

Lin Zhao's expression remained indifferent. "He's so-so. For a male idol, I prefer Lian Xiao."

Question marks appeared over the faces of Mo Xiaoxiao and Li Zi, but they did not want to appear too uneducated in front of

Lin Zhao. Hunching over their phones, they began to check who Lian Xiao was on the internet.

Looking at the results, the girls' faces turned blank.

Lin Zhao continued writing solemnly. "As for female idols, I like Choi Jeong the most. She's now ranked at ninth dan, and her Go skills are extremely impressive."

Mo Xiaoxiao and Li Zi were both speechless.

Nevertheless, the girls got along well. After washing her face, Lin Zhao too grabbed a bowl of steamed egg. As she was reading the group chat, Lin Mu happened to tag her.

"Are you awake yet?" Lin Mu asked.

Lin Zhao replied while eating, "Yes."

"I'm at the organic farm with Lu Rong and Meimei now. Are you coming later?"

Looking at the map, Lin Zhao thought for a moment, then typed, "I want to go to the Rainbow Path."

Lin Mu did not reply for a while, perhaps looking at where the path was located. Instead, An Jincheng suddenly started typing, "I'll go with you."

Lin Zhao was surprised by that message.

Reflexively, she lifted her head, looking for him. An Jincheng was standing at the bottom of the stairs. Unlike other boys his age who loved wearing T-shirts, wife-beaters and shorts, An Jincheng seemed to have nothing to do with the possibility of perspiration—he was dress in a collared shirt and casual trousers.

An Jincheng's appearance was a different sort from Lin Mu's eye-catching looks. He belonged to the pure and simple type of beauty, his brows and eyes exquisite, and he looked just like a painting.

He signed towards Lin Zhao, "I'll go with you to the Rainbow

Path."

Lin Zhao blinked. Li Zi and Mo Xiaoxiao were also a little surprised.

Lin Mu sent another text message in the group chat. "*Jie*, are you alright with that?"

There was nothing that Lin Zhao was not fine with. In fact, she would also be fine going there alone. However, Lin Mu always seemed to worry that things would be inconvenient for her, and he believed that it would be better if there was someone accompanying her.

Cao Zhan and Xu Yilu wanted to go to the reservoir, and so Jiang Tianhe and Sun Hai formed a group with them. As for Li Zi and Mo Xiaoxiao, they wanted to ride horses, and Mo Xiaoxiao even put on her athletic prosthetic limb for this purpose.

"Everyone, remember to take photos." Lin Zhao wrote on her writing pad. Holding it up, she flipped to the next page. It said, "Have fun, everyone."

The Rainbow Path was a little difficult to find, and it was the furthest away as well. It was located near the Xihu Dingshengtai Tea Plantation, so An Jincheng booked a car to take them there.

On the way there, Lin Zhao remained quiet. She knew that An Jincheng understood sign language, but she had no interest in interacting with him, only chatting away in the group chat, and looking at the photos Lin Mu sent.

"We picked a bunny for Meimei." Lin Mu's photography skills were horrible. Somehow, the grey rabbit's eyes were like two spotlights.

He also sent some photos of the scenery and people. Scrolling through them, they turned out to be all of Lu Rong only.

Sun Hai could not take it anymore. "Stop sending the *xuedi*'s photos. What are you doing? Creating a photobook of him?"

Jiang Tianhe joined in the ribbing. "Who would take such ugly photos for a photobook?"

Lin Mu sent a row of ellipses in the chat.

Lin Zhao was very amused, and she could not help but smile. When she raised her head, she discovered An Jincheng looking at her. Lin Zhao did not avoid his gaze, only tilting her head in puzzlement.

An Jincheng lifted his hands, moving his fingers. "We're almost there."

Lin Zhao nodded, not understanding why he needed to say that. The scenery outside the window clearly showed that they were already at the tea plantation. Clumps of tea plants covered the slope of the mountain, and all over was green. This was the first time that Lin Zhao had seen so much greenery. Plastering to the window, her mouth fell slightly open, and a rarely seen excitement appeared on her face.

The driver said something to An Jincheng, and the car stopped. An Jincheng alighted first, then turned to nudge Lin Zhao's arm.

"It's just ahead." He pointed. "Can you see it?"

Lin Zhao held onto her sunhat on her head. She looked up, and the view was clear to her eyes.

Winding through the tea plantation was a colorful trail, and in the distance was a red windmill. Summer was when the tea plants were the lushest, their branches clustering thickly, and some of their leaves had even scattered all over the trail, paving the path with green.

Excitedly, Lin Zhao signed at An Jincheng. "It's really pretty!

It's so beautiful!"

An Jincheng was considerably calmer, but it could be seen that he was delighted as well. Lifting up his phone, he took a photo of Lin Zhao.

"Send it to Lin Mu and let him have a look." Lin Zhao leaned over. A lock of hair fell off her ear, and she tucked it back without thinking.

An Jincheng was standing very close to her. His hand trembling a little, he sent her photo to the group chat.

Lin Zhao looked at it for a while, commenting, "Your photography skill is so much better than my brother's."

An Jincheng did not know what to say to that.

Lin Mu was currently milking a cow with Meimei and Lu Rong. Only when his hands were empty was he then able to look at his phone. Removing a glove and biting onto it, his thumb slid down the screen of his phone, and he saw a few solo shots of Lin Zhao.

Standing next to him, Lu Rong saw them too.

Lin Mu flaunted a little. "Isn't my sister very pretty?"

Lu Rong nodded. "Yes."

The twins looked so much alike, so to praise Lin Zhao meant that he was also praising Lin Mu for being pretty.

Happily, Lin Mu saved the photos. But when he realized who sent the photos, his expression became a little unfathomable. Thinking it over, he could not help asking Lu Rong, "Do you think An Jincheng likes my sister?"

Lu Rong glanced at him in astonishment. "You've only just realized that?"

"What?!"

Lu Rong removed his gloves. Their milk had just been packaged, and holding onto a bottle, Chen Meihua was sipping at it.

"Sometimes, you twins are extremely sensitive, but other times, both of you can be rather obtuse." Lu Rong opened a bottle for Lin Mu. "Not only did An Jincheng learn sign language, he even wants to learn Go as well. Who do you think he's doing this for?"

Lin Mu nearly choked on this gossip about his sister. Frowning, he said a little disapprovingly, "The issue is, how is he going to chase after my sister? He might be going abroad next semester."

"I'm going abroad soon." An Jincheng looked at Lin Zhao. She currently had her hand stretched out, plucking the tea leaves by the side of the trail. When she saw An Jincheng signing, she froze for a moment.

Lin Zhao seemed a little surprised, but soon she regained her calm. She asked, "Has it been confirmed?"

An Jincheng nodded. He hesitated for a moment, then suddenly moved his fingers quickly. "Do you want me to go overseas?"

Lin Zhao's brows creased slightly, and her fingers moved a little forcefully. "This has nothing to do with what I want. The only thing that matters is what you actually want for yourself."

An Jincheng tightened his fists. His expression was cold, but the tightness in the corners of his mouth betrayed his anxiety. His eyes were like the light of fireflies, bringing along with them a passionate heat.

"I just want to know your answer, and I don't care about the rest."

Lin Zhao did not avert her eyes. Facing the flames in front of her, she was like a cool, flowing spring. "I'm not your answer."

Her slender fingers were like delicate blades, slicing through the current situation. "You should know what you have to do, and what you want to become. This is the question you have to ask yourself, and not me."

She paused before continuing, "I play Go, not because of my parents, or for Lin Mu."

Lin Zhao pointed at herself, her expression a little proud. "I'm doing it for myself."

"In some sense, Go is the most impartial." Lin Zhao stood up. The movements of her fingers slowed down a lot, and she clearly wanted An Jincheng to be able to understand what she was conveying. "Once I sit at the table, my rival won't care whether I'm a male or a female, or if I'm healthy or disabled."

She looked at An Jincheng, smiling slightly. "On the board, there's only winning or losing, and there's no pity."

"Go has proved that I can win, that I can be just like any healthy individual. I can even compete and make money." Lin Zhao raised a brow a little wickedly, looking very pleased. "I'm a rich woman, and I have a lot of spending money."

Lin Zhao emphasized, "I will earn even more in the future, and I will be able to support my parents and Lin Mu."

An Jincheng could not come up with a response.

Lin Zhao studied him for a few moments. No happiness could be seen from An Jincheng. His mood was a little low, mixed with traces of embarrassment and he was a loss for what to do.

"You should be fair to me," Lin Zhao signed suddenly.

An Jincheng frowned, signing a question mark.

"If you want to confess that you like me, you should say it openly, instead of asking me if I want you to go overseas. Doing things like this is sly, and it's also very unfair to me, as you're irresponsibly making me decide your future. Even if I like you, I still don't have the right to decide your future."

Lin Zhao pursed her lips disdainfully. "That's not liking me, but the actions of a coward."

"So," Lin Zhao proudly raised her chin, her fingers drawing gracefully through the air, "I have the right to reject you now. Come and talk to me again once you think things through."

Lin Mu did not seem to be worried over the matter of An Jincheng liking Lin Zhao.

"Lin Zhao was already going to the Go institute to learn Go when she was about five or six years old." Lin Mu picked up the rest of the milk, accompanying Meimei to feed the rabbits with Lu Rong. They had already selected a gray one to bring home with them. There was a greenhouse at the organic farm, and there happened to be a bridal couple taking their wedding photos outdoors. Chen Meihua was very curious, and, after feeding the rabbits for a little while, she kept looking over in their direction.

"At that time, Lin Zhao was very young. She could not hear, nor could she speak. In the institute, she was bullied. During winter, they would throw the Go pieces she had washed back into the cold water, forcing her to retrieve them." Lin Mu's expression was very calm. He continued, "That's when I learned to fight."

At that age, little children were too young and foolish to truly understand what bitterness was. It seemed as though happiness and liberty were things that were always present, but the truth was that hardship and hard work would also be present along with them.

Lin Mu thus grew up sturdily, fighting along the way.

"Back then, I was only in the first year of primary school, and I couldn't beat most people in a fight." Lin Mu looked back at his memories. Realizing that he was more often the one bruised and battered, he did not really want to reminisce anymore. He went on, "In the eyes of outsiders, they all thought that I was the one taking care of Lin Zhao, the one protecting her. But in fact, that's not the case. Lin Zhao doesn't need me to protect her. She's a goddess of war."

Lu Rong did not believe that Lin Zhao could fight, but he acquiesced with what Lin Mu said.

He actually pitied An Jincheng a little more.

"It's highly likely that my sister will never marry," Lin Mu sighed, feeling a little conflicted. "In order to take revenge on my behalf, in less than two years, she defeated all the adults and children of that Go institute. Ever since then, no one dared bully her again."

The wins and losses on the board meant greater than anything else. This was Lin Zhao's way of Go.

Lin Mu said, "Her goal is to become a world-class Go player, and then earn lots of money to perform her filial duties."

"She doesn't need to rely on anyone. Even if she's disabled, she still wants to prove that she can support herself and her family as well."

Lin Mu paused, then continued, his tone a little complicated. "It sounds a little crass to talk about money, doesn't it?"

Covering his mouth, Lu Rong coughed slightly. "My family owns some stores, and I collect rent from them to support Meimei and myself."

Surprised, Lin Mu nodded, then spoke solemnly, "Don't worry. When I become a doctor in the future, my salary will not be too bad, and I'll be able to support both of you."

Their conversation took a turn, and they were now talking about who would be the one to support the other. Lu Rong had not thought about this issue before, while Lin Mu already had a rather concrete plan, as though this future was right in front of his eyes.

Lin Mu actually gave this far more thought than Lu Rong did. He had been taking a few points into deep consideration—Chen Meihua's health condition, Lu Rong's education, his national college entrance examinations, the universities he wanted to attend... The more Lin Mu pondered over it, the more troubles he had.

However, it seemed that he was the only feeling a sense of urgency over it, while Lu Rong seemed to be completely unbothered. Whenever this topic was mentioned, Lu Rong would divert it to something else. It was true that he would only be in his second year of high school when the semester started and that there was no need for him to be in such a hurry. There was no need for them to argue over it.

The young bridal couple was posing in the greenhouse. Chen Meihua insisted on going over to take a look, and Lu Rong and Lin Mu could only follow her.

The photographer and his assistant did not require everyone to clear the room, only requesting that no one affect the background. They allowed the visitors to peruse the area, and Lu Rong quietly reminded Chen Meihua not to run around. The old lady agreed obediently, her eyes glued to the bride in the greenhouse.

"Her dress is so beautiful," Chen Meihua said enviously.

Lin Mu asked, "Does Meimei wants to wear one too?"

Chen Meihua gazed at the couple for a while, then nodded. "Yes."

Before Lin Mu could speak, they heard the photographer teaching the couple how to pose. "The groom has to take more initiative. Hold your bride's hand, kiss her forehead, that's it! The bride, look a little happier!"

The bride seemed to be a little shy, giggling softly.

The groom complained, "Be a little more serious. I'm going to kiss you now."

Only then did the bride hold back her laughter as she closed her eyes.

At that moment, the sun was shining in at a perfect angle. The rays gently cascaded onto the bride's face, with flowers of all colors blooming around her, and the groom kissed her tenderly.

Lu Rong could not help turning to look at Lin Mu.

The latter happened to be looking over as well.

Chen Meihua's attention was still fixed on the bride's dress. Lu Rong suddenly lowered his head, asking, "Meimei, where's the rabbit?"

The old lady exclaimed, instantly crouching down to look. Just as Lin Mu wanted to bend down, Lu Rong reached out, holding onto the back of his neck.

Chanting "good little rabbit," Chen Meihua then saw the little gray rabbit popping out from the bottom of its cage. She quickly picked up the rabbit, carrying it in her arms. Standing up, she looked up towards Lin Mu. "Meimei found the rabbit!"

Lu Rong's heat still lingered on Lin Mu's lips, but the person who kissed him seemed to be acting as if nothing had happened.

Crossing his arms, Lu Rong spoke sternly to Chen Meihua, "Meimei must watch over the rabbit properly. If the rabbit runs away, Meimei will not be able to become Chang'e and fly to the moon."

...This person's bullshitting ability is becoming more and more impressive! Lin Mu thought.

The couple finished their photoshoot, and Chen Meihua was very satisfied with having watched them. For lunch, they decided to fill up their stomachs at a place nearby. While waiting to order their food, Lin Mu and Lu Rong looked through the photos posted in the group chat.

Jiang Tianhe and the other three boys had taken the most photos. The scenery in the reservoir was indeed beautiful, and Mount Mogan's nickname, "Little Jiuzhai," truly lived up to its reputation.

However, boys being boys, their photos were a little lacking in aesthetics. They took turns, sitting by the lake and giving a victory sign. Behind them was azure water surrounded by swaths of bamboo. Though they looked a little foolish, the scenery was still gorgeous.

Lin Mu's focus was actually on Xu Yilu's clothes. Looking at them for a long time, he could not help but ask, "Who chose Little Heron's clothes?"

Sun Hai was very proud. "Me! Why? Isn't he handsome?"

Lin Mu was speechless.

He had never seen anyone think it acceptable to match green with blue.

Cao Zhan seemed to think that the colors didn't match either, and he only dared not mention it at first. Since Lin Mu kickstarted the topic, he cautiously spoke up, "Does Little Heron know that he's wearing green pants?"

Jiang Tianhe was baffled. "What's wrong with green pants? It's not like he's wearing a green hat, making people think that he's being cuckolded or something."

Lin Mu nearly died laughing because of these people. After Lu Rong ordered the food, he rinsed the bowls and utensils with hot water for Chen Meihua and Lin Mu. Mo Xiaoxiao then posted a few photos of them on horses.

Photos taken by the girls were obviously of a different level— the angles they used, and their positioning were all perfect. If they added a filter, they'd be good enough for magazines.

"Xiaoxiao, how's your leg?" Sun Hai proclaimed himself to be Kunqian's number one "warm-hearted knight." He would always be very solicitous towards every pretty girl, flattering them as much as possible. "With your prosthetic limb on the horse, you look just like a steampunk character!"

Mo Xiaoxiao's reserved character from when she had just enrolled into Kunqian had long since disappeared. Having been nurtured over the past year, she was a lot more confident, and she no longer minded letting others see her leg.

Li Zi said, "She rode much better than me. All the instructors were praising her."

Mo Xiaoxiao's last photo was of the two girls standing next to a horse. Both of them were dressed in riding outfits, and each of them held a horsewhip in their hands. Her metal leg was showing, and it had a checkered scarf tied around it.

"You're my most outstanding knight." Mo Xiaoxiao wrote on it.

The first to return to the villa in the afternoon were An Jincheng and Lin Zhao. They had taken a car there and back, so naturally, they would be a lot quicker than the rest. Lin Zhao did not feel any embarrassment or self-consciousness from having rejected An Jincheng. She took out her Go set, asking him, "You wanted to learn Go?"

Previously, Lin Mu had asked her how much her lessons cost. Thinking about it now, he was probably asking on behalf of An Jincheng.

An Jincheng sat down across her, a little awkward. He signed, "How much are the fees?"

Lin Zhao was expressionless. Puffing out her cheeks, she signed as she set up the board, "It's free."

An Jincheng looked at her questioningly.

Lin Zhao lifted her lids, glancing at him. She seemed to smile, signing, "Because you're good looking."

When Lin Mu and Lu Rong returned with Chen Meihua, many white and black pieces were already on Lin Zhao's board, looking very much like a territorial war. When Lin Zhao saw her brother, she raised her chin towards him, signing, "You're back?"

Lin Mu nodded. He asked An Jincheng, "How many times have my sister thrown the game?"

An Jincheng gave him a look, his expression clearly showing his complete despair and hopelessness of having been abused. Coldly, he said, "I'm just helping her put the pieces down."

Lin Mu took a look at the board. Sure enough, where Lin Zhao pointed, An Jincheng would place a piece. His sister now had someone assisting her in her practice.

Chen Meihua's little rabbit needed a nest. Lu Rong found a few wooden boards, wanting to set a temporary one up. Lin Mu went over to help. Halfway through, Mo Xiaoxiao and Li Zi returned.

Still tied around Mo Xiaoxiao's prosthetic was the scarf. When

Lin Mu saw it, he laughed. "The knight has returned?"

Mo Xiaoxiao stretched the limb out graciously. Proudly, she said, "Isn't the knight handsome?"

Lin Mu whistled. "It's way too cool."

The two girls had a great time, and now they asked Lu Rong and An Jincheng for their photos to edit. As Chen Meihua fed the rabbit, Lu Rong sawed at the wooden boards, glancing over at his grandmother. "Meimei, don't feed the rabbit too much food."

Chen Meihua agreed, but she still continued shoving leaves at the rabbit. Seeing that his reminders did not work, Lu Rong took the rest of the vegetables away. Chen Meihua made a fuss for a little while, but she stopped very quickly.

In the sweltering evening heat, the sunset's glow slowly crept its way towards the surroundings. The mountain was lush with trees, the lake and the sky contrasting beautifully against each other, and even the clouds were pink. Lin Mu raised his head, the swath of pink in the sky reflecting in his eyes.

Due to the physical labor, Lu Rong was only wearing a dark colored wife-beater. Between his teeth were nails, and he was hammering at the wooden boards, his actions smooth and deft. Lin Mu looked at the setting sun for a little while, and his eyes were again drawn to Lu Rong's arms.

When he had just met Lu Rong, it was also summer, and the latter's skin had been dark and swarthy. This year, although he was still a little tanned, it was more of a healthy glow. Beads of sweat rolled down his neck, leaving cool trails behind.

Lin Mu was a little envious of his muscles. Boys their age were always a little competitive. If others were to judge Lu Rong's build, he might not even lose to others who worked out regularly.

Lu Rong bent over to pick up another wooden board, and Lin Mu could not resist pressing a hand against his abdomen.

Lu Rong froze, motionless. He asked, "Where are you touching?"

Lin Mu did not consider the implication behind his actions at all. Very innocently, he asked, "Do you have a six-pack?"

"Yeah."

"Show me."

Lu Rong shot him a look, his expression a little peculiar. "Now?"

"We're all men here, there's no need to be shy. Come, lift up your shirt and show me."

Lu Rong was speechless.

Holding onto the board, he stood still, not moving. Lin Mu's impatience grew as he waited—his hands held out, pulling Lu Rong's shirt up directly. Lu Rong tried to dodge him, but failed. Just as Lin Mu leaned in, Sun Hai's shouts came from the entrance.

"We're back! What are you guys doing?!"

Lin Mu wanted to turn his head around, but Lu Rong suddenly lowered the hem of his shirt, pulling it right over Lin Mu's head.

Lin Mu was stunned.

His nose was pressed right up against Lu Rong's six-pack, and his breaths were trapped within the tight constraints. The other boy's skin would occasionally brush past his tightened lips. The smell of Lu Rong's sweat was not strong, and it was mixed with a trace of last night's soap.

Out there, Sun Hai probably never expected to come across such a sight. Standing there frozen for a long time, ellipses seemed to appear above his head. "Why are you giving yourself a big belly? And why are you covering Lin Mu's head like this?"

Lin Mu's nose and mouth were muffled against those gorgeous abs. He wanted to know the answer to this question as well. Lu Rong's arms were on his shoulders now, as if they were hugging each other.

"We're just playing around," Lu Rong said.

As he spoke, his chest vibrated slightly, constantly coming in contact with Lin Mu's face. Lin Mu stared at Lu Rong's muscles for a while, and as though possessed, he stuck his tongue out, licking him lightly.

Lu Rong froze.

The rest of his words were caught in his throat, neither able to exit nor be swallowed down. A pink noticeable tint spread over his cheeks, and a faint crease appeared on his brows.

Lin Mu seemed to want to lick a few more times, but Lu Rong, discovering his intentions, pressed onto Lin Mu's head through his shirt.

Sun Hai was very simple-minded, and he had no doubts about their horseplay. He even added mockingly, "Why are you pressing on his head? Is he biting you?"

Lin Mu was wordless.

Probably to prove that Sun Hai was right, Lu Rong's abdomen was really left with a bite mark from Lin Mu. When showering at night, Lu Rong removed his shirt, standing in front of the full-length mirror. The bitemark was a little high up, and it was not very deep. The imprint of teeth looked neat and straight, and the mark would most likely fade by tomorrow.

Lu Rong stared at it for a little while. Reaching out, he brushed his fingers against it, smiling slightly.

Lin Mu knocked from outside. "Are you done showering?"

Lu Rong paused, about to remove his pants. With a bare upper body, he pulled the door open, tilting his head down at the boy outside.

Lin Mu seemed to be feeling a little guilty. His eyes darted all around as he handed Lu Rong a towel. "Here."

Lu Rong took the towel.

Lin Mu released a breath in relief, and he could not stop himself from looking at Lu Rong's abdomen. His teeth marks were still there, and embarrassment finally overtook him.

Lin Mu asked, "Does it hurt?"

Lu Rong looked at him. "What do you think?"

Lin Mu could only claim, "I didn't use much strength... See, the skin didn't even break!"

Lu Rong laughed aloud. "What? Were you actually thinking of ripping the flesh off?"

Lin Mu, of course, did not really want to injure Lu Rong. Shamefacedly, he mumbled, "Why are you being so petty? I'll let you bite me in return then."

Lu Rong's brows twitched. Just as he was about to say something, Xu Yilu's voice rang from outside their room. "Mumu, do you want to play Truth or Dare? Everyone's downstairs."

Lin Mu froze. Just as he was about to reply, his chin was suddenly grabbed by Lu Rong. The boy covered his mouth, pulling him into the bathroom.

Xu Yilu repeated his question. After waiting patiently for a little while, he looked a little doubtful. "Is he not in his room?"

"He might have gone out for a stroll. Mama said that walking after eating is good for digestion," said Cao Zhan, who had helped Xu Yilu here. "Shall we go out and take a look?"

Lin Mu could not make a sound. They listened as the voices outside gradually faded away, and Lu Rong, who had been holding him still, finally lifted his head, looking down at Lin Mu from his height.

Lu Rong released his hand from Lin Mu's mouth.

Anxious, Lin Mu said in a low voice, "They shouldn't go out and look for us, it's not safe at night."

Lu Rong seemed to be unbothered. His eyes were fixed on Lin Mu's lips, and his tone was lazy. "An Jincheng is there."

Lin Mu urged him on, "Hurry up and shower, Meimei is waiting for us too."

Lu Rong still did not move.

Puzzled, Lin Mu blinked. "What's wrong?"

"I'm thinking." Lu Rong bent down. He suddenly lifted the hem of Lin Mu's shirt, dragging his waist closer. Slowly, he continued, "I'm thinking about where I should bite you."

Lu Rong had always known that Lin Mu had very fair skin, seen from his exposed limbs and neck.

Lin Mu's T-shirt was pulled up to his shoulders, revealing his smooth, fair waist that looked as though it was carved from marble. Lu Rong half-dragged him up, seemingly considering where he should bite him.

The person being half-carried dared not move. However, after waiting for some time, Lin Mu did not want to passively wait for his doom. Standing on tippy toes, he resisted. "Put me down first..."

Lin Mu felt a heat along the back of his waist. The rest of his words were stuck in his throat, as he realized that on his back were Lu Rong's lips.

"There's no meat around your waist," Lu Rong said, his voice muffled.

Lin Mu lowered his head, stammering an explanation, "Neither do you have any."

Lu Rong seemed to chuckle a little.

His kiss was not hurried, and it was very meticulous. Lin Mu could feel the warmth of Lu Rong's gaze drawing across his waist. The phrase "where to bite you" was like a blade hanging in mid-air, causing Lin Mu to feel a shy anticipation, as well as a vague sense of fear.

Lu Rong's kisses went up his back, and he finally paused as he approached Lin Mu's shoulder blade. Opening his mouth, he nibbled gently at the skin there. Not much force was used, but Lin Mu still shuddered.

"I used to think that your Adam's apple and collarbones were beautiful." Lu Rong pulled Lin Mu's shirt down from his shoulders. Looking at Lin Mu, he continued, "Now, I've discovered that your waist and your back are beautiful too."

Lin Zhao and the rest were gathering in the living room, playing Truth or Dare. Cao Zhan wanted to go out to find Lin Mu and Lu Rong, but was denied from doing so by An Jincheng.

"It's getting dark outside. Why are you looking for them?" An Jincheng was like a mother taking care of her children. He was unwilling to play that role, but he could not just leave them be. "Dopey, take good care of Little Heron."

Xu Yilu used to be a little afraid of An Jincheng, but he slowly became more familiar with him after being in the same group chat. When they came back from the reservoir, they heard that Lin Zhao and An Jincheng had been playing Go the entire afternoon. Xu Yilu at first did not think too much about it, but later on, he felt that there was something not quite right.

It felt as though his ship was about to sink.

Jiang Tianhe's luck in Truth or Dare was horrendous. His face had already been drawn all over, and Mo Xiaoxiao and Li Zi were practically rolling on the floor, laughing. When Lu Rong and Lin Mu came out of the room, no one noticed them, and Chen Mei-hua was instead the first to realize.

"Mumu!" The old lady tossed away the cards in her hands, running over to hug him. "Where did you go?"

Cao Zhan got a shock too. "You guys were in your room?"

Lin Mu could only say, "We fell asleep, so we didn't hear anything."

Cao Zhan was not very smart, and he believed everything he was told. However, Xu Yilu was not convinced, and he asked doubtfully, "You guys fell asleep after dinner?"

Lu Rong explained, "We took a shower as well."

Xu Yilu was wordless.

Why did the explanation make the situation sound even more ambiguous?!

A trip lasting three or four days to Mount Mogan was the perfect length. On the way home, they were all a little reluctant. Sitting in the front, Chen Meihua hugged her rabbit happily. Her rabbit was lively and active, and had even put on quite a bit of weight.

Lin Mu was speaking with Jiang Wan on the phone. Her mother was mostly asking about Lin Zhao, and after answering her questions for quite some time, he said helplessly, "There's so many of us together, what are you worried about?"

"No matter where you all go, I'll always be worried. So, where are the photos? Share them with me."

"The photos are still being edited. Why are you in such a hurry?"

"As if I don't know what my own children look like. Why are

you still editing them?!"

Lin Mu had no response to that.

Li Zi created a shared photo album on Weibo, and it was not set to private. After editing the photos, she made them into a collage and uploaded them. Some of the boys did not have Weibo accounts, and therefore they looked at the photos on her phone instead.

Lin Mu saved the photos from the group chat into his phone. Pausing for a moment to consider it, he then set a photo of Lu Rong from the back as his background photo.

The journey back home was not quick. As the bus jolted along the road, Lu Rong's head drooped, resting on Lin Mu's shoulder. The boy did not wake up, breathing slow and deep with his eyes shut. Lin Mu turned to look at him, discovering that he was holding a glass bottle in his hand.

In it was a beetle.

Lin Mu looked at it for a little while, unable to keep himself from smiling.

There was still half a month left in the summer break, but the students heading into their third year had to start preparing. Although Kunqian did not require them to attend extra lessons before school started, there were many private tutoring classes available. For some reason, Jiang Wan had started paying more attention to her son, enrolling him in one of such classes. Lin Mu now had to brace himself and attend these classes every week.

"I wish I could skip these lessons." It was already five when the class ended. Bringing Chen Meihua along, Lu Rong waited in the lounge below the office building. Lin Mu was sprawled across the desk, only raising his head after complaining. "Why are you here?"

Lu Rong said, "Meimei wanted to come out to play, so I accompanied her."

"Oh." Lin Mu was weary. His class was held in an office building located in the city center, and all three floors were occupied
with students attending classes. In just the tiny amount of time
they spent talking, there had been many other students from the
same class walking past. They greeted Lin Mu as they saw him,
and many of them looked at Lu Rong and Chen Meihua in curiosity.

Lu Rong fell silent for a while, a little unused to it. Quietly, he
said, "Shall I go first?"

Lin Mu frowned. "I'm leaving too. Let's go together?"

Lu Rong nodded, not saying a word.

A student who came in to buy coffee chatted with Lin Mu. "Is
this your classmate?"

Lin Mu smiled. "He's my friend."

"He's not attending the classes?"

Lin Mu said, "He'll only be in his second year of high school."

The student did not have any malicious intentions, only his
gaze towards Chen Meihua was a little curious. Lin Mu blocked
her from his sight, speaking to Lu Rong, "Let's go."

When the three of them left the office building, the sky outside was dark and gloomy, looking as though it was about to
rain. Lu Rong thought for a moment, and he said, "I don't think I
should come again."

Lin Mu frowned. "Don't overthink it. I'm not bothered by
them at all."

Lu Rong pressed his lips together, seeming to be smiling in
resignation. "I know."

Chen Meihua's rabbit was a little too fat. Looking at it from a distance, it looked like a puppy instead. Lin Mu was always worried that the rabbit would get diabetes, hypertension, or high cholesterol. As such, he had been telling Meimei in private not to feed it so frequently.

"It will die from being too fat." During the afternoon break the next day, Lin Mu bought a slice of cake for Chen Meihua from the shop in the lounge room. "Then it would no longer be able to go to the moon with you."

Chen Meihua widened her eyes, feeling very anxious. "Really?"

Lin Mu nodded seriously, "Yes."

Chen Meihua seemed to believe him, quietly telling Lu Rong that she wanted to put the rabbit on a diet.

Lu Rong simmered with laughter. Just as he was about to speak, out of the corner of his eye, he saw another group of students come in.

They clearly all knew Lin Mu. From a distance, they waved at him. "Your friend's here again."

"Yeah." Lin Mu's attitude was very natural. "He came to look for me."

The students nodded, sitting down at a table slightly further away.

Chen Meihua was halfway through her cake, and her mouth was smeared with cream. Lin Mu took out a piece of tissue paper to wipe her mouth. The old lady giggled, reaching out and smearing the cream on Lin Mu's face.

"Meimei." Lu Rong frowned, reprimanding her softly. "Stop it."

Chen Meihua froze. She looked over to Lin Mu, then turned back to Lu Rong. Pursing her lips in grievance, she seemed as though she was about to cry.

Lu Rong raised his voice. He said, "You're not allowed to cry."

SILENT HEARTS

Our Future

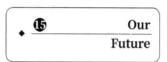

⓯   Our
              Future

Chen Meihua did not burst into tears, but because of Lu Rong's berating, people around them still looked over.

Lin Mu ignored how his face had been smeared with cream. Holding Chen Meihua like a child, he tucked her into his chest, patting her back lightly. "Don't cry... Meimei has to finish the cake, or else the cake will be sad."

Chen Meihua gulped a few times, nodding. "Meimei understands."

Seeing that there was nothing out of the ordinary, the people nearby all turned back to their friends and continued chatting, no longer paying them any attention.

Lu Rong released a breath of relief. He looked at Lin Mu, speaking quietly, "I'm sorry."

Lin Mu smiled. "They all know that Meimei is ill."

Lu Rong seemed a little surprised.

"There's nothing to hide," Lin Mu grumbled a little. He wiped the cream off his face, speaking frankly, "I've told you before, I want to help you take care of Meimei."

As he had to attend classes, Lin Mu had been unable to go to Lu Rong's place as often as he used to. Chen Meihua would frequently throw a tantrum over this matter, and Lu Rong thus had to spend more time and effort in cajoling her.

In the evening, the grandmother and grandson were washing her hair in the courtyard. Chen Meihua was no longer afraid of the water now, but she was still a little resistant to getting her hair wet.

"Why isn't Mumu coming anymore?" The old lady asked.

Lu Rong poured some shampoo into his hand, rubbing it into Chen Meihua's scalp and spreading it through her hair. Bubbles slowly appeared, foaming up. "He has to attend classes."

A pause, and he continued, "He will be very busy for a long time, so we can't disturb him."

Chen Meihua said, "He can live with us."

Lu Rong was a little helpless. "He has his own family too, and he can't only take care of you."

Chen Meihua was not very happy. She turned her head away, making it easier for Lu Rong to rinse her hair with water. Quietly, she asked, "Would Mumu not want us anymore?"

Lu Rong paused in his actions. He lowered his eyes, speaking softly, as though to himself, "He won't."

A few days after school started, mock exams piled upon the third-year students like snow. Lin Mu was not afraid of taking exams, but he felt that they were a waste of time. Going through the exams caused their lessons to end late, and so Lu Rong and Chen Meihua had to wait for him.

The new batch of first-year students had already started their military training. When Lin Mu walked down the corridor, carrying the exam papers, he could see the contingents on the sports ground. Next to him, Sun Hai sighed, "Ah, to be young."

Lin Mu looked at them for a little while, saying suddenly, "Back then, someone secretly took a photo of Lu Rong."

Sun Hai nodded. "And the next day, he became the most handsome boy in the forum."

Lin Mu laughed. Leaning against the railings, he looked downwards. A second-year class was getting ready for their physical education lesson. Mo Xiaoxiao was the first to notice him, and when she shouted "Lin Mu-*xuezhang*," many heads looked up.

Lu Rong was there too. Holding Chen Meihua's hand, he tilted his head back slightly.

Lin Mu's eyes fell onto his face.

"Meimei," Lin Mu shouted abruptly, "do you miss me?"

Everyone around them all knew that Lin Mu was always very concerned over Lu Rong's grandmother, so it was not surprising that he would ask such a question.

Lu Rong fell silent for a moment, then he answered, "Yes."

Lin Mu grinned. He said, "I miss you too."

The scores of their third mock exams were to be ranked against the students of the entire city. The pressure on Lin Mu's class was immense. Even Lin Mu himself had not been able to get enough sleep over the past few days due to studying, and the dark circles around his eyes were startling.

Lin Zhao dropped by her brother's class to see him a few times.

"If I knew, I would have become a Go player too."

As a professional Go player, Lin Zhao did not need to take the national college entrance examinations. Soon, she would be participating in an international competition as the youngest female competitor.

"I'm going to have a match with Choi Jeong," Lin Zhao signed. She then emphasized, "Choi Jeong!"

Ninth Dan Choi Jeong, who was currently the strongest professional female Go player in South Korea. Other than losing to China's Sixth Dan Yu in the Mt. Qinglong competition, she had pretty much never been defeated before.

Lin Zhao poked her head through the doorway of Lin Mu's classroom.

Lin Mu asked, "What are you doing?"

Lin Zhao asked, "Where's An Jincheng?"

Eager for gossip, he looked at his sister for a bit, then he turned to shout, "Young Master An, come here for a moment."

An Jincheng lifted his head from his practice book. When he saw Lin Zhao standing at the door, he froze.

Lin Mu had an expression of awaiting a great show. He said, "My sister's looking for you."

Lin Zhao had no qualms or embarrassment about calling An Jincheng out alone. The break times for the third-year students had been reduced by half, and one of them had to study, while the other one had a Go game in the afternoon. Neither of them had much time to waste.

"When are you going abroad?" Lin Zhao went straight to the point.

An Jincheng seemed to be more comfortable with sign language now. "If everything falls into place, I'll be leaving during the winter break."

Lin Zhao was not surprised. "Oh."

An Jincheng hesitated for a moment, and suddenly said something off-topic. "Even after I leave, my father's donations to Kunqian won't stop."

Lin Zhao did not get it, blinking in incomprehension.

An Jincheng moved his fingers swiftly, "You asked me what sort of person I would like to be in the future. Although it might sound like I haven't got much aspirations, I'll most likely be taking over the family business."

Recalling the businesses An Jincheng's family ran, Lin Zhao was a little speechless. To rich people, was this considered being without aspirations?

An Jincheng continued. "I want to do something more for you ... all of you."

After saying that, he felt that his words might have been disrespectful to Lin Zhao. After all, she had worked so hard for so many years, just to be like other "ordinary" people, rather than simply be labelled as a "disabled person," and showered with sympathy.

Fortunately, Lin Zhao did not mind.

She smiled, her fingers dancing lightly, "I understand what you mean."

Her face lit up, her expression joyful. Clenching her fist, she raised her thumb, shaking her hand lightly a couple of times.

"Thank you," she said.

Other than Lin Zhao, Cao Zhan also did not need to attend his cultural classes in the afternoon. He wanted to enter the Central Academy of Fine Arts, and for their entrance exam, the applicants would be tested on drawing and sketching. These skills needed time to practice, and Ji Qingwen had specially hired a professional tutor to guide him.

"I want to make a sculpture." Cao Zhan decided to show off the new vocabulary he had learned. "A Su Gong jade sculpture!"

Jiang Tianhe clicked his tongue. "To make a jade sculpture,

you need to know how to recognize all the different types of stones. How are you going to deal with that? Don't end up getting sold off by others when you go to Hotan in Xinjiang."

Cao Zhan had never thought about this. Racking his brain for some time, trying to think of a solution, he asked slowly, "How about you go with me?"

Jiang Tianhe was baffled. "Why should I go with you?"

Cao Zhan said very naively, "Because Jiang Tianhe, you're a very nice person."

Jiang Tianhe was speechless.

Across them, Lin Mu and Sun Hai nearly fell off their seats laughing. After all, Jiang Tianhe had started off with a script for a "delinquent," but slowly progressed to having "impotent rage" and he was now declared "a very nice person." He himself probably could not imagine how the entertaining shifts in his character had happened.

To no one's surprise, Xu Yilu's entire family would be going overseas together. His parents were highly qualified technical engineers, as well as geniuses that had been repeatedly offered positions with North American companies.

Most importantly, they were going overseas to treat Xu Yilu's eyes.

"Frankly speaking, the possibility of recovery is not high." Xu Yilu had always been very open-minded about his vision issues. "However, since there's a chance, we should give it a try."

He did not wear his special glasses today. Because of his very fair skin, even the color of his irises seemed very faint.

Xi Yilu faced his friends, smiling. "I really hope that there would be a day where I can see all of you clearly."

As youths, things existed that one would never be able to

escape from. One of them was growing up, and another was separation. News about An Jincheng going overseas soon spread through the class. Lin Mu was not very surprised, but when he was alone with Lin Zhao, his gossipy self could not help but ask, "So what did the two of you agree on?"

Lin Zhao was baffled. "What do you mean by agree on?"

Lin Mu felt that she was not following any normal rules. "Why are you still pretending? Will you be in a long-distance relationship?"

Lin Zhao looked at him as though she was looking at an idiot. "What relationship are you talking about? You better focus on your studies. Have you finished your papers yet?"

Lin Mu was left with nothing to say.

In comparison to those who had already decided on going abroad, going to an arts school, or was in such a unique position that they had no intention of participating in the national college entrance examinations, Lin Mu, Sun Hai, and Jiang Tianhe, who followed convention and walked down this solitary path, had it the hardest. This was especially so for Sun Hai and Jiang Tianhe, whose grades were very mediocre. In their lifespan of around seventeen years, neither of them had probably ever worked so hard before.

Even Lin Mu was a little overwhelmed with his own studies, and he could barely spare time for others.

Other than doing more practice papers, the third-year students also had to attend enrichment classes during the weekends. The time available for Lin Mu to meet Lu Rong was now reduced to an hour or two after the classes on Sunday. This could also not be considered a date, as no matter where Lu Rong went, he would have to bring Chen Meihua along.

"Are you guys splitting streams soon?" Now, other than worrying over his own upcoming exams, the only other thing Lin Mu was worried about were Lu Rong's grades. "Do you plan on taking liberal arts or STEM?"

Lu Rong glanced at him, and he seemed to have no opinions on this matter. "STEM, probably... I have no time for the memorization required for the humanities."

Just before the winter break, the temperature had dropped so much that Lin Mu had to wear a down jacket. The two boys stood at the subway platform, and Lu Rong took a heat pack out from his bag, signaling Lin Mu to turn around.

"You're just like Doraemon." Lin Mu felt the warmth on his back. With his scarf wrapped around half his face, his voice was muffled.

Lu Rong seemed to smile a little. He held onto Chen Meihua with one hand, holding his other hand out to Lin Mu. "Like this, you won't be cold anymore."

Their hands were hidden in the pocket of Lin Mu's down jacket. Many people were waiting for the train, but no one noticed them. With his free hand, Lin Mu tugged at his scarf, hiding his flaming red ears.

The three of them held on to each other, quietly standing in a row.

Before getting onto the train, out of concern, Lin Mu reminded Lu Rong, "You have to consider which stream you want carefully, don't be all slipshod about it."

Lu Rong nodded obediently. "I know."

After the exams, as always, it was time for the second-year students to decide which stream they wanted to focus on.

Li Zi and Mo Xiaoxiao had both decided on the liberal arts

stream, and the two girls surrounded Lu Rong's table, looking at his grades, trying to come up with a decision.

"It'll be better for you if you choose the STEM stream." Li Zi concluded after looking at his results for mathematics, physics, and chemistry. She then asked, "Is Lin Mu-*xuezhang* still tutoring you?"

Lu Rong shook his head. "He's too busy, he doesn't have time."

Mo Xiaoxiao was a little surprised. "Then you're very impressive! Your grades in your STEM subjects are among the top in our class, right?"

Lu Rong did not pay any special attention to the class ranking. He tended to favor certain subjects over others, and at the same time, he had to take care of Chen Meihua too. Hence, he did not have the attention span to focus too much on his education.

The application form for the stream selection did not need to be submitted immediately. The students could bring the application form home to discuss with their parents, and they had the entire winter break to decide.

In the end, Lu Rong shoved the piece of paper all the way inside his bag. If not for his form teacher calling him just before the new year, he probably would not even have remembered about it when school started.

"If Lu-*tongxue* doesn't have anyone to discuss this with, I can help you." Although the form teacher was very young, she was very responsible. Lu Rong's class was the first class she ever taught, and she felt she should pay more attention to her two special needs students.

Holding onto his phone, Lu Rong felt a little awkward. His brows creased slightly, while Chen Meihua was next to him, fooling around. She fiddled with the loudspeaker mode, turning it on and off, chattering away as she wanted to speak into the phone as well.

Lu Rong spoke quietly, "Meimei, stop messing around. My teacher is on the phone."

Chen Meihua pouted. "Who is this teacher? Hurry up and hang up."

The form teacher heard her, and she felt a little embarrassed. "Is your grandmother there?"

Lu Rong's tone sounded very resigned. "Yes."

The form teacher immediately said, "Then I'll make a trip to your place, and we'll discuss this face-to-face."

Lu Rong refused without thinking, "There's no need."

The form teacher made a questioning sound.

Lu Rong paused for some time. He seemed to have made his decision, and softly, he spoke into the phone, "*Laoshi*, next year, I don't plan on coming to school anymore."

The form teacher sounded as though she was in disbelief. "What did you say?"

Through the phone line, Lu Rong's voice did not sound real. It was soft and thin, like a wisp of a cloud. "I don't plan on continuing my education anymore."

In a quiet voice, he continued, "*Laoshi*, I'm sorry."

During this year's Chinese New Year, Lin Mu was forced by Jiang Wan to stay at home and receive guests. Looking down at his phone, he texted away, and Lin Zhao did not even need to think to know who the recipient of the texts was.

"Little Deer is very busy too, don't keep disturbing him." His sister was like a wet blanket. "Our aunt has been looking at you a few times already."

Lin Mu could only look back. Sure enough, his aunt was again looking at him, her eyes bright and full of questions.

"Does Mumu have a girlfriend now?" The Lin family were all rather open about such matters, and they were not against students being in a relationship. Lin Mu remembered how his relatives would often ask if he had any girls he liked when he was still in primary school.

The corners of Lin Mu's mouth twitched. He thought about how he did not have a girlfriend, but a boyfriend instead.

However, he could not say this now. After dodging the question for quite some time, he finally managed to change the topic.

Lin Mu was a little resentful about the questions. He signed at Lin Zhao, "Why didn't they ask you?"

Expressionlessly, Lin Zhao signed haughtily, "I'm a world-class professional Go player. Everyone is aware that most mortals are not worthy of me."

Lin Mu was wordless.

Lin Zhao asked, "What are you and Little Deer chatting about?"

Lu Rong's name was not easy to sign, and so the twins were used to using the sign for deer to refer to him. Face to face, they seemed to be "calling" each other with their hands.

Lin Mu said, "I'm discussing with him what stream he should choose."

Lin Zhao rolled her eyes. "You're not his mother, why are you so concerned over this?"

Lin Mu was unable to clearly explain this "beautiful love story" of his. He could only wave his hand, feigning the arrogance of an elder as he said, "You don't understand."

After replying to Lin Mu's message, Lu Rong returned to the dining table in the living room. Chen Meihua was currently eating a bowl of Eight Treasure Rice, looking at the person across her with great curiosity.

The form teacher did not actually want to come knocking on their door, and disturb them during the festive season. However, Lu Rong's statement of not coming back to school had been too shocking, and she thought she had to drop by.

"Lu-*tongxue*, don't make a decision so quickly," the form teacher tried her best to convince him. "Let's think of another way."

A high school education was not within the bounds of the nine-year compulsory education. This meant that if Lu Rong made the decision not to go to school anymore, there truly would be no one who could force him.

Chen Meihua spilled the rice all over herself. Distracted, Lu Rong cleaned her up. With a dirty hand, the old lady wanted to grab the bowl again, but was stopped by Lu Rong.

The form teacher did not know how to react to the scene.

It took Lu Rong about five to six minutes before he could settle Chen Meihua and clean her up. He looked a little weary. "*Laoshi*, as you can see, my grandmother's illness is getting worse."

A pause, and he continued, "I'm sorry, we've caused you so much trouble."

The form teacher opened her mouth. She was really only a young lady, and before she could speak, her eyes reddened abruptly.

She asked, "Are you unhappy in Kunqian? Is someone bullying you?"

Lu Rong shook his head. "No, I'm not unhappy, and no one is bullying me."

"Then why?"

She could not understand, and she repeatedly asked why.

However, even until the end, Lu Rong still did not give her

the answer to her question.

By the time the form teacher left, it had started snowing outside. Lu Rong stood in the yard, raising his head up towards the
dark, inky sky, where small, scattered pieces of white were drifting down.

Lin Mu sent him an image of crabapple blossoms over the
phone, adding a line, "Happy New Year."

Lu Rong looked at it for a while, and he could not help but
smile.

"I can't come out tonight, so I won't be able to deliver any
flowers in the snow." Lin Mu seemed a little regretful as he texted
Lu Rong. "I'll come and look for you tomorrow morning."

Lu Rong replied, "OK."

His phone buzzed non-stop with notifications. Cao Zhan and
the rest had sent their new year greetings as well. An Jincheng
was already in the United States, and despite the time difference,
he started distributing red packets to everyone.

Lin Mu sent another text privately, "Quick, grab some red
packets and then buy some new study materials with the money.
I've kept Qidong's papers for you, and you must practice them
when school starts again."

It sounded as though he was talking about something delightful, and his messages came in very quickly, one after another.
"Choose the STEM stream, as you're very good at the sciences.
You'd have me as well. I'll tutor you, and you'll definitely be in
the top three in our school, and the top five in the city!"

"Then, you can also study medicine, and go to the same university as me. You'll continue to be my underclassman, and I'll be
doing my clinicals while you study the foundations..."

Before Lin Mu could finish texting, he suddenly received a call.

Shocked, he quickly ran to the balcony and answered it in secret. "Hello?"

Lu Rong's voice sounded, calling out his name. "Lin Mu."

Lin Mu pressed a hand to his chest. Lu Rong's voice made his ears heat up, and he stammered, "W-why did you suddenly call me?"

Lu Rong laughed. "It's nothing, I just missed you."

"Oh." Lin Mu was rather dazed. He looked into the house, and seeing that no one noticed him, he covered his mouth and whispered to the phone, "I miss you very much too."

A muffled laugh came from Lu Rong's side. He said, "It's snowing."

Lin Mu told him that he saw the snow too.

Lu Rong suddenly recited a line from an old poem: "We share this moment while being apart."

Lin Mu wanted to laugh. "This is used for the moon, not the snow."

"It's the same to me," Lu Rong said. "Whether it's the moon or the snow, I only want to look at them with you."

On the first day of the new year, Lu Rong had to go to the hospital to collect Chen Meihua's medication. He had contacted a doctor he was on familiar terms with, arranging to go at an earlier timing so that he could avoid a long queue.

Chen Meihua did not like to be woken up so early. She made a fuss over it, and no matter how hard Lu Rong tried, he could not calm her down. When they arrived at the hospital, the old lady was still crying.

Lu Rong coaxed her to the point where even he himself found the situation amusing. Chen Meihua was sitting, while he was in a half-crouching position. He lifted his head, looking at his grandmother. "Meimei, what are you not happy about?"

Chen Meihua sobbed, "I haven't finished my dream."

Lu Rong then asked, "What did you dream about?"

Chen Meihua said, "Meimei dreamed that she was with Mumu in a garden. There were many many flowers, and they were all very pretty. Mumu made a flower wreath, and then placed it on Meimei's head."

Lu Rong thought for a moment and said, "How about this? Meimei will go with me to collect the medicine, and then we'll go buy some flowers to make you a flower wreath?"

Chen Meihua was not satisfied with that. "I don't want you to make it, I want Mumu to make it."

Lu Rong had no choice but to say, "Then after collecting the medicine, we'll go look for Lin Mu. How about that?"

Coaxing an old person was like coaxing a child. No matter what Chen Meihua decided on, they still had to collect the medicine first, and it was a bargain between the two.

Chen Meihua was still not very happy, but she had no choice other than to go with Lu Rong and join the queue for the medication. The number of people in the hospital gradually increased, and Lu Rong pulled Chen Meihua to his side, afraid that she would be separated from him.

After collecting the medicine and meeting the doctor they knew for a consultation, Lu Rong coaxed and wheedled Meimei into doing a routine checkup. It was nearly noon by the time what felt like torment to the old lady ended, and she was no longer in the mood to mention Lin Mu and the flower wreath anymore. Instead, she sat there wearily.

Lu Rong coaxed her again, "What does Meimei want to eat?"

Chen Meihua pouted, refusing to speak. Lu Rong again asked, "Is Meimei hungry?"

Chen Meihua thought for some time before replying, "I want to eat at Pizza Hut."

Lu Rong had no opinions about it. To him, as long as Chen Meihua was willing to eat, anything would be fine. He packed away the medicine and the medical result slip, bringing his grandmother out to lunch. In the end, before the pizza was even brought to the table, Lu Rong received a call from Zhong He.

"Where are you?" No students would save their principal's number, and Lu Rong at first thought it was a call from a telemarketer. When he heard Zhong He's voice, he was a little stunned.

Zhong He sounded very stern, and again he repeated, "Where are you?"

Lu Rong finally answered after some silence. "I'm at The First Affiliated Hospital..."

"You brought your grandmother to see the doctor?"

"Mn." Lu Rong made a sound of acknowledgement.

"Give me the address, I'll come to you."

Lu Rong was not so daring as to hang up on Zhong He. As such, about half an hour later, Zhong He was sitting across the grandmother and grandson, looking at Lu Rong with a severe expression.

"I heard that you want to withdraw from school?" Zhong He went straight to the point.

Lu Rong had no intentions of hiding this matter anyway. After some hesitation, he nodded. "Yes."

Zhong He frowned. His features were already quite harsh, and whenever he had an unhappy expression, his face would look even harsher.

"How's your grandmother?" Zhong He asked abruptly. "Are

you able to take care of her by yourself?"

"I can still manage for now." Lu Rong paused, then continued, "Her progression of Alzheimer's disease would only get worse, so I don't plan on attending school anymore, as it would be difficult bringing her along."

Zhong He exhaled slowly. Rubbing at the point between his brows, he said, "You want to withdraw from school, but how many years will this withdrawal last? A year, two years, five years or ten years?"

Lu Rong did not respond.

Zhong He asked, "Do you really have no plans to go to university?"

Lu Rong hung his head. A while later, he finally said, "Right now, I have no way to even consider such matters."

Zhong He was a little agitated. "That's your future! Do you not want to consider it?!"

Lu Rong slowly lifted his eyes. The corners of his mouth twitched, as though he wanted to laugh.

He said, "With my current situation, there's not much of a future to be seen."

It was a little noisy in Pizza Hut. Carrying the pizza, the server brought it to the table. Chen Meihua did not really know how to eat it by herself, so Lu Rong cut the slice up for her before feeding her bit by bit.

Even so, his grandmother was still not cooperative. Whenever there was something she did not want to eat, she would reach out and grab it, then toss it to the side.

Zhong He looked at the messy chunks of pizza on the plate, then turned towards Lu Rong with a complicated gaze.

The latter seemed to exhale slowly. He coaxed Chen Meihua,

fed her, wiped her mouth, then cleaned up the table. Everything he did was in perfect order, as if he had done it a million times.

"If you're still willing to come to school next semester, I'll arrange for one more teacher that will be dedicated to accompanying you and your grandmother," Zhong He suddenly said as he looked at Chen Meihua.

Lu Rong lifted his head, looking at Zhong He with a bit of surprise.

"Don't say things like not wanting to attend school anymore," Zhong He looked calm as he spoke. "My original intention for building this school was to let children like you receive an education like any other ordinary children, to be able to study and enter universities, and have a chance at a decent future."

Lu Rong opened his mouth. He seemed to want to say something, but Zhong He held his hand out, stopping him.

"Perhaps you may think that I'm an adult, that I'm not you, and I'm not standing in your shoes, and yet I'm still saying something so arrogant."

Zhong He adjusted his glasses, speaking quietly, "Just let me be a little arrogant for now, based on the years I have on you."

"Don't give up, and take some time to consider for yourself," Zhong He continued. "Don't try to put everything on your shoulders alone, and don't say that you have no future. Your life shouldn't be like this."

After lunch, Zhong He went to the counter to pay the bill. It was a rare occasion for Lu Rong to not reject the offer, and the three people left Pizza Hut in silence. Before Zhong He left, he again repeated his suggestion, reminding Lu Rong again.

"If you need money, I can also be the guarantor for your loan application." He paused, then added, "Also, with regards to the teacher, Chu Lin and I can make arrangements to help take care of your grandmother while you're in class."

Lu Rong did not know how he should reply. After some silence, he could only thank Zhong He repeatedly.

Zhong He seemed to worry that Lu Rong still felt conflicted, and so he added Chu Lin's phone number into Lu Rong's phone. "If there's any issues, you can contact Ms. Chu directly. She'll also come and meet you. Whatever you're thinking about, or worried about, you can tell her anything."

Lu Rong nodded.

Seeing that Lu Rong was able to accept all that he had told him, Zhong He finally released a breath of relief. With a dinner appointment later, he could not stay too long with Lu Rong, and he had to leave first.

"Don't think about withdrawing from school anymore," Zhong He said before leaving. "Even if the sky were to collapse, there would still be us adults to support it. How bad can things get?"

After Chen Meihua walked for some time, she stopped and refused to continue. Lu Rong had no choice but to squat down and let her climb onto his back.

On their way home, they went past a florist. The old lady finally remembered her flower wreath. She made a fuss about buying flowers, and Lu Rong could only carry her on his back as they went inside the shop.

After picking out a few stalks, Lu Rong received a text from Lin Mu.

He took a photo of baby's breath and sent it in response.

Lin Mu's reply came almost instantaneously. "Meimei wants to make a flower wreath?"

"Yes. Are you still in class?"

"It's about to end soon. Will you be coming to see me?"

Lu Rong replied, "Sure."

After paying, Lu Rong once again carried his grandmother on his back and walked down the road.

"Where are we going?" Chen Meihua asked as she swayed her legs happily.

Lu Rong answered, still looking straight forward. "Didn't you want to make a flower wreath? We're going to see Lin Mu now."

"Is Mumu really making one for me?"

Lu Rong said, "Yes, it's true, we'll see him soon."

Chen Meihua was clearly delighted. On Lu Rong's back, she chattered away noisily. Lu Rong supported her with his arms on his back, afraid that she might fall. However, he was not angry, only saying helplessly, "Meimei, be good."

Chen Meihua clasped her arms around his neck, falling quiet for a while before murmuring softly into his ears. "Rongrong, school is starting soon, right?"

Lu Rong's footsteps came to a stop.

Chen Meihua continued quietly, "Rongrong, Granny has saved some money for your university fees. Are you happy?"

Lu Rong did not state if he was happy or not. He remained standing there, his head hanging down. Chen Meihua was a little muddled. She stretched her head out and saw a few dark, wet spots near Lu Rong's feet. It looked as though they were going to spread and turn into puddles.

After accepting the offer from the overseas university, An Jincheng returned home to complete the last bits of paperwork. His father even organized a "coming of age" party, which basically was the family of three having a meal at a fancy restaurant.

Setting up something like this was not very creative, and it even felt a little deliberate, but An Dayou liked it. Just like his name, the relationship between him and his wife was derived from "My Old Classmate." He was a businessman, but for some reason, he had a very literary side to him as well.

While waiting for the dishes to be served, An Jincheng kept fiddling with his phone. After seeing his son do so several times, An Dayou could not help but ask, "Who are you texting? Are you in a relationship?"

An Jincheng looked up from his phone, glancing at his own father expressionlessly.

He had inherited his mother's looks. When Zheng Yannian had been younger, she'd been famously beautiful. An Dayou loved his wife more than himself, and he naturally accommodated every request of his only son as well.

"I'm going to the washroom." An Jincheng stood up.

An Dayou was dishing out the food to his wife, and he spoke without looking up, "Come back quickly."

Silently, An Jincheng rolled his eyes. He stepped out of the private room and was led to the end of the corridor by the waiter. After dealing with his physiological needs and moving to the sinks, he realized that there were a few people smoking by the plants next to the door.

Washing his hands, he perked his ears, eavesdropping.

"Principal Zhong, that Young Master An in your school is going abroad soon, right?"

Zhong He's voice was a little hoarse from too much smoking, but his tone was very courteous. "An Jincheng-*tongxue*'s grades are excellent, so it's no surprise that he would go abroad."

Another person asked, "Then wouldn't An-*laoban*'s sponsorship fizzle out?"

Zhong He paused for a while before saying, "It's hard to say, I have yet to ask him about this."

The group of people laughed, and their tone sounded very casual. "With Principal Zhong being this hardworking, it wouldn't be difficult to get more sponsorships."

"Isn't there a student learning Go in Kunqian?"

An Jincheng's hands paused when he heard this. Frowning, he considered the situation for a moment, then took his phone out and turned on the voice recording function.

That person was still speaking. "That little girl's in the newspapers again this year. She's very pretty indeed, and her Go skills are good too. What a pity she's deaf and mute."

Zhong He interrupted, "Wang-*laoban*, let's go back and have a drink."

"*Ai*, Principal Zhong, it's not that I want to criticize you." It sounded as though that man might have drank too much, and he spoke very freely, "You've accepted so many special needs students, and you've spent so much money with nothing in return. I remember that the professional Go player can teach Go, right? I know a little about Go too. If there's time, how about you set up a meeting between us, and let the child teach me?"

Zhong He answered calmly, "Wang-*laoban*, you've drank too much."

"No, stop. Although I haven't donated as much as An Dayou, it is still quite a substantial amount. Look at those students of yours. They're either missing a limb, blind, or stupid. I heard that there's even one who brings his grandmother to school? How interesting, treating the school like a nursing home. In my opinion, if that sort of student doesn't want to attend school, then just don't. Yet you even went to him and persuaded him to continue studying. Principal Zhong, you're really a great philanthropist."

An Jincheng felt a fury well up in him, and his brain buzzed angrily. But before he could step outside, he heard a commotion. Someone was holding onto Zhong He, while others were pulling up that Mr. Wang.

The plants by the door had blocked most of his view, and An Jincheng could only see that Mr. Wang lying on the floor. Despite being held back, Zhong He was still desperately trying to kick Mr. Wang, but the man was not the kind of person who would fight back. Instead, he covered his head, shouting that he was going to withdraw his sponsorship, and that he was going to call the police.

Zhong He refused to concede, pointing at him and cursing, "You think I need that pittance sum of yours?! Withdraw if you want! However, I'll make it clear today! Don't even think about having any filthy intentions towards a single one of my Kunqian students!

"What's wrong with my students?! My students are great! You're the blind one, the heartless one, and you're worse than a beast! Even if I have to kneel at An Dayou's feet, I will never again take a single cent from you!" After saying that, Zhong He went up and gave Mr. Wang a few more punches, taking advantage of the inattention of the others. In the end, when he yanked his tie loose and turned his head around, he saw An Jincheng standing by the washroom door.

Zhong He looked a little embarrassed. Not because his student had witnessed him fighting, but because he felt it was shameful for his student to hear such disgusting things.

An Jincheng took his phone out, turning off the recording. He looked at Zhong He and suddenly said, "I'm having a coming-of-age party with my family today. Principle Zhong, please join us."

When Zhong He arrived at the An family's private room, he had yet to realize what had just happened. Despite having already drank quite a lot of liquor, reflexively, he wanted to toast An Dayou as well, and the latter pushed it off sheepishly. "Principal Zhong, this is a family dinner, there's no need to drink like this."

Zhong He was a little embarrassed, and he replied obligingly, "Look at me, it's already become a habit."

An Jincheng was still playing with his phone, and he did not mention what had happened just now. Zhong He could not figure out the reason why An Jincheng had invited him here, and so he could only enquire about him going abroad.

An Dayou only had this one darling son. An Jincheng himself was also hardworking and showed great promise, and the father was very proud of him.

Zhong He was very gratified as well. "Jincheng definitely has a bright future ahead of him."

An Dayou waved him off, laughing. "*Aiyah*, the child's health, safety and happiness are the only things that truly matter. His mother and I have no other expectations."

Pointing at his son, he continued, "I was originally afraid that he'd be rebellious, and refuse to take over my company."

An Jincheng finally had a reaction when he heard this. He said indifferently, "I have to earn as much money as possible, to have the capital to marry and settle down."

His father laughed at him. "You're thinking so far ahead. Why? You've already decided which school your child will go to, and where your house will be?"

Zhong He did not know how to react to this conversation between the father and son.

It was not appropriate to mention anything about donations

or sponsorship during a family dinner, and Zhong He also did not want to mention such matters in front of his student. However, when the meal was over, An Dayou took the initiative to speak up.

"An Jincheng has had ownership over some assets ever since he was a child," An Dayou shook hands with Zhong He, smiling as he spoke quietly. "Before he went overseas, he reached an agreement with me, and one of the conditions was that I would continue my sponsorship for Kunqian."

Zhong He's mouth fell open. He was speechless.

An Dayou continued, "He has always been a child who is cold and aloof in all matters. My wife and I are so busy with our careers that we've neglected him for too long, causing him to cultivate such a personality. I had always been worried that he didn't know about love, and doesn't know how to love."

Zhong He spoke a little urgently, "He's not like that..."

"I know my own son," An Dayou interrupted. He continued sincerely, "It's because of Kunqian, and that's why he's able to grow into such a warm person."

After dinner, Lin Mu was a little puzzled when he received a recording. He looked at the sender, then sent a voice message in reply, "What's that?"

An Jincheng was rather impatient. "Have you listened to it yet?"

Lin Mu turned on his computer, logging into wechat and saying perfunctorily, "I'm listening, I'm listening."

He then thought of something else and asked, "Are you still coming back to school when it starts?"

"I'll be attending for a few days, there are some things I need to hand over."

Lin Mu sniggered. "Then you're still able to meet my sister a few more times to improve your relationship."

An Jincheng did not know how to respond to that.

He could no longer stand it, and so he urged Lin Mu, "Listen to the recording first."

At first, Lin Mu was not paying any attention to it, thinking that An Jincheng was playing a prank on him. Halfway through, he finally realized what was wrong. Furious, he said, "What does that Wang fellow mean?! How dare he have such intentions towards Lin Zhao?!"

"In any case, it's over for him," An Jincheng said coldly. He took a deep breath, no longer able to wait. "Did you know anything about Lu Rong wanting to withdraw from school?"

There was no buffer or slowing down for the second semester for the third-year students. About to take the national college entrance examinations, the students went straight into the final stretch of preparation. During the first mock exam, there was not much of a difference in Lin Mu's results. Mr. Yang called him over to his office to collect the exam papers in the morning, and he took the chance to discuss his university applications with him.

"If you want to study medicine, it's a bit of a waste not to go out of the province." Kunqian would ask their third-year students to fill out surveys on which universities they were interested in applying for. Lin Mu had written down a university within their province all three times, and Mr. Yang was not very reconciled to it. "The universities in Jiangsu are not considered to be influential. Your aim is to become a clinical doctor, so would you not consider choosing a university outside the province?"

Lin Mu hesitated for a while, but he still replied, "I don't want to be too far away from Suzhou."

"What about Shanghai? Shanghai's nearby too."

Lin Mu said lazily, "I have to be able to meet its entry requirement first."

Mr. Yang was exasperated. "With your grades, you only need to put in a bit more effort and you can get into Tsinghua or Peking. Why are you suddenly so unsure of yourself?"

Lin Mu did not speak, and he was actually a little distracted. Ever since that call from An Jincheng, although he had remained in contact with Lu Rong, they had yet to have the time to see each other face to face. It had been less than a week since school started, and Lin Mu did not make any deliberate trips over to the second-year classroom. When An Jincheng came back to handover the affairs of the school committee, he shared that he had bumped into Li Zi.

"She didn't mention anything about Lu Rong's withdrawal." An Jincheng was leaving in the afternoon. Standing in the corridor, he spoke to Lin Mu, "However, she did say that he's only been attending the morning classes during the past few days."

Lin Mu was silent. An Jincheng sighed and said quietly, "You need to talk to him."

"About what?" Lin Mu asked suddenly. He was expressionless, and his tone was a little aggressive. "Would he listen?"

An Jincheng frowned. "What are you talking about? Calm down."

Lin Mu took in a deep breath. "Don't bother about our matters anymore."

When Lu Rong wanted to be excused in the afternoon, he had to look for the head of his level to approve his excuse slip. Chu Lin led him upstairs, and the third-year students just happened to have finished their lessons. Jiang Tianhe and Cao Zhan saw him from a distance, and both called out, "Little Deer."

Lu Rong turned his head around, and Cao Zhan hurried over. "Where are you going?"

Perhaps because of his low IQ, Cao Zhan never beat around the bush, and his words were always direct and frank.

Lu Rong thought for a moment and replied honestly, "I'm applying to be excused, there's something I have to do."

Cao Zhan nodded. He could not think about what else to ask, only envious that Lu Rong did not have to attend classes in the afternoon.

"Where's Lin Mu?" Lu Rong could not help asking. "What has he been doing recently?"

Cao Zhan blinked, answering innocently, "He's doing his homework. Just now, he even went to the teachers' office."

Lu Rong opened his mouth, wanting to enquire further, but up ahead, Chu Lin urged him on.

"Hurry up and go." Cao Zhan's smile was cute and silly. "You don't have to attend classes!"

Lin Mu stood there, his hands behind his back. Mr. Yang was once again nagging at him with kind intentions, but it went in through one ear and out the other for Lin Mu. Behind him came the sound of the door opening, and Chu Lin's voice was very energetic. "Mr. Chen, you have to sign an excuse slip."

Lin Mu turned his head around reflexively, and his eyes met Lu Rong's. He stiffened up like a rock.

Lu Rong was looking at him as well. There was a warmth in his eyes, a flowing affection within them.

Lin Mu tightened his lips, inexplicably feeling a swell of anger rushing through him. He turned his head away, refusing to look at Lu Rong.

Lu Rong was confused.

Chu Lin said, "What are you looking at? Come here and sign this."

Lu Rong was a little baffled by what Lin Mu was angry about. He suppressed the puzzlement within him, taking a pen and bent down, signing his name on the excuse slip. However, just when he finished signing, someone suddenly reached out from behind him and snatched the paper away.

Chu Lin was startled. "Lin Mu, what are you doing?"

Lin Mu said stiffly, "Lu Rong is not withdrawing from school. He has to continue studying, and this signature is invalid."

Question marks appeared all over Chu Lin's face. "What?"

Just as Lu Rong opened his mouth, wanting to explain, Lin Mu glared at him, speaking sternly, "I have yet to settle this account with you."

He said, "In any case, don't even think about withdrawing from school."

Chu Lin did not know whether she should laugh or cry. "Who said Lu Rong's withdrawing? This is just an application to be excused for the afternoon, and Lu Rong is going home to deal with his shop rental issues. Why are you butting in?"

Lin Mu was stunned. The excuse slip in his hand was taken away by Lu Rong, and the latter said helplessly, "I'm not withdrawing from school. I've only applied for a few afternoons off, as I have some things to settle."

Chu Lin shared, "The shop owned by Lu Rong's family is going to be rented out. He's underage, and cannot sign the lease agreement, so he has asked Principal Zhong to be the guarantor. The paperwork has been prepared over the past few days, and he is requesting to be excused to go to the intermediary and meet the client during the afternoons."

Chu Lin poked at Lin Mu's head, speaking unhappily, "You're not allowing him to withdraw? No one did!"

Pressing a hand to his head, Lin Mu could not force a single sentence out. Chu Lin was no longer concerned with him, taking the slip of paper and leaving to look for Zhong He. Standing by the office door, Lu Rong was in no hurry to go, and he waited for Lin Mu, who staggered outside.

"Why are you avoiding me?" Lu Rong tilted his head down at Lin Mu, asking softly.

Lin Mu was stubborn. "I haven't been avoiding you."

"Even your text replies are slower."

Lin Mu had no response to that.

Lu Rong was a little aggrieved. "There were some replies that took more than two minutes."

Lin Mu shot him a look. "You even check the time when looking at messages?"

"Of course." Lu Rong made it sound very natural. "I'm afraid that I'll miss the messages and cannot reply to you in time."

Lin Mu nearly choked listening to him.

"Let me ask you." Lin Mu did not mean to go through their issues right here, but if they did not settle this now, he would feel upset over it for the rest of his life. "Did you plan on withdrawing from school?"

Lu Rong never thought that he would be able to hide it from Lin Mu, but he still tried to deceive himself about it, telling himself that Lin Mu would never find out.

Seeing that Lu Rong was not responding, Lin Mu's eyes gradually started to redden. He asked, "Am I that untrustworthy?"

Lu Rong jerked his head up, a little panicky.

Lin Mu looked at him, asking questions one after another. "What are you afraid of? Are you afraid that I cannot bear with the work? That I cannot take care of Meimei? Or are you afraid that I don't like you enough, and I'll get tired of you after some time, that I'll get tired of Meimei?"

Lu Rong's chest heaved unsteadily. He choked out, "No..."

"What's going on here?" The door to the teachers' office was suddenly opened from inside. Mr. Yang was standing in the doorway, looking at them strangely. "Why are you two standing here and not going back to your classes?"

Lin Mu stared at Lu Rong for a beat, and he was the first to avert his eyes. Walking past Lu Rong, he headed for the stairs.

Lu Rong nodded hurriedly towards Mr. Yang, then followed behind Lin Mu.

He dared not stick too close to Lin Mu, and there was half a flight of stairs between the two. It was only when the person ahead stopped, then standing a few steps above, Lu Rong gazed down at the person in front.

The skylight in the stairway was half-opened, and the afternoon sun came streaming in, falling at Lin Mu's feet. He turned around, his face hidden in the shadows, as though a dim light was cast around them.

"Lu Rong, I cannot dig my heart out for you to see." Lin Mu sighed, long and slow. He was silent for a few moments, then continued desolately, "But I really wish I'm able to dig it out and let you examine it."

SILENT HEARTS

Meimei

=

═══

⑯   Meimei

◆

Zhong He signed on the line meant for the guarantor. He looked like someone not to be trifled with, and every clause in the contract was studied carefully by him. The intermediary that came with the client was so nervous that his forehead broke out in sweat, afraid that if he offended this man, this deal that was already in hand would go up in smoke.

Lu Rong sat by the side with Meimei. He signed on the line meant for the landlord and helped his grandmother press her thumbprint onto it. Meimei quietly asked him, "What are we doing?"

Lu Rong said patiently, "We're renting the shop to earn a living, and we'll hire a nanny for Meimei."

Chen Meihua understood the meaning of "nanny," and she was not very happy. "Why do we need a nanny?"

Lu Rong replied, "Because I have to study, and I need someone to help me take care of you."

Chen Meihua reluctantly accepted this reasoning, but she grumbled unhappily, "Meimei doesn't need to be taken care of by someone else."

"Then who do you want to take care of you?" Lu Rong asked.

"Meimei can take care of herself." Chen Meihua's expression was very naive. "Also, there's Mumu. Why isn't he moving in with us?"

Lu Rong was a little helpless. "Lin Mu has his own family, and he needs to take care of his sister too. Meimei cannot be so selfish."

Chen Meihua pouted in grievance. She said, "Then you can get married with him. When you're married, you can live together."

Lu Rong was speechless.

He did not know how he should explain to Chen Meihua that two men could not get married here. Chen Meihua took things too much for granted, but to be able to have such daring thoughts seemed to be something worth being happy and blissful about.

Zhong He had to return to school in the afternoon. Lu Rong received quite a large sum of money, and it was definitely enough to cover the cost of hiring a nanny.

"Chu Lin and I will help you keep an eye out." Zhong He was clearly afraid that Lu Rong would mention that he wanted to withdraw from school again, and he wanted to help Lu Rong sort everything out, to settle everything for him. "We'll try our best to find a nanny with experience in taking care of an Alzheimer's patient. Also, Chu Lin has already arranged for another teacher to assist you. When you officially return to class next week, there will be someone taking care of your grandmother with you."

Lu Rong felt as though he had been thanking people around him countless times over the past few days. Of course, he had made his apologies as well, but he did not know if the receiver's anger had subsided yet.

Looking down, he sent Lin Mu a text, taking a photo of the lease agreement and sending it to him. The latter replied after some time, "Everything's settled?"

"It's settled."

It took Lin Mu a long time before he replied, "Hmph."

Lu Rong felt that this boy was way too adorable. Tapping on his phone, he sent a message, "Are you still angry?"

"Of course." Lin Mu's response came quickly, and his anger was evident. "You were planning on hiding your withdrawal from school from me, how can I not be angry?"

Lu Rong might be very adept at coaxing Meimei, but now facing Lin Mu, he could only send a simple apology. As though trying to make up for it, he added, "I'll study hard and go to university with you."

This time, Lin Mu did not send a reply. Lu Rong was not anxious either, tucking his phone back into his pocket. Crouching down, he spoke to Chen Meihua, "Meimei, I'll piggyback you."

Chen Meihua clambered onto his back in delight.

"Mumu hasn't come to see me in a long time." Sprawled across Lu Rong's back, Chen Meihua complained softly. "Does he not like Meimei anymore?"

"How could that be?" Lu Rong said. "He's been busy recently; he's preparing for his university entrance exams."

When Meimei heard the words "university entrance exams," her expression went a little muddleheaded. Lu Rong turned his head to look at her, saying, "I'll also get into a university, so Meimei must live to a ripe old age and watch over me."

In his English class, Lin Mu had handed in his mock exam early. Leaving the classroom, he leaned on the corridor's railings, looking down and texting on his phone. It seemed as though he had seen something interesting, and he could not help but laugh.

There were a few teachers hanging a banner downstairs. Lin Mu took a look, discovering that it was to celebrate An Jincheng's admission to a prestigious school in the United States.

Zhong He was there directing them himself, instructing the teachers on where to hang the banner, how high it should go, and whether it was hanging straight or not. For him, it was not enough to have only one banner. There was another one by the sports ground, as well as by the gate.

Resting his chin in his palm, Lin Mu watched him busy about, and his friends were still chatting away in the group chat.

"I think they're going to have a fourth banner." Jiang Tianhe was sneakily texting under his table. Out of the ten words in a message, half of them were wrong. "Young Master An is now a hot commodity for publicity, and that scoundrel Zhong He would most definitely make full use of it."

Li Zi said, "It's not just the third-year students. Last semester, a second-year student won the first prize in a science and technology competition, and the certificate is still hanging by the school gates."

"It's the same for Lin Zhao-*xuejie*'s Go competitions." Mo Xiaoxiao glanced at a newspaper. "Kunqian High's Student—Third in Go Competition. I heard that Principal Zhong had paid for this headline to publicize our school."

Cao Zhan looked at it for some time before sending a text, confuddled. "Why does he have to pay for it?"

Lin Zhao sent a reply, harsh and heartless, "For money."

Lin Mu laughed himself silly. Before he could reply, he was discovered by Zhong He downstairs.

The principal looked up, his harsh features wrinkling. Pointing at Lin Mu, he said loudly, "Why aren't you in class?"

Lin Mu blinked. Due to them being on different floors, they had to shout at each other. "I just finished my exam."

Zhong He was not very pleased. "You handed your paper in early again!"

Lin Mu was not afraid of him, and answered gleefully, "I can still get a perfect score!"

Zhong He placed his hands on his hips, a resigned look appearing on his face. Lin Mu looked down at his phone, noticing that Lin Zhao had once again edited the name of the group chat.

"Cheering on Robber Zhong He..." Sun Hai had submitted his paper too. When he saw the name of the chat, he froze for a moment. He asked, baffled, "Why are we cheering him on? Didn't you use to hate him?"

Lin Mu replied leisurely, "As you said, it's 'used to.'"

Sun Hai sent a reply. "?"

Lin Mu stuck his head out, shouting down, "Principal Zhong! Do you want me to help you hang the banners?!"

Zhong He's hair nearly stood up in exasperation, and he swore before shouting back, "Go back to your class! Study hard! Don't fool around!"

Carrying Chen Meihua on his back, Lu Rong had to stop a few times as they walked. His grandmother had many issues, and with her age, she needed to go to the toilet frequently. Lu Rong brought her to a public restroom and then asked a passerby to help take care of her. The one who accompanied her in was a very responsible middle-aged woman. When she brought Meimei out, she even reminded Lu Rong to change her pants.

It's too tight," the woman said mildly, "I don't think she's comfortable."

Lu Rong thanked her, then tilted his head down to his grandmother and asked, "Did Meimei say thank you?"

Chen Meihua smiled brightly. "I've said it, and I even sang."

The woman praised her singing before leaving. Holding Chen Meihua's hand, Lu Rong took his phone out to discover that Lin Mu had replied to him.

"Zhong He has hung up quite a few banners." He took a few photos, all of which were the banners publicizing An Jincheng's acceptance into an Ivy League school. He sounded jealous. "If I were to study abroad, I might get this kind of treatment too."

Lu Rong was silent for a few moments, and he sent "I'm sorry" in reply.

This time, Lin Mu responded very quickly. He seemed to be whining, sounding like a spoilt and pampered child. "See how good I am to you."

Lu Rong laughed. Just as he was about to type his reply, he received another text from Lin Mu.

"The next time we meet, you must remember to kiss me first."

Lu Rong sent a question mark.

Lin Mu said, "As long as you kiss me, I won't be angry with you anymore."

It was not just Lu Rong. Chen Meihua was also eagerly waiting for the weekend to see Lin Mu. Unfortunately, the students preparing for their national college entrance examinations were very busy with their studies. Even Jiang Wan, who seldom managed her son, had been strangely proactive.

"Don't drive me there." Sitting at the porch, Lin Mu was speaking helplessly. "I'll go by myself, and come back home by myself too."

Jiang Wan was unhappy. "The sun is so bright. Wouldn't it be nice if I drive you there? Don't get distracted now, is it because you're dating? Tell your little girlfriend to endure a while more, and once your exams are over, I'll immediately go over to their family and propose a marriage."

Lin Mu was speechless.

He stared at his mother with a particularly tragic expression. When Lin Zhao walked past, she was a little curious, and so signed a question. "What's wrong?"

Jiang Wan continued spewing nonsense, singing, "Your brother is getting married."

Lin Zhao's eyes widened. She raised her hand, waving it by the side of her temple and asked suddenly, "With whom? Little Deer?"

Lin Mu got a shock, thinking that Lin Zhao had discovered them. But looking at how unconcerned she was, it seemed like she was cracking a joke.

Jiang Wan however took it seriously, signing, "Who is Little Deer? Is she pretty?"

Lin Mu's head hurt. Afraid that the more they discussed about it, the more real it would sound, he braced himself and said aloud, "He's a boy."

Jiang Wan was baffled. "So what if he's a boy? I'm not a stick in the mud."

Lin Mu had no response to that.

As though his heart had turned to ashes, Lin Mu sat in Jiang Wan's car. His mother's driving was pretty good, and while steering the car, she was even singing as well. The music played in the car was alternative western rock, and it could be seen how trendy the owner of the car was.

"Have you decided which university you'd like to apply for?" Jiang Wan could not be considered to be a very qualified mother.

Due to Lin Zhao's special situation, her heart had been wholly placed on her daughter since a long time ago. Lin Mu could be said to have grown up having been allowed to do whatever he want, with the occasional guidance from Lin Yanlai.

Fortunately, her son had always done well since he was a child, and in the matters of his education, he had never caused the adults any worry.

"I'm thinking of a Shanghai university," Lin Mu said. "The medical schools at Shanghai Jiao Tong and Fudan are pretty good."

Jiang Wan was a little startled. "You want to study medicine?"

Lin Mu nodded. "Yes, I want to be a clinical doctor."

Jiang Wan never thought that her son would have such a clear, well-defined goal. She was even ready to be a "concerned mother" for once, listening to the student's worries and troubles. But in the end, her son was not worried, and neither did he have any trouble. In comparison, she was instead the one who was a little foolish.

Cars were not allowed to stop for too long at the door of the tutoring class. Before Lin Mu went in, he bent down, speaking to Jiang Wan in the driver's seat, "I'll go back by myself after class."

"Why don't you let me drive you home?"

Lin Mu decided to be frank. "I have a date."

Jiang Wan was not angry at all. She realized that since there was nothing to chat about with regards to school, she could still do so about his relationships. "Have you really found a little girl-friend? How about introducing her to me?"

Lin Mu said resignedly, "So that you can propose a marriage?"

Jiang Wan considered it for a moment, and she answered thoughtfully, "It's not impossible."

Lin Mu was speechless.

Even in the tutoring class, Lin Mu was still the teacher's favorite student. He sat in the middle row, and he was not overly conspicuous. However, he also would not just muddle along and sleep in class, and his grades in his STEM subjects were so excellent that no one could find fault with them.

Exams and rankings also occurred in this class. Lin Mu was the first to collect his papers from the teacher, so he thought that the class would end early, and he could leave. Instead, the teacher had called upon him to explain his solutions, and Lin Mu had to waste another hour or so. By the time he left the classroom, it was almost past dinner time. Looking down at his phone, he wanted to send a message. Halfway through typing, his eyes happened to slide past the lounge downstairs.

He did not know what time Lu Rong had arrived. Next to him was Chen Meihua, and the old lady was currently eating ice cream. Now that the weather had warmed up, Lu Rong finally agreed to let her have an ice cream a day to satisfy her cravings.

"I can only have one?" Chen Meihua was eating it very carefully, afraid that she would finish it too quickly. "Can I have another one when Mumu comes?"

Lu Rong had to say, "You can't ask Mumu for one, that's against the rules."

Chen Meihua pretended not to understand. "What's against the rules?"

Lu Rong was a little exasperated. Rudely, he pinched his grandmother's cheek. Chen Meihua cried out a little, then refused to acknowledge him again.

Lin Mu pushed the door open, going in and calling out, "Meimei."

Lu Rong turned his head around. He looked at Lin Mu, and it

seemed as though two tiny flames were burning in his eyes.

Looking at him, Lin Mu smiled.

The two boys had not seen each other in a while, and for a moment, they did not know what they could say. Lu Rong sat across from Lin Mu, his hands properly placed on the table. After a short silence, he suddenly asked, "Are you hungry?"

Lin Mu smiled. "I'm fine. Are you hungry?"

Lu Rong also said that he wasn't. He was still looking at Lin Mu, as if he were trying to absorb a few days' worth of Lin Mu all in one glance. Chen Meihua had already finished her ice cream, and spoiling the atmosphere, she grumbled quietly, "Meimei is hungry."

Lin Mu could only ask, "What does Meimei want to eat?"

Chen Meihua herself did not know what she wanted to eat, but she was truly hungry. Shaking her head, she repeated, "I want to eat."

Lu Rong had no choice but to pull her up. "Shall we get something to eat?"

Lin Mu nodded. He opened an app on his phone, searching for a nearby restaurant. As students, the money they had was limited. This was especially so for Lu Rong, and so Lin Mu had to consider their spending and food wisely.

The three people were a little conspicuous standing by the door to the tutoring class. Seeing them, the departing students and teacher would all exchange a greeting with Lin Mu, and those who had often seen Lu Rong around would nod at him too, smiling as they praised Chen Meihua, "Meimei is dressed so beautifully today."

The old lady spun in a circle, displaying her tulle skirt. "Little Deer picked it."

Even though Chen Meihua's brain was no longer as agile, her intuition could still tell her clearly whether a stranger was kind or malicious. She did not have much of a coherent ability to think, and when her illness played up, she could not even communicate regularly with others. However, she would still carefully avoid those who bullied her.

She could not control her emotions, and sometimes she would even end up embarrassing Lu Rong. However, even if she was bullied, she still wanted to protect her own grandson.

A girl said that her braids were very pretty. Chen Meihua was too shy to say that they were tied by Lu Rong, afraid that it would cause him trouble. Faltering awkwardly, she refused to say anything.

Lu Rong looked up from Lin Mu's phone, calling out to Chen Meihua, "Meimei, come here."

"*Aye.*" Chen Meihua ran over to him.

Lu Rong apologized to the girls. "Please excuse us."

The girls waved their hands hurriedly, saying, "It's fine, Meimei is very adorable."

Chen Meihua poked her head out from behind Lu Rong, speaking cautiously, "Little Deer tied my hair."

The girls laughed, then praised Lu Rong for his deft hands.

Lin Mu coughed. He shook his phone, saying, "I've decided. Shall we go?"

Holding onto Chen Meihua, Lu Rong bade the girls farewell. When he walked over to Lin Mu, the latter gave him a profound look.

"You're pretty popular." Lin Mu's tone was a little jealous.

Lu Rong was stunned for a moment, before he laughed. "They just like Meimei."

Lin Mu was vexed. "What do you know? This is called making use of someone to achieve their own gains." He paused, and grumbled, unreconciled, "Didn't I use this method right at the beginning as well? And that was how I won you over."

Probably because his life had been too hard and tough, and he had no time to pay attention to anything else, Lu Rong did not realize how popular he was. Both boys and girls had appeared in front of him before, expressing their feelings for him timidly and shyly. However, that bashfulness seemed to be only for a spur of the moment. It did not last long, nor was it pressing. It was like a poor imitation of wind, sweeping through the hearts of the youths perfunctorily.

It was only a casual remark when Lin Mu talked about "using others to achieve their gains." He sent Jiang Wan a text, saying that he would not go home for dinner, and his mother gave him a call.

"You're really on a date?" Jiang Wan was curious. "Did you bring enough money?"

Lin Mu resisted the impulse to roll his eyes. "I've told you already, it's a boy."

"It doesn't matter. In any case, you have to be the one paying on the date. Don't let the other party take out their wallet."

Lin Mu did not know what to say to that.

He finally understood that no matter what he said, Jiang Wan and he were on different wavelengths. His mother's girlish, imaginative character had never dissipated with age, only becoming even more intense over the years, and it was completely out of control.

Of course, as students, they would not choose restaurants that were too expensive. Besides, Meimei was with them, and they could not spend too much time eating either.

The restaurant by the street was not big, and the three people at the table had to lean in close. Lu Rong was feeding Meimei, and halfway through the meal, Lin Mu held his hands out to him.

"I'll do it," he said. "You should eat first."

Lu Rong did not stand on courtesy, handing over the chopsticks and spoon to Lin Mu. Chen Meihua giggled at Lin Mu, her hands stained with grease and gravy. Picking up a napkin, Lin Mu carefully wiped her fingers clean.

"Mumu, the rabbit has grown up," Chen Meihua informed him softy. "When will the osmanthus tree bloom?"

Alzheimer's patients had no logic to their words, and they would ask whatever they thought about. Lin Mu did not feel annoyed, and he answered patiently, "Osmanthus flowers will only bloom in autumn, it's not even summer yet."

Chen Meihua thought for a moment, "Rongrong will be taking his university entrance exam in summer."

Lin Mu paused in his actions of wiping Chen Meihua's hand, asking softly, "Meimei remembers?"

Chen Meihua's expression was a little lost. She seemed to not understand what Lin Mu meant when he asked her if she remembered. Lin Mu smiled and continued, "Lu Rong will take the exam next year, so Meimei, you don't have to worry so much."

With only a hazy sense of comprehension, Chen Meihua nodded. She asked Lin Mu, "Is Mumu taking the exam then?"

"Yes." He held the bowl up, scooping up some soup and changing the topic. "Meimei, open your mouth."

Chen Meihua opened her mouth. As she ate the soup, she still wanted to speak, and she did not realize the soup was spilling from the corners of her lips. Lin Mu could only tilt her head up and help her wipe her mouth.

"What does Mumu want to be when you grow up?" Chen Meihua asked.

Lin Mu said, "I want to be a doctor."

"Not a scientist?"

Lin Mu laughed. "A doctor can be a scientist too, and then we
can cure Meimei's illness."

Chen Meihua was suddenly unhappy. "Meimei has no illness."

Lin Mu coaxed her. "Yes, yes. Meimei only forgets things easily."

Chen Meihua could not tell the difference between "illness"
and "forget things easily." However, she seemed to be much more
able to accept the change in words, and now she was willing to
eat obediently again.

After feeding her a few mouthfuls, Lin Mu suddenly remembered something. Sticking out his little finger, he spoke mysteriously to Chen Meihua, "Can Meimei promise me something?"

Chen Meihua imitated him, carefully hooking her little finger
with his. "What is it?"

"If I'm going to study elsewhere in the future, tell Lu Rong
something when he starts to miss me." Their little fingers hooked
together, Lin Mu leaned into her ear and whispered.

Chen Meihua asked curiously, "Tell him what?"

"Tell him that I'm thinking about him every day," Lin Mu
whispered secretly, "and that he is the one I like the most in the
world."

Since he had already told his family that he would be having
dinner outside, and Jiang Wan had also accepted that her son
was on a date with his "little girlfriend," Lin Mu was in no hurry
to return home. He sent Lu Rong and Chen Meihua home, and
Chen Meihua told him that they had to feed the rabbit first. Lin

Mu crouched with her in the yard, with leafy vegetables in their hands. The rabbit seemed to have a fear of making decisions, and it did not know from whose hand it should eat from first. With its nose twitching, it sniffed here and there.

Lu Rong had finished heating the water and making the bed. When he stepped outside, he saw Lin Mu and Chen Meihua chattering away, and he only managed to make out their conversation when he came closer.

"Don't make it too fat." Lin Mu had reminded Chen Meihua countless times about the rabbit's weight, and he even explained it in great detail. "You should only feed it at the right time and in the right amount every day. If it's too fat, it will fall sick, and it's not good for its digestive system too. What happens if it dies?"

Right now, Chen Meihua no longer had any desire to fly to the moon. She thought for a moment, then said, "If the rabbit dies, can we buy a new one?"

Lin Mu remained silent for a while before refusing her staunchly. "No, we can't."

Chen Meihua pursed her lips, seemingly about to cry. Just as her eyes were filling up with tears, behind her, she heard Lu Rong say calmly, "If this rabbit dies, I'll cook it and feed it to you."

Chen Meihua was stunned.

Her expression clearly declared that Lu Rong was a monster, but Lu Rong was not moved by it at all.

"It's time to wash your feet and go to bed," Lu Rong said, "Lin Mu has to go home. He can't stay too long."

Chen Meihua asked. "Can't Mumu sleep with us?"

Lin Mu shook his head. Jiang Wan was not so liberal as to allow him to spend a night at his "little girlfriend's" place. It was not that she was afraid someone would take advantage of Lin Mu, but rather he would take advantage of his "little girlfriend."

Chen Meihua could only obediently follow Lu Rong back into the house to wash her feet. After doing that, she insisted on Lin Mu telling her bedtime stories. When they finally coaxed the old lady to lie down, Lin Mu had already received many text messages from Jiang Wan.

"You can't stay overnight!" That was the final ultimatum from the mother to her son. "You're not allowed to do anything that the girl doesn't agree with!"

Lin Mu was wordless.

If he really wanted to do something, Lu Rong would most definitely agree.

Of course, he could not say such things. As he replied the messages, he walked out of Chen Meihua's room carefully. Lu Rong was doing his homework in the living room, only looking up when he heard him, and he mouthed silently, "She's asleep?"

Lin Mu nodded. He sat down next to Lu Rong, looking at his homework. "Any issues?"

Lu Rong turned to the last page. "If there are any problems, there are answers and steps available to solve them."

Lin Mu smiled. He looked at Lu Rong, and Lu Rong was also looking at him. The boy's eyelashes were long, sweeping downwards before lifting up again. Lin Mu had yet to react when he leaned in, until Lu Rong reached out and covered his eyes with his palm.

It was a long and slow kiss, so long that it seemed as though they could map out the lines on each other's lips. In the shadowy darkness, Lin Mu tasted the flavor of plain water, and Lu Rong's breath held the scent of flowers from the yard. The heat and moisture of the early summer lingered between their lips.

"I'm sorry," Lu Rong said quietly. He paused, then continued, "I truly, deeply love you."

When Lu Rong walked Lin Mu out of the lane, Lin Mu finally turned around, speaking helplessly, "Go back, you don't have to walk me any farther."

Lu Rong had his hands in his pockets. He did not move from where he stood. Agreeing with Lin Mu, he tilted his head down, kissing him again. Lin Mu cupped his face in his hands, and they shared more than one kiss.

"Stop apologizing," Lin Mu said. "I'm already tired of hearing it."

Reflexively, Lu Rong wanted to apologize again, but he managed to stop himself in time. Thinking for a moment, he reached out and hugged Lin Mu. The two people stood under the streetlight, hugging for some time, and then Lin Mu's phone rang again. It was Jiang Wan calling him to urge him home.

"It's already ten." His mother's voice sounded quite excited. "What are you doing?"

Lin Mu replied, exasperated. "I'm coming home."

Unexpectedly, Jiang Wan's tone sounded a little regretful. "You're really coming home?"

Lin Mu laughed. "What are you thinking about?"

He looked over at Lu Rong and suddenly said, "Would you like to speak to my 'girlfriend'?"

Jiang Wan got a fright, half nervous and half excited. "Really?! Then what should I say? Will I come off too scary?"

Lin Mu turned his phone to the loudspeaker mode and then got Lu Rong to speak into the phone.

"Hello Auntie, I'm Lu Rong."

Jiang Wan was speechless.

Lin Mu was about to die laughing, but he was also afraid of scaring his mother to death. Just as he was about to explain, they suddenly heard Jiang Wan jerkily, yet solemnly say, "Little Deer, don't be nervous. I have no prejudice at all, and I'll definitely support you both!"

Lu Rong did not know how to react.

In April, Xu Yilu went to the United States with his parents. There were now two people in a different time zone in their "Good Luck for Finals" group chat. Almost every morning, when Lin Mu woke up, he would be able to see last night's conversation between An Jincheng and Lin Zhao.

"Why aren't the two of you messaging in private?" Lin Mu signed at his sister over breakfast. "You guys were even using voice messages."

Lin Zhao was very frank. "We're not dating, why do we need to send messages to each other in private? Also, Little Heron's there too."

Due to Xu Yilu's vision issues, other than the voice messaging function on wechat, everything else would not work. Each time he was by himself, people in the group would switch to voice messaging function, and the duty of translating for Lin Zhao would naturally fall to Young Master An.

An Jincheng was also very busy. In the end, Lin Zhao and Xu Yilu were the ones talking to each other more often instead, while An Jincheng was only a tool to pass messages. Other than the second-year students, the third-year students who did not need to take the national college entrance examinations were Sun Hai and Lin Zhao. Sun Hai would be going to Australia in May, while Lin Zhao was focused on moving up the Go rankings. Only Jiang Tianhe, Cao Zhan, and Lin Mu were left huddling together for warmth in the cold left by the pending exams.

Of course, the only ones who needed the warmth were Cao

Zhan and Jiang Tianhe. Lin Mu alone was a source of heat.

During the last stretch of preparation, even Lin Mu, a monster at defeating examinations, could no longer digest the number of mock papers raining upon them like a storm. Questions from Qidong were so difficult that it made the students want to vomit. When doing practice questions for Mathematics, the teachers had selected over a hundred of them, and the students had to complete every single one of them. Jiang Tianhe complained that for questions worth thirty marks, their difficulty was set at three hundred marks, and all of them could be found in one paper. By the time he finished the paper, he was about to claim PTSD.

Although Cao Zhan could take two fewer papers, with his brain, there was not much of an advantage for him. Furthermore, he had to spend half his time preparing for his fine arts exams, and the rest of the time was not enough for him to catch up and practice.

Lin Mu could only take some time out to prepare a study plan for him. "For Math, just focus on geometry, your geometry's pretty good. As for Mandarin and English, just memorize them, and try writing a bit longer for reading comprehension."

Cao Zhan said, "But there's still essay writing."

Lin Mu took a deep breath. "Let me take a look."

Cao Zhan's essay writing skill was similar to that of a primary school student. For his argumentative essay, he was completely off topic, and his essay usually ended up contradicting itself, with no clear train of thought.

Lin Mu could not think of a better solution either, so he could only advise Cao Zhan to work on narrative essays.

"Just write according to the title. Ignore the inscription. Whatever topic they give you, just write about it." Lin Mu flipped through Cao Zhan's essay workbook. Although his argumentative essays were off topic, his narrative essays were not too bad, partly because his way of seeing the world was different from that of ordinary people. For example, the descriptions he used sometimes could be rather bizarre, but they strangely fit very well in the essay. If not for the fixed model standards of the national college entrance examinations, Cao Zhan would most definitely become a great literary poet.

When the results of entrance examinations for the Central Academy of Fine Arts were released, Lin Mu and Jiang Tianhe accompanied Cao Zhan to take a look.

The three people stood solemnly in front of the noticeboard, holding Cao Zhan's admission form in their hands and comparing it with each identity number. When they reached the third row, Jiang Tianhe shouted loudly, "1302! 1302! I found it!!"

Cao Zhan had yet to register what was happening. In his ears were the yells of Jiang Tianhe, and other than screaming incoherently, Jiang Tianhe was unable to say anything else. He hugged both Cao Zhan and Lin Mu, jumping on the spot excitedly, as though he was the one who had been accepted.

Lin Mu gripped onto Cao Zhan's hand tightly, shouting, "Dopey! You passed your fine arts exams! Did you see it?!"

Cao Zhan had just seen the numbers "1302." His hands were shaking, and he was still in slight disbelief. "I-did I really passed?"

Jiang Tianhe said, "You passed! As long as you meet the requirements for your humanities exam, you'll be going to university!"

Cao Zhan's face was flushed a bright red, and it was unclear whether he was happy or excited. He confirmed the number against his admission ticket a few more times, and unable to control his emotions, his tears slid down his face, unimpeded. Choking, he said, "I, I really got in."

"Don't cry, Dopey." Lin Mu wiped away his tears, not knowing whether to laugh or cry. "Now that you've passed your fine arts exam, you still have your humanities exams. Don't relax now, and just endure for a little while more."

Sobbing, Cao Zhan nodded. The moment he started crying, Jiang Tianhe felt tears welling up within him as well. He turned away, wiping his eyes with his sleeves, and spoke feebly, "Fool, don't be scared. You'll definitely be able to study here."

Cao Zhan smiled through his tears. "I'll definitely study hard. I still want to go to university."

The group chat was filled with messages asking about Cao Zhan's results. The ones who had not been able to go were even more nervous than the ones who had gone. Some messages were like essays, first analyzing the situation, then giving a conclusion, even attaching a Plan B just in case Cao Zhan did not manage to make the cut. In any case, no matter the results, there would be a solution.

Jiang Tianhe took a photo and sent it to the chat, his tone sounding as though he himself had passed the ancient imperial examinations. "Here here here, it's time for all of you to give out lucky red packets!"

After two seconds of silence in the group, An Jincheng and Lin Zhao both sent out huge red packets. While thanking the "bosses," Sun Hai congratulated Cao Zhan too, flattering all parties very well.

Xu Yilu sent a rare voice message in the chat. "Well done, Dopey. You've worked hard."

"Little Heron, you said that I'm only a point below the seventy points score of ordinary people." Cao Zhan thought for a long time before recording this voice message. "I might never be able to gain this one point in my entire life, but it doesn't matter. Even if it's sixty-nine points, it's still me, it's my entire being, and so I'm not envious of that one point at all."

Cao Zhan remembered that during one occasion when he was still very young, he was held in his mother's arms, and his mother was weeping. As he was stupid, he could never do the homework set by the teachers, and the school had suggested that he attend another school for mentally handicapped students. He always envied people of the same age with normal intelligence, and he used to be upset and felt he was stupid too.

Until he came to Kunqian.

Cao Zhan did not know what had transpired between Ji Qingwen and the school. His mother only told him that he could continue to study in high school. Cao Zhan was at first unwilling, but Ji Qingwen and Cao Nian both firmly insisted on it.

"You're only a little slower than others," Ji Qingwen told him gently. "Just try for a little while more, alright? Even if you're unhappy with studying, you can make friends too."

Cao Zhan did not feel that he would be able to make friends. He had constantly been bullied, and had been given all kinds of strange nicknames. He would always be the one with sixty-nine points, and he was different from the rest.

And after that? After that...

Someone did give him a nickname, but he liked to be called Dopey.

Someone told him, "You're only one point below seventy, it's alright."

Someone was clearly always very fierce towards him, bullying him all the time. But that person never hit him, and when there was actually a fight, that person would even try to protect him despite getting beaten up.

The crafts he did, the drawings he drew, the items he sewed, so many people liked them. The boys wore the skirts he modified, and hanging on the girls' bags were the little items he made.

Because of the banners he sewed for the sports meet, he even scored points for his class.

He had a "revolutionary friend" named Meimei. They both disliked eating mushrooms, and they both liked rabbits.

On Monday, when the students returned to the school, Zhong He had added four more banners to Kunqian's grounds. On them were written, "Congratulations to Cao Zhan from the special needs class for passing his fine arts exam."

Lin Mu laughed when he saw them, telling Lu Rong, "Look at how grand this is, it's even grander than Young Master An getting into a famous school!"

Cao Zhan thought, he would no longer be envious of seventy points anymore. His sixty-nine points was excellent too.

SILENT HEARTS

NCEE

The students had three days off before the National College Entrance Examinations. Lin Mu was no longer in the mood to continue revising. Recently, Jiang Wan had been doing what a good wife and mother would do, cooking meals and making soup, the flavors everchanging, and she put great effort on making all kinds of soup. During one hot day, when Lin Mu drank the soup she made with aged hen and ginseng, he dared not make even a peep when his nose started bleeding in the middle of the night, instead running over to Lin Zhao's room to seek his sister's help in stopping the nosebleed.

Recently, the group chat had been fairly quiet as well. The third-year students were preparing for their exams, and the underclassmen from second year were all very sensible. Afraid of disturbing their upperclassmen, they remained extremely quiet. When Lin Mu finished consolidating his notes of the past few years, he made a copy and sent it to Li Zi and Mo Xiaoxiao.

Lu Rong of course got a copy too. On the second day of the school break, Lin Mu personally delivered it to him.

June's weather had gradually turned warmer, becoming more humid. Lin Mu dragged his bicycle out from the basement, bumping into his mother in the main hallway.

Jiang Wan had just finished brewing another pot of soup, and she was wiping her hands as she walked out of the kitchen. Seeing Lin Mu, she was startled. "You're going out?"

Lin Mu nodded. "I'm bringing something to Lu Rong."

Jiang Wan asked, "What are you bringing?"

Lin Mu showed it to her. Jiang Wan glanced at it, and, upon seeing that it was studying material, she did not ask any further.

It was the middle of the day. The sun was like a freshly cooked coddled egg, the sweltering heat oozing out like yolk, scorching the clouds surrounding it. Lin Mu stood up as he cycled, and his shirt billowed in the wind like a mini parachute. The bicycle passed through the Taohuawu district, the foliage lush and green. The gardenia flowers were in bloom, their fragrance filling the air, and people's eyes were drawn to the blossoms.

Lu Rong was standing at the gate of his yard, waiting for him. Lin Mu stopped his bicycle at the gate. He was perspiring, beads of sweat rolling down his cheeks to his chin. Lu Rong could not help but laugh when he saw him.

"Why are you laughing?" Lin Mu asked.

Lu Rong shook his head. "When you first came to my place, you were also on a bicycle, just that it was during a snowy winter night. You were pretty much exuding cold air, and even your brows were white."

Lin Mu was a little embarrassed. "Wasn't it just because I was eager about bringing you the flowers?"

"Today, you came under the blistering sun, and you're now soaked in sweat. It feels like it's always a difficult trip for you

459

each time you come over."

Lin Mu laughed. "It is through hardships and obstacles that one's sincerity and heartfelt feelings can be seen. I have to imprint myself deeply in your heart, so that you'll always think of me."

Perhaps Lu Rong had never expected that Lin Mu's tongue could be so honeyed, for in response to that his expression was a little helpless. As they were speaking, Chen Meihua's chattering could be heard coming from the house.

"I've hired a nanny for Meimei," Lu Rong told Lin Mu after a small pause. "Today's her first day."

Lin Mu had not expected that. As he walked into the yard, sure enough, he saw an unfamiliar middle-aged woman braiding Chen Meihua's hair. Meimei was very delighted when she saw him, calling out loudly, "Mumu!"

"Auntie Luoyao, this is Lin Mu," Lu Rong introduced. "He's my friend."

Fang Luoyao seemed to be in her forties. She had a round face, and she liked to smile. Giving off an image of youthfulness and amiability, she had a very good temper. She was not the chatty type, and she smiled at Lin Mu, greeting him, "Hello, would you like some green bean soup?"

The temperature outside was too hot, and Lin Mu's forehead was covered with sweat. Green bean soup was perfect for warding off the heat, and Lin Mu did not stand on courtesy. Sitting down, he took the bowl handed to him by Fang Luoyao, gulping down half its content at once.

While Lin Mu was drinking the soup, Fang Luoyao finished tying Chen Meihua's hair.

"Is it pretty?" She held up a mirror to the old lady, carefully showing her the hairstyle from behind. Chen Meihua turned here and there for a while, as though she was examining homework, then spoke with feigned sternness after some time, "It's not too bad."

Fang Luoyao laughed, giving Chen Meihua a bowl of green bean soup as well.

When she went to wash the bowls, Lin Mu could not help commenting to Lu Rong, "She's quite good."

Lu Rong glanced at him, holding back his laughter. "Are you interviewing her on my behalf?"

Lin Mu answered thoughtfully, "You can't treat this too casually. It's not easy to take care of an Alzheimer's patient, and not all nannies will be good. You should pay more attention to it."

Lu Rong sighed. "I don't hold out hope that I'll be able to find a good one on the first try either. It's all up to luck, and we'll just take it slow."

Fang Luoyao was someone Chu Lin had found for Lu Rong. She said that Fang Luoyao had many years of experience in caring for a disabled elderly. However, she refused to continue working for the last family due to some issues, so Chu Lin invited her over to come help Lu Rong out.

Lu Rong was not a curious person, and he did not ask her why exactly she left her former workplace. Chen Meihua's situation was rather special, so her nanny would have to stay with them. Fortunately, despite the age of their house, it was a stand-alone house, so it was easy for them to empty a room for her.

"Auntie Luoyao has a son who's still in junior high." Lu Rong and Lin Mu sat in the yard, chatting. Chen Meihua wanted to take an afternoon nap, and Fang Luoyao accompanied her back into the house. "She's taking care of him alone."

Before Chu Lin brought Fang Luoyao along with her, she even gave Lu Rong her resume. In the column for marital status, she

had stated that she was widowed. Lin Mu flipped through the resume, and his expression was a little complicated. After a bout of
silence, he suddenly said, "Life is actually quite tough."

Lu Rong glanced at him, smiling, "It used to be tough for me."

Lin Mu sighed. "It's not easy for you now either, but fortunately, you've hired a nanny. I've been worried over what you'll do
when you're in the third year of high school."

"It's doable," Lu Rong said. "I just feel that time is passing too
slowly, and I want to skip a grade."

Lin Mu gave him a questioning look.

Lu Rong lowered his voice, sounding as though he was speaking to himself. "You're about to go to Shanghai soon, and I feel
anxious about it."

Lin Mu's heart pounded loudly, and his blood heated up. It
was already past the hottest time of the day, but he still felt as
though his head was burning hot.

"I'll come back to see you every weekend I'm free." Lin Mu felt
as if something was stuck in his throat. Placing his arm in front
of his eyes, he tried to hide. "Your words are making me not want
to study anymore."

Lu Rong did not know whether to laugh or cry. "What nonsense. Don't say such things."

Later on, he asked Lin Mu why he was not studying during
these three days, and Lin Mu said that he would throw up if he
were to continue studying anymore. He even complained about
the soups Jiang Wan had been brewing, and how both his stomach and brain were now basically swimming in oil.

Lu Rong laughed until his belly ached. After laughing, he
gazed at Lin Mu again for a moment.

The two had leaned towards each other very closely when they
were chatting. Lin Mu lifted his head, kissing Lu Rong's chin.

"You have to study hard." Lin Mu reached out, caressing Lu Rong's cheek. "You must get into a university."

Lu Rong paused before answering, "I won't be able to go to Shanghai."

Lin Mu replied calmly, "I know. Don't be afraid. Even if I go to the South Pole, I won't break up with you."

Lu Rong smiled, feeling a little low. "Fortunately, there's no university in the South Pole."

At dinner time, Jiang Wan called, urging Lin Mu home. Lin Mu hemmed and hawed, answering her perfunctorily, then heard his mother say warmly, "Pass the phone to Little Deer, I'd like to convey my regards."

Lin Mu was baffled. "What are you trying to do?"

Jiang Wan spoke as though nothing could be more obvious, "Isn't he your 'girlfriend'? Can't a mother-in-law talk to her 'daughter-in-law'?"

Lin Mu could not tell whether his mother was being serious or joking at all. Resigned, he handed his phone over to Lu Rong, letting him speak instead. Turning around, he discovered Fang Luoyao looking at him, her gaze a little strange. When she saw him looking over, she immediately turned away, adjusting her expression before asking with a smile, "Is Lin-*tongxue* staying for dinner?"

Lin Mu did not think too much of it, and his response came naturally, "I'll be taking the national college entrance examinations the day after tomorrow. My mother has been keeping a tight watch over me, so I won't be staying."

Very sincerely, Fang Luoyao said, "Good luck with the exam, don't be nervous."

She, too, was someone with a son, and thus would show great

concern over students. She could not help but give him a few reminders about revising his notes, not forgetting his admission pass, and bringing more 2B pencils to the exam venue. Before she could finish speaking, she looked up to see Lin Mu smiling at her, and she then realized how much she had said. Awkwardly, she said, a little self-mockingly, "Just look at me, I'm too naggy."

Lin Mu's smile was very bright, and he hurriedly said, "Auntie, don't say that. I'm more than happy to listen."

Fang Luoyao pressed her lips together, smiling sheepishly.

When Lu Rong hung up, he turned his head around to see his grandmother's nanny and Lin Mu smiling at each other strangely, and he asked, "What's going on?"

In a good mood, Lin Mu replied, "It's nothing."

He went to the yard to get his bicycle. Swinging a leg over, he supported himself on the other leg and held one arm out to Lu Rong. "Come here for a hug."

Lu Rong walked over, hugging him tightly.

"I'll go to your exam with you in a couple of days," Lu Rong said quietly into his ear.

Lin Mu said carelessly, "Everyone has their parents waiting outside the hall. What, will I be the one to have a boyfriend waiting out there?"

Lu Rong ruffled Lin Mu's hair with some force, and he could not be bothered with Lin Mu's flirtatious teasings.

In the car, Jiang Wan helped her son examine the items in his folder again. She looked so nervous, and even wanted to buy Lin Mu some Redbull.

"I really won't be able to finish it." Lin Mu was not joking, and he was afraid that it would make him need to go to the washroom. "Why are you so nervous? It's your son taking the exam, not you."

Jiang Wan glanced at him resignedly. "I took the exams thirty years ago, and that trauma still haunts me to this day."

Lin Mu had nothing to say to that.

Other than his mother, Lin Yanlai and Lin Zhao came along too. As his sister, Lin Zhao was completely stress-free, even bringing along a camera to take photos of Lin Mu.

"It's a milestone in life," Lin Zhao signed, "we should commemorate it."

Truthfully, Lin Mu was a little jealous of her. "Aren't you going to play Go?"

Lin Zhao lifted the camera, aiming it at him. Fiddling with it for a while, she then answered, "We'll be heading out tonight. This time, it's an international competition, the Samsung Fire Cup. If I win, I might be Sixth Dan Lin when I come back."

International Go competitions brought a lot to the table for the players. With the gradual decline of Go in Japan, the professional players of China and Korea flourished. Unlike the strict postgraduate system in Korea, China's Go style was in between the two countries, developing in a more uncivilized manner, growing out of collective strength. There were few sects or schools, but it was still a tradition for the old players to guide the new. When Lin Zhao entered the professional rankings, she had once been under the guidance of a famous teacher and institution to practice her skills. Through a journey bathed in blood, she slowly formed a style that suited herself.

If it wasn't easy for Lin Mu to be participating in the national college entrance examinations, it wasn't much better for Lin Zhao before a competition either. Even late in the night, around 2 or 3 AM, Lin Mu could still hear his sister practicing Go in her room.

"Do well." Lin Zhao raised the camera again. "Smile."

Standing at the exam venue entrance, Lin Mu gave a victory sign to the camera, along with a dazzling grin.

On the last day of the exam, Lin Mu received a phone call from Jiang Tianhe as soon as he left the exam venue. Sounding like a pig that had been released from its pen, his yells were earth-shattering. "Are you out yet?!"

Lin Mu laughed. "I'm out."

"The fool is waiting outside, has he called you yet?"

He then realized that there was an issue with his question, and he said straightforwardly, "I'll hang up first, you answer his call."

Sure enough, less than two seconds later, Lin Mu received a phone call from Cao Zhan.

"Lin Mu!" Cao Zhan shouted his name.

"Hey, Dopey!"

"Is the answer to the last question of the English comprehension passage C?!"

Lin Mu did not expect Cao Zhan would immediately be checking his answers with him. Taking some time to recall, he answered uncertainly, "I think I chose C."

"Wow!" It was unclear who was next to Cao Zhan, and the boy chattered away excitedly, "Lin Mu chose C! He really chose C! I guessed correctly!"

... Choosing C when he did not know the answer was actually a trick Lin Mu taught him.

Cao Zhan was still cheering away incoherently, and Lin Mu followed the crowd, slowly walking out. The school gates were half open, and many excited students started running. However, Lin Mu was in no hurry. Today, Lin Zhao was playing an entire day of round-robin matches, and there was a live broadcast for it. Although Jiang Wan felt that she was letting her son down, it was physically impossible for her to attend both events simultaneously, and she was now at home, waiting for Lin Zhao's results in front of the television.

On the other side of the phone, Cao Zhan was still saying something. He had probably caught sight of Jiang Tianhe, and quickly urged Lin Mu, "Hurry up, Lin Mu, you're the only one left!"

"I'm coming, I'm coming." Lin Mu asked, "Who else is there?"

Cao Zhan answered honestly, "Little Deer and Meimei are here too, they're all waiting for you."

Lu Rong stood head and shoulders above the crowd. Even with so many people around, Lin Mu still saw him from far away. The boy was standing in the shade of a tree, his head turning to the side as he spoke with Cao Zhan. On his face was the dappled sunlight shining through the leaves, the mottled shadows enhancing his good looks.

Chen Meihua was the first to notice him, and she smiled as she shouted, "Mumu!"

Lu Rong turned his head around. His eyes fell upon Lin Mu's face, and after studying him for a while, he gave a somewhat reserved smile.

"Congratulations on graduating," Lu Rong said quietly after Lin Mu came closer.

Standing next to them, Cao Zhan heard him as well. In all apparent seriousness, he said, "We haven't graduated yet. We'll need to come back to school a few days later and attend the graduation ceremony."

Jiang Tianhe added, "Sun Hai and the rest are coming back. We can take this opportunity to meet up."

"Where's Fairy Zhaozhao?" Cao Zhan asked.

Lin Mu replied, "It's the last day of her round-robin matches today. My mother says she's in the semi-finals now, and she'll rank within the top four."

Jiang Tianhe was a little astonished. "She's so awesome, jumping ranks like this."

As soon as the national college entrance examinations was over, the group chat became lively again, and the second-year underclassmen quickly congratulated their upperclassmen. As for how well they actually did in the exams, no one cared except Cao Zhan.

Although Sun Hai managed to avoid China's national examinations, he still needed to study a preparatory course in Australia for half a year. In a foreign country, he was all alone, and the degree of difficulty he was facing there was no easier than that of his friends back in China.

An Jincheng acclimatized the fastest. He was now a student at a prestigious school, and he had also become very famous among the Chinese students in less than half a semester—due to his good looks, his wealth, and his stellar grades. Lin Mu was actually worried that his potential brother-in-law might be faced with relationship troubles. If there were too many temptations by Young Master An's side, and if he couldn't resist them, what would happen to Lin Zhao?

However, the situation clearly was one where the party actually involved was not anxious at all, while the bystander was. His sister seemed to never be troubled about this, and the anxieties and unease that typical young girls usually had did not seem to exist in Lin Zhao at all.

Among those who went overseas, Xu Yilu was naturally the one with the most special circumstances. Other than it being a little troublesome for him when applying to schools, he also had to treat his eyes first. As such, studying was not the most important factor in his life for now.

Li Zi cracked a mild joke in the chat. She said, "It seems that the upperclassmen have all turned into adults overnight."

Cao Zhan did not really understand. He asked Lin Mu, "Is it bad to be an adult?"

"Well, it isn't bad, I guess." Lin Mu thought about it, then smiled. "Dopey, you're different, you'll never become an adult."

Muddleheaded, Cao Zhan nodded. He seemed not to be bothered about whether he would become an adult, and he was not conflicted over it in the slightest.

The news of Lin Zhao beating Ninth Dan Choi only reached Lin Mu in the evening. With the advance of the Internet, information could be received in real-time. Even though Go competitions were not very popular, due to Lin Zhao's deaf and mute status, the Samsung Fire Cup became one of the most widely searched topics for the day.

Lin Mu and the rest were not aware of this.

That very night, Jiang Wan bought flowers and made a reservation at a restaurant, wanting to have a good celebration for when her daughter came home. Lin Mu took the opportunity to hide at Lu Rong's place, not wanting to be dispatched on errands by his mother.

When Lin Zhao got her phone back, she started texting her brother.

Lin Mu sent, "This time, when you're back, it won't just be our neighbors anymore. I think the entire zone will know your name."

Lin Zhao sent a series of ellipses over before sending a message: "As long as no firecrackers are set off."

Lin Mu replied, "But our mother wants to hold a three-day banquet. It's quite embarrassing."

Lin Zhao probably felt that life held nothing more for her, and there was no reply she could give either. She still had several interviews to attend, so she could not chat with Lin Mu for too long.

"How would you be doing your interviews?" Lin Mu asked. "Did they hire an interpreter for you?"

"Such good treatment doesn't exist. Dad is here, he has taken up the role of the interpreter."

Lin Mu was not very happy. "This just shows that they're not fully prepared. Before the competition, they must not have thought that you would do so well! They're looking down on us!"

Lin Zhao sent a smiley face over. "Ninth Dan Nie has already highlighted this issue. He has given a tongue-lashing to the media, and he has vented my anger on my behalf."

Holding onto his phone, Lin Mu chuckled. Upon looking up, he saw Lu Rong carrying plates out from the kitchen, and he hurried over to help.

"Sit down, don't move," Lu Rong said. "I'll do it."

Lin Mu followed behind, as though he was Lu Rong's tail. When all the dishes were placed on the table, Fang Luoyao went to coax Chen Meihua out to eat.

"Auntie," Lin Mu asked casually, "where's Fang Nuo?"

Fang Nuo was Fang Luoyao's son. As a nanny, she needed to stay with Chen Meihua, but Fang Nuo was still underaged, so he should be living with his mother.

Fang Luoyao said bashfully, "The school holidays had just

started, and Xiao Nuo will be staying with his friend for now."

Lin Mu had no other questions. Picking up some vegetables, he placed them in Chen Meihua's bowl. Fang Luoyao seemed to be used to serving others, and besides taking care of Chen Meihua, she also tried to serve Lu Rong and Lin Mu rice and soup.

In the end, Lu Rong could not help but persuade her. "Auntie, just go ahead and eat, don't worry about us."

"*Aye.*" Fang Luoyao was still very reserved. "I'll just eat later, it doesn't matter."

Lin Mu gave her a few looks, but he did not say anything. When clearing the plates after they finished eating, he asked Lu Rong in private, "Did something happen to Auntie Fang in the past?"

Lu Rong remained silent for a few beats before speaking slowly, "I'm not bothered by it, but there recently have been strangers hanging around our place. It should be because of her."

Lin Mu's expression turned ugly. Frowning, he asked, "Can they be caught?"

Lu Rong sneered, "In any case, they have to be caught. We have to get everything out in the open."

It was only when the summer break started that Fang Luoyao accepted the job with Lu Rong. Before that, she had given many job agencies the impression that she was being particularly picky.

In fact, Chu Lin had not held much hope either. However, Fang Luoyao was a good match for Lu Rong and his grandmother, and since they fit her request to take care of only female elderly, she braced herself and asked Fang Luoyao if she would like to try it out.

It took Chen Meihua some time to get used to the situation.

Fang Luoyao was very patient. She clearly was very experi-

enced in taking care of the elderly, and she was very knowl-
edgeable about Alzheimer's disease as well, able to maintain the
balance of treating Chen Meihua both like an old person and a
child perfectly. By the end of the month, Chen Meihua had pretty much accepted her.

One morning, when Lu Rong woke up late, he hurried downstairs to find Fang Luoyao feeding Chen Meihua steamed egg
with a spoon.

"Meimei wants to eat fish." Chen Meihua had just eaten a
spoonful of egg. Before she had even swallowed the bite, she
spoke up eagerly.

Fang Luoyao smiled as she wiped her mouth, "We'll go out and
buy some later."

Chen Meihua nodded. "We have to buy some flower hairclips
too."

The old lady had many flower hairclips, many of them made
by herself. After Fang Luoyao came, she helped her tidy them up
so that she could have access to them anytime she liked.

"We can buy flower hairclips, but Meimei cannot cry when
we're outside." Fang Luoyao bargained with her. "if you don't cry,
not only can we buy flower hairclips, you can also have some
candy."

Chen Meihua's eyes rounded. "Then I want candied hawthorn!"

It was easy to make her requests to Fang Luoyao, and Fang
Luoyao replied, "Then we'll buy candied hawthorn."

She tidied up Chen Meihua's bowl and cutlery, and then looked
up to see Lu Rong standing by the stairs blankly. She smiled as
she greeted him, "Young Master, come and have breakfast."

This was not the first time she'd called Lu Rong "Young Master," and the self-conscious boy nearly could not bear it. He
forced out, "Auntie, just call me *Xiao* Lu will do."

Fang Luoyao smiled, but she did not reply. She got Chen Meihua ready, preparing to go to the market to buy groceries.

Lu Rong was still a little dazed. This was the first time he overslept, and Chen Meihua was not crying in front of him. There was no need for him to coax her, the breakfast was ready, laundry was done, and there was a clean and refreshed Chen Meihua.

Fang Luoyao said, "I'll bring Meimei along with me to do some grocery shopping."

Lu Rong stood up. "I'll go with you."

Fang Luoyao shook her head. "You haven't finished your holiday homework, have you? Don't work too hard, finish your homework first."

As a mother herself, whenever it came to schoolwork, she behaved as though she was talking to her own child, and she could not help but nag a little.

Lu Rong agreed obediently, watching Fang Luoyao and Chen Meihua leave together. Before going to the kitchen to get a bowl of steamed egg, he sat there in his thoughts for a moment. For the first time in a long while, he enjoyed a free and leisurely breakfast.

On the way to the market, Fang Luoyao bought a stick of candied hawthorn for Chen Meihua. Chen Meihua ate them as she walked, spitting out the hawthorn pits in her hand. When she could no longer hold onto them, Fang Luoyao took out a small plastic bag and got her to toss the pits inside.

"What kind of fish would you like to eat?" Fang Luoyao asked.

Chen Meihua stared at the fish in the pool. Pointing here and there for some time, she finally said, "A bream."

Hence, Fang Luoyao bought her a bream. After that, they went to buy vegetables. In the past, Chen Meihua often came here with Lu Rong. The stall owners all recognized Meimei, and they now found out that Lu Rong had finally hired a nanny to help him.

"It has been too hard on *Xiao* Lu." The friendly older lady selling bamboo shoots gave them some extra scallions. "He's been taking care of his grandmother since he was a very small child, and we've seen how he grew up. It's a good thing that he now has someone helping him out."

Fang Luoyao was not a talkative person. She was a little shy, but she was steadfast with her work. If she came across people with whom she could have a conversation, she would tend to listen more than she spoke. As for Chen Meihua, ever since she became ill, she liked to chat with people. Although she often sounded incoherent, people could understand what she meant if they were willing to take some time to listen.

"*Xiao* Yao's cooking is delicious," Chen Meihua praised Fang Luoyao solemnly. "Both Little Deer and I have gained weight."

The lady laughed. "You don't look like you've gained any weight at all, but your complexion looks great."

Chen Meihua touched her face, turning around to ask Fang Luoyao, "Is my complexion good?"

Fang Luoyao hid her smile behind her hand. "Yes, it's great."

Chen Meihua nodded. "Then, if my complexion is good, can I have candied fruit?"

Fang Luoyao started to become familiar with Chen Meihua's tricks in getting snacks and candy, and she responded calmly, "You can, but we have to go home first."

Chen Meihua blinked. She could not see any deceit or conflict between "going home" and "candied fruit," so she innocently agreed.

Fang Luoyao went to the stall next door and bought some strawberries. Picking up the fish and vegetables, she held onto Chen Meihua's hand and walked home together.

When they were nearly home, Chen Meihua suddenly pulled at Fang Luoyao's arm.

"What's wrong?" Fang Luoyao tilted her head down, asking. She thought the old lady was asking for candied fruit, so she explained, "I'll be making the candied fruit at home, so could you wait a little while more, Meimei?"

Chen Meihua shook her head. She stared at the osmanthus tree next to the courtyard gate, leaning close to Fang Luoyao and whispering, "There's someone there."

Fang Luoyao looked up. Her face froze for a couple of seconds before she slowly frowned.

Once Lin Mu's exams were over, he spent almost all his time at Lu Rong's place. As Lin Zhao had just finished with her competition, she was now on a break. Feeling bored at home, she wanted to come out and play too. Although she had a tough battle and defeated Ninth Dan Choi, she lost to Yu Xiaoqing from her own team in the finals by just a very slight difference. Despite so, she won her first international ranking, and advanced two ranks in one fell swoop, becoming the youngest professional Go player in the Jiangsu team.

"I can't always be number two," Lin Zhao reflected. "I have to win first place in the Nongshim Cup."

Lin Mu was riding his bicycle, and his sister sat behind him. As she signed, he had to stop and turn to look at her. Finally, at the last traffic light, Lin Mu signed at her, "Why are you in such a hurry? Slow down, take your time."

Lin Zhao shook her head. "When Ke Jie was my age, he had already won all his competitions."

"You're nearly there."

He thought for a moment, then asked, "Do you want to go to Beijing for Go?"

Ever since Lin Zhao started learning to play Go, she had only been honing her skills under famous Go institutions and teachers in the Zhejiang province. However, China was a vast country with abundant resources. The Go circle was deep and broad, and there were also excellent teachers in Beijing and Guangdong. Due to the distance, she could only meet them annually during various competitions.

"I'd like to visit Nie-*laoshi*," Lin Zhao signed. "He was one of the teachers guiding us during the Samsung Cup, and he taught me a lot."

Lin Mu asked reflexively, "You're going alone?"

Lin Zhao shot him a look. "I've grown up already, do I still need Dad to accompany me?"

Lin Mu really wanted to say that with her condition, she definitely needed someone to accompany her. However, he was afraid that his words would hurt his sister's pride, and he still remained a little doubtful. Lin Zhao naturally knew what he was worried about, and she signed swiftly, "I know you're worried about me not being able to hear."

Lin Mu sighed. They were quite close to Lu Rong's place, and he decided to get off the bicycle and push it instead. "This is not a small issue. Without anyone around to help you in regard to communication, what happens if something goes wrong?"

Lin Zhao pursed her lips. Surprisingly, she did not protest. After all, what Lin Mu said was true, and she had no better solution yet. However, before she could think up of anything as an objection to her brother's words, in a blink of an eye, Lin Zhao's sight was caught by something.

She quickly knocked on her arm, tugging at Lin Mu's sleeve.

"Look there, isn't that Meimei?"

Lin Mu looked over to where Lin Zhao was pointing, only to see Fang Luoyao standing in front of Chen Meihua, shielding her. Fang Luoyao was glaring at a couple in front of her with an awful look on her face, and the three people seemed to be arguing over something. Suddenly, the man held his arm out, attempting to drag Chen Meihua out.

Lin Mu felt all his blood rush to his head. Without a word, he ran over.

"Let go." He gripped the man's wrist, while behind him, Lin Zhao was hugging Chen Meihua, glaring at the couple with a look of warning.

The man had probably not expected that people would come over in aid. He froze for a moment, then spoke angrily, "Who are you?!"

Lin Mu gnashed his teeth. "I should be the one asking you that! Who allowed you to touch my grandmother?!"

Throughout the entire situation, Chen Meihua was completely confused. Her wrist ached very badly, but she endured it and did not cry, as Fang Luoyao had told her that as long as she did not cry, she would have candied fruits to eat later.

Lin Mu grabbed the man's arm, forcing him to let go. Aggrieved, Chen Meihua's lips were pursed in a pout, her eyes swimming in tears.

The man was still shouting, "You've already got the money, and you've found a job too! It should be time for you to give us a letter of forgiveness, right? Framing an old man like this, how shameless can you be?!"

Fang Luoyao's face paled, either from anger or from fear. Trembling, she gritted her teeth and forced out, "I didn't frame anyone. Your entire family is aware of what your father did, and the police have it on record as well. You think I don't know about what disgusting things you said in front of my son? If I were to just let it go so easily, I'd be letting myself down, I'd be letting Fang Nuo down!"

"Bullshit! What can my father do?!" The man refused to give up, becoming very aggressive. "He's half paralyzed, and he's always either lying in bed or sitting in his wheelchair! How could he have taken advantage of you?! And committing obscenities towards your son... Aren't you embarrassed saying that?!"

Fang Luoyao's appearance was fair and clean, and her pale face swiftly reddened. In a miserable state, she glanced over at Lin Mu and Chen Meihua, closing her eyes in despair as she no longer objected. Seeing her like this, the man gloated, as though he now had the upper hand. Just as he wanted to humiliate her further, his vision suddenly blacked out. Lin Mu's fist had flown over.

Lin Zhao could not hear anything, and she did not know what they were arguing about. However, looking at Lin Mu's expression was enough to tell her that it was nothing good. Hugging Chen Meihua, she calmly withdrew from the battlefield. Panicking, Fang Luoyao wanted to stop the fight, but she too was held back by Lin Zhao.

After that punch, Lin Mu shook his fist out. Behind the man was a woman, and they seemed to be siblings. The woman's screams pierced the air, and it was fortunate that Lin Zhao could not hear. Fang Luoyao covered Chen Meihua's ears, and the three of them stood a large distance away, looking like obedient bystanders.

"You—How dare you start hitting people?!" Pointing at Lin Mu, the woman shrieked. "We've called the police! Just you wait!"

Lin Mu was not afraid of her at all, and he calmly said, "Since there's no letter of forgiveness yet, it means that the case isn't concluded, right? And you dare come here to harass the victim when the case is still open? Exactly who's the one who should call the police?"

The expression of the man lying on the ground was stiff. The punch had not been a soft one, and there was a bruise clearly forming under his eye. They had only come here to get Fang Luoyao to personally write a letter of forgiveness for them, as with such a letter, the case would be concluded, and they would only have to pay a small fine. Finally, after hanging around this place for so long, they managed to catch Fang Luoyao and the old lady with dementia. However, Fang Luoyao refused to write the letter, looking as though she wanted to have this matter handled officially, and she seemed to have no intention of compromising.

As a widow with a child, Fang Luoyao was always a little more disadvantaged. When the offending old man had taken advantage of her, Fang Luoyao initially endured it. However, the old man had become even more audacious, turning his eyes onto Fang Nuo. With the desire to protect her son, she could not stand it any longer, and she finally exposed the wretched things the old man had done.

The family had felt that a nanny with no power was very easy to control, and that Fang Nuo would be Fang Luoyao's weak spot. If they targeted him, they would be able to gloss over this matter. However, they had not expected that the mother and son would share the same beliefs. Although Fang Nuo was young, he refused to be deluded by these people, and he stood firmly on his mother's side through it all.

After the matter blew up, to not let it affect her son, Fang Luoyao did not bring her son along when she found a new job. Since the school holidays started, Fang Nuo had been staying with his classmate. After trying for so long, these two people could only find an opportunity to duke it out with Fang Luoyao.

"She's framing us, she wants to get money out of this!" The man was still being stubborn. "Why? Are you her new employer? You'd better watch out; you'll never know what she can do. Your grandmother's an idiot, right? If she starts abusing her, I'll see what you'll do about it!"

Lin Mu had to laugh out of anger. "Who are you calling an idiot?"

The man saw his expression. His lips moved, but he did not dare repeat what he had just said. The woman behind him helped him up, and they wanted to walk away, only to be stopped by Lin Mu.

"Don't come again," he said expressionlessly, with his hands in his pockets, "if you dare to come again, we'll call the police and tell them you're threatening us. The case hasn't been closed, and there will be no letter of forgiveness either. We'll just drag it out. If the half-paralyzed old man is now in the police station, who knows when he'll be gone? It could be any moment. You'll even have to worry about his funeral."

Lu Rong only found out that there was a fight going on outside when his neighbor came knocking on his door. The commotion had been too great, and the houses in Taohuawu district were situated closely together, so everyone was able to see what was happening. The neighbor shouted a few times, "*Xiao* Lu!"

The siblings who caused the ruckus ran off in a hurry, while the friendly neighbors surrounded Chen Meihua like a wall, chattering away as they showed their concern and asking what had happened. Lin Zhao looked lost, and as she could neither hear

nor speak, she signed reflexively. An old lady next to her flamed
up with indignation. "What do those bastards want?! How could
they bully such a beautiful young lady!"

Lin Zhao was completely confused.

The old lady stroked Lin Zhao's head. With a face full of concern as well as her mouth opening and closing, she wished for
nothing more but to tuck Lin Zhao into her arms.

With much difficulty, Fang Luoyao tried to take control of the
situation. She had to protect Chen Meihua from being squeezed
or pushed down, as well as enduring the waves of sympathy coming from the neighbors.

"We're fine..." Fang Luoyao stood in front of Chen Meihua and
Lin Zhao, shielding them. "The two people had been chased away
by Lin-*tongxue*, and they won't be coming here again."

The wall of people refused to disperse, and they continued
chattering away. Some asked Fang Luoyao what was going on,
while others showed concern over Chen Meihua and Lin Zhao.
When Fang Luoyao could no longer handle the crowd, Lu Rong
finally made his way through.

Lin Mu was crouching down and looking at Chen Meihua's
wrist, which had reddened. The old lady looked very fragile, her
mouth fixed in a pout. However, she fortunately was not crying,
only sniffling away.

"Does it hurt?" Lin Mu asked.

Chen Meihua shook her head, then nodded. Finally, she said
quietly, "Meimei has to be strong."

Lin Mu froze, not knowing whether to laugh or cry. "Meimei
doesn't have to be strong now, just say it if it hurts."

Chen Meihua did not say that it hurt. Bending her head down,
she blew softly across her wrist.

Fang Luoyao dared not speak to Lu Rong. She felt that this

was her fault, and she was about to lose her job. Her face was full of a conflict she could not conceal. Lu Rong first took a look at Chen Meihua's injury, then at Lin Mu's hand.

"I'm fine." Lin Mu raised his fist, showing it to him. "I'm very experienced. It's only just hitting a piece of trash; I won't get hurt."

Lu Rong sighed. "But you still can't be so impulsive. He didn't cause you any trouble this time, but no one knows what will happen next time."

Lin Mu snorted. "He dares come here again? That paralyzed old beast of theirs is still in the station. If they come and cause a ruckus one more time, they can just wait and collect his corpse."

Lin Mu's harsh words sounded as though everything would be just as he said. His honeyed tongue could melt anyone's heart, but his poisonous tongue was also savage.

Lu Rong helped Lin Mu up, then turned to ask Fang Luoyao, "Auntie, are you alright?"

"What could be not alright about me?" Fang Luoyao forced out a smile. She quietly said, "I've caused you trouble."

Lu Rong looked at her. After a few moments of silence, he slowly said, "I've just received a call from Fang Nuo, he says he's coming over tonight."

Fang Luoyao blinked, looking a little baffled. "Isn't he staying at his classmate's house?"

Lu Rong only replied, "He's probably worried about you."

Fang Luoyao's mouth fell open. Abruptly, her eyes reddened.

Lu Rong waited for her to compose herself before speaking gently, "Let's talk tonight. There are some things should always be clarified, and there are some matters should be settled."

SILENT HEARTS

Life

═══

⬧ **⑱** _____ **Life**

Fang Nuo would be entering his second year in junior high school, but the boy looked as though he had yet to even reach puberty. He was thin and fair, his voice small and soft. He came with a big bag full of clothes and toiletries, and his attitude was shy and reserved.

Fang Luoyao asked him why he did not continue to stay with his classmate.

Fang Nuo replied, a little aggrieved, "I miss Mama."

Fang Luoyao was feeling both sorrow and joy. "Did they come to look for you?"

Fang Nuo hesitated for a moment, before nodding slightly. "They did. I was worried about you, so I quickly came here."

Fang Luoyao's eyes reddened, angry with how far those bullies were pushing it. When the incident just happened, in order to stop Fang Nuo from saying anything, both siblings did not hold back on humiliating Fang Luoyao in front of Fang Nuo, accusing her of being indiscriminate and seducing her employer. They had called her all sorts of awful names, trying to denigrate her by all means.

"Later on, that old man and his family wanted to use Fang Nuo to coerce me." When Fang Luoyao explained the situation to Lu Rong, she no longer had the initial rage of wanting to destroy herself along with that family. During that period, her life had been both difficult and hopeless. Even after the police took the old man away, she was still very anxious and fearful.

Most employment agencies were concerned that she had such a matter attached to her, and they even refused to accept her resume. "Slut," "vixen," and "seductress" were names that were now attached to her like shadows, yet she had no ability to refute them.

Fang Luoyao deeply cherished the opportunity to work for Lu Rong's family. She was raising Fang Nuo alone, and she was very in need of money.

"I will never write the letter of forgiveness." Fang Luoyao wiped her face, speaking calmly, "If I write it, it means that I accept the names they've given me, the things they've done to me. I will never admit to things that I've never done."

Lin Mu and Lu Rong exchanged a look. Lin Mu thought for a moment before speaking, "Don't you worry, Auntie. We're not the sort to listen to others' opinions and follow the crowd."

Fang Luoyao was clearly prepared to explain further. Her mouth fell open, her expression confused. Relaxing her tightly clenched fists, at a loss, she stammered, "W-what do you mean?"

Lu Rong smiled. "Meimei likes you very much. These few days, she keeps praising your cooking. She even says that you're willing to buy her candy and ice cream, and you're treating her much better than I ever did."

Chen Meihua heard her name. Pursing her lips, she said, "Yaoyao is better than you, she's much more obedient."

Lu Rong narrowed his eyes. He wanted to reprimand her, but due to the number of people present, he held himself back.

Fang Luoyao had yet to register what was happening, but Fang Nuo's face turned red with joy. He could still be considered a child, and he was easily shy, tucking himself behind his mother. Both the mother and son were so delightfully surprised that they could not speak a word for some time.

Now that Fang Nuo was living here with them, they had to prepare a room for him. There happened to be a small storeroom next to Fang Luoyao's room, which had to be cleared out first. Lin Mu went to help, while Lin Zhao accompanied Chen Meihua in the living room.

Fang Luoyao did not know sign language, and so she could only list down the names of the dishes on paper and show it to Lin Zhao.

"Are they biological siblings?" Fang Luoyao could not help being curious, and she quietly asked Lu Rong.

Lu Rong nodded. "They're twins. Haven't you noticed that they're almost identical?"

Fang Luoyao looked carefully, exclaiming, "They really do look alike. The only differences between them are their demeanors and temperaments."

Lu Rong did not speak anymore. People who did not know the Lin twins would easily be confused when looking at their facial features. Still, as long as they had interacted with them for a long enough time, they would discover that the two people were completely different, and they could be differentiated with just one glance.

Drifting from the storeroom were snippets of conversation between Lin Mu and Fang Nuo. While preparing food, Fang Luoyao could not help looking over. Lu Rong saw her glancing over a few times, and so decided to speak up, "If you're worried, you can go help them too."

"No," Fang Luoyao answered, a little awkward. She hesitated for a while, before quietly saying, "*Xiao* Nuo doesn't like to be alone with males."

"Oh." Lu Rong was not surprised. Having had that sort of thing happen to them could easily leave some trauma on the individual.

It was just that Fang Luoyao looked as though she wanted to say something, but she was too embarrassed to do so.

Secretly glancing at Lu Rong a few times, she finally said something, beating around the bush. "Are Lin Mu and you... Is it out of your own free wills?"

Lu Rong was baffled at first, and then he immediately understood. Half a beat later, he said uncertainly, "We're that... obvious?"

"No, not really." Fang Luoyao smiled when she saw his expression. "I just happened to notice."

She paused, then continued, "In the past, because of *Xiao* Nuo's incident, I was prejudiced towards such matters. However, it's been so many days, and both you and Lin Mu are good children. He even helped me today, beating up that man..."

Fang Luoyao glanced at Lu Rong, asking cautiously, "You're not coercing him, right?"

Lu Rong did not know whether to laugh or cry. "You saw for yourself today how good he is at fighting. How can I make him to do anything he doesn't want?"

Due to the trauma left by her former employer, Fang Luoyao

was more inclined to like Lin Mu more than Lu Rong. Besides, Lu Rong was not a chatty person. He was used to being calm and silent, his emotions rarely displayed on his sleeves. He did not embody the characteristics of other young people of his age at all, nor was he full of laughter and recklessness, so he was naturally less likeable.

Other than Fang Luoyao, even Chen Meihua held some fear for him. Not just fear, either—there was also dislike.

Lin Mu was lively and cheerful, and he was very good at speaking. In no time, Fang Nuo started addressing him as "Lin Mu-*ge*." The two people finished tidying up the storeroom, making the bed, and were even discussing what games they had been playing recently.

Lu Rong had to go in and hurry them. "It's time to eat. You can continue tidying up later."

Lin Mu smiled. "We're almost done. Where's my sister?"

Lu Rong pointed at the living room. Lin Zhao was quietly playing with her phone, and when Lin Mu went over to take a look, he discovered she was playing online Go.

Speechless, Lin Mu signed, "Didn't you say you wanted to take a break?"

Lin Zhao was not very serious about the game, and she laid her pieces down without much thought. Taking her attention from her phone, she signed, "I'm just playing for fun."

"You're usually playing Go already, and now you're even playing Go during your break. Don't play until you become a fool."

Lin Zhao raised a brow, not very happy. "Not using your brain will be the thing that makes you a fool."

Lin Mu hummed noncommittally. Online Go was usually a fast game, in which players must place their piece within thirty seconds. While speaking to him, Lin Zhao had already placed about seven to eight pieces, and her opponent soon forfeited the match, admitting defeat. Lin Zhao did not say anything, leaving the match and joining a new one.

Fang Nuo helped Fang Luoyao carry the dishes out, and Fang Luoyao then led Chen Meihua away to wash her hands.

Chen Meihua was still thinking about the candied fruits. She asked, "When can I eat them?"

Fang Luoyao pumped some soap into her hands, saying, "I'll make them for you once we finish dinner, so tonight, you must eat well, and eat more vegetables."

Chen Meihua's logical reasoning was nonexistent. If one tried to reason with her, forcing her or requesting her to do something, she would usually throw a tantrum. However, as long as one made things clear, making a trade-off with her, she would normally capitulate.

Lin Mu observed their interaction. Feeling very complicated, he asked Lu Rong, "Does this count as lying to her?"

Lu Rong shook his head. "Auntie Fang will really make candied fruits for Meimei later."

Lin Mu did not expect that. "She's really going to make some?"

Lu Rong laughed. "What were you thinking?"

Lin Mu felt a little wronged. "You can't blame me. You've always lied to her, telling her all sorts of nonsense. Whenever you lied to Meimei, your expression never changed."

Lu Rong did not know how to react to that.

He did seem to behave like this.

Fang Luoyao started making candied fruits after dinner. Chen Meihua deliberately dragged a stool over, sitting next to her and watching her melt the sugar. Lin Zhao continued playing her online Go matches, occasionally looking up. When the scent of sugar started filling the air, there was an obvious increase in the frequency of her looking up.

Lin Mu and Lu Rong were sitting in the yard together. The sweet smell of sugar in the air grew heavier, wafting out with the wind. Fang Nuo handed the sticks of strawberries to his mother, and Lin Mu twitched his nose, unable to stop himself from smiling. "It smells good."

Lu Rong glanced at him, not saying a word.

Lin Zhao finally could not resist putting her phone down and hurrying to the entrance of the kitchen. Together with Chen Meihua, they stood by the door like guardian statues.

"It's too sweet." Lu Rong looked at Lin Mu, suddenly saying, "Right now, just looking at you tastes sweet to me."

That night, Lin Mu and the others all had a stick of candied fruits each. Fang Luoyao made a lot, storing them in the refrigerator. In Lu Rong's eyes, when Lin Mu was eating the candied fruits, he basically seemed to be coated with sugar, his entire being suffused with sweetness.

When the twins were on the way home, sitting on the back of the bicycle, Lin Zhao signed at her brother, "Are you two dating?"

Lin Mu's foot nearly slipped off the pedal. He looked at Lin Zhao's unconcerned expression, and he felt a little conflicted over whether he should admit the truth or not.

Lin Zhao stared at him for some time, then signed, "Okay, I know now."

Lin Mu gave her a confused look.

What do you know?!

Until they got home, Lin Zhao had yet to tell Lin Mu what she knew.

It was a rare occasion for their children not to be at home, and so Jiang Wan and Lin Yanlai managed to enjoy an entire night of being together alone. In Lin Mu's words, the house was filled with the stink of romance.

After a day of rest, Lin Zhao again returned to her daily schedule of going to the Go institute and meeting her teachers. She had talked to Lin Yanlai about wanting to go to Beijing, and the Lin family once again had a large-scale family meeting.

"I will go with Zhang-*laoshi*." This time, Lin Zhao had considered this issue from all facets. Zhang Mei, Ninth Dan Zhang, was Lin Zhao's teacher here, as well as one of the few Ninth Dan female players in the country. She valued Lin Zhao greatly.

Lin Yanlai was hesitant. "It's not that we don't trust Ninth Dan Zhang, but your situation is rather unique. If you want to go, I'd want to go with you too."

Lin Zhao sighed. This time, she was not angry, only thinking for a moment before signing slowly, "I know you're worried about me, but I'm already of age. Like other students going to university, I'm also going to Beijing to a university of sorts. During the three years in Kunqian, didn't I acclimatize very well? It's only a change of place, and it doesn't make any difference to me."

Jiang Wan disagreed. "Kunqian is different. It's a paradise, it's very tolerant."

Lin Zhao raised a brow, refusing to compromise. "I know, and it's because of this knowledge, Kunqian is my strength and support. I won't be afraid no matter where I go, because I'm a Kunqian student."

Lin Yanlai seemed a little astonished, and he exchanged a look with Jiang Wan. They both had a hint of hesitance on their faces. This time, Lin Mu surprisingly was not on the opposite side from his sister. He had his arms crossed, and Lin Zhao and he sneaked looks at each other.

Jiang Wan looked at her son, finally remembering that she should treat her children equally. As such, she shifted her sight, asking Lin Mu, "Have your results been released yet?"

Lin Mu deliberately put on a sour tone. "Oh? You've finally remembered about me?"

Jiang Wan feigned picking up her slipper to hit him. Lin Mu blocked his face, speaking loudly, "May Master be relieved, the results are adequate!"

Lin Yanlai was at a loss for words.

Lin Mu's scores were estimated to be enough to guarantee him a spot in Shanghai Jiao Tong University. He did not need his parents' help in filling in the application, and halfway through filling out the online form, he even sent Lu Rong a photo.

"Congratulations." Lu Rong's reply came very quickly this time, and he also sent a photo of his own revision back.

Lin Mu teased him. "So hardworking?"

"My results dropped quite a bit. If I don't work harder, I'm afraid I really might not make it into university."

Lin Mu considered it. "Do you want me to tutor you?"

"You've finally graduated, and you're now on break. Just go ahead and play. We'll start the tutoring when school reopens."

Lin Mu sent a "hurt" emoji in response. "I'll be going to Shanghai once school reopens, and I can only come back once a week."

In reality, he hadn't finished his sentence, because, for medical students, they might not even be free on weekends, and once his clinical placements started, he would not be able to return.

Lin Zhao had changed the name of the group chat to "Dreams

Come True." The first to post their results was Cao Zhan. His luck was astonishingly good, and he scraped a pass for his humanities exam. However, he did not manage to meet the requirements for the fashion design course he wanted. Therefore, after enrolling, he would have to make up for it according to the school regulations.

"I can go to university!" This was the thing Cao Zhan was the most ecstatic about. He still was not sure what it meant by having to make up for it, but in any case, Ji Wenqing would worry about it on his behalf.

Sun Hai was now in an Australian time zone, and he was frequently online at night. His response was very supportive, "You'll be a famous artist in the future!"

Cao Zhan was very excited too. "Then I'll be able to make more things for you. What do you all want?"

Lin Zhao did not stand on courtesy at all, piping up, "I want a bag."

Jiang Tianhe said, "In the future, you can set up a brand. Who knows, it might even be China's future version of Chanel, Hermès, or Prada."

In the eyes of outsiders, these words might seem a little overconfident, even comical. However, in this group chat, none of the members felt that they were only spouting nonsensical dreams. Youths were fearless, and they did not know how big the world outside was. Courage was the thing that led them, and breaking through the limits was the only thing they wished desperately for.

Other than Cao Zhan, Jiang Tianhe too had successfully made it through the second batch of admission. He had chosen a university in the central region, ready to experience a flourishing lifestyle.

There was not much sorrow of departure in the chat. In to-day's times, communication was very well developed. Even if they were all in different places, it felt as though they could still be right next to each other.

In mid-July, Lin Mu received an acceptance letter from the university. He and his friends arranged to return to Kunqian to-gether to attend the graduation ceremony. Although it was called a ceremony, they were basically going there with their acceptance letters, reporting the good news to their teachers.

Zhong He would definitely appear during such occasions, and the man only wished he could hang banners all over the school grounds to welcome the graduates back.

The students started streaming in during the morning. Al-though it was not an official event, some procedures still had to be followed. Zhong He cleared half the hall, placing a small table there. Chu Lin then gave everyone their transcripts and gradu-ation books in sequence. Different from their graduation certif-icates, the books had been designed with great care. There were several pages within, depicting the students' lives in Kunqian over the past three years.

When Lin Mu collected his graduation book, he had no time to look through it. Cao Zhan was the first to flip through Lin Mu's book, and on the very first page was Lin Mu standing on the rostrum in a skirt. Jiang Tianhe exclaimed loudly, immediately opening his book and discovering that everyone had a photo too.

Lin Mu was stunned. "People were taking photos that day?"

Cao Zhan and Jiang Tianhe looked muddleheaded as well. It was not just the three of them. In nearly every boy's book was a photo of themselves in a skirt.

This matter had been instigated by Lin Mu and organized by An Jincheng. It was the work of the entire level, and no one was able to escape.

Jiang Tianhe gnashed his teeth. "That scoundrel Zhong He is too ruthless!"

Lin Mu was speechless. Taking out his phone, he updated the chat about this, and the other three people who were coming later in the afternoon felt as though they had been struck by lightning.

Sun Hai asked gingerly, "Is my leg hair long?"

Lin Mu replied, "Not only is it long, it's in high definition too."

Sun Hai was speechless.

An Jincheng, however, was pretty calm. "The photo's already taken. I'll just burn it when I go back."

Lin Zhao sent a stream of emojis asking them to show her their photos.

Lin Mu could not help but smile. "How long will it take you guys to get here?"

Sun Hai said, "I've already arrived at the airport. We'll probably need another couple of hours. Young Master An and Little Heron are on the same flight, they might be a little late."

Lin Mu sent a message, inviting them to have dinner together. Just as he kept his phone away, he saw Lu Rong bringing Chen Meihua along, appearing at the hall entrance.

Mo Xiaoxiao and Li Zi came too. The girls even brought a stalk of flower with them, tucking it into Cao Zhan's arms.

"Let's take a photo together." Mo Xiaoxiao extended her selfie stick. She called out to the rest, "Lu Rong, you're the tallest. Stand towards the back."

Lu Rong shifted accordingly. Standing next to Lin Mu, he saw the other flipping through the graduation book.

"What are you looking at?" Lu Rong asked quietly.

Lin Mu looked up, shooting him a smile as he closed the book on its last page.

"You'll find out next year." He stood next to Lu Rong, shoulder to shoulder. A while later, he could not resist saying, "Don't look at me, look at the camera."

As for the content on the last page of the graduation book, Lu Rong finally received his own version one year later.

Before the release of the results of the national college entrance examinations in September, Lin Mu had to rush back to his university because of a pressing experiment. As such, the couple only had time to speak to each other over the phone after the release of Lu Rong's results, and Lin Mu's anxiety over this matter was finally settled.

"Media studies?" Lin Mu seemed to be still busy with something, and rustling sounds could be heard over the phone. "Sure, but if your score isn't high enough, you'd have to settle for back-up majors."

Lu Rong did not speak. He quietly listened for a while, until Lin Mu asked, "What are you doing?"

Lu Rong responded, "Nothing much."

After a pause he then laughed, his laughter oddly sounding like a sigh. "Everything feels like a dream."

Lin Mu laughed as well. There were others with him, and some of them were calling his name. Lu Rong asked if they should hang up, but Lin Mu was unbothered, saying that there was no need for that.

Lin Mu continued, "How could this be a dream? This is what you should do. Study hard, go to university, then come be with me."

Lu Rong laughed when he heard the sudden turn of Lin Mu's words. He suddenly recalled something and said, "I've received the graduation book."

It took Lin Mu a beat to catch up, and he chuckled as he asked, "You saw what's on the last page already?"

"I saw it," Lu Rong answered. He lifted up the book, his eyes falling on the words below the school motto.

"The road ahead may be long and lonely, but no matter what, please never stop, because one day, in this life, you will arrive among the stars."

Lin Mu chuckled. "Zhong He has to be a little more longwinded, so that some of the special needs students will be able to understand him."

Lu Rong did not catch his drift. "What do you mean?"

"It's a Latin proverb," Lin Mu smiled, his voice travelling through the phone from one city to another.

He explained, "*Per Aspera Ad Astra.* Through hardships to the stars."

The two people spoke for a little while more before Fang Luoyao came to call Lu Rong for dinner. Fang Nuo was taking his high school entrance exams this year as well, and he could be considered to be Lu Rong and Lin Mu's underclassman in the future.

Compared to Lu Rong, Fang Nuo clearly idolized Lin Mu more.

"Will Mu-*ge* return for the school's anniversary celebration?" Carrying a bowl, Fang Nuo asked Lu Rong. He was a lot less timid, unlike how he was before, and he seemed to be more energetic now. Once he grew some more he would no longer appear weak and easily bullied.

Fang Luoyao and he were both living on the first floor, making it more convenient to take care of Chen Meihua. Throughout the past year, the old lady's physical condition had not deteriorated, but her mental status had not improved at all, and the times she was alert had been even fewer than before. If not for Fang Luoyao's great efforts, Lu Rong might not even have been able to complete his high school education due to having to take care of Meimei.

Chen Meihua would always react upon hearing Lin Mu's name. She asked, "Mumu is back?"

Ladling soup for her, Lu Rong quietly said, "Not yet, he's not coming back this week."

Chen Meihua pouted, clearly unhappy. "He hasn't been back in so long. Does he not want Meimei anymore?"

At a loss for words, Lu Rong did not know where her girlish affections came from, but since she was an old lady, he had to cajole her. As such, he patiently said, "No, that's not the case."

Chen Meihua stared at him.

Lu Rong did not stop her from staring, instead speaking with solemnity, "Also, Lin Mu is not your boyfriend, he's my boyfriend. You can't say things like that again, understand, Meimei?"

Chen Meihua was a little resentful, but it could still be seen that she was more afraid of Lu Rong. Finally, she unwillingly said, "Alright."

Holding back their laughter, Fang Luoyao and Fang Nuo both buried their heads in their bowls, pretending to eat. Fang Nuo was still thinking about the school anniversary celebration, and Lu Rong promised to ask Lin Mu about it.

After the meal, Lu Rong had to deal with his university applications. He was not like Lin Mu, whose grades were so excellent that there were quite a number of prestigious schools he could choose from. Instead, his grades barely scraped through the first round of applications. As he was only considering the universities in Suzhou, Lu Rong was prepared that in the end, with his score, he would have to settle for backup majors.

As for Li Zi and Mo Xiaoxiao, one would be going to Sichuan, and the other to Wuhan. Although they would be separated, they would always be best friends, and they made arrangements to go out and play together.

"Lin Zhao-*xuejie* is going too." Mo Xiaoxiao sent the itinerary to their group chat. The three girls had started calling themselves the "Around The World: Disabled in Body, but Abled in Spirit" group, and they had already gone on a few trips together.

Lin Zhao was now studying Go in Beijing, and she was preparing to attempt the seventh dan ranking within two years. A few months ago, she won the women's international championship, and was now one of the top female players in the country.

Compared to professional male players, there were very few international events for female players, and it was tough for female players to gain a foothold in the battle for titles. Lin Zhao's situation was a little more unique than others, and so the media paid great attention to all her competitions.

Many times, Lin Mu had been worried over this issue, saying that such attention would affect Lin Zhao's mental state. By focusing on her disability alone, they were basically making use of her to make headlines, and now, many people outside the Go circle were paying attention to her. Although it gained her some popularity, she would also be criticized for seeking sympathy with her disability if she lost a game.

Outsiders were only looking for gossip. Her disability, being a professional Go player, a woman, a champion—all these were used as fodder for hot topics. Regardless of whether Lin Zhao had won or lost, none of that could compare to her "title" as a disabled person. However, Lin Zhao had worked so hard for so many years just to get rid of this label of disability. She did not need anyone to pity or feel sorry for her, as she had always felt that other than being unable to hear or speak, she was no different from anyone else.

This matter reached its peak during the interview after Lin Zhao won the women's international championship.

Lin Zhao had refused all interviews, posting a statement on her social media that from now on, she would reject all requests for interviews regardless of winning or losing. She had decided to use true silence to confront these reporters who were only using her to gain viewership.

Towards this resistance, there were people who thought that they could get around it. If they could not interview Lin Zhao, they thought they would be able to interview Lin Zhao's family.

Lin Mu had been harassed a few times. Finally getting irritated, he mocked the reporters right into their recorders, "You know very well that my sister is a deaf-mute. Why do you want to interview her?"

Obviously, the reporter did not register the subtlety of his statement, instead explaining foolishly, "We have a sign language interpreter, so translating is very convenient."

"I've said it, my sister is a deaf-mute," he said icily as he looked at the camera. "Do you not understand that?"

The reporter blinked, his smile a little forced. "Umm... The Go player Lin Zhao is a role model for the youth. She's inspirational, she's positive..."

"Stop." Lin Mu cut him off impatiently. "My sister is not any-one's role model, and she cannot afford to carry this label. Every-one is just ordinary, and in the 365 days of the year, all she did was to just play Go every day."

The reporter did not know what to say.

Lin Mu looked at the camera. "My sister cannot hear you, nor can she speak to you—that's why she's able to resist your attempts to make her into another headline. As for those who can't, they can only force themselves into becoming 'deaf and mute.' You should try it yourselves next time and see which method exactly is more lamentable."

When Lin Mu's words were shared on the Internet, it caused quite a big stir. After finding out about it, Jiang Wan gave him a scolding, feeling that he had been too outspoken, and would end up creating trouble for his sister.

Lin Mu disagreed. "Was I wrong? In today's world, anything we say can be easily twisted. Lin Zhao has won so much prestige and so many titles, but they still cannot hold up to her label of being a disabled person. People only see what they want to see. Who cares if she broke through her opponent's strategy on the chessboard?"

Jiang Wan said patiently, "You're looking at it from a pro-fessional angle, but not everyone is a professional. People and readers want entertainment, and your sister is no longer a pro-fessional Go player in her little pond. Other than looking at her accolades, they will also pay attention to other things about her. You can't tar everyone with the same brush."

Lin Mu was very disdainful. "If not the accolades, what else should they look for in a Go player? They're not part of the entertainment industry, and yet they have to entertain everyone."

Her son's point of contention left Jiang Wan with no response. No matter what she tried to think up, she was unable to rebut him. Her children were truly outstanding in every way, the only issue being that they were too individualistic.

Despite being so young, Lin Zhao had already reached a global height in her career as a Go player. Other than remaining humble and unassuming in the Go circles, working hard and constantly perfecting her skills, she did not give any thought to what was happening outside her circles. As such, during her interviews, she often showed impatience as she signed, or she would sign too fast, leading to the interpreter failing to keep up with her. Rather than regarding her as a Go champion, most media agencies treated her as an object to gain readership. Their readers wanted entertainment and drama, and hence, the agencies would edit the videos they captured in the most attention-grabbing way possible.

"People often think that champions should be perfect," Lin Mu sighed. "But Lin Zhao isn't perfect. She has worked hard for so many years, and the reason she's standing up there right now is to prove that she doesn't need anyone's sympathy."

"The rights and wrongs on the chessboard, the wins and the losses, they're all in black and white. However, the world is not that way. She is well aware of this, and that's why she refuses to say anything."

Before Lin Zhao won her first international championship, she did have a short period of time where she was in the troughs of her career. Besides being affected by what was going on in the outside world, part of it had to do with her bottleneck in Go. During that time, in various national competitions, she had more losses than wins. As such, Lin Yanlai and Jiang Wan made several trips to Beijing, and when she was not playing Go, they would accompany her on strolls around the city.

During those days, Lin Mu would often receive video calls from his sister when he was in the dormitory late at night. Lin Zhao had a little lamp switched on next to her, and she was seated in front of a chessboard, the black and white pieces arranged accordingly. Lin Mu was exhausted from doing his research the entire day, and he signed, "Why aren't you sleeping?"

Lin Zhao raised her phone, moving her fingers, "Am I bothering you?"

"No." Lin Mu waved his palm. He sat up slightly, resting his head on his hand. "You lost?"

Lin Zhao was rather expressionless. She had always been a rather aloof beauty, and after playing Go for so long, she rarely expressed her emotions on her sleeves. Whether she won or lost, she would still look the same. "I've been losing the whole time, and I didn't win once."

She paused, then added, "It's been a few days already."

Unlike other young Go players, Lin Zhao was not the sort of person who only reported good news and concealed her sorrows. She rarely hid anything from Lin Mu, and she did not think that it was shameful. "I'm taking a few days off. If I continue losing, my mental state will collapse."

Lin Mu could not help laughing. "If you know that you're about to collapse, it means that there's really nothing wrong."

He stared at the board for a little while, asking, "Is that the game you lost today?"

Lin Zhao nodded. She aimed her phone towards the board, showing it clearly. "Can you understand it?"

Lin Mu shook his head, signing, "I haven't been able to understand any of this for a long time already."

Lin Zhao sniffed haughtily. "Even An Jincheng can see why I lost."

Lin Mu rolled his eyes at her.

Lu Rong did ask once exactly what sort of relationship An Jincheng and Lin Zhao shared, but Lin Mu was unable to put it into words either. After finishing his research, he finally managed to get a two-day break, but his parents were in Beijing with Lin Zhao, leaving him alone at home.

Lu Rong was on his summer holidays. Other than worrying over his university applications, the two people were basically glued to each other the entire time.

"In any case, you've submitted your applications already. If you cannot be admitted to your chosen major and only have backup major available, then we'll accept it." Lin Mu was holding onto the watermelon that had just been taken out from the fridge. He held out his hand, stroking Lu Rong's chin from behind the couch, consoling him. "You can change your major when you're enrolled, and we'll think about it then."

Lu Rong caught his hand, pressing it to his lips. His voice was a little muffled as he said, "You're really relaxed when it comes to me."

"This is me being strict with myself, and lenient with others."

Lu Rong smiled without responding to that. He looked up at Lin Mu, asking, "How is *Jiejie*?"

Lin Mu sat down on the couch, tucking his legs behind Lu Rong's waist. Unconcerned, yet a little sulky, he said, "For a while, she was calling me every night to seek consolation. She later realized that there was an even better option, and she hasn't given me a call for the past few days."

Lu Rong was speechless. Despite knowing the answer, he

asked, "An Jincheng?"

Lin Mu could not keep himself from rolling his eyes. "Who else? Even their time difference is perfect."

Lu Rong did not know what to say to that.

Their conversation topic naturally drifted to Lin Zhao's rumored partner.

Americans had a long break around Christmas time, and last year, Young Master An had stayed for quite some time when he came back. Lin Zhao happened to be on a break from Go as well, and Lin Mu could sense that something had happened between them. However, it was unfortunate that the two did not have much time to spend with each other. An Jincheng had to return to the United States to continue his studies, while Lin Zhao had to return to Beijing once the year was over and continue her training.

It took Lin Mu quite a bit of effort to dig out whatever "gossip" he could get his hands on. For example, during the period when Lin Zhao was experiencing a series of losses, other than harassing her brother, An Jincheng was also her pillar of "strong support," to the point that Young Master An, who initially did not know anything about Go at all, could now understand a Go practice book when he looked at it.

"It hasn't been easy for An Jincheng either." Lin Mu sighed as he thought about it. "He can be considered to be wooing his partner over such a long distance. I only found out later that he would watch Lin Zhao's every live match, and I heard that he would even take notes later. My sister has probably had over a hundred matches, or even a thousand. His stack of notes must be very thick now."

Lu Rong too had an expression of disbelief.

Lin Mu continued, "Also, my sister is the sort to want to be a strong career woman. When she's playing Go, she recognizes neither friendships nor bonds of family. An Jincheng has been my sister's tool for a year already, and even I feel upset on his behalf for not having any actual or official status or title."

Lu Rong did not know whether to laugh or cry. "It might be better if you didn't take the side against your own sister."

In the evening, Fang Luoyao gave Lu Rong a call. The implication was that his presence was being missed, and so she was urging him to return home. Lin Mu packed up the watermelon, along with some other fruits. He carried his bicycle out from the basement, prepared to go with Lu Rong.

He hung the watermelon on the handlebar, with one foot on the ground, supporting the bicycle. "Hurry up and get on."

Carrying the box of cherries, Lu Rong seemed a little resigned. "How about I cycle?"

Lin Mu turned to look at him.

Lu Rong was now around 188 centimeters tall. It was unclear how he had been exercising, but the lines of his shoulders were like those of a model. Perhaps his third year of high school had been very tough, and his slightly round jawline had sharpened and become a lot more defined.

It took Lin Mu quite some time to think of a word to describe him, and he finally came up with—manly.

"Get on the seat first." Lin Mu patted the backseat.

Lu Rong had no choice but to climb up. He was too tall, so there was no place for him to put his feet, and they would naturally press against the ground.

Lin Mu flexed his arms for him. "Look at my muscles, I've been carrying cadavers for more than half a year."

Lu Rong looked at them obligingly.

"You should gain some weight" was Lu Rong's final conclusion. With his feet on the ground, he shifted forward a little. The bicycle shifted together with him, and Lin Mu nearly lost his balance.

"Be good," he warned.

Lu Rong held onto Lin Mu's waist, resting his head on Lin Mu's back. With a muffled laugh, he said, "I'll cycle, just sit in the back."

Lin Mu gave him a questioning look.

Lu Rong smiled, teasing him. "This is your highness's little pumpkin carriage."

There were quite a number of people living in Lu Rong's place. After dinner, Lin Mu hesitated for some time, but he still felt too embarrassed to continue remaining there. Fang Luoyao knew about their relationship, and every time she looked at him, her expression was always motherly. She was like mothers in their forties who loved to take photos in their red scarves, gossip becoming their nature. Lu Rong was half a son to her now, and she definitely had to pay more attention to her son's boyfriend.

Fang Nuo was a little clingy, behaving a little like Lin Mu's shadow. He probably thought that his landlord and his Mu-*ge*'s relationship was a bromance, and that their actions were mainly horsing around. He would even occasionally be jealous of Lu Rong, feeling that it was due to his young age, and that was why he was unable to be closer to Lin Mu.

"Mu-*ge*." Fang Nuo stared at him. "Are you returning to Kunqian for the celebration?"

Lin Mu joked, "I'll go if Zhong He invites me."

Fang Nuo blinked. "When we went to collect our enrollment

letters as new students earlier, Principal Zhong still had your banner hung up."

Lin Mu thought that this was nothing strange. One of Zhong He's favorite things to do was to wring out every drop of value from the students' accolades, and he would never let go of an opportunity to have the honor reflect off him, giving people a lasting impression that they could also be the pride of Kunqian in the future.

Chen Meihua wanted to take a stroll after eating. Now, she basically could not recognize anyone anymore. Even if she did, she was more likely to mistake Lu Rong as Lu Zhengnian. However, for some reason, she never forgot Lin Mu. The only time she would misidentify him would be like the period when they had just known each other, and she would call him "*Jiejie.*"

Lin Mu would not deliberately correct her. With no one else around, it did not hurt his dignity being referred to in this manner.

"Shall I wear a dress the next time we go out to play?" Lin Mu had the wildest idea. To him, crossdressing was not shameful at all, as the only distinction to be made about crossdressing was in having never done it at all and doing it all the time—and his situation was clearly the latter. There had not been a significant change in his appearance, other than his features becoming more handsome. When he stood next to Lin Zhao, everyone could see that they were twins.

Lu Rong glanced at him helplessly, shaking his head. "Don't do that. Meimei has finally managed to understand that you're a man. If you do this, she'll forget it."

Lin Mu accompanied the grandmother and grandson on the stroll around Taohuawu District. The peach blossoms only bloomed in spring, but it was now currently the season for gardenias, and their scent filled the air strongly. Over the past two years, many shops had opened along the streets, and streetlights shone brightly at night. With the cluster of old bungalows tucked within the area, the contrast of liveliness and sobriety complemented each other very well.

The evening's summer breeze could not be described as warm, but neither was it very cool, and the humid air clung gently to their limbs. Lin Mu was wearing a pair of slippers, choosing ice popsicle flavors from a roadside stall. The neon lights reflected upon his hair, and the image he presented was like a retro poster.

Lu Rong could not help but reach out to touch, and Lin Mu turned to look at him.

"What flavor do you want?" He asked in the Suzhou dialect.

Lu Rong said, "How about grape?"

Lin Mu took his money out, buying three grape flavored ones. Out of habit, he broke the popsicle into two when it was still inside its packaging. With one in each hand, he passed it to Chen Meihua.

"Is it cold?" He asked Meimei.

Chen Meihua's answer was wide off the mark. "It's sweet!"

Lin Mu laughed. Lu Rong was a lot stricter, and he said sternly, "You can only have half."

Chen Meihua had a shocked expression on her face, looking at her grandson indignantly.

Lu Rong was not moved at all. "It's too cold. If you eat too much, it will hurt your stomach."

Chen Meihua was furious, and she feigned crying for quite some time. She had not many teeth left, and to not waste the popsicle, she sucked on it as she cried. Lu Rong kept a watch over her, and seeing that she had finished half of it, he immediately took the other half back.

"You're not allowed to have anymore," he emphasized again with no partiality.

Chen Meihua sobbed, looking at the half-empty popsicle packaging, reluctant to part with it.

Lin Mu would never get tired of watching the interaction between this pair of grandmother and grandson. It was fascinating, with how the older one was like a child, while the younger one was like the adult. Although Lu Rong did not mention it, his final year of high school had actually been very tough.

Fang Luoyao and Chu Lin were both assisting him at home and at school, respectively. With their help, Lu Rong managed to complete his education. He did not usually share his troubles with Lin Mu, but Lin Mu was still aware of it.

When Chen Meihua learned that Lu Rong would be going to university, she miraculously had a few moments of clarity.

Lu Rong showed his acceptance letter to the old lady. She was not able to say too much, and her hands trembled fiercely.

"Meimei has saved up some money." Lu Rong watched Chen Meihua trying hard to suck at the last bits of the melted grape popsicle. "It's for my university education."

Lin Mu asked, "How much is it?"

Lu Rong stated a sum. He remained silent for a while, then laughed gently. "It's not a lot. She had saved it up too early, and she has no idea about the price of things now."

Lin Mu contemplated his words, and he managed to understand what he meant.

Lu Rong sighed. He looked up, and the summer breeze blowing by caused a stir in their emotions. "Knowing that she was ill, she started saving this money a long time ago."

"Whenever she remembered, she would add a little to the savings, all the way until now," he said quietly, "she understands everything."

The youths had already grown up, and they rarely cried anymore. Furthermore, this was a joyous thing, and to tear up now would seem to be too delicate a behavior. Chen Meihua was in delight. Just a second ago, she was feigning tears over the popsicles, but the next moment, she could be seen smiling brightly over the gardenias by the road.

Standing under the flowering tree, she called out to Lin Mu, "*Jiejie*! Let's take a photo!"

Lin Mu teased her, "Are we taking a photo of you or the flowers?"

Chen Meihua took it seriously, considering it for a moment before answering, "Both! We'll take a photo of everything!"

Lu Rong took a photo of her with his phone. His photo album consisted mainly of photos of Chen Meihua and Lin Mu. When he could no longer store them on his phone, he would print them out and store them in the photo album at home.

"Are you attending the school celebration?" Lu Rong asked.

Lin Mu was amused. "Why are you asking the same question as Fang Nuo?"

Lu Rong looked at him from the corner of his eye, a little scornful. "Am I the same as him?"

Lin Mu finally registered the situation, and asked if Lu Rong was jealous.

Lu Rong did not deny it. He usually looked reticent and reserved, but in actual fact, he was very possessive. During the busiest time of his third year in high school, he still insisted on contacting Lin Mu five to six times a week, beating around the bush to find out what was going on in his life. In this one year, Lu Rong could even remember how many times Lin Mu's room-mate had gone to the toilet in a day.

"Medicine students work like dogs every day," said Lin Mu frankly. "Other than my syllabus and my research, there's only room left for you in my heart."

Thinking about this, he cast Lu Rong a side-eye look, warning him, "You're the one who has to behave properly in university."

Lu Rong said calmly, "If you're worried, I'll just take Meimei to class."

Lin Mu was completely silenced by his words.

Regarding the school celebration, even if Lu Rong and Fang Nuo did not ask, Lin Mu would still attend. It was not that Zhong He had invited him, but because Cao Zhan was going.

As for why Cao Zhan was attending, he was the only one who had been specially invited by Zhong He to attend the celebration.

Three years ago, if someone were to say that Cao Zhan would accomplish great things, the entire school would probably think that that person's brain was damaged from too much dreaming, that there was something wrong with them.

However, Cao Zhan did go on to accomplish great things.

Although Cao Zhan managed to pass his humanities exam during the national college entrance examinations, he was assigned to the sculpting major as he did not meet the minimum requirements of the major he wanted. Suzhou was well-known throughout the country for its unique way of sculpting, whether wood, stone or jade. Like Suzhou's embroidery, it had won fame both at home and abroad.

At first, Ji Qingwen had only wanted to give it a try, to let Cao Zhan have a chance. She did not need Cao Zhan to become a master at it, only hoping that he could become an apprentice in the future and earn some money from it. As a mother, she was very aware of what her son was like, and she did not need him to stand out among others. To her, it was pretty good that he could support himself. Furthermore, Cao Zhan came from a well-off family, and they did not expect too much from their disabled son, only hoping that he would not go astray. If he could be a kind, pure and diligent person, that would be more than enough for them.

Cao Zhan finally settled on majoring in jade carving, and he would be fiddling with rocks every day. Ji Qingwen allowed him to do as he wished. Suzhou's sculpting style emphasized on an ingenious conception, its lines exquisite, and looking just like nature itself. Besides knocking on stones every day in class, Cao Zhan even went out to find a master to accept him as a student. In a moment of coincidence, he ended up finding an expert.

The circle of such a sculpting style could not be considered very big, but it was not small either. It was mainly divided into two groups—the northern and the southern. The northern group focused on sculpture in the round, which was basically carving a sculpture right out of a large item. On the other hand, the southern group was famed for their relief sculpture, carving a scene out from an entire piece of jade without destroying the shape of the jade itself. Carving a story out from the stone, it seemed even more skillful.

When the division occurred, many people from the northern group came to the south of Suzhou to learn this skill. Now, there were five pillars in the Suzhou jade carving circles, as well as many other skilled artists. However, the ones that were most recognized by the people within the circle were still those five masters.

Two masters, Yang and Jiang, had long made their names. Anything that went through their hands were notable works of art, displayed in national museums, and their names renowned. Below them were Gong, Fang and Gu, who could be considered as juniors of the two masters. Their creations were exquisite, their craftsmanship superb. Between Gong and Gu, one was good at carving monkeys, and the other lotuses. Master Fang was good at both concurrently, excelling at both monkeys and lotuses.

"Master Gu's lotuses are fresh and zen-like, while Master Fang is the opposite, the petals of his lotuses lush and luxuriant." Jiang Tianhe was now half an expert. Both Cao Zhan and he had been very lucky, stumbling into Master Fang during the school celebration of Suzhou Art & Design Technology Institute. After seeing half a piece of Cao Zhan's work, Master Fang had asked him if he would like to practice at his studio.

Cao Zhan's reaction was very calm at that time, while Jiang Tianhe almost fainted on the spot. He always worried that Cao Zhan would be bullied, and would often run over to the art institute whenever he had time. The bus drivers who drove the route between their schools all knew him, and they all thought that he was visiting his little girlfriend from the art institute.

"I'm going to see a fool." On the day of the art institute's school celebration, Jiang Tianhe had basically been conscripted into attending to show support for Cao Zhan. He said churlishly, "I wouldn't have such a stupid girlfriend."

In summary, the beginning of Cao Zhan's university life was not as blissful as how it had been in high school. After all, social relationships in university were more complicated, and the utopia created by Kunqian was easily destroyed without any effort.

Although Cao Zhan had low intelligence, he was not so stupid as to not realize the difference and changes in his surroundings. He had always been reticent with people he was unfamiliar with, and his initial silence and distance were at first able to conceal his differences from others. However, as their interactions started increasing, they would always discover that he was cognitively deficient.

Relationships between people were always so complicated. In Kunqian, the only person who would bully him was Jiang Tianhe, but now, in university, the only person who could help him was also Jiang Tianhe.

Fortunately, for the jade sculpting major, lectures were not the focus of their education, and the interactions between the students were not so frequent that the bullying became very serious. However, Cao Zhan was still ostracized, and if he were to return to his dormitory just a little late, he would run the risk of getting locked out by his roommates.

He did not understand many things, but he understood very well what malice was.

His classmates' groundless chatter; their periodic probing and scornful glances; how no one was willing to sit next to him in class; how he would always be interrupted when he was speaking; how he could rarely select any good material when practicing, only left with scraps and poor-quality ones; how, because of his wealthy family background, they refused to return the money they borrowed from him; how they casually used his belongings— these were all common occurrences.

Cao Zhan had once quietly given Jiang Tianhe a phone call in private, tears falling from his eyes as he spoke. Repeatedly, he asked, "I didn't do anything bad. Why don't they like me?"

Jiang Tianhe did not give him any platitudes like "this is how the world works" or "this is the true reality." He even skipped his own classes, spending a lot of time with him. After some time, everyone knew that the jade sculpting major had an external student who was a layman.

When Cao Zhan found out about this, he was a little embarrassed. He asked Jiang Tianhe to return to his classes, and to not let anything affect his grades.

Jiang Tianhe was not bothered. "Too bad Lin Mu isn't here. Otherwise, he'd come as well."

Of course, other than Jiang Tianhe, the underclassmen in their busiest semester of their third year in high school took some time out to visit Cao Zhan occasionally as well. Mo Xiaoxiao and Li Zi were stuck to each other like glue, while Lu Rong brought Chen Meihua along.

The group of four, two of whom had unique appearances, attracted quite a lot of attention when they were at the art institute.

Chen Meihua's mind was even slower than Cao Zhan's. When she saw him, she called out "Dopey" a few times. In the heat of the day, Mo Xiaoxiao was dressed in shorts, her prosthetic limb openly on display, and she did not care that others were looking.

Jiang Tianhe clicked his tongue when he saw them, joking, "What a grand entrance."

Li Zi glanced at him, speaking calmly, "If we don't open these people's eyes, they'd still think that they're the light, they're bright, and they're the only legends around."

Li Zi had always had a vicious tongue and an icy expression. She did not keep her volume down when she said this, and the other students around them all heard her. The faces of the people who often led the way in ostracizing Cao Zhan visibly turned ugly, but because of the intimidating presence of Lu Rong and Jiang Tianhe, they did not have the guts to come challenge her.

Cao Zhan was delighted upon seeing them. He pretty much dragged them to the art institute's cafeteria, telling them that the food there was both good and cheap.

"I have to submit my homework first!" Cao Zhan remembered suddenly. Going to university was no different from going to high school for him, and he still thought that he should be doing homework every day. As such, as long as there were any classes with practical work, he would be knocking and grinding determinedly every day, and he never dragged it to the next day.

Jiang Tianhe leaned over. "Master Fang set the homework?"

Last month, it was as though Cao Zhan had struck the lottery. Master Fang had taken a liking to him, accepting him as his apprentice. Every morning, he would attend classes in school, and then head to Master Fang's studio as a disciple in the afternoon, learning from him. He would spend every weekend there, and this surprisingly solved a portion of the issue of him being ostracized.

"I can use the machines now!" He was very excited, and he took out the models he made to show his friends.

The higher the quality of nephrite jade, the more detailed and softer it was to touch. The pores would be very fine, the stone smooth. Logically speaking, carving the jade by machine would be very different from doing it by hand, and amateurs would normally practice by using small pieces of low-quality material. Few would carve such high-quality stone directly with machines.

Cao Zhan took out a small piece of stone from a fine woolen

bag. Although it was not big in size, it was a complete piece of nephrite jade. On one surface was carved the image of a lotus flower. The black outline was still visible, and it had yet to be waxed and polished.

Jiang Tianhe and the rest naturally did not have much expertise in this matter. Looking at the item for some time, they were unable to come up with any great compliments.

Cao Zhan carefully kept the stone, unbothered by their non-reaction. "I'll have to hand this in to *shifu* later, and it will be graded."

Jiang Tianhe choked. "He's not running a school, yet he's grading every item?"

Cao Zhan looked very earnest. "*Shifu* is very fierce! If the item isn't passable, he will scold us! Last time, Zhang-*shixiong* carved the head of a monkey crooked, and was scolded by *shifu* until he peed his pants!"

Zhang-*shixiong* himself had been the one who'd first used the phrase "peed his pants" himself; Cao Zhan was only repeating what he said.

Li Zi frowned, a little worried. "Did he scold you?"

Cao Zhan blinked, giving a response that seemed as though nothing could be more natural. "Of course! *Shifu* doesn't treat me like someone stupid, but treats us all equally. Whoever doesn't do a good job will be scolded."

He thought for a moment, and then felt that there seemed to be something wrong with what he had just said, so he hurriedly corrected himself. "Of—of course, I've always been a little stupider anyway."

His friends were speechless.

Cao Zhan broke out in sweat from his anxiety. "It just means, it means that he wouldn't scold me more or less than the others.

I'm just like the others, and we're all treated the same!"

None of them had ever been accepted as an apprentice by a famous master, but looking at how happy Cao Zhan was, they could not say anything that would be too shocking. Beating around the bush, they hinted to Dopey that if there were any physical contact, by which they meant corporal punishment, he must tell an adult immediately instead of hiding it.

Dopey was still dopey, and he was completely lost. "We don't fight here. The senior apprentices are all very nice, and they'd even help me select materials."

Lu Rong sighed, finally deciding, "We'll come to visit you when we're free."

These words were not just empty talk. When Lin Mu returned to attend Kunqian's school celebration, he made time to visit Master Fang's studio a few days before the celebration itself. With such a lineup, it felt as if they were going down to deliberately find fault.

"It's the summer break, but there's no holiday, and Dopey is still there working five days a week with two days off." Jiang Tianhe was very biased, and he kept grumbling the entire way. "If they don't pay him, that's illegal child labor!"

Lu Rong could not help but interrupt, "With Dopey's age, it's no longer child labor."

Jiang Tianhe's explanation actually sounded convincing. "It's the same. His mind is like that of a child. How is that not child labor?"

However, Lin Mu was not so critical. "Dopey is learning how to sculpt there, and he should stay there a little longer. The more he learns, the more he'd know. After all, slow birds need to start

519

flying earlier."

Jiang Tianhe said, "Cao Zhan even won an award with his work previously. Didn't you guys see it? It was shared by an official social media account. Although it's not a big prize, people have begun to call him Little Teacher Cao."

Lu Rong considered it. "Normally, in this line, when apprentices represent their studio in competitions, they would be using the name of their masters, and they might not even be able to have their own name on it. However, Master Fang did not do this, but directly used Cao Zhan's name."

Jiang Tianhe opened his mouth. He seemed to have just thought about this, and with a frown, he was left speechless.

Lin Mu slapped his thigh, saying, "Let's not twist ourselves over this anymore. In any case, we'll know once we get there."

Suzhou had a couple of relatively huge streets famed for jade sculptures. The first street in the city was Shiquan Street, and next to Guanqian Street was Yuehai Square. Master Fang's studio was located in the lower half of Shiquan Street, occupying nearly one entire row of shophouses. On the door was a signboard with only the word "Treasure" in traditional Chinese, and below it was Master Fang's name.

Looking at the entire street, this was the only place who displayed their name and seal in such a public manner. Lin Mu and his friends stood in front of the magnificent and imposing shopfront, their legs feeling a little weak.

The arrogance that Jiang Tianhe had displayed on the way here had long disappeared. Faltering, he asked, "A—are we going in just like this?"

Lin Mu sighed, "We can't just leave, can we?"

Lu Rong was rather expressionless. Today, he brought Chen

Meihua along, and the old lady surveyed the place curiously. Without thinking, she reached out, wanting to push the door open.

Before Lu Rong could stop her, the door was pushed open. A person was sitting by a rosewood tea-bench, brewing tea. The other person in front of him looked like a guest, and they turned their heads neatly around.

The man brewing the tea was of some age, and he wore a pair of glasses. From head to toe, he looked extremely plain. He seemed like the sort who often flared up in anger, and the lines on his forehead were very deep. Coldly, he looked at Lin Mu and the rest.

"Who are you looking for?" He asked.

Lin Mu recovered from his shock, answering calmly, "I'm looking for Cao Zhan."

That man raised a brow, looking cautious. "How are you related to him?"

Lin Mu said, "I'm his friend."

That man studied him for a few moments, then looked at Jiang Tianhe and Lu Rong as well. His eyes finally fell onto Chen Meihua, and after a thoughtful pause, he called out gently, "Meimei?"

Seeing someone she did not know calling out to her, the old lady did not make a sound. She seemed to finally know how to be scared, and she hid herself behind Lu Rong. That person finally understood who they were, and he raised his chin slightly towards the stairs. "Dopey's upstairs. You can go ahead."

He reminded them, "Don't go around touching things willy-nilly. If they're damaged, Dopey will not be able to pay it off even if he signs a slave contract."

Lin Mu was at a loss for words.

SILENT HEARTS

19 **The World
Is Round**

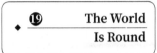

The second floor of the jade carving studio was different from the first floor. There were no displays of jade pieces, only having around seven or eight jade carving machines.

When Lin Mu and his friends went upstairs, Cao Zhan was seated at the machine right in front. A man and a woman were standing next to him, and the woman was currently bowing her head, looking at his work.

"Does this place need to be a little thinner?" There were very few female craftsmen in the world of jade carving, and this was the first one that Lin Mu had ever met. When she finished speaking, she looked up and was a little surprised to see them. "Who are you looking for?"

In Cao Zhan's hand was a stone, and the machine was still in operation. The drill whirled loudly, beads of clarified water dripping down onto the carving.

Jiang Tianhe clearly remembered what Master Fang had just said. He pointed at the machine with a trembling finger, saying, "S-switch it off first..."

Cao Zhan was baffled, but as he was not very smart, he listened and obediently switched the machine off. Very excited, he introduced the group to the woman, "Song-*shijie*, they're my good friends!"

Song Jiuling studied the group, seemingly enlightened. Pointing at them one by one, she could even say their names. "Jiang Tianhe, Lin Mu, Lu Rong... and Meimei?"

They were all a little shocked, clearly not expecting that people in Master Fang's studio would recognize them. Song Jiuling did not act like a stranger to them. She greeted them warmly, finally explaining how she knew them. "Dopey mentions you guys over eight hundred times daily. I feel like I've been friends with you all for a long time already!"

Since his friends were here, Cao Zhan naturally could not continue working. The senior apprentices all looked to be slightly older than Lin Mu and Jiang Tianhe, and Song Jiuling was in charge of hosting them. Enthusiastically, she brewed tea and brought them snacks, inviting them to eat as much as they wanted.

There was definitely no way to be familiar and free in other people's territory, but Cao Zhan, with no brain or any consideration, had no such reservedness at all. He seemed to enjoy a very good relationship with Song Jiuling, and the other apprentices all took good care of him as well.

"The works *shijie* made this year have all gone on auction." Cao Zhan started counting on his fingers. "It's a sum with... seven zeroes!"

Jiang Tianhe leaned into his ear, whispering, "Didn't you win an award... Is there no competition between you all?"

Cao Zhan blinked. He understood what competition meant, but he did not understand how it applied to him. "No, everyone is just dedicated to art!"

Lin Mu nearly spat out the tea in his mouth. Wiping his lips, he asked, "When did you learn to say such lofty words?"

Cao Zhan answered honestly, "*Shifu* always said so."

He was basically regurgitating what he heard.

Jiang Tianhe covered his face, realizing that he could not be subtle with Cao Zhan. The boy was not clever enough, and he had to speak frankly. As such, he directly asked, "We just want to know, are you being bullied here?"

Cao Zhan's eyes widened as if he had been wronged. Loudly, he protested, "Of course not! The senior apprentices are all very kind to me! They don't bully me at all!"

Lu Rong said, "Keep your voice down."

Cao Zhan froze for a moment. "Oh," he quietly said.

Deliberately lowering his voice, he repeated to his friends, "*Shifu* and the team are very kind, and they don't bully me at all. They even take the initiative to teach me, and everyone here is a good person!"

There was a variety of complicated expressions on everyone's face, the only exceptions being Cao Zhan and Chen Meihua. Perhaps because they shared a brain between them, they looked at things very simply.

With how loud Cao Zhan had been, Song Jiuling naturally heard him. She was not angry in the slightest, instead looking at them with interest, exclaiming, "You all truly share an excellent relationship."

Lin Mu and Lu Rong exchanged a look. Lin Mu smiled. "Dopey is a little different from others, so we'll always worry more about him."

Song Jiuling understood it very well. She nodded, then suddenly changed the topic. "By the way, there are very few female sculptors in the world of Suzhou style carving. You're aware of that, right?"

Other than the jade carving students from the art institute, in the circle of Suzhou sculpting, there were also "non-students" who, once they reached a certain age, were sent to the masters to become apprentices due to the lack of money in the family. Although there were no stipulations that the jade carving skills should only be passed down to men and not women, it was still relatively rare for masters to accept female apprentices.

"Unsteady hands," "lack of strength in the wrists," and "girls from the village will go back to marry and have children when they're of age" were all common reasons given by jade carving masters when they did not accept female apprentices.

"*Shifu* has an admonition here." Song Jiuling removed a jade tablet tied on her waist, showing it to the group. There were only eight characters carved on it. "Share both joy and sorrow; Enjoy both beauty and ugliness."

Song Jiuling kept the jade tablet. With a mischievous smile, she said gently, "Since we're to share both joy and sorrow, there's not much difference between Dopey and us."

Eating snacks in such an exclusive jade carving studio was not something to be casually done, especially as Cao Zhan still had to work. He took the phrase "hard work can make up for the lack of intelligence" to the extreme, and the homework assigned by the Master today must never be left until tomorrow. Even with his friends around, his heart was completely with his work, and he would never be affected by the outside world's influences.

Master Fang even came by when they were there, inspecting

everyone's work that they did today. Cao Zhan had carved a little lotus flower. Unlike his teacher's ostentatious style, his lotus flower had yet to bud, looking like a bashful little girl. Master Fang dabbed a brush in water, sweeping away the dust left from the carving. Examining it while wearing his reading glasses, he called out, "Dopey."

Cao Zhan immediately went over, carefully listening to what he had to say.

Master Fang stated, "The lines where they meet should be smooth, and the roots should be carved clearly and not indistinctly."

It seemed as though he was worried that Cao Zhan would not understand. Taking a thin brush, he added a few strokes to the carving and handed it back to Cao Zhan. "Carve along the drawn lines."

Cao Zhan acknowledged his comments. Just when he was about to start the machine, Master Fang caught his hand. "Do it tomorrow. Your friends are waiting; you should go and play."

He then asked Song Jiuling to keep away all the jade pieces. She even cleared away the snacks and tea, and they deftly began to chase their guests away.

Lin Mu and the rest no longer had any reason to stay. After all, it could be seen that Dopey was extremely happy in this place. His teacher regarded him highly, and the senior apprentices all took care of him very well. None of what they were worried about had occurred at all. Jiang Tianhe, had at first imposingly wanted to pick faults with the studio, but later on, he did not even remember about this matter, instead praising the studio non-stop.

"Don't come again." Cao Zhan looked very solemn. He said earnestly, "I want to focus on my carving. If you come, I can't focus properly."

Surprised, Lin Mu had never expected that there would be a day when he would be scorned by Dopey. Feeling a grief that was not unlike that of a father, he said, "If anything happens, remember to call us."

Cao Zhan nodded. "I know."

Jiang Tianhe then asked him, "You have to give a speech during Kunqian's school celebration, right? Have you memorized it yet?"

Speaking of this, Cao Zhan suddenly recalled something. He took his phone out, showing them. "Do you know that Little Heron is coming back too?"

Lin Mu tilted his head to read the message. He did not know about this, and Sun Hai had not told him about it either.

Lu Rong asked, "He's coming back for the school celebration?"

Cao Zhan shook his head. "No, he's back to collect the dog."

"Collect the dog?" Lin Mu did not understand. "What dog?"

Cao Zhan said joyfully, "The dog, the guide dog! Little Heron's application for a guide dog has been approved!"

They all knew that Xu Yilu had been trying to apply for a guide dog ever since high school. He had only mentioned it once before that he would not study abroad if his application was approved. However, even after the university entrance exams, there still had been no news about it.

They had thought that this matter might continue dragging on for a few years. No one expected that this approval would come out of the blue.

The requirement for having a guide dog was stringent, and there was also a limited availability of guide dogs available. Xu Yilu's parents had considered it very carefully before finally returning to the country and letting their son have a guide dog.

"The dog has to be shipped here from Dalian." Xu Yilu was now still overseas, and they could only meet each other online. To be able to gather everyone together was truly left up to fate.

Lin Mu grumbled, "You didn't mention anything."

Xu Yilu responded, "I wasn't sure either. It's hard to say anything when nothing's set in stone."

Jiang Tianhe counted the days. He said excitedly, "So this time, you'll be able to come back with Sun Hai?"

Sun Hai had already loudly announced the news of his return countless times in the chat. His grades had always been average, and he had thought that he would be free once he was overseas. In the end, he found out that no matter where it was, people's expectations towards education were the same. A poor student would be a poor student everywhere, and he would have to put in effort wherever he was.

Xu Yilu laughed. "There's Young Master An too."

He called out Lin Mu's name, and Lin Mu answered him.

"An Jincheng went in person to Lin Zhao's match in Japan."

The Nongshim Cup was recently held in Tokyo, Japan, and Lin Mu paid close attention to the reports about it. This time, Lin Zhao had performed very well in her round-robin matches and successfully entered the knockout stages. Other than her, the other world-class female players included Korea's Choi Jeong, as well as Shanghai's Han Rui.

"Did An Jincheng quit school?" Lin Mu could not resist jabbing at him. "Are they coming back together after the competition?"

Although Xu Yilu was blind, he had always been an avid consumer of gossip since high school. "Did Lin Zhao not tell you?"

He gloated a little, "Their rooms are now even booked together. An Jincheng is currently the leader of the support group for the whole Chinese Go team, and the media has shone a spotlight on him as well. If Lin Zhao makes the headlines again, the label for this love of a century between a pair of childhood sweethearts will definitely be placed on them!"

At first, Lin Mu could still listen calmly, but as soon as he heard that "Their rooms are now even booked together," his brows started creasing. Upon hearing the words "love of a century" and "childhood sweethearts," he only felt a heat rush up into his head, and the vein on his forehead nearly burst.

It was already too late for Lu Rong to try and calm him down.

Suppressing his anger, Lin Mu said icily, "Who is his childhood sweetheart? They only met in high school, and they weren't even from the same class. Childhood sweethearts, hah, what sort of stupid rumor is this?!"

The after-effect of Lin Mu's words was evidently quite impactful, and next to him, Lu Rong fell silent. When Lin Mu realized that he had gone a little overboard, he hypocritically changed his tune, "You're different."

Lu Rong held his smile back. "But what you said is true."

Knowing that Lu Rong was not angry and was only teasing him, Lin Mu said helplessly, "Don't joke around."

Jiang Tianhe and Cao Zhan were unaware of their relationship. Dopey's head could not process such complicated relationships and romance, while Jiang Tianhe was too much of a straight guy, and he ultimately did not see them in an ambiguous light.

Chen Meihua was the only one who seemed very upset. She stared at him suspiciously, her aggrieved expression looking as though she was asking if Lin Mu was going to abandon them after the dalliance.

Little Heron had already hung up, but Lin Mu had yet to feel reconciled to the situation. On the way back, he kept texting Lin Zhao.

She would be returning home from Tokyo in a few days, and this was the first time that the younger brother harassed the older sister like this during her competition. When Lin Zhao saw the endless list of notifications, she cocked a brow, trying to recall how she had managed to offend this little brother of hers.

Lin Mu had sent many messages, and Lin Zhao's brain had no juice to comprehend them after a match. Selecting one with more words and many exclamation points, she read that first and then replied to him.

"I won today." This was the main point. "I'll be back the day after tomorrow."

Lin Mu's reply came in an instant. "Where are you sleeping tonight?"

"The hotel room."

Lin Mu asked ferociously, "What about An Jincheng?!"

Lin Zhao did not give a direct answer. She had learned to speak in a roundabout manner. "We're in a suite, and he's in another room."

Lin Mu was speechless.

Lin Zhao had a tone of a wise and worldly person, her response sounding very sensible. "Your sister has to study her guides tonight. Do you know how tiring that is? What if I'm hungry or thirsty in the middle of the night? Someone needs to be here to serve me."

Lin Mu's eyes were finally opened. An Jincheng and his sister had long been carrying out their liaison in secret. Xu Yilu, the walking talking gossip radar, even sighed about how his previous ship had sunk. After all, he had genuinely believed that he was sailing an actual ship, but had ended up supporting the wrong pairing of Lu Rong and Lin Zhao for several years. Now, he upheld the belief that as long as he sailed his ship fast enough, the bad ending would never be able to catch up with him. So, with great acceptance, he started to ship this new pairing.

Cao Zhan's speech had been written by himself. Afraid that it would be unsatisfactory, he wanted Lin Mu to help him edit it while he was writing it.

Lin Mu looked through it. "It's quite good; you should be confident in yourself."

Cao Zhan was still worried. "Does it sound boring?"

He did not know how to use extremely nice sounding or flowery words, and his speech was generally frank and straightforward. There were even some sections where it rambled on a little, and the sentences did not flow well. Halfway through, Lin Mu had to ask Cao Zhan what some of his sentences meant, and then he helped him restructure those parts.

"It's really quite good," Lin Mu comforted him. "Don't be afraid. Just read it on the day itself, don't look at the expressions of the people below, and don't bother about what they're saying."

Cao Zhan asked pitifully, "What if they scold me?"

Lin Mu's expression was very stern. "I'll scold them for you."

Before Lin Zhao returned, there was no one at home. Jiang Wan and Lin Yanlai were pretty much running around with their daughter. They basically raised their son like a free-range bird, and their concern for him was expressed through a daily call.

During the summer holiday, Lin Mu did not have any place he

wanted to go. Lu Rong finally finished his applications, and was just waiting for the final confirmation of his major. He was not anxious, but Lin Mu was tossing and turning around every night, worrying over whether his score was enough to get into the major he wanted.

"If I can't get into media studies, I can go elsewhere too." Lu Rong did not have any strong opinions about it. "In any case, there will be a place somewhere for me."

Lin Mu looked at him with a puppy-like resignation in his eyes. "Majors are very important. You chose three, and if you're lucky, you have a chance of getting into one of them. If you're unlucky, you'll need to make an alternative choice."

After a while, Lin Mu mumbled to himself, "You won't be unlucky."

A laugh spilled from Lu Rong. Hugging Lin Mu, he swayed with him, then buried his head in his shoulder, not saying a word.

Xu Yilu had returned with Sun Hai. When Lin Mu and the others met them, they saw the dog at the train station.

A teacher from the Dalian Guide Dog Center was accompanying it, and he placed the leash of the white Labrador into Xu Yilu's hand. There was a period of adaptation they had to go through, and only after an assessment would Xu Yilu then be able to keep the dog.

"I can see a little." Xu Yilu crouched down, patting the dog's head. "It's so adorable."

None of the others spoke, feeling even more emotional than Xu Yilu. The Labrador stuck its tongue out carefully, licking Xu Yilu's hand a few times. He seemed to find it ticklish, and he chuckled aloud, hugging the dog's neck in great satisfaction.

"Lin Zhao will be coming back with An Jincheng tomorrow."

Before he left, Xu Yilu deliberately pulled Lin Mu aside for a private conversation. "They'll head straight to the school celebration. You can't break their relationship up, got it?!"

Lin Mu was no longer as angry as when he first heard about their "love of the century." Lu Rong had said he had a bit of a "sister-complex," but Lin Mu did not really admit to it. He disagreed that it was a complex, and it was just that his entire family was very protective of Lin Zhao, afraid that she would get hurt. He also did not go along with his sister all the time, and if she needed to be criticized, he would still do so.

Both Lu Rong and Xu Yilu seemed to be quite afraid that he would make a big fuss after seeing Lin Zhao and An Jincheng tomorrow. Lin Mu had no choice but to vow not to do anything stupid.

The main focus of the school celebration was not on those who had already graduated, but on welcoming the new students who were about to start. Fang Nuo had just enrolled into Kunqian, and he was naturally very enthusiastic about such matters.

Lin Mu actually felt quite sympathetic towards him. After starting school, if he were to have any achievements, once he was faced with Zhong He's extreme passion, he probably would no longer feel that attending the school celebration was anything good.

However, Lin Mu did not tell him that. He was now standing on the same line as Zhong He, and was very supportive of Kunqian's "greed for vanity."

Mo Xiaoxiao and Li Zi arrived later. After they decided on their universities, their dress sense had become more stylish. Not only did they curl their hair, they had even dyed it. Mo Xiaoxiao was wearing a pair of shorts, revealing her legs, and all the under-classmen could not help sneaking looks at her.

"There's a child in a similar situation as you." The good friends gathered together, chatting. It was something Sun Hai had noticed, as he pointed at the new students.

Interested, Mo Xiaoxiao looked in that direction. "Where?"

Li Zi was looking for that student too. Her eyes were sharp, and she spotted the student immediately.

"In the fifth row, that little boy." Li Zi pointed the boy out to Mo Xiaoxiao.

Perhaps the boy realized that his upperclassmen were looking at him. He bowed his head in embarrassment. A slow flush of red crept up his face to his ears, and he shifted about, trying to hide his left arm.

"Look at how shy he is." Sun Hai laughed.

Mo Xiaoxiao looked at him for a little while, and she smiled as well, saying softly, "It's fine. Slowly, he will grow up."

Lin Zhao and An Jincheng stood on the edge of the group while Lu Rong and Lin Mu stood together. The two couples were face to face with each other, trapping Xu Yilu in the center as he held onto his dog's leash.

This three-way communication was actually fascinating. Lin Zhao and Lin Mu were signing at each other. Both Lu Rong and An Jincheng could understand, but it was not convenient for them to join the conversation. The gestures of the two siblings' four hands were already exaggerated. If they joined in, they would basically look as though they were having a fight.

Xu Yilu's eyes were not good, so he could only rely on Lu Rong translating the conversation aloud for him. However, he was not a frequent sign language user, and his translation was rough and jerky. Unable to continue listening, An Jincheng joined in the translation too.

In the end, as the twins "spoke," Lu Rong and An Jincheng were like voice dubbers. With his Labrador, Xu Yilu listened with great interest.

"You're too long-winded." Lin Zhao's fingers moved very forcefully.

An Jincheng obviously had a personal investment in this, and he brought his own emotions in as he translated this sentence.

Lin Mu glared, his fingers moving swiftly. "An Jincheng spoke ill of me just now! Will you help him or me?!"

Lu Rong jammed up. He glanced over to An Jincheng, and finally, under the eyes of Lin Mu, he translated what he said with great emotion.

After listening to them, Xu Yilu paused for a while before asking uncertainly, "They're the ones fighting, but why are the two of you playing along with so much feeling?"

Standing on the stage, Zhong He had finally finished bragging. With a bright smile on his face, he looked out at the students. Cao Zhan was still going over his speech, and Jiang Tianhe was listening with a face full of annoyance, correcting him, "It's Wu-*laoshi*, not Hu-*laoshi*. Repeat after me, Wu Wu Wu!"

Cao Zhan repeated after him obediently, but his "Wu" and "Hu" still could not be distinguished clearly, and he was so anxious that he was about to cry. "What should I do?"

Jiang Tianhe rolled his eyes, deciding to go for broke. "Just skim it; no one's listening anyway."

Zhong He was at a loss for words.

Only after he coughed did Jiang Tianhe and Cao Zhan realize that his speech was over. Facing the new students, Zhong He said,

"Now, let's invite Cao Zhan-*tongxue* on stage to give a speech."

Cao Zhan's name was not widely known in high school, and the current second and third-year students were all fans of Lin Mu and An Jincheng instead. Once, they had even started individual threads for the two people on the school's forum, everyone so interested that it seemed like as though they would only stop after one was crowned the title of the school's best-looking boy.

In the end, when these two threads were still going on, a new competitor arrived. A new thread had appeared, and attached to it were Lu Rong's photos taken during graduation.

As such, there was no end to the competition among the three solid competitors. When the students heard that the school had invited an alumnus to give a speech, most thought it would either be Lin Mu or An Jincheng.

This was also the first time Fang Nuo had met Cao Zhan. He could not help but slip out from the crowd, asking Lu Rong, "Who is he?"

Lu Rong had his arms crossed. Lin Mu and Lin Zhao had stopped quarreling too, and they were all paying great attention to the stage.

"Listen well." Lu Rong was rather expressionless. He had always been a little strict with Fang Nuo.

When Cao Zhan began to speak, the crowd was still a little noisy. His slight cognitive deficit was quickly noticed, and some of the new students were in disbelief, their faces full of amusement and incomprehension.

However, when Cao Zhan got to the middle of his speech, the entire ground fell silent.

Cao Zhan did not have much talent in writing, and Lin Mu had read the entirety of the speech's content before. Just like a little hamster hiding its winter hoard, in scattered pieces and chunks, he included his own experience of his three years in high school.

Hugging his dog, Xu Yilu listened earnestly.

In front, Mo Xiaoxiao was wiping her tears away. Li Zi was hugging her, and with their heads bent together, nobody knew what they were sharing in secret.

Sun Hai turned to look at Lin Mu, the latter waving and pointing at the stage.

Leaning close to Lin Zhao, An Jincheng gently interpreted everything for her. Lin Zhao looked at his hands seriously. This person again added some of his own agenda into the interpretation, and with a cock of her brow, Lin Zhao reached out and pinched An Jincheng's cheek.

Lu Kong quietly extended his hand. Without looking down, Lin Mu intertwined his fingers naturally with him.

"I-I'm very stupid." About to finish his speech, Cao Zhan was still very nervous. He glanced over at Jiang Tianhe, who had been standing on guard backstage. The boy gave him a thumbs-up, looking to be even more anxious than him.

Cao Zhan looked back out to the students, saying slowly, "In the past, I was terrified that people would scold me, that they would beat me, and that they would borrow my things and not return them to me."

When he said this, peals of laughter rang out from the crowd, and the laughter was friendly. Sun Hai cupped his hands around his mouth, shouting at the stage, "Who bullied you? We'll help you beat them up!"

Cao Zhan shook his head solemnly, refusing the offer. "No, you can't. Fighting is wrong."

More laughter burst out, and Cao Zhan paused for a bit before continuing, "However, now, if there are people bullying me, I'm no longer scared."

He said, "I have Kunqian, I have all of you. I have a lot of love, and I'm not afraid of anything."

He looked down at his speech, then raised his head again, smiling as he said, "Hello everyone, I'm Cao Zhan. You can call me Dopey."

Methodically, he gave a bow. "Today, I'm proud of Kunqian, and tomorrow, Kunqian will be proud of me. Thank you, everyone."

SILENT HEARTS

The Future

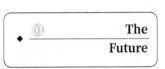

The
Future

By the time Lin Mu and Lu Rong were done with their long distance relationship, they had already graduated with their postgraduate degrees. As the distance between where they were located were not too far apart, it had to be said that the difficulties they endured over the past few years had faded into insignificance when the two people were about to move in with each other.

Meimei had not been in the best of health over the past two years. Lu Rong quit his nine-to-five job at the newspaper company, becoming a freelance writer instead as he focused on writing articles for some platforms and social media accounts. Lin Mu never interfered with his career choices at all, because as long as Meimei is still alive, to a certain degree, Lu Rong would never be able to live like a normal adult.

Fortunately, he had Lin Mu.

Returning to Suzhou, Lin Mu successfully applied for a position at a top-tier hospital. His area of expertise was in neurology, and during this time when Meimei was feeling unwell, Lin Mu was the one worrying over her hospital admission. Only when Meimei's condition had stabilized did Lin Mu then take the first step in approaching Lu Rong about moving in together.

"Taking care of her alone would never be as easy as two people taking care of her together." Lin Mu had a heart-to-heart talk with Lu Rong after dinner. "You have to write your articles every day, and there will be times when you're overwhelmed with work. I'll be able to help."

Lu Rong folded the lid of his computer down. They were still living in the old house in the Taohuawu District. Ever since he found a steady job, Fang Luoyao had gone to the city where her son's university was to accompany him, so there was one fewer person to take care of Chen Meihua. Looking at Lin Mu, Lu Rong asked, "How about you move in?"

Lin Mu nodded. "Of course I'll be the one moving in."

Lu Rong smiled. He did not ask Lin Mu if he had spoken to his family about him before, but since his return from Shanghai, Lin Mu was basically staying in his place. If it was getting late in the night, he would just sleep over, and this house was just like his own home.

"Ever since my sister achieved her ninth dan ranking, she no longer competes every year." Whenever Lin Mu mentioned Lin Zhao, he would sound very proud. "Also, she's preparing to get married."

Lu Rong seemed a little surprised. Due to worrying over his grandmother, he had been rather out of touch with what was happening around him. Other than knowing that Cao Zhan had started his own jade carving studio, that Mo Xiaoxiao and Li Zi seemed to have joined some cycling trip that would be travelling along the Sichuan-Tibet Highway, and that Xu Yilu had made a associate professor in an university , he was not very certain as to what the others were doing.

Counting on his fingers, Lin Mu told him, "Jiang Tianhe invested in Cao Zhan's studio, and he's in charge of dealing with all of Dopey's business-related matters. A few months ago, Sun Hai jumped ship over to JZ Bank. Young Master An has inherited the family business, he's also..." Lin Mu held up a finger, waving it. "Getting ready to marry my sister."

Lu Rong laughed. "Time has passed by so quickly. I never thought that An Jincheng would actually be able to marry your sister."

Lin Mu clicked his tongue, speaking in an insouciant manner, "This is how complete sincerity can carve through even metal and stone. He's after all my sister's first fan. Having followed her competitions for so many years, even if her results had nothing to do with him, he still showed tremendous effort."

He then leaned in closer to Lu Rong, pressing their heads together and softly saying, "We can attend my sister's wedding together."

Lu Rong did not speak. He reached out, hugging Lin Mu from behind, bowing his head and kissing the tip of his nose.

Lin Zhao's wedding preparations could be said to be filled with tedious tasks. Just the wedding dress alone required them to visit quite a number of stores. Other than Mo Xiaoxiao and Li Zi accompanying her the entire time, Li Mu had originally been expected to be one of the advisers as well. However, as he was really too busy with his work in the hospital, this formidable task finally fell onto Lu Rong and Chen Meihua.

The new Suzhou Wedding Mall was extremely big, and this was the first time Lu Rong took Meimei there. Lu Rong was not very much surprised, but Chen Meihua was just like a very much aged-up child, exclaiming in delight over everything. Li Zi and Mo Xiaoxiao were already in the shop, and they sent him a text, asking him to hurry over.

Holding onto her grandson's hand, Chen Meihua wanted to look at all the wedding dresses in the window displays. Lu Rong accompanied her, and by the time they reached the shop where Lin Zhao was choosing her dress, the bride-to-be was already trying one on, standing there and examining herself.

Mo Xiaoxiao and Li Zi were helping Lin Zhao to arrange the skirt of the gown. The latter saw Lu Rong, and raising a brow, she signed swiftly, "Is it pretty?"

Lu Rong studied the bride-to-be carefully, then gave her a thumbs-up.

His compliment was not the perfunctory sort from most guys. After complimenting the dress, he continued signing at her, "The color complements you very well, and the style makes your figure look perfect. You really do look wonderful in it."

Lin Zhao was clearly in an extremely good mood. She rarely smiled, and in the world of Go, she was known as the "Fairy on The Moon." Now, draped in a wedding gown, she looked to be enveloped in the air of spring, both gentle and blissful.

Chen Meihua was evidently very interested in how Lin Zhao was trying on wedding dresses. The old lady's health had finally improved in recent days, and, pointing at Lin Zhao's dress, she whined, "It's so beautiful. Meimei wants to wear one too."

Lu Rong coaxed her, "Once *Jiejie* is done, then it's Meimei's turn, alright?"

Chen Meihua gave it some thought. That seemed acceptable, and so she sat obediently on the couch, watching Lin Zhao change into the next dress.

Lin Zhao's second dress was for her wedding toast, and it was a traditional qipao style. She looked in the mirror for some time, then seeing Chen Meihua's expression, she signed at Lu Rong. "Meimei likes it?"

A little resigned, Lu Rong signed as he said, "She has always liked pretty things."

Lin Zhao signed back. "Then let Meimei try on a dress too."

Lu Rong was a little startled by that. It was not that he minded buying pretty clothes for his grandmother, and a wedding dress was no big deal to him. However, today was an important day for Lin Zhao, so Lu Rong did not wish to trouble her because of Chen Meihua.

Chen Meihua clearly understood what had just been signed, and her eyes brightened. Turning her head between Lu Rong and Lin Zhao, her legs swung happily as she sat on the couch.

Mo Xiaoxiao and Li Zi picked out a wedding gown. The two girls pulled Meimei up, and the old lady turned to look at Lu Rong, who then made a shooing motion at her.

Mo Xiaoxiao said, "Don't bother about Little Deer, Meimei just has to look pretty."

Feeling a little helpless, Lu Rong said, "Don't pamper her so much."

Li Zi laughed. "The old gets younger at heart. If we don't pamper her, who else shall we pamper?"

With the help of the girls, Chen Meihua changed into a wedding gown. Lin Zhao even styled her hair and picked out a veil for her. Standing by the side, Lu Rong watched on, only to be scorned by Li Zi and Mo Xiaoxiao. They asked him to stop standing there like a stone, and to help take photos and videos.

Lu Rong had no choice but to pick up his phone. With great responsibility and professionalism, he took photos from all angles possible.

The old lady was naturally delighted. Dressed in a wedding gown, she spun around in circles happily. Lin Zhao stood next to her, hand in hand, and the two people posed away. In the end, they all decided to buy Meimei a wedding dress.

Lu Rong looked through the photos taken, selecting some and sending them to Lin Mu who was at work.

He was probably busy with work and did not text back until noon.

"My sister has decided on her wedding dress? Have you bought the one Meimei is wearing?"

Lu Rong laughed, replying, "Why are you saying the same thing? They all said to buy one for Meimei too."

Lin Mu's reply came very quickly. "Of course we have to buy it! Meimei is so pretty in it, we should buy at least eight of them!"

Lu Rong was speechless.

There was a break in the afternoon at the hospital, but for the ones working in the outpatient clinics, it did not make much of a difference. Scrolling through the photos in his phone, Lin Mu looked at the few dresses Lin Zhao tried on.

Lu Rong had taken many photos, and it could be seen that he was trying his very best to elevate his unaesthetic sense of photo composition. There were a few where they even seemed as though Lu Rong had lay on the floor to take them, and Lin Mu could not help but laugh. Tapping on his phone, he saved some of the photos.

Lin Zhao sent him a text, asking him which gown looked best.

Lin Mu picked out the satin wedding gown with a long train, replying, "This one looks best. It makes you look very elegant, just like a goddess."

The praises left Lin Zhao very happy, and she responded, "We also bought Meimei quite a number of gowns."

"I saw that."

He then photoshopped the few photos taken of Meimei alone, and forwarded them to Lin Zhao.

"... You remember to photoshop other people's photos, and yet left out mine?"

Lin Mu said with a honeyed tongue, "You're already so ethereal-looking, do you even need editing?"

His head bowed, Lu Rong texted Lin Mu. Chen Meihua had already changed back into her own clothes, and with Lin Zhao making the decision, they packed up the dresses Meimei tried on. Lin Zhao's intention was that the old lady could wear them on her wedding day.

"Meimei can be my bridesmaid." Lin Zhao signed.

Lu Rong held his hands apart, looking a little resigned. "It's your big day, and you'll be the star. Whatever you say goes."

Lin Zhao looked at him, her expression saying "how clever of you." Li Zi and Mo Xiaoxiao were also bridesmaids, and the two had to pick out their bridesmaid dresses as well. Lu Rong followed them for a while, before he finally thought to ask who the best man was.

Li Zi laughed. "You'll have to ask Young Master An."

Lu Rong did have An Jincheng's contact details. However, the groom-to-be seemed to be doing things a little slower. The bridesmaids had already been decided upon, yet there was nothing heard from An Jincheng, and when Lin Zhao wanted to probe into it, she was unable to get any information at all.

Lin Mu seemed very unconcerned. "Young Master An has always been ice-cold on the outside, and deeply passionate within. He likes surprises and romantic gestures, so you'd just have to wait and see."

After they accompanied Lin Zhao with her wedding gown shopping, they also picked out the flowers they wanted for the ceremony on the way back. Lin Zhao would be having dinner with An Jincheng that night. The couple was already semi-cohabiting with each other already, and they no longer had to inform their respective parents about their daily comings and goings.

Lin Zhao reminded them repeatedly that they were not allowed to share with An Jincheng any photos of her in the gowns. Her friends did not wish to burst her little dream of seeing An Jincheng's first-hand reaction to her in her dress, and so they would naturally keep this secret for her.

That night, An Jincheng finally made his move.

When Lin Mu and Lu Rong were invited into the group chat, they had just only coaxed Meimei to sleep, and were about to enjoy their time alone together. Lin Mu had only just finished his shower when he saw his phone buzzing non-stop with notifications.

Lu Rong picked up a hairdryer, his other hand scrolling down the screen of his phone.

Sun Hai and Jiang Tianhe were arguing noisily in the chat. It seemed like both of them wanted to be the best man, and no matter how Xu Yilu and Cao Zhan persuaded them, they did not stop.

Lu Rong was blow drying Lin Mu's hair as Lin Mu sent a voice message. "My sister has two bridesmaids. Both of you can do it together."

Jiang Tianhe blustered, "There's no way I'll do it with Sun Hai!

If I have to, I'll be the best man together with Dopey."

It took some time before Cao Zhan replied. "I- I don't want to be the best man. I'm afraid that I won't be able to find my shoes..."

Sun Hai was left with no words.

Lin Mu nearly died laughing. Holding his phone, he chortled away, while Lu Rong held his head straight and aimed the hairdryer at his fringe. The chat was very lively, and when An Jincheng sent a message, no one paid attention. He asked Lin Mu if Lin Zhao had bought her wedding gown already, and Lin Mu told him she had. However, he was most definitely not going to tell him anything about it, and that he would only be able to see it on the day itself.

"Should we go and buy our suits together?" Xu Yilu laughed as he asked the group.

Buying suits was naturally not as particular a task as the bride choosing her gown. However, even if there could only be two best men, having been good friends and schoolmates of Lin Zhao and An Jincheng for so many years, this group of people would still have to dress themselves up properly to rise up to the occasion.

Considering it, Lin Mu felt that there was no issue in doing so, and so answered on Lu Rong's behalf as well. An Jincheng sent a red packet too, indicating that they could just go ahead with the purchases, and he would foot the bill.

Happily, Lin Mu accepted the red packet. His hair was nearly dry, and so Lu Rong kept the hairdryer. Looking at his expression, Lu Rong asked, "You're that happy?"

Lin Mu smiled. "Of course I am! We've benefited from Young Master An's generosity."

Lu Rong raised a brow. He had received An Jincheng's red

packet as well, but he did not have any opinion with regards to buying his suit. Having just dried his hair, Lin Mu seemed to be feeling a little warm. His cheeks were pink, and behind his longish hair and parted fringe, a pair of starry eyes peeked out.

Suddenly reaching out, Lin Mu threw his arms around Lu Rong's neck, and the two exchanged a kiss.

After some time, they finally parted. Lin Mu's breaths sounded a little heavy, his lips slick and shiny, and he felt even warmer than before. Lu Rong adjusted himself to face him directly, hugging him as his hand slid into his clothes.

"Have you locked the door yet..." Mumbling, Lin Mu bit at his lip.

Softly, Lu Rong told him that the door was already locked. His palm was slightly calloused, and slid up from Lin Mu's waist to his shoulder blade. They did not have sex frequently, but, after so many years, they could be said to be an old married couple already. In bed, it had always been Lin Mu who was more proactive.

Lu Rong's enthusiasm today left Lin Mu a little surprised.

The foreplay went on for a good while, and Lu Rong's desire was exceedingly intense. He held Lin Mu's legs apart in the shape of an M, admiring how the two people were joined together.

Unable to bear how Lu Rong was looking at him, Lin Mu moaned as he covered his face with his arm.

Lu Rong grabbed his hand, watching the pink on Lin Mu's cheeks spreading down to his neck.

The house in Taohuawu District was rather old, and the soundproofing rather poor. The entire time, Lin Mu tried his best to keep his voice down, afraid to wake Meimei next door. However, there seemed to be a spark of wickedness in Lu Rong, always pausing at the critical moment. It was either a flurry of activity, or he would take his own sweet time. His actions left Lin Mu feeling as though he was about to meet his end in bed.

When Lin Mu finally came, he was nearly at the point of collapse. Exhausted, he lay there limply, letting Lu Rong clean him up, even changing his clothes for him. Once satisfied, Lu Rong lay back down, hugging Lin Mu from behind.

"You were so intense today..." Lin Mu exclaimed huskily.

Caressing the ends of his hair, Lu Rong smiled. "When have I been not intense?"

Thinking about it, Lin Mu realized that although Lu Rong had always been very careful and gentle in bed, every single time, Lin Mu was always the first one to come. Lu Rong would only be willing to stop only after fucking him into orgasm.

Their arms around each other, they chatted for a little while more, and Lu Rong said out of nowhere, "You should buy a white suit."

Lin Mu was somewhat baffled. "Why?"

His expression a little secretive, Lu Rong only said, "You look better in white."

Lin Mu shot him a few strange glances, but as he was really too tired, he did not want to think further about it. Groggily, he prepared to fall asleep.

Just as his consciousness was about to fade away, he suddenly felt something cool slid down the ring finger on his left hand. Squinting his eyes open, he discovered a wedding ring there.

Lin Mu was stunned.

Lu Rong thought that he had already fallen asleep. Completely unaware, he helped Lin Mu adjust the position of the ring, his tone satisfied as he murmured, "How fortunate, it fits perfectly..."

Lin Mu suppressed the urge to "wake up." Warm wetness welled up within his eyes, and all he could think of was how Lu Rong wanted him to buy a white suit.

His stream of thoughts started jumbling and turning blurry. Lin Mu seemed to be dreaming about the past, that high school graduation trip to Mount Mogan, where he and Lu Rong accidentally stumbled into a wedding in a garden. It was there that they stood together, hand in hand, and, under the bright sunlight, they looked just like two grooms getting married.

· END ·

SILENT HEARTS

Afterword

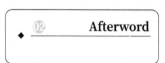

Afterword

I feel that youth is like the breeze, the clouds, the flowers and snow.

It's romantic, adorable and warm.

In conclusion, this is a story about growing up, love, and the many, many instances of warmth in humanity.

I had once thought about ending it all
I had yet to meet YOU
Because of an existence like yours
I fell a little in love with the world
Because of an existence like yours
I started to having a little more hope in the world
— Boku Ga Shinou To Omottanowa by Mika Nakashima

While writing this story, I kept thinking, and I earnestly hope that when everyone is feeling extremely exhausted, or extremely unhappy, you would be able to gain a little warmth and strength, even if it's just the tiniest bit, and you'll be able to bravely continue endeavoring on.

The path ahead might be long and lonely, but I hope that no matter what, you would never stop walking, as in this life, you will one day arrive at the stars.

Per Aspera Ad Astra.

I hope that everyone can become "gege" and "jiejie," and, just like Mo Xiaoxiao in the story, you'd all be able to find love and gentleness.

I want to give all the children, whether extraordinary or not, whether typical or not, a beautiful future and a gentle happily ever after.

The things that cannot be done in reality, I still hope to present it to them through the story. At the same time, I also hope that all of you, outside of this story, will be able to gain some warmth from the words written within.

Now that all of these little friends have had their beautiful and gentle happy ever after, I'm really ecstatic!

Thank you everyone for accompanying me, I'll see you again in the next story!

Love,

AGeng

Silent Hearts

Via Lactea
Publishing Co.